DETOUR

Janice Richards

Windy Ridge Publications

ISBN-13: 978-0615736662 (Windy Ridge Publications)
ISBN-10: 0615736661

Cover design by Robin Ludwig Design, Inc.
www.gobookcoverdesign.com

This book is dedicated to Marcia Lutz, one of the most amazing women I've ever known. Our world is a lesser place without her laughter and smile. May her toes be ever in the sand, and may her sunsets be ever glorious.

*What lies behind us and what lies before us
are small matters compared to what lies within us.
Ralph Waldo Emerson*

ONE

Pulling back on the throttles, Jayne descended, banking her plane for a closer look at the Seven Mile Bridge, connecting Marathon to Little Duck Key halfway between Miami and Key West. Dotting the narrow ribbon of concrete, several motorcycles passed each other in a game of leapfrog. One of the riders waved, so she dipped a wing twice, receiving several waves in return.

Righting her course, she squinted as the blazing sun tossed diamonds across the mass of turquoise water sprinkled with watercraft, and slid her sunglasses back on. A thin line of showers had come and gone, leaving the air crisp. God, flying on days like this was the best—days when the weather was glorious and her agenda was wide open. Big Pine Key came into view brief moments later. Then she spotted it—the little yellow beach house along the shore.

So much for her plans to spend February there...

Jayne still couldn't believe the news. After everything she'd been through in the past few years, she didn't deserve this. But at least she'd have this weekend with her girlfriends before all hell broke loose. She'd have to tell them, but not yet...not for a few more days.

1

They'd spend this weekend catching up and catching rays. She'd drop the bomb later.

Closing in on Key West, Jayne shut out the tormenting mental commentary and radioed air traffic control to obtain her landing clearances. She lowered the flaps and lined up for her designated runway, the land of sunset celebrations and key lime pie racing toward her.

Greg Halverson admired the flashy twin engine Beechcraft taxiing past. And when a woman exited the cockpit, wind swirling her dark blonde hair, his focus shifted. She walked with confidence, sleek as a panther in a pair of worn jeans and a tight, low cut sweater that hugged some intriguing curves.

"Sir, what day are you departing?"

Halverson returned his attention to the agent. "Monday. That Baron's sharp. Know the pilot?"

"Sure. Ms. Morgan flies in a few times a year."

"She from around here?"

"Kansas City." The agent placed papers on the counter, tapping on the bottom of the page. "Sign and date here, sir."

Halverson skimmed the document, then peered at the agent over the top of his reading glasses. "She any good?"

The agent nodded. "One of the best I've seen. We've watched her nail landings in screaming cross winds most pilots would fear. Nerves of steel."

"Married?"

"No, sir. I don't think so. Excuse me a second."

The fellow raced around the counter to greet the blonde, reminding Halverson more of an eager puppy than the manager of a private air terminal.

"Welcome back, Ms. Morgan. Be right with you. Good flight?"

He was treated to a glimpse of charming dimples and an alluring smile as the woman shook the agent's hand.

"Great , thanks. Take your time, Tim."

When she pushed her sunglasses up, corralling that tumble of tawny hair, her eyes sparkled with intelligence in the afternoon sun. And the sultry purr of her voice cinched the deal, making his blood hum in his veins.

Single, huh? Watching the exchange, he decided he needed to know more. She was quite a beauty... curvy, long legs... *Hmm, she'd make an exceptional weekend distraction...* A flash of her legs wrapped around his neck swung through his mind and lingered. *Oh, definitely...*

Jayne stepped back, her eyes landing on the attractive man at the counter. Refined Patrician features met a full head of thick blonde hair. He was about six feet, tan and lean, a few years her senior. Creased jeans and a starched white shirt, what appeared to be hand-made Italian leather loafers and belt. *Crisp.* The sparkle from a large diamond flashed against a ray of afternoon sun, drawing her eye to his wedding band. He folded a sheet of paper and put it in his briefcase, snapped it shut and turned to her, his gaze direct.

"That's a sweet little plane you've got. Always liked the Barons."

Jayne smiled. "Thank you."

"Sharp detail work. Like that bright red striping. Did you have it added, or was she that pretty when you bought her?"

"Thanks. I ordered her that way."

"*Sweet.* And you're lucky you got hangar space this weekend. Appears my bird will be parked outside for a couple of days." He shrugged, gesturing toward the window.

She didn't respond but her eyes followed his hand

to a jet parked on the tarmac. So he flew a Lear. Nice, but she preferred the Gulfstream or the Hawker for that kind of money.

He flashed an eighty-watt smile that gave her the impression he was evaluating a dessert cart. "Here for the regatta?"

"No. Just meeting friends." They always watched the race, but she didn't want to give him an opening.

"You should join us. My boat's entered." He extended his hand. "Greg Halverson."

She accepted the proffered hand, wondering what type of work he did to look so polished, yet have such calloused hands. "Jayne Morgan." She turned back to the desk, her eyes on the documents the agent placed on the counter.

Halverson slid his business card along the desk toward her, pointing to the photo of an impressive sailboat. "Here she is."

Jayne studied the picture. "High Class Looker— interesting name. She's beautiful. Good luck, Mr. Halverson. Now, if you'll excuse me."

She turned back to the agent, offering an apologetic smile. She signed the forms, willing Halverson to disappear. The last thing on her mind was attracting the attention of some slick, married, wanna-be player. But he hovered, leaning closer to her, his cologne a bit cloying and sweet.

"Greg, please. And Jayne, could I interest you in drinks or dinner this weekend?"

"No, thank you." She kept her eyes on the contract. Even if he'd been single, he wasn't her type. She preferred bigger, broader men. Her mom's words flashed through her mind. *Never date a man who wears smaller jeans than you.*

"In case your plans change, my number's on the card. The invitation stands."

Jayne shook her head and tossed him her best withering glare. "I'm fully committed this weekend." Then she eyed the ring on his third finger. "And I don't go out with married men."

His brows drew together, confusion on his face. "I'm not married."

Jayne glanced at his left hand, and his eyes followed. "*Right.*"

"Oh, this?" He brought his ring up, inspecting it. "This was my father's. I wear it for good luck." He looked back at her. "That change your mind?"

"I'm sorry, I'm afraid not."

She returned to the paperwork, signed the last page and pulled a credit card from her pocket, passing it to the agent. "Tim, would you please have the guys wash the Baron, top off the tanks and check the oil before next Thursday?"

"Sure thing. You need anything else, let us know. And happy birthday—Saturday, right?"

"Thank you. How'd you ever remember?"

"You're easy to remember, Ms. Morgan," he stammered, lowering his eyes, his cheeks going pink through his tan. "Will you be staying at the Westin again?"

"Yes, out on Sunset Key, but call my cell if you need to reach me."

Jayne turned, startled to find Halverson still standing behind her, cell phone to his ear. She gave him a brief nod and slipped around him, a crewman following with her suitcases.

Halverson was on her heels. He stepped up and placed his hand on her forearm. She looked down at his hand as if it were a reptile, then raised an eyebrow.

"Let me give you a lift. I have a car and a driver."

"No thanks. I'm all set. Enjoy your weekend." Spying a ready escape, Jayne jumped into the back seat of the waiting cab, pulling the door shut as the crewman hefted her bags into the trunk.

Halverson squinted, chewing his lower lip, watching the cab disappear. Jayne Morgan was stunning—no doubt about that...and not easily impressed. That alone excited him—made his blood race a bit. She was a woman of means, if the price tag on her plane was any indication. Those were what, a couple to three million brand new? Oh yes, confident, beautiful and wealthy—his favorite combination.

He pursed his lips, planning ahead. Ms. Morgan would add an interesting dimension to the weekend...a challenge he hadn't anticipated. A good chase, from what he could see so far. And it was always about the chase. Such a pity women couldn't figure that out. Once they let you catch them, it was over. And he was definitely over his last one.

"Mr. Halverson? Ready to go?"

Leveling his assistant with a glare, he hissed, "No, Bennett, let's just stand here all day."

The young fellow's face fell as he slammed the rental car's trunk closed. Halverson blew out a breath, stemming his impatience with the kid. Bennett wasn't the brightest bulb in the box, but he was resourceful and he knew his place.

Halverson's phone buzzed. He glanced at the number on the screen and groaned under his breath. "Hello, my dear."

"I've been trying to call you all afternoon. I've rearranged my schedule. I'll be there tomorrow night."

His jaw set. *Friday. Shit.* "Hmm...sorry sweetheart, but that's not such a good idea after all."

"What do you mean? I've booked a flight and cancelled my other plans so we can be together."

The edge of a pout flavored her words and he

detected a full-out tantrum heading his way. Masking his annoyance, he softened his tone and said, "Listen, I'm going to be tied up all weekend and you'll be bored. I'll call you later. Cell service is weak and I can barely hear you." He could hear her perfectly, he simply wasn't interested in what she had to say. She'd been far more entertaining when she was unavailable and cheating on that asshole she called a husband. Now she had expectations he had no intention of meeting.

Deciding appeasement was his best course of action to keep her from going postal, he lied, "We'll do something next weekend."

"But I haven't seen you in three days!"

God, she was wearing on his last nerve. "My car's here. I've got to go. Later, dear."

He hit end and called information as Bennett opened the car door for him. He settled into the back seat of the Town Car and made the call, his game plan formulating. *Jayne Morgan just thinks she doesn't have time for me this weekend...*

Clicking off his phone, he chuckled, "Change of plans, Bennett. We'll be staying out on Sunset Key."

<u>TWO</u>

Screaming down I-275 is one helluva ride doing eighty on a Harley. Nick McCord rode the only way he knew—full out. He squinted against the early morning sun glinting off Tampa Bay. A bracing wind whipped around the cowling and windshield of his bike. His best mates, Andy Jameson and Jimmy Langston, were just ahead and the other riders were close behind as they sped down Florida's Gulf Coast.

He needed this trip with the guys for his sanity as much as anything. Didn't seem possible it'd been a year since Paris, but it was finally over. The growl of the engine dulled thoughts of the shit he'd been through, allowing him to focus on the shimmering girders and support cables of the Sunshine Skyway Bridge ahead. Experts tagged it one of the ten most beautiful bridges in the world. Nick agreed. He'd built many skyscrapers, but never a bridge, and he was in awe.

Mile by mile, Nick's shoulders relaxed and the knot in his neck loosened. No better way to decompress than rolling down a road with nothing on the agenda but beers with his buddies for the next few days. He'd made it through the worst of it, and he'd be licking financial wounds for a while, but his business was intact. Just thinking about the insane amount of money he'd parted with in the past ten months made his gut churn, but hey…easy come, easy go. He'd be fine. No, he'd be *better*. Already was. He'd shifted focus, and so far he liked the view.

Hours passed, and Nick soaked up the sun and wind. Cheap, idyllic therapy. Temperatures climbed as they hit Florida City. Nick slowed when tail lights flashed ahead, then followed the group into a crushed shell parking lot. Pulling alongside Andy, he shut off his engine and glanced at the tin buildings lining the waterfront. Then he studied the collection of big, rigged-out Harleys. Their polished chrome reflected scattered rays of sunlight in a refracted glare, each bike projecting the personality of its owner.

Nick swung off, ran his hands through his tangled hair and swiped a bandana across his face, removing his sunglasses to wipe them. Like the rest of the crew, he started shedding his leathers, stowing them in his saddlebags.

Andy's voice boomed behind him. "Gotta love the Tiki Bar."

Tucking in his shirt, Nick responded, "Yeah. It's a regular welcome mat to the Keys."

Andy's beefy hand clamped his shoulder. "Don't know about you, but I'm *hungry*. Been a while since breakfast. We're making good time, though. Should hit Key West by five."

Nick squinted as he inspected the approaching line of smudged, rolling clouds. "Maybe. Afternoon monsoon's on its way."

"Shouldn't last long." Andy touched the screen on his phone and passed it to Nick. "Look here. Doppler shows that thin line passing over. This'll give us time to eat." He exhaled deeply, gesturing toward his bike. "So how do you like my new baby? Sweet, huh?" He stood back, then ran a hand across the cowling of his Ultra Classic.

"Andy, it's *orange*." Nick winced. The bike had great lines, but black was the only color for anything he drove. He watched his friend wipe road grime from the chrome pipes. He'd known Andy Jameson since they were kids playing hockey in middle school. They'd collaborated to win league titles and young girls' hearts. Now they collaborated to win construction bids and design awards, and he'd never had a truer ally. Andy was big, boisterous, and outrageously flirtatious, just like the blinding orange bike. In many ways, he and Andy were polar opposites. But they were alike where it counted and they covered each other's backs on a routine basis.

"Hey, hey, don't be making fun of the pumpkin," Andy chided, wiping a bug off the windshield.

"Wouldn't dream of it..."

"*Right*...let's go. Whoa, here comes the rain."

"You better go easy on the chow or you're gonna blow a tire, big guy." As a couple of fat drops splattered on Nick's face, he smacked Andy's broad back and took off for cover at a jog, the other riders following suit.

"Yeah, yeah, fuck you." Andy patted his wide stomach, hurrying next to Nick. "Besides, this is muscle."

"Table muscle." Nick rolled his eyes, chuckling.

"At forty-two, I'm done worrying about the six-pack."

"Six-pack, hell. It's a *keg*."

Gathering under the canopy of a thatch-roofed hut, Nick got in line behind his friends to order lunch, the rain rattling the tin roof of the adjoining building providing a rhythmic soundtrack.

He leaned against a post, taking in the volley of bullshit. He'd ridden with some of these men for years. Trips they'd taken through the Colorado Rockies, down the Baja Peninsula, and up the Iceland Highway flashed through his mind. Good times with good men. If it hadn't been for these guys, he wasn't sure he'd have survived the past twelve months.

Nick retrieved his order from the counter and parked on a bar stool next to Jimmy Langston. Jimmy was right up there with Andy in his book. Always game and willing to push the envelope, Jimmy hid his bashful nature behind a mask of aloofness strangers mistook as arrogance because he was the unrivaled heartbreaker of the group.

Women fell all over the guy, but Jimmy was married to the love of his life and dodged the constant advances. After a drink or two, he'd flirt and kid around, talking smack, but Nick knew better—Jimmy was as humble and loyal as the day was long. Until he got pissed—then he got scrappy. And he could back his bark. Two decades of working in the concrete business resulted in upper body strength that surpassed his average height and stature. Nick had watched Jimmy muscle equipment men half again his size couldn't maneuver, and his sheer brute power came in handy when they needed to heft bikes and gear on their trips.

"So?" Jimmy cocked an eyebrow at Nick, speaking over a mouthful of shrimp taco, "Get things taken care of this week?"

Nick took a big bite of his grouper sandwich, nodding while he chewed. Swallowing, he answered, "Yeah. Yesterday. Before we took off."

Jimmy tapped his bottle to Nick's. "Good deal."

Andy joined them, pulling up a stool. "Doesn't get any better than this." He raised his beer in a salute. "To getting away from ice, snow and work."

Jimmy nodded and took a swig. "Speaking of work, hear our *friend's* sucking hind tit."

Andy threw Nick a sidelong glance, unfazed by the new direction of the conversation. "'Bout damn time, that prick. I'm still blown away that one of your own sold you out, Nick."

"No. She was on his payroll even before she came to work for me. And she was coerced. That makes it different. Not better, but different."

Andy and Jimmy were among the few who knew the full details of why his company had lost some major bids over the past two years. At first, Nick thought his wife was selling him out, but it turned out to be one of his engineers. In fact, the engineer had been blackmailed to hire on with McCord Construction nearly three years earlier and when required, to forward critical bid details to Nick's biggest competitor. He'd suffered some losses. Then he'd gotten even. *No, he'd gotten ahead.*

"Damn. Wish I'd been a fly on the wall when that bastard heard he'd lost those bids to you," Andy chortled.

"Yeah—the explosion heard across the continent. Gotta hand it to you, Nick, your timing was spot on."

"He asked for it. And I knew we'd only get one shot."

"Word on the street, he's taking it in the shorts. Like my momma always said, time wounds all heels. Glad the asshole's going down."

Shaking his head, Nick drew out a breath. "Bottom feeders always survive. Doubt I've seen the last of him."

"Probably not." Andy got up and tossed his bottle in the trash.

"He's the last person I want to think about now," Nick said, taking his last swig and setting the bottle on the counter. He wiped his mouth and threw the napkin in the basket with the remnants of his fries. "Besides, I made him bleed the green stuff—*lots* of it. Cold day in hell before he gets the jump on me again."

"Don't be too sure. He's a mean son-of-a-bitch. And he still blames you for that mess with his brother.

You need to watch him."

Jimmy pointed at the patch of blue sky peeking through the gray. "Rain's over. Let's go."

"Look out, here comes Mother." Nick watched Gene Caruso march toward them. A short, wiry fellow with olive skin and thick dark hair, Gene was their self-appointed travel director who had an annoying tendency to try to make the guys keep schedules. Sometimes they humored him, often they ignored him, and occasionally they hid from him.

"Guys, listen up. We need to go straight to the hotel when we hit Key West. Our rooms only have a six o'clock guarantee and the resort's sold out."

Andy gave Nick and Jimmy an eye roll, wiping the last vestiges of the brief rain from the pumpkin. "Gene's such a girl, but he's entertaining."

"Careful Gino, your slip's showing," Jimmy called, giving his seat a quick swipe with a rag. He straddled his mustard yellow Fat Boy and hit the starter switch, the rumble of the engine drowning out Gene's retort.

Nick followed Jimmy, rolling onto southbound Highway One. The pavement was nearly dry and the wind whistled in his ears. This was his favorite part of the ride—roaring through the Lower Keys with nothing but blue water as far as the eye could see and the salty ripe smell of the mangroves heavy in the air. He took in a deep breath. *God, I needed this.*

Just past Marathon, another of Nick's favorite bridges beckoned. The Seven Mile Bridge was a kick—long, sleek and close to the water. Nick capitalized on the lack of traffic and the smooth pavement. He opened up the throttle, throwing a thumbs-up and laughing as he blew past Andy and Jimmy, wondering which of his friends would rise to the bait and be the first to roar past him.

A flash of light caught Nick's eye and he squinted

to see a shiny plane flying low. On impulse, he waved, and the pilot dipped a wing in greeting. He laughed out loud, then grimaced as he spat out a bug.

Pulling into Key West ninety minutes later, Nick took the lead position and signaled to Andy and Jimmy when they came to the Duval Street intersection. The light turned green and he watched Gene turn left, amused as he imagined the fit the man would throw when he realized several of the guys were ignoring his instructions to get checked in. Hotel or no, it was time for a beer. Besides, he made it a practice to aggravate Gene from time to time.

Nick yelled to Andy as he turned right, "Last man to Hog's Breath buys."

THREE

"I'm sorry Ms. Morgan, but we had a late departure and your cottage isn't available just yet. We can store your luggage, and call your cell phone when it's ready."

Jayne retrieved her credit card from the clerk. "No problem. I'll just grab a couple of things from my bag and take a walk around Old Town."

She sorted through her tote and pulled out a tee shirt, more than ready to shed her cashmere sweater. Jayne slipped into the powder room to change, and upon rounding the corner to the lobby, she spied Greg Halverson standing at the front desk. *Ah, crap.* To avoid a second encounter, she slid through the side door and handed her bag to the doorman, then headed down the front drive.

Turning left, she came to the red brick Custom House, pausing to take a look at the newest addition to the bronze lawn sculptures. At some point, she needed to stroll through the building. She couldn't get over the structure's resurrection. When Key West was the richest city in the country, this had been the courthouse and post office. But a century later when she was making her first visit to the island, it was boarded up and in grave decay. Now, it stood proud and housed famous works by local artists.

Winding her way farther down the sidewalk, she stopped in front of the old cigar factory to allow a tour bus to pass. While sorting through her purse for her sunglasses, she ran across Greg Halverson's card.

He was certainly attractive, and seemed friendly enough, but something about him put her off. Besides, she wasn't interested—in him or any other man for that matter. Right now she only had time to focus on important things, and a vacation romance didn't make the top twenty.

Jayne stopped at the corner of the street, taking in the eclectic combination of tourists and locals meandering through Old Town—the tacky couples in matching outfits and the waiflike old women peddling jewelry and baked goods from bicycle baskets. No telling what was in those brownies. She breathed in, almost tasting the interwoven combination of saltwater brine, coconut oil, and fried seafood.

So familiar and welcoming…the lazy attitude of the island settled over her. She was an addict and this was her drug. Key West and all its craziness made her deliriously happy. A smile stretched across her face, her whole body taking an audible sigh at finally being back in her Nirvana. Here, for a few days, she could postpone her troubles and pretend all was right in her world.

Music, conversations and laughter drifted through the streets, intermittently drowned out by the rumble of a passing motorcycle or the high-pitched *beep-beep* of a scooter horn. Jayne soaked it in, reveling in the cheerful noise.

Crossing to her favorite bar, she paused at the fenced courtyard entrance. Welcoming her like an old friend, the Hog's Breath Saloon opened its arms and embraced her with the unmistakable aroma of greasy cheeseburgers mingled with the tang of stale beer. Branches from an ancient live oak reached down to tap her shoulder as she passed beneath it, and when she glanced at the uneven bricks paving the patio, she could swear they smiled up in a crooked grin.

Spying the profile of one of her favorite bartenders, the first local friend she'd made, she snuck behind him. "What's a girl gotta do to get some service around here?"

The bartender kept his back to her. "Stand in line like all the other ugly women." Then he whirled around and bounced from behind the bar to give Jayne a crushing hug, lifting her off her feet. "Jayne Morgan! Welcome back."

"Ahh, Brian—how're you doing? You look fantastic." And she meant it. Brian was a handsome guy, the black patch covering his left eye lending a roguish quality. His athletic body was bronze, most likely from days spent running on the beach. Jayne ruffled his dark hair, cocking an eyebrow at the silver dusting the temples—something new since her last visit. "What's this I see? Very distinguished."

"Andrew's idea."

"Tell him I agree."

"Tell him yourself. He's dying to see you."

Brian gave her another hug. He was the kind of guy she'd have enjoyed dating if he'd been straight. Instead, they'd become friends and he kept watch over her and her gal pals any time they visited his domain.

He looked her up and down. "You're looking fantastic. Just get in?"

"'Bout an hour ago."

"Thirsty?" Brian stepped back to his post behind the bar. "Can't believe it's January again."

"Yeah—the year went way too fast. Guess I'll have my usual."

"You look like all's good with you." He mixed and handed her the drink. "This one's on me." He passed beers to a server, then returned his attention to Jayne. "Where's your entourage?"

"They'll be here later, depending on how the

weather's affecting flights. The eastern seaboard's a mess."

"So I hear. Cheers to this eighty-degree paradise."

Jayne raised her glass. "Amen. How's the band this weekend?"

"Good." He glanced behind Jayne, "Let me take care of those guys. Hang tight."

Jayne watched with amusement as Brian handled the boisterous group of men just congregating at the back of the bar with his usual skill. Then she twisted the opposite direction on her stool to survey the rest of the crowd. The restaurant side was full of diners and older folks relaxing at tables, their low hum of conversation underscored by an occasional rise of laughter from the crew of men behind her.

Brian returned, pointing out a fellow walking toward them. "That's the lead singer with the band."

"He looks familiar."

Brian waived him over. "Mike, I've been telling my friend she's gotta stop in to listen to you guys this weekend."

"Remind me to increase your cut." The short, stocky man grinned and turned toward her, offering his hand. "Hey. Mike Vincent."

His energetic hazel eyes appeared to take in everything at once and she accepted his hand. "Jayne Morgan. I hear you know how to pack a dance floor."

Grabbing the stool next to her, he laughed, "Sugar, a bunch of drunks will dance to anything."

His baritone was strictly South Georgia with a little gravel and smoke tossed in for good measure. She recognized his voice and the unmistakable graying buzz cut that worked into a little cowlick at the top of his forehead.

He caught a passing server. "I called in an order fifteen minutes ago under the name Vincent. Think it might be ready?" Then he turned back to her. "You should come by tonight. We start at ten."

"Count on it. I've heard you down here before. Sloppy Joe's or Captain Tony's?"

"Yeah, I've played here quite a few times with different bands. You on vacation?" Mike asked, accepting the bottle Brian placed before him.

She nodded, taking a sip of her vodka. "Meeting some friends for a few days."

"It's her annual birthday trip," Brian offered.

Scrunching her nose, Jayne conceded, "I love birthdays, but growing older *sucks*. I figure Key West is one of the few places where a gal over thirty can stay perpetually young."

"We'll help you celebrate." Mike tapped his bottle against her drink. "So Jayne, where's home and what do you do?"

"Kansas City and I do a little writing," she answered, shooting Brian a look she hoped would encourage his silence.

"What do you write?"

"Travel articles for starters." Not a lie, just an understatement. "Ever been to Kansas City?"

"No. But our guitarist, Steve Mitchell, spent some time there with a band several years ago. Says it's a great town." Mike looked up as the server approached, laden with bags, "Listen, Jayne, I've enjoyed visiting, but the guys are waiting on supper. We'll catch you tonight." He tipped the waitress and grabbed his bags.

Jayne's stomach heaved as she fought to force breath back into her lungs. *Steve Mitchell?* Could it be the same guy? Images of her husband, on stage with the Steve Mitchell she knew, flew before her eyes and snapshots of her former life flooded her brain. *Ah, Mack...*

No matter how deeply she'd buried her past, it had

a tendency to resurface in the blink of an eye. Sometimes it only took the notes of a song or the mention of a name, but it was always a paralyzing blow to her heart. Like now. Taking a breath, and then a generous swallow, she willed her stomach to settle.

A commotion rumbled behind her. Taking another sip, she turned to investigate and in that instant, a slam to her back threw her drink in the air. Liquid shot up and back down, landing squarely on her front, drenching her chest in an icy bath.

A shrill gasp escaped her lips as she flew from her bar stool, the cold shock taking her breath a second time. Dripping, she stared at her soaking shirt, grabbing the towel Brian tossed her way. She tried blotting her white top, now all but transparent, but it remained glued to her torso, revealing every detail of the lacy pattern on her bra.

"Whoa, I'm so sorry. You okay?"

The deep voice invited her to look around, and then up into a pair of the most intensely green eyes she'd ever seen, an immediate appeal drawing her to further explore his face. Tilting her head back to get a better angle, she swallowed, taking in the hard planes across his cheekbones. Unruly dark hair curled at the back of his neck, a day's growth of dark beard, and white, even teeth now posed in a flirtatious grin framed by dimples so deep you could disappear in them… Jayne gulped—a modern day Marlboro Man had simply walked out of a magazine ad to dump a drink all over her.

Shaking off the hum of electricity zooming through her blood, Jayne backed up a step and took a visual sip of this tall drink of water and savored the taste as if sampling a rare Bordeaux. He was a good bit taller than she was, with broad shoulders and narrow hips. She assumed he was a rider as she took in his jeans, boots, T-shirt with a Harley-Davidson logo, and black bandana knotted around his neck. Wind and sun had etched a pattern where his sunglasses had been, leaving a pink tinge across his cheekbones and the bridge of his nose.

He was entirely rugged—handsome in a way that grabbed the wind from her sails and made her stare. His gaze held her prisoner for an excruciating moment—a moment so potent she was in danger of being taken into permanent custody.

Jayne's heart was hammering and the reaction pissed her off. She figured he could see the *bam-bam-bam* through her skin and soaking shirt. Only one other man's eyes had ever taken such complete possession of her. But that was a lifetime ago.

She snapped her mouth shut, embarrassed when she realized she'd been gaping and he was regarding her with amusement. She must look like the village idiot. His companions had gone silent and were peering at her with interest when she glanced at them.

Exhaling, Jayne offered a quick smile and shrugged. "No harm done. I'm machine washable." She stepped away, blotting her shirt with the towel again. "I'll scoot down to give you guys more room."

Distance would be a good thing...a *very* good thing if she had any desire for self-preservation.

"No, no. Please don't. Let me buy you another drink."

His tone was friendly and sincere, but Jayne watched his eyes lower, taking in her wet shirt and the shift in his expression made her face grow hot. No doubt he'd noticed how tissue paper thin her top had become and now he was taking advantage of the view.

She crossed her arms in front of her chest, her face radiating heat. "No, it's okay. Really."

He frowned and stepped toward her, his voice a

21

deep purr. "Please. It's the least I can do. And I'll be happy to replace your shirt."

Backing up as he moved toward her, Jayne became the mouse under the watchful eye of a tomcat, his predatory posture exhibited by the sparks shimmering in his eyes. She jumped when her cell phone rang, holding up her index finger to halt his advance, indicating her phone.

Turning away from the noise, Jayne cupped her ear. "Hi, Cara. Where are you?"

"I just checked in, but I missed the boat to the island. Where are you?"

"I'm at the Hog. Come on over. I could use some back up." A loud roar from the men interrupted the call. "Hear that? Hurry."

"On my way. Have a drink waiting for me."

Jayne clicked off her phone and caught the Marlboro Man still checking her out. He met her gaze and offered up a lazy smile, shrugging his shoulders. She had to laugh. She'd busted him and he had the good grace to roll with it.

A gigantic hand pressed her arm from her other side. Jayne turned to a big fellow positioned strategically between her and an escape route. She raised her eyebrows. "Hello."

"What brings you to Key West?"

"Usual vices. How about you?"

"Running from the law." He removed his hand from her arm and extended it. "I'm Andy."

"I'm Jayne." She grinned, her hand completely dwarfed in the enormous paw. "Did I mention I'm a bounty hunter?" She cocked an eyebrow, "Is there a decent price on your heads?"

"Probably, but we're way too much trouble."

Laughing, she nodded. "No doubt. Where's home?"

"Toronto area. You?"

"Kansas City."

Jayne spied Cara at the entrance and waved her over. "Hey, you! I'd give you a hug, but I'm wet and sticky. Had a little mishap."

"Who cares? I'll take one anyway." Cara Allen, a feisty blonde stick of dynamite packaged in a curvy five-foot-two bundle, looked at Jayne's shirt and laughed, then gave Jayne a tight squeeze. She added under her breath as she eyed the group of men, "Just what do we have here? Give you thirty minutes alone and you've got a whole pack nipping at your heels."

"Aha. Reinforcements. How'd you manage this?" Andy interrupted, laughing and laying his arm across Jayne's shoulder as if they'd been buddies for years.

"Silent decoder ring. All the rage these days."

"Oh man, I want one. Does it come with a shiny red cape?" he asked, stepping back to allow Cara into the circle.

"Yeah, and a tiara. A really big tiara. Very *you*," Jayne teased.

She accepted the drink the Marlboro Man handed over just as Cara caught the group's attention.

"You guys ride Harleys or something?" She waved to the various Harley-Davidson logos adorning their shirts, mock innocence plastered across her face.

"Naw, we just wear this gear to look sexy. Those are our Vespas out there," Andy yelled over the deafening response, pointing to a line of pink scooters in the parking area.

"I understand the concept. I'm not a stripper but I wear the lingerie," Cara shot back and received a roar of approving laughter.

During the exchange, Jayne gave the Canadians her full attention. Rambunctious? *Definitely.* Jovial, friendly? *Oh, yeah.* Obnoxious? *Not really.* Ticking off their attributes in her mind, she tallied them up on the plus side of the column. Late thirties to late forties, mostly nice looking—some more interesting than handsome, the majority were tall and rugged—a couple sporting slight paunches, but overall in good shape.

Listening more closely to their banter, she recognized an educated vocabulary with an absence of improper grammar and vulgarity, a big plus as far as she was concerned. They all showed signs of being fairly well-heeled and of sufficient means, and bore confidence without arrogance. Vacationing in the Keys during high season required financial resources and catching a glimpse of the impressive Harleys lined up in the parking area confirmed that thought. Bikes of this caliber and the gear these men wore were no small investment. Just an impression, but she'd bet most of them had some type of success story. Vacation liars were a dime a dozen, but Jayne's career was devoted to reading people and telling their stories, and if her instincts were accurate, these guys were the genuine article.

"We haven't officially met. I'm Nick McCord."

Her concentration broke when she realized *tall, dark and dangerous* had addressed her. She shifted her eyes upward to meet his, and extended her hand. "Jayne Morgan. And this is Cara Allen."

Nick shook their hands, then pointed to his friends. "You've met Andy, the fellow with the white hair is Colin, and this heartbreaker beside me is Jimmy, but we call him *Hollywood* for obvious reasons." He pointed to the other fellows and rattled off their names but Jayne lost track after one look at Jimmy Hollywood. He was heart-stopping, drool-inducing handsome with a mischievous light in his crystal blue eyes. Yeah, she could see how he'd earned the nickname. Nick was more handsome in a rugged, masculine way, but Jimmy was a smokin' hottie.

"Are there any more of you?" Colin, the one with the gorgeous mane of white hair asked.

"Why? Aren't we enough?"

"For *me*, sure...but I'm thinking of my friends..." he gave her a friendly grin and a wink.

"In that case, there should be five of us by the time everyone gets here. How about you?"

"There's a bunch of us. But some of the guys are just along for the ride. You probably won't see them out and about."

Cara, true to form, was speaking in exclamation points and working the crowd with single-minded determination to get the scoop on each of the men.

"So, Jayne, where are you guys staying?"

She felt Andy's hand on her shoulder again and turned to answer him, "We stay on Sunset Key."

"That's the resort over on the little island, right? Nice place?"

She nodded, "Very. We like it because we can stay together in one cottage."

"Yeah, we looked into staying there, but these lunatics would never be able to get back and forth on that little boat without falling overboard. We'd have casualties."

Jayne laughed. "It's a challenge for us some nights, and it gets embarrassing when the late-night captain knows you by first name after a couple of days."

Her ears perked up as she overheard Cara and Nick in a spirited exchange behind her.

"Where are your husbands?" Nick asked her friend.

"Chained in the cellars at home. Where are your wives?"

"Doing time for spousal abuse." Nick's chuckle was a rich, vibrant sound Jayne decided she liked.

"Then we should get along just fine. So, you're all married?" Leave it to Cara to cut to the chase.

"Pretty much, and the wives don't care to come on these trips."

Jayne was surprised by the disappointment that slipped over her. Why should she care if the Marlboro Man was married or not? She had no interest in wasting time on someone who wasn't part of her inner circle, especially now. She had to give him credit, though. At least he'd been up front about their status. Men who appeared this substantial were rarely unattached even if they chose to forego wedding rings. Not that there weren't plenty of men who would lie about being divorced. Didn't matter, but her radar was clearly off. She'd gotten the vibe Nick was available. And interested.

Nick stepped around Andy and faced Jayne. "What are you girls doing later?"

Jayne sipped her drink. "Oh, we'll probably grab dinner and head back to this place. I hear the band's good. Any of you like to dance?"

"Sure. Some of us. And after a few drinks, we'll all make fools of ourselves."

"Hmm, if you're lucky we might just put you on our dance cards." Jayne smiled and tapped her finger into his chest.

Nick grabbed her finger and a little buzz rolled through her system. If she hadn't been looking right into his eyes, she might not have seen them widen for a split second. She'd lay odds that he'd noticed something, too. The little robot from *Lost in Space* flew through her mind. *Danger! Danger Will Robinson!* Yeah. Danger in the form of a tall, handsome, *married* Canadian who made her skin itch. And not in a bad way...

Dammit, she was being ridiculous. He released her

finger and she gathered her wits. This guy was off limits—on several levels.

Nick said, "Right now we should head to our hotel and clean up. We need to get some supper or it's gonna get ugly real fast. We'll track you down later tonight."

"O—kay...," Jayne hesitated, lowered her voice a notch, and laid her hand on his arm, "Nick?" Her eyes locked on his as she continued, "I overheard you say that you're all married. If you guys want to dance and drink with us, that's great, but if you're looking for a more adventurous weekend, you should find other talent. Those of us who are married are *very* married, and those of us who are single aren't looking to be on the wrong side of a wedding band. We've been kidding around a lot, but I'd hate for you to get the wrong idea."

Nick frowned, a confused expression crossing his face, then he nodded. "No worries. We're on the same page." Then he tilted his head at her, "And by the way, I didn't say we were *all* married..."

He held her gaze a little longer than necessary and she pulled back, determined to ignore the warm familiarity that vibrated between them. A rumble of engines from the parking lot broke the spell.

"Sounds like they're about to leave me." Nick squeezed her shoulder and pivoted for the parking lot. "I'll see you later."

Jayne watched the big bikes crowd a path down Duval Street, their roar all but drowning out the early evening entertainer who was strumming a guitar. She turned back to Cara, who was now hitched up on a bar stool and leveling her with an arched eyebrow. Jayne shrugged.

"Oh, no you don't. Don't give me that innocent *whatever* look. There's a hunky Canadian with his sights set on you—and did you get a load of those *sights*?"

Cara laughed and tapped her hand on her chest in a mock thump-thump of a heartbeat.

"Yeah, I noticed. Jumped in and nearly drowned for a second or two....," Then Jayne muttered under her breath, "No lifeguard on duty...."

FOUR

"Hey, gals. 'Bout time ya'll showed up. I was fixin' to send out a search party."

Jayne stepped onto the porch as Leigh Wallace, her business manager and attorney for the past ten years, greeted them from the cottage door.

"Hey, yourself." Jayne grabbed Leigh in a rib-crushing hug, "I'm a mess but I think I'm dry enough that I won't get you sticky." She leaned back, reaching up to flip Leigh's blonde bob. "Hey—love the new do."

"Thanks. Needed something more stylish as I'm heading for forty." Leigh turned and hugged Cara, then waved her empty glass in the air. "Just mixing myself a little toddy. You obviously started without me, and Jayne, appears you took one for the team. You gals go ahead and get settled while I bartend. Cara, nice job provisioning the kitchen and bar. We're set for a month and I vote we extend this trip for at least that long."

"No arguments from me. The concierge made it easy. I just faxed the list and *voila*," Cara waved a pretend magic wand at the kitchen with a laugh. "Now, which room do Meg and I get?"

"I grabbed the one on the left for Jayne and me. I figured you two would want the room across the hall from us. Liz gets the single since she won the coin toss. By the way, where are those two?"

"Dealing with weather delays. I have no idea where they are at this point," Jayne answered, her eyes roaming over their accommodations.

Leigh pushed Jayne toward the hall. "I'll make your usual while you dump your gear. Cara, you still swilling G&T's?"

"Of course. And don't bruise the gin with too much tonic," Cara called over her shoulder.

Jayne located the room she'd be sharing with Leigh, her bags already perched on a luggage valet. She unpacked a few items, traded her damp tee shirt for a clean one, tossed her makeup bag on the bathroom counter and returned to the kitchen.

Leigh was stretching to put chips and munchies in an upper cabinet—her contribution to Cara's request for help with her ongoing diet plan. She'd been known to plow through entire bags of chips in late-night feeding frenzies. Cara would need a chair to reach what Leigh could grab with ease.

Classic features and five-ten barefooted, Leigh had a voice full of tupelo honey and referred to herself as *a good ole' suthren gal.* She was smart as a whip and touted a law degree from Georgetown, often using her down-home manner to her advantage in business. Jayne pitied the idiot who mistook the lazy southern drawl for a slow mind. Her friend reeled her opponents in and filleted them like the catch of the day on a regular basis, and Jayne was grateful to have that intelligence and savvy at her disposal, not to mention the sister-like bond that had grown between them over the years.

Cara returned from her tour of their digs, adding her signature trill of excitement to her words. "This place is fabulous. They really outdid themselves with these new cottages. I could move right in. And the bathrooms...wow! Jayne, you must be in heaven."

Jayne nodded. Giant showers, whirlpool tubs, marble, granite, glass. Didn't matter what the rest of the place was like as long as the bathroom reeked of over-indulgence.

"How about this rigged-out kitchen?" Jayne waved toward the space, acknowledging Cara's hot button.

Cara studied the layout, ran her fingers along the granite island and opened the oven door, peering in. "Sub-Zero...Viking. *Nice.*" She pulled open the door of the upper cabinet and laughed. "Thanks for stashing the goods. Do. Not. I repeat. Do not let me near those cookies. I ordered those for Meg. My jeans are tight enough without me going face down in that bag."

"We've got your back, kiddo." Leigh patted Cara's shoulder. "We'll tackle you if we see you inching toward that cupboard."

Jayne mentally shook her head as she witnessed the exchange. Leigh could eat anything, Cara only had to look at dessert to gain five pounds and she was somewhere in the middle. The three of them shared many similarities, but style of dress wasn't one of them either. While Cara favored trendy, colorful clothes, Leigh was in her typical uniform. Custom-tailored from her monogrammed silk shirt and ivory linen walking shorts to her well-worn cordovan Tod loafers. Her jewelry rarely varied, and why would it? A diamond pendant big enough to choke a horse graced her neck, rivaled only by the four-carat solitaire she wore on her left hand. Matching stud earrings in platinum finished the set—big family diamonds that she was as comfortable wearing as old sneakers. Somehow Leigh managed to make the most traditional attire appear *en vogue*, pulling off old money like nobody's business.

"Now that we've established house rules, we'd better head on over to the pier or we'll miss sunset." Jayne grabbed her drink from Leigh, leading her friends out the door.

Vibrant red and orange hibiscus lined the walkways leading them to the pier, and brilliant purple and fuchsia bougainvillea cascaded over courtyard walls, swaying in the early evening breeze. Kansas City was dormant and cloaked in snow right now, and this resplendent beauty was refreshing.

They rounded the corner and joined a small group of residents and guests congregated on the dock. Viewing Key West sunsets was a time-honored tradition. The daily performance, featured on the giant screen of the western skyline, entertained visitors with swirls of crimson, tangerine and maze brushed in splendor only God could orchestrate, and never failed to draw rave reviews.

Jayne watched the sailboats, catamarans, and wave runners crowding the harbor to capitalize on that last hour of daylight. She and her friends had attended countless sunset celebrations, yet year after year they trucked down to the waterfront and happily chatted with complete strangers for that blissful ten-minute interval.

As they circled on the dock with glasses raised, Jayne offered the initial toast, "To good friends and southernmost sunsets."

"To another trip around the sun," proposed Leigh.

Cara added, "May we live to tell the tales and return next year."

Those words, so innocent, slammed Jayne sideways, hitting their mark as they echoed her thoughts from earlier in the day. *May we live to tell the tales and return next year...* She fought to hold her smile in place as their glasses touched.

Then Leigh added, "Here's to good women. May we *be* them, may we *know* them, may we *raise* them. And to Jayne, who always manages to rally us troops. Happy birth *week*, honey."

Jayne smiled and nodded, more somber as she added, "And here's to Madeline—our own diva extraordinaire. We're carrying on, just as you wanted, dear friend. We know you're here with us in spirit, and we miss you so." She touched her glass to theirs again, feeling her lower lip begin to quiver, the death of their friend still cloaking their gatherings with a profound sense of loss. Leigh's eyes were watery, and Cara was running a delicate finger below one eye.

"Amen to that," Leigh's voice cracked and she tossed back the remnant of her drink.

When the sun plunged into the ocean, Jayne could almost hear the sizzle of heat meeting liquid. In unison, they turned and wound their way down the path to their cottage.

Jayne was silent, choking on a wave of sadness. Toasting Maddy had sliced through her thinly woven mantle of control, and it was all she could do to keep from breaking down as she hurried along the path. Maddy had been on this trip with them from the beginning, and two years ago when she'd told them of her illness they never dreamed she wouldn't beat ovarian cancer. But it was a short fight that left everyone reeling in disbelief when they gathered to toss her ashes in the ocean.

She blinked to keep the tears from spilling down her face. So much to think about. *People come in and out of our lives. Some stay a while and others leave all too soon.* How well she knew this. She caught little of Leigh and Cara's chatter, happy they were oblivious to her mood, and went straight to the shower.

Hot spikes of water energized and soothed as she considered the evening ahead and another thought returned. *Steve Mitchell?* If it really *was* him, would he recognize her? Did she want him to? He could be the catalyst that gave her the nerve to open the sealed door. And it was high time she started peeling off some of the suffocating layers, especially *now*. Had it really been thirteen years since she'd lost Mack? Didn't seem all that long since her life had been twisted into a pile of smoldering rubble. Some days, it seemed more like last week. She'd moved beyond the bitterness and anger, but just barely. For all anyone knew, she was thriving, like the mythical phoenix that emerged from the ashes. One day at a time.

Grief never completely disappeared, and boy had she learned that simple fact the hard way. It could lay dormant for long periods of time, but nudge it and it sprang to life, snarling and snapping as it backed you into the corner. Just like now, when she thought of Mack. She squeezed her eyes shut, the memories of her husband flooding over her. He'd been so vibrant, so much her other half that she hadn't been whole since she'd lost him. He'd seen through her masks, accepted her flaws and had loved her with his whole being. Something no other man would ever be able to do. *No.* Something she could never *allow* another man to do.

No matter how lonely her life might be at times, opening her heart again was out of the question. It wasn't up for discussion or negotiation—for very private reasons. Jayne couldn't let anyone know how close she'd come to losing her sanity. Thirteen long years—she'd climbed back inch by slow inch—scaling Kilimanjaro would've been easier—and she couldn't fathom making that trek ever again. Instinct told her she wouldn't survive another emotional hit and that made her avoid any man who could make her want more than a friendly no-strings-attached relationship. She'd gotten pretty good at casual dating. Now she'd get pretty good at not dating at all. What sane man would want anything to do with her, considering what she faced?

But Mack's image continued to float before her closed lids, the green eyes twinkling in mirth. Then the green eyes twinkling at her became Nick McCord's. *Ah, shit!* She shook her head, dislodging the vision. He was off-limits. If she let him get close, he'd threaten her emotional well-being. That made him doubly dangerous. She had to avoid him. He was too much of everything she craved. Shutting off the water, she mentally shut off thoughts of Nick with that same twist of the faucet.

Jayne opened the door for ventilation and wiped steam from the mirror. It was high time to face her past head on. She'd kept it locked away, only doling out the absolute basics when necessary to her girlfriends. Now might be the perfect time to lower her walls…

Leigh lounged in an overstuffed club chair, browsing through a magazine. She glanced up and took a sip of her drink. "Long shower—you get it all worked out?"

"Ah, you know me…soaking in the steam as a form of self-analysis." Jayne toweled her hair and brushed the wet strands, continuing, "I might be cruising into a head-on collision tonight. Looks like my past may be center stage at the Hog's Breath this weekend."

"Huh?"

"There's a guitarist playing at the Hog's Breath named Steve Mitchell. Might be a coincidence, but I'm betting he's an old friend—someone who played with Mack."

"Hmmm. How do you want to handle this? Think he'll recognize you?"

"I can't imagine he wouldn't recognize me. I haven't changed all that much. I'll just have to see how it plays out. Could be interesting…"

Leigh met her eyes straight-on. "Far as I know, I'm the only one who knows the whole story. Would it be so bad to tell the others?"

"I'm thinking about it—maybe later this weekend. I just wanted to give you a heads up in case I need a save tonight."

"We don't have to go to the Hog's Breath—"

"No. It'll be okay. I've been gearing myself up for the last couple of hours and finished it off in the shower. But the story itself is on hold for tonight. Plenty of time for that later."

"Good enough. You lead, I'll follow."

Just then Cara popped in, clad in a robe and hot rollers. "Jayne, have you told Leigh about the Canadians we met?"

"No. Be my guest. I need to dry my hair. And you tell a much better story—be sure to add a few exclamation points," Jayne teased, closing the door so the dryer wouldn't drown out their conversation.

Jayne finished spraying her hair and re-opened the bathroom door. "What's our dinner plan tonight?"

"Half Shell." Leigh said, rising from her chair. "Need a refresh?"

"Just a bottled water, please." Jayne went to the closet and pulled out a pair of her favorite jeans—slightly faded with a low-slung waist. Standing at the vanity in her jeans and a La Perla black bra made of delicate French lace, the straps and edges sewn with tiny pearls in soft taupe, she applied lipstick and mascara.

Leigh set Jayne's water on the counter. "Well, look at you. Bet that bra set you back a pretty penny. Gorgeous, but what a waste."

"You think I'm crazy for what I spend on lingerie, but I could no more wear those cotton granny panties of yours than I could stroll down the street naked."

"Like I always say, it all looks the same on the

floor, which is where it usually ends up thirty seconds after a man sees it." Leigh plopped back down in her chair.

Debating between two tops, Jayne held them both up for an opinion. "Which one?"

"Black one."

Jayne pulled it on and assessed her look in the mirror. The top, a low V-neck with a jagged ruffle around the neck and at the wrists, flattered her figure. Her eyes fell to her chest and the cleavage that peaked above the neckline. Too much? *Naw.*

Leigh glanced up and caught her eye in the mirror. "What's wrong, Miss Jayne? You look great."

"Oh, nothing. Just wondering if these jeans make my ass look like the broad side of a barn," Jayne lied. She knew her jeans were loose. She'd been so upset since she'd gotten the call that her appetite had been nonexistent.

"Are you kidding? You've lost weight since I saw you in November. And that top was made for you. If I had a set of knockers like yours, I'd flaunt 'em, too."

Flaunt them? Was that what she was doing? Might as well...

Jayne rolled her eyes, laughing. "Right." She sorted through her jewelry bag and decided on silver hoop earrings and a simple onyx necklace. Then her toes found their way into a pair of black Donald Pliner stacked heel sandals that added a couple of inches to her five-seven frame.

Cara posed in the doorway, propped on her platform sandals.

Leigh teased, "The wicked Dallas socialite emerges from her lair, out for a night on the town. Where's your brush and bucket of red paint, Miss Cara?"

"Back pocket, Ms. Wallace, where I keep the number for my bail bondsman."

These friends were exactly what Jayne needed to keep her attitude light. In the past ten years, she and Leigh had been through a lot—personally and professionally, and Jayne could always count on Leigh's dry sense of humor and level head to keep her centered. Leigh had become the sister Jayne never had, though they were smart enough to keep business and friendship separate. And Cara's exuberance was nothing short of contagious. Yeah, she was in good company.

Walking toward the dock, Jayne's phone jingled. She glanced at the screen before answering, "Hey Meg. You just get here?"

"Nope. Still in Lauderdale. At this rate, I should've rented a car and driven down. I'm scheduled to land at ten."

"Skip going to Sunset Key when you get here. That'll take too long. We're just heading over to the Half Shell to eat and then we'll work our way to the Hog."

"That'll work. I started drinking on the way down so I may be bulletproof and invisible by the time I see you."

"Join the club. You know how it goes on our first night. We started early. Be safe. Call when you land."

Jayne clicked off her phone and followed Leigh and Cara onto the little boat that taxied guests back and forth from the pier at Sunset Key to Key West proper. She sat on the long leather bench and started to convey Meg's status when her phone buzzed again.

She looked at the screen. "It's a text message from Liz. She's stuck in Atlanta tonight. Should be here by eleven tomorrow morning."

"Well, ladies, looks like we'll need to get into extra mischief tonight to make up for our absent diva," Cara chuckled.

Leigh shook her head. "I don't know…Liz has a way of making up for lost time."

FIVE

"We're so predictable. First night we eat at the Half Shell and then we hit Sloppy's Joe's for the first round," Leigh mused, then shook her head. "And no matter when you come here, this place is always packed."

"Just like us, everyone stops in at some point. And I like the bartenders." She waved a greeting to one of her preferred *mixologists*. The historic bar was filling up as Jayne surveyed her surroundings. Not much had changed in the place over the years—enormous black and white photos of Hemingway hung on the walls, along with smaller photos of men who had won the annual look-alike contest. An array of flags from various nations and military units fluttered from the rafters a story above them, a huge wooden airplane propeller swayed, suspended from cables above the bar, and industrial strength ceiling fans hummed overhead.

"Order me a G&T. I'm gonna snoop through the gift shop," Cara said, walking away.

They snagged three stools and ordered drinks.

Leigh propped an elbow on the bar and turned to face Jayne. "So, what's been going on? With the craziness of the holidays, it feels like we haven't had a chance to catch up in ages. Anything changed between you and the handsome doctor?"

"No. Harrison calls to check on me occasionally, and he gave me a signed, first edition of Hemingway's *A Farewell to Arms* for Christmas, but since he wants to get married and I don't, I've insisted that we keep things strictly platonic since last September."

"Nice gift. Any significance with the title?"

"Probably. Leigh, he's a good man, but I drive him nuts because I won't commit. He wants all or nothing. So I checked option B."

"Most women would kill for a guy like Harrison. Handsome, rich, smart...you sure about option B?"

"Positive. I love him, but I'm not *in love* with him. We're companionable, but we want such different things out of life. You know how much I like to travel, spend time by the ocean, take an occasional run-away play day. Harrison's so regimented. He insisted on an itinerary for everything we did. No spontaneity whatsoever."

Leigh frowned. "Do you think it's because he has to keep such a tight schedule at the hospital? Could he loosen up, with a little nudge?"

Jayne shrugged. "Maybe, but that's not the only issue. I can't imagine getting married again—and he's convinced a woman can't be happy unless she's being supported and taken care of. I baffle him because I don't fit into any of his compartments. There's a better fit for him out there. When I tried telling him that, he just held up his hand and said he disagreed. Six months later, he's still calling and I don't think he's been dating much."

"He's still pining for you."

"Maybe, but he's too proud to renege on his ultimatum. I went to a couple of black-tie fundraisers with him last fall, but we haven't done much together since. We'd be there for each other if either of us needed something, but it's over as far as I'm concerned."

"Do you miss *anything* about him?"

"Sure. Lots of things, but he wants more from me than I can give. He's a great conversationalist, he's considerate, he's generous to a fault...but I've been so busy with the new book I haven't had time to miss him."

"There you go, then. I never take a trip that I'm not excited to get back to Charlie."

Jayne nodded. "You two were lucky to find each other."

"Yes we were. And one of these days, some dreamboat will waltz in and sweep you off your feet when you least expect it."

Jayne stared into her drink, twirling the ice cubes with her finger. "Honestly, the thought of meeting someone scares the hell out of me. Good thing— because the odds aren't in my favor. I had the real deal with Mack, and my chances of finding it more than once in a lifetime are slim to none." She took a sip and tapped her glass against Leigh's. "So on I go."

"You aren't even forty yet, so don't bet the farm on it. Life's full of surprises." Leigh tapped her glass to Jayne's, offering an end to the topic. "On a different note, how're the final edits coming along?"

"Slow. I've been...distracted."

"Think your month in Big Pine Key will allow you the time and solitude you need?"

"I've changed my plans. Think I'll just stay here in Key West for three or four extra days and knock it out. I'm going—"

"Look who's bellied up to the bar—" a deep male voice boomed behind them.

Jayne jumped and Leigh's head whipped around, her eyes and mouth flying wide open as she gasped, "Omigod. What in the world are *you* doing here?" Leigh jumped up to hug the man.

"Fishing, drinking and flying for the U.S. Navy. And *you*, holding down the bar...explain yourself, darlin'."

"Pleading the Fifth on that count." Leigh put her

Jayne strolled the quick block and found her favorite spot at the end of the bar partially taken, so she grabbed the last three empty stools and signaled to Brian. Customers were crowding in and the band was setting up.

"Hey Brian. Just a Diet Coke for now, please."

Brian slid a couple of waters with limes in front of the other two bar stools and handed over her soda. "Gotta mark your territory."

Conversations flowed around her. She caught a glimpse of someone out of the corner of her eye and turned to get a better look. Thirteen years, but she'd have known him anywhere.

A hand landed on her arm and she turned to find Mike Vincent standing on her opposite side. "Hey, Jayne. Glad you made it."

"We want to be front and center."

Mike signaled to someone over her shoulder, "Steve, this is the gal from Kansas City I told you about."

She turned to follow Mike's wave. Steve's face was partially blocked by a pair of women who'd leaned in to order drinks. "Hey, Steve." Jayne called over to him, still unable to fully see him.

"How's it going?" he said, distracted by two women vying for his attention, the barrier preventing eye contact.

Jayne's throat grew tight at the familiar sound. Steve's voice was a sexy drawl, mellow as fine-aged Kentucky bourbon, and it brought the past tumbling forward. When she finally caught a good look, he was the same, yet different. A bald pate replaced a pony tail, a goatee replaced a mustache, and a slight paunch replaced his washboard abs, but Steve was none the worse for the wear. In fact, he was more attractive now that he'd grown into himself.

She caught him shooting her a sideways glance from his awkward vantage point. But his expression remained neutral. He hadn't figured it out.

Watching the band as they ran through their checks, Jayne closed her eyes. Remembering the rush that ran through her when the surroundings and music were in sync, a familiar tingle of adrenalin raced down her spine. Steve was giving his guitar a final tuning when a whiff of cologne wafted past. She'd know that fragrance anywhere. Armani's Aqua Di Gio. Mack's cologne. Sensing someone directly behind her, she opened her eyes and looked around, feeling a whisper of a breeze float across her cheek. *Huh. No one was there.*

Her phone vibrated, Meg's name showing on the screen. "You here?"

"Just landed and I'm catching a cab. Where will you be in about twenty minutes?"

"Meet us at the Hog's Breath."

"On my way."

Jayne clicked off her phone and turned to find Steve Mitchell at her side, smiling down at her, his caramel eyes dancing.

"Ah, Steve, you remember. I wasn't sure you'd recognize me after all this time." She paused, sighing a smile as she stood. "Been a lotta miles...lotta years, my friend."

"Come here, you." Steve wrapped his arms around her and crushed her to him. "Too many. Took me a minute, but I'd know your sweet smile anywhere. You have no idea how often I think of you and Mack."

She allowed Steve to hold her close for another minute, comforted by a hug that made her eyes well. Her past had indeed come full circle, and the avalanche of emotions consumed her—the joy, the grief, the anger, and finally, the acceptance—all squished into an untidy package that opened up and sprang at her like a jack-in-the box.

Steve drew back, his eyes searching hers. "Aw, sugar, don't cry. I didn't mean to make you sad. I'm just glad to see you again."

Jayne gave him a watery smile. "You're not making me sad, Steve. I couldn't be happier."

"So tell me about *you*. What are you doing now? You still sing? You had a set of pipes that could've paid the rent for all of us."

She blinked and ran a finger under her eye. "Just enough to kick off the rust now and then—weddings mostly." She laughed, waving toward the stage. "Nothing like back then. I'm too old for that shit. After everything happened, I left it behind me."

"Where'd you go? You vanished."

"Steve, I hope you'll forgive me for that. You guys were so good to me—all the hospital visits, all the calls...but when I got back home, I couldn't handle being there. I had to go away. Survival mode, you know? I moved out to my folks' place on Hilton Head for a few years—didn't do much for a while. Played a lot of golf with my mom, did a lot of flying with my dad and brother. Then I started writing stories instead of songs—it was the only way I knew how to cope. Escapism at its finest." Jayne took a breath and shrugged, "So here we are. Like my dad always said, you never go so far that your tail doesn't follow you."

"Jayne, it's all good." Steve put his arm around her shoulder and pulled her close again. "So, how are your folks? They were so great to all of us—even afterwards."

"I've lost both of them. Dad had a massive heart attack seven years ago and Mom died of pancreatic cancer two years later."

"Aw, sugar—I'm so sorry." Steve frowned and shook his head. "I hadn't heard. They were *good* people.

That must've been tough."

"Like you can't believe." She was silent for a moment, recalling the numbing desolation that had encompassed her as she'd stood at her mother's grave when she'd realized she was a widow and parentless before her thirty-second birthday.

She forced herself to brighten. "But running into you like this is terrific. Best birthday present I could ever imagine."

"Back at ya, gal. Let's get together sometime this weekend and catch up."

"I'd love it. Right now it looks like the guys need you on stage."

"How about joining us for a couple of songs?"

"Thanks, but I'll pass. I'm *way* too rusty. Besides, none of my friends even know that I was ever *on* a stage."

She shook her head more emphatically, not trusting the wink he gave her as he picked up his guitar. He said something to Mike, then Mike grinned and nodded.

No, she didn't trust this at all...

Jayne was blown away by the voice emanating from Mike Vincent's compact stature. He possessed a powerhouse of a voice that jumped from Joe Cocker to Donald Fagan in a heartbeat, and paired with Steve's skill on the guitar, she was mesmerized. As the band wound into a rendition of Van Morrison's *Brown Eyed Girl*, Jayne spied her girlfriends weaving through the crowd flanked by Leigh's cousin and a couple of men who appeared to be his fellow pilots. No disguising that solid, dignified military bearing or the haircuts.

"Look who we found!" Leigh pulled Meg forward.

Jayne jumped up to embrace her friend. "Meg! Glad you finally got here."

"Wasn't sure I ever would—but hey, looks like you got the party started. And I can't believe you're not dancing yet."

Meg's eyes were a little over-bright, no doubt the result of the long travel delays where she'd parked at the bar. *Good for her.* It was usually tough to get Meg to relax. And she was sporting new duds. Her stylish top and jeans were a welcome replacement for her usual khakis and polo shirts. Hmmm, so Meg had listened to their advice and indulged in a new wardrobe now that she'd liberated herself from her asshole of a husband.

"Just waiting for all of you to get here. You look beautiful, Meg. Love your hair down." Jayne tucked a curl of Meg's long dark hair behind her ear and gave her friend another hug.

"Just following your lead, Miss Jayne." But Meg beamed, her cheeks pink.

A hand clamped around Jayne's wrist and she spun to find Nick's friend, Jimmy Hollywood, standing next to her, tugging her toward the dance floor. "Let's dance, Kansas City."

After the third song, Jayne followed Jimmy off the dance floor. "That was fun, Hollywood. Are you flying solo tonight?" What she really wanted to ask was *where's Nick?* But she was loathe to admit she was hoping to see him.

"No—Nick and Andy should be heading in this direction, and some of the other guys are around here somewhere."

Cara tapped Jimmy's shoulder. "Hey, trouble, next dance is mine."

"Absolutely. Buy you girls a drink first?" Jimmy grinned and hailed Brian.

Jayne could hear Mike's voice on the mic, partially audible over the din her friends created next to her. She thought she heard her name and strained to hear what he was saying, his words static like an out-of-tune radio station.

"—got a little surprise...you tonight—hell, it's a surprise for *us*. An old friend of Steve's from Kansas City... might need a little coaxin' ... her to sing ... or two for us. Jayne? Come on up here, gal..."

Customers were beginning to glance around as Mike continued talking, his words now startlingly clear, "Seriously folks, she hasn't been on a stage like this for a long time, so we need your help. Jayne, where are you hidin'? Oh, *Jayne*..." The last was said in a sing-song that made everyone laugh.

At Mike's initiation, the crowd started clapping and chanting, "Jayne, Jayne, Jayne."

Flabbergasted, Jayne's mouth gaped open. "*Oh shit,*" escaped her lips. Her girlfriends fell silent, standing beside her, their eyes wide. Still holding the Lemon Drop shot Jimmy had placed in her hand, she looked first at Leigh, then at Meg, raising her eyebrows in a nonverbal *what do I do now?*

Leigh and Meg turned to one another, then just shrugged their shoulders and shook their heads.

Thanks, guys, big help.

A couple of seconds felt like minutes as she read Cara's lips, mouthing to Leigh, "*What the fuck?*"

She sought out Steve, shaking her head. But the crowd had identified her and starting pushing her toward the stage.

Cara grabbed her arm, eyebrows raised. "What's going on?"

Jayne squeezed by and hollered over the roar, "I'll explain later. Just cover my back." She downed the shot in one quick swallow, the liquid scorching her tonsils. *Liquid courage...*

She accepted Steve's outstretched hand and rolled her eyes at him. "I told you *no*."

Steve winked, a broad grin plastered across his face, diffusing her aggravation. Even though she trembled at the prospect of embarrassing herself, a small voice deep down was screaming in delight. Once upon a time in her life, singing with the band had fed her soul.

He pulled her close for a hug and purred into her ear, "You weren't very convincing, so we decided to Shanghai you."

"No joke." Her heart was hammering. It had been years since she'd stood on a stage with a band. She wasn't sure she still had the strength in her voice to pull it off, but she was determined to try. Her knees were shaky until she caught Steve's reassuring smile.

In that instant, the years melted away. She was once again center stage, Mack beside her and Steve behind her. A tiny thrill bloomed as that familiar rush of adrenaline took over. She welcomed it—that nervous peak-alert of her senses had always been a friendly companion any time she took the mic.

Jayne straightened her shoulders and said under her breath, "I'll need some help out of the chutes, Mike. Let's do something fun."

Mike nodded, handing her their play list. "Sure. Pick anything."

She looked it over and nodded when her eyes landed on a song she used to sing with Mack. She pointed. "How about this?" Mike nodded, so she added, "You start and I'll jump in."

Mike turned and filled the band in on the plan. With a wink at Jayne, he sang the first line of the old Joe Cocker recording, *Unchain My Heart*.

Jayne caught her cue and joined him, fighting to still the tremor in her hand as she pressed the mic to her lips. Looking at the group of patrons watching her, she read curiosity and apprehension in their expressions. They were wondering if she'd be any good. Praying she wouldn't make them cringe.

As she nailed the first line, a tangible sigh of relief rippled through the crowd. She knew exactly what was running through their minds. Nothing worse than being embarrassed for and enduring a lousy singer. When she saw the expressions on her girlfriends faces' change from unyielding support to absolute approval, her jitters vanished. From their posts next to the stage, they clapped and cheered, along with the Navy pilots and Jimmy Hollywood, having crowded the dance floor as Jayne took the platform.

Applause greeted her as she and Mike finished the song. Jayne gave a half bow to the crowd and handed her mic to Steve, smiling and mouthing her thanks to the band. She turned and took the first step off the stage when Steve's hand caught her arm.

"Not so fast, Jayne…." He turned to address the crowd, "Let's keep her up here as long as we can. Don't you agree?"

☼☼☼

"Come *on*. You've seen this late night freak show before," Nick muttered, his patience wearing thin. Nothing he'd seen on the Duval Street sidewalks interested him. He wasn't remotely in the market for female companionship. But the image of Jayne Morgan's pretty smile kept paging through his brain, beckoning him to find her. If they crossed paths, it couldn't hurt to buy her a drink…just to make amends for trashing her shirt. And he liked her direct approach. She'd posted the rules from the beginning even though she had no idea getting laid and cheating on the wives wasn't what this trip was about, or what they were about for that matter. He respected the fact that she'd clarified her position, even if it meant alienating him. That took her up a few more notches in his book.

Andy lagged, his head swiveling back and forth, "I know, big guy, but the women get younger, their clothes get smaller and their boobs get bigger. Can't help myself. Just because I'm on a diet doesn't mean I can't look at the menu. What's your rush?"

"No rush. Just hate sauntering…"

"*Right…*" Andy picked up his pace. "For you, I'll put my blinders on."

"If you hadn't seen it before, you wouldn't know what it was." Nick detected strains of a familiar song as they neared the entrance of the Hog's Breath. "Band sounds good."

They passed the bouncer and Nick scanned the crowd. The singer was knocking the crowd out—she owned the old Linda Ronstadt hit. He spied Jimmy and the back of Colin's white head on the edge of the dance floor. "Found 'em," he tossed back to Andy.

"Yeah, they managed to beat us here," Andy said, then grabbed Nick's shoulder. "Hey—isn't that the gal you doused this afternoon? Jayne?"

"Where?"

Andy pointed at the stage. "Singing."

Nick looked at the stage, his mouth falling open. Then he muttered, his eyebrows knitting, "Holy shit." *Damn.* She looked hot, her hair falling on her shoulders…her jeans and shirt hugging all the right curves…and she sounded every bit as good as she looked as she sang. He could apply the words to how good she looked. *Oh, baby, baby, indeed.* Glancing around the bar, he could tell the crowd was eating her up like cotton candy at a carnival. Something about her tempted *his* sweet tooth, for sure. And that same something had his heart in a flat out race for the first time in ages. *Not good*—run far, run fast, old man…you *do not* want to go there.

Jayne was aware of Nick even before she saw him on the edge of the dance floor. Something instinctive made her knees threaten to pool beneath her. One step behind Nick was his sidekick. She watched as Andy spotted her and grabbed Nick's arm, saying something. Finally, Nick looked up at her.

He stopped at the edge of the dance floor and leaned back, his feet spread and firmly planted, a beer bottle in one hand while his other hand rested in his jean pocket. She looked at her friends, laughing and dancing, but she sensed Nick daring her to make eye contact. Finally meeting his gaze, she detected something challenging and predatory that smoldered beneath his cool veneer.

Focusing on the song, she shifted her gaze to the bartender at the oyster bar. If she kept looking at Nick, she'd forget the words. Her heart revved, drowning out the base drum behind her. A familiar face peered at her from the edge of the crowd. When she looked more closely, Mack's face was gone. *Mack? Oh, hell...now I'm imagining things.*

Andy yelled into Nick's ear, "You should grab that one and buy her a drink... Hell—you should buy her *breakfast*." Andy chuckled and slugged Nick on the back.

"Asshole." Nick shook his head.

"Good thing you're *not interested* 'cause some other guys are already staking claim." Andy needled, nodding in the direction of some military types who stood sentry next to Jayne's friends.

Nick took one look at the group of men, feeling his blood pressure rise. He shook off the irritation. Still, he elbowed his way into the throng, positioning himself beside Cara, who offered him a smile and a nod.

Jayne was just hitting the last notes of the song. Nick cheered as she gave the crowd and the band a dazzling smile. She had star quality in spades.

He leaned over to Cara and waved toward the stage. "Didn't realize she was with the band."

"She's not. We had no idea she could do this."

"No kidding?"

"We've heard her sing, but never like—wait, what's she saying?"

Nick's attention returned to Jayne, listening as she addressed the crowd.

"Thank you for humoring us tonight. It's been too long since I've had the privilege of singing with such talented guys. I'll sing one more and turn it back to them. Steve, this one's for you."

So who was this guy she was singing for? A pinch of jealousy snapped Nick as Jayne smiled back at the guitar player. He had no right to care one way or the other who she sang to or with, but it didn't set well. She looked out at the crowd, making eye contact with different people, then she appeared to take a breath and brace herself as her eyes closed.

Curiosity piqued, Nick listened, goose bumps climbing up his arms as she slid into the first notes of one of his favorite songs.

"All I needed was some time away, time to clear my head, time to clear my heart of all you'd done and said...."

Nick let her voice resonate through him, deciding she could put him in a trance. Her eyes focused in his direction, but she was somewhere else entirely. He whistled and clapped right along with the crowd when she finished—and reconsidered his initial thoughts about keeping his distance, for the weekend anyway. Was getting to know her really such a bad idea?

She was speaking into the mic, but he missed her

first words because of the applause.

"—real treat for me. Thanks for letting me have some fun. Give it up for the Mike Vincent Band— they're great, aren't they?"

She hugged the lead singer and kissed the guy named Steve, then stepped down from the stage and joined her girlfriends. Okay, why'd she kiss that guy? First she sings him a song, then she gives him a kiss. *Huh...*

Jayne rejoined her friends at the edge of the dance floor, tugged along to the bar in an onslaught of whoops and hugs. Nick was leaning against it, one elbow resting on the ledge, just staring at her. She caught his eye, and a warm sizzle cruised from her scalp to her toes, altogether exhilarating, but she wasn't sure what to make of his expression. Was he scowling at her?

"Hi Nick." She offered a tentative smile.

His features softened as a smile spread, deepening his dimples, just before he leaned into her ear. "Can I have your autograph?"

Those five simple words, asked in that sexy growl, turned Jayne's insides to molten lava, bringing on a tingle where her thighs met black lace. *Yikes...*She drew his gaze, pretty sure a slow simmer of heat lurked there.

How could a complete stranger bring on such intense *want*? She'd just met this guy, but instinctively she'd known him forever.

Pushing fear aside, she laid her hand on his arm and flashed him a wink. "Only if you dance with me first."

Nick nodded and set his beer on the bar. Then he took her hand and led her through the packed space. Walking behind him was like following Moses across the Red Sea. He was a head taller than most other men and carried himself with a commanding swagger that made him stand out. His broad shoulders made an easy wake for her, and then he carved a slot for them on the crowded dance floor.

To Jayne's astonishment, Nick swung her around in a smooth version of a Carolina Shag, practiced and light on his feet. When he smiled down, the glow in his jade eyes put her off balance and it was all she could do to follow the quick steps without stumbling. As the song wound down, Nick offered her a playful grin, then twirled and dipped her.

Laughing, she allowed Nick to pull her upright. "That was fun. You can be my dance partner any time."

"Back at you. Another?"

"Sure."

Jayne heard the first notes of a familiar slow song and her eyes flew to Steve. In turn, he offered a nod and a knowing smile. She'd sung it a hundred times, but it was still painful to hear.

Nick, unaware of the song's significance, merely pulled her against his chest, taking her hand as he led. Leaning into his taut strength, she recognized the fragrance of his cologne and fell headlong into the scent. With her eyes closed, her olfactory senses kicked in and tried to take her to another time and place, and into the arms of another man.

But being here with Nick was somehow different, somehow *more*. Nick exuded power and confidence with every breath, and the crinkles at the corners of his eyes spoke of life's lessons and experiences.

As Steve sang the last words of the song, Jayne looked up at Nick, struggling to shake off the hunger those memories evoked, afraid Nick might see the vulnerability resting beneath the fragile veil of confidence she wore. "Thanks for the dance."

"Any time." He offered his hand, his eyes settling

on hers, questioning.

His gaze heated her blood, making it flow through her veins like a sip of cognac. She clasped his hand and followed him back to their post at the bar. With a racing heart, she excused herself and took off for the ladies room—high time to distance herself from *tall, dark and dangerous*. Between her own rampaging memories of Mack, and a little too much alcohol, she couldn't get a grip on her attraction to Nick and the heat simmering under her skin when he touched her. He'd as much as said he wasn't married, but he was still a very bad idea, on so many levels. Especially now.

Crowding into the small space, Jayne ran into Meg and Cara.

Meg called from the other side of her stall door, "Okay, Jayne. Need some Cliff Notes. The minute I arrive, you're brandishing a microphone, belting out songs like nobody's business, which I had no idea you were capable of. Then there's Tom Selleck's younger brother who seems to have you on his radar screen, four adorable fly boys vying to be the sultans of our harem, and a pack of rowdy Canadians intent on getting themselves and all of us really shit-faced. Did I leave anything out?" Meg finally took a breath.

Cara giggled from the next stall, hiccupping just before she said, "Meg, those *are* the Cliff Notes. How much have you had to drink, anyway? I've never heard you talk so much at one time."

Jayne turned on the faucet to wash her hands, amused as she listened to her friends, both clearly intoxicated. Quiet Meg had become chatty and Cara was finding everything comical, her giggle contagious.

She made room for Meg at the sink. "You're seeing everything pretty much at face value. And here's the deal. I need to keep my distance from Nick. He's a little too much of what I like. I was doing fine until we slow danced and I realized he's wearing Armani's Aqua di Gio..."

"Hmmm...that's been your undoing on more than a couple of occasions if I recall." Meg scrunched her face. "What is it about men's cologne anyway? If it's good, you'll follow them to the devil's den, and if it's bad, it doesn't matter how hot he is. It's like mosquito repellent."

Cara emerged from the stall, and added, "Amen to that, sister. Don't know what the deal is, but Jimmy and Andy smell good, too. Is it a Canadian thing?"

Jayne shook her head, then said deadpan, "No. it's a Canadian *biker* thing."

Cara giggled hysterically. "Must come with the motorcycle license. And it's *so* obvious Nick's called dibs on you. Whether you like it or not, you've been tagged and the rest of them are giving him a clear path. Send up a signal if you need a save."

"Trust me, I have no intention of getting close enough to need a save."

"Why not? What's the harm in hanging out with him this evening? He's all that and a slice of cake. Your *birthday* cake, so to speak..."

Jayne shook her head, frowning. "The last thing I need is a weekend Romeo. He's definitely a slice of cake, but I'm on a diet."

"Jayne, this is just vacation. You don't have to *marry* him. Why not have a little fun? He sure can dance." Meg cocked an eyebrow, "And a man that can dance like that can..."

Meg and Cara burst into laughter, so contagious Jayne joined in. "Well, now that you've put it that way..."

"Atta girl."

Jayne scolded herself. She had to stop taking everything so seriously. Any other trip and she'd be flirting and having the time of her life. Why shouldn't she let loose for the evening? But she needed to be careful—Meg and Cara weren't the only ones feeling the effects of the alcohol.

☼☼☼

Greg Halverson listened to the message from his assistant, his blood pressure rising with every word. Bennett was advising him, just in case he was interested in knowing, that he'd just seen Nick McCord walk into Sloppy Joe's with the pretty blonde they'd met at the airport. He checked the time stamp. Just before midnight.

What the fuck? He slammed his phone back into his pocket, his jaw clenching as he whirled on his heel and charged back down Duval Street to Sloppy Joe's, pushing against pedestrians who strayed into his path. White hot anger flashed, boiled over and scalded him. How in the hell had this happened? What was that prick, McCord, doing in Key West? And what was he doing with Jayne Morgan?

Halverson shoved through the bar, finally spotting Bennett. Heading to him, he scanned the crowd. *There.* McCord and that lug, Jameson, were easy to find. Then he recognized Langston. No surprise to find that band of idiots roaming together. But what the hell were they doing in Key West this weekend? He finally spied Jayne Morgan, in the middle of a group of women. She was laughing and then McCord stepped beside her and pressed his hand against her back. Halverson sucked in a breath between his teeth, blinding dots dancing before his eyes. Why was she letting him touch her?

He watched Jayne follow McCord to the dance floor. He nearly stroked out when McCord placed his hand on Jayne's back, pulling her toward him. *That bastard can't have her. I won't allow it...*

Halverson swallowed the bitter taste flooding his mouth. McCord was always in the middle of everything. The Halverson family business had been vilified and bankrupt because of McCord, and now that it was once again thriving, Nick was stealing construction projects from him left and right. Now *this*? How in the hell did McCord manage to be here in the middle of *this* game. *Nick Fucking McCord...*

Steadying himself, he exhaled and reined in his ire as an interesting realization struck—seeing Jayne as an object of McCord's attention made her that much more appealing. He chewed his lower lip as a revised plan formulated. He gave Bennett a few instructions and retreated to the shadows.

From all appearances, Jayne had just met McCord and he'd obviously failed to mention his current marital status or she wouldn't be getting so cozy with him. She'd made it clear married men were off limits when he'd asked her to dinner that afternoon. Halverson smirked, picturing the scene playing out.

SIX

Jayne wasn't exactly sure how Nick happened to be lip on lip with her, but he was. Not a quick smooch, but a big, whopping, lip nibbling, tongue swirling kiss that left her breathless. She wasn't sure if it was the kiss or the alcohol that made the ground roll beneath her feet. Maybe a little of both, but one thing was certain—if he let go of her, she'd melt into the floor.

"Ohhh..." was all she could manage as he pulled back.

"Yeah..." He breathed, peering into her eyes.

Jayne's world shrank to only her and Nick as dancers gyrated all around them in the dark.

Nick leaned down and kissed her again, more aggressively this time, his lips strong against hers, the blood sizzling beneath her skin where he touched her. The song ended and he led her off the dance floor to a bar stool where Meg babysat their drinks.

"Here Jayne, take this seat," Meg offered, accepting Jimmy's hand as he invited her to the dance floor.

"I'd rather stand. I'm afraid if I sit, I'll never get back up," Jayne said, her head a little woozy.

"Okay. Then I'll sit." Nick perched and pulled her between his legs, wrapping his hands around her back.

Taking a pull on his beer, he realized that he might be just a little drunk, but hell, who wasn't? He'd have to watch himself, though. This pretty woman had the goods to make him rethink how he'd like to spend the rest of his time away. He pulled her close and kissed her again, enjoying the way she fit perfectly against him. Her lips were warm, and in the dark bar with the crowd paying them no heed, it was easy to forget they weren't alone.

What had possessed him to kiss her in the middle of a dance floor, anyway? He'd always been so private, so careful to refrain from any kind of public display. But now he wanted more. It'd been so long since he'd connected on a physical level with someone. Hell, even the touch of her firm breasts molding against his chest unleashed a need so raw it was throwing his brain function below his belt, surprising him as he felt his body respond. He'd been celibate for over a year. After Paris, all desire for sex had flat out deserted him. But it was back—in a big way. A virtual tidal wave of need was sweeping fire straight to his groin, reminding him of everything he'd missed.

And the way she tasted…warm, sweet, peppermint and orange. He breathed in the scent of her perfume. She smelled as good as she tasted in spite of their dank surroundings. For the first time in months, he wanted to take someone to bed…*this* someone—and the sooner the better.

Nuzzling her neck, he purred, "You know, we could go somewhere more private…"

Jayne took a breath, willing her heart to slow. Her head was swimming and this man was addiction personified. She drew back, unsure how to respond to his proposition. As much as she'd love to give in to the pure lust, it was way too soon to be going *there*. And she knew better than to take him seriously. Sure, he might mean it, for this moment, anyway—he was tanked and he'd just uttered the typical drunk-guy-in-a-bar invitation. They'd shared a couple of hot kisses and he was sporting major wood. *That* was pretty obvious. He had to know she'd never accept the offer, but as a member of the male tribe, he had to make the play. It was part of the code. Just the same, knowing he wanted her translated into a surge of power that put every nerve ending on high alert.

"Ah, you're such a charmer. Every girl dreams of being picked up in a bar. How could I possibly say no?" she chided as she teased her fingertip across his lower lip, then tangled her fingers in the curls at the back of his head. She held on for a moment, imagined twining her fingers through his hair while she wrapped her legs around him and a dormant twinge flashed through her core.

Nick leaned back, a chagrined expression planted on his face. "You're right. That was...umm...tacky. I'm—"

Jayne laid her finger across his lips. "Understood." She braced his face with her hands, looking into his eyes. "We're on the same page, but it's all about timing."

Did she dare make some time for him this weekend? Would it be so bad to see how it played out for a couple of days?

Cara was leaning on the bar, watching the crowd when a young man, cute in a wet-behind-the-ears manner, took an open spot next to her, offering her a friendly nod.

"Wanna dance?"

"Sure." Cara followed him to the dance floor. She loved to dance. Didn't matter if it was with someone old, young, fat, skinny, cute or not. Hell, she'd even dance with her gal pals to the right music.

After ten minutes, they exchanged names between songs and left the dance floor as the band announced a break.

Bennett motioned to the bar. "Can I buy you a drink?"

"Thanks. I have one sitting over there with my friends." She pointed to Jayne and Nick.

He took a couple of steps forward, then pulled back, a shocked look spreading across his face as he stopped short and said, "Hold up." He gestured in the opposite direction. "I'll wait for you over there."

"What's wrong?" Cara asked, puzzled.

"I see someone I know and he's not with his wife. It'll be awkward if he recognizes me."

"What guy?"

"That guy on the bar stool with the blonde," he answered, giving a slight nod toward Nick.

"The blonde is my friend. How do you know Nick?" Cara asked, her stomach knotting for her friend.

"Nick McCord's in the construction business in Toronto. I know his wife, and that's not her," he said, pointing toward Jayne. "What he does is his own business, but I'm steering clear. I don't need problems back home with a guy as important as he is, and he may not be happy to run into someone from home. No offense if he's a friend of yours."

"None taken. We just met him tonight. So, thanks for the dance, but right now I need to find someone…"

Fuming, Cara scanned the crowd, but Leigh and Meg were nowhere to be seen. Dammit, she needed them to help her with this. Blowing out a breath, she figured a direct approach would be best. She stepped over to Jayne, tapping her on the arm. "Join me for a sec, will ya?"

"Sure." Jayne set her drink on the bar and followed.

Once they wound their way to the back corridor near the ladies room, Cara took Jayne by the shoulders, her voice hushed, "I'm very sorry, but I need to tell you something. That guy I was dancing with? He knows Nick from Toronto." Cara took a breath, pausing, then frowned, trying to soften the words. "Says he knows Nick's *wife*. Jayne, I hate telling you this, but it seems Nick's married after all." Cara put her arm around Jayne's shoulder. "I'm so sorry, but I knew you'd want to know."

Jayne's stomach fell like an elevator car with a broken cable. It took a second for Cara's words to fully register, then color exploded before her eyes. Hot. Blazing. Red.

Damn him! Furious with herself for being so naïve, the acid raged inside, but she squelched it, refusing to lose her cool in public.

Taking a deep breath, she met Cara's eyes. "Thanks, sweetie. I know it was hard to tell me, but I should've known. He's too good to be true." She blew out a calming breath, shaking her head. "Dammit, I'm such a fool—a drunken fool."

Shit! And she'd just about talked herself into a little weekend romance—a last dance, so to speak. And this was the reward for letting her guard down...

"What do you want to do? If you want to leave, I'll go with you."

"Thanks, but I'm not about to ruin the rest of the night for you guys. I'll slip out the back. Nick McCord can go to hell. Feel free to tell him so once I'm gone."

"We're in this together. You're not leaving alone."

"No. I need to disappear without a scene. Just let me get out of here. Okay?"

Cara bit her lip, nodded, then gave Jayne a hug. "I'll get Brandon to walk you back. Hang here for a few minutes."

"Fine. I'll be around on the side."

Greg Halverson watched fury slide across Jayne's face as she listened to her friend, and a spurt of satisfaction sped through him. Bennett had done his job. He slid off his bar stool as Jayne came toward him, catching her as she passed. "Jayne? Hoped I'd run into you tonight."

"Oh, hello."

He chose to ignore the lackluster greeting. "Have a drink with me?" He watched the play of emotions filter through her eyes, but he had to give her points for composure. She was one cool number, and he was even more fascinated now that he'd seen some of her colors. He'd seen an angry flash of fire in her eyes. Now he'd like to see that same flash in the heat of passion. Oh, what he could do with her... *to her.* There was no end to the pleasures he'd share, and in time, when she was ready, he'd introduce her to some of his more... *satisfying* preferences. All in good time... God, he was getting hard just thinking about it.

"Thanks, but I'm calling it a night." She continued toward the door.

"Could I walk you somewhere?"

She offered him a half smile. "No thanks. Good night."

"If you're sure. Good night." *I'll be seeing you, my lovely.*

He'd follow her at a distance, but first he had a message to send along with one of the photos his assistant had snapped of Nick mauling Jayne. He tapped out a quick note on his phone.

Who's with Nick? You should find out. Could change your $$$ settlement. BTW Nick's trading down.

He hit *send.* He'd made it a personal mission to find every way, no matter how small, to make McCord's life hell. Like Chinese water torture, he'd slowly and painstakingly continue making Nick pay for what he'd done to his brother.

Jayne stormed down the sidewalk. She'd allowed her defenses to slide and now she was paying the price. Humiliated beyond words, but also embarrassed, she wondered how she could have been such an idiot. She cringed, as the descriptives *cheap* and *bimbo* reared their ugly heads. She wanted the sidewalk to open up and swallow her.

No...she wanted the sidewalk to open up and swallow *Nick Asshole McCord,* then chew him up and spit him into the ocean as chum. Why in the world had she ignored her better judgment? Now he'd played her for a fool. *Aargggh...frigging cretin!*

She'd only kissed him...but she'd made damn sure he knew she was interested. He was a cheat and she'd played right into his hands, oh so willingly. If she hadn't made it clear from the beginning that she didn't play this game, she could chalk it up to typical man-on-a-holiday behavior and blame herself for being naïve. But *this?* She'd told him—explicitly—that married men were off limits. And he chose to lie. *Arrogant, self-serving piece-of-shit-rat-bastard.*

Anger grew with each pounding step. By the time she reached the corner of the street, she didn't care if she made a quiet retreat or not. She was ready to rip Nick a new one. Hadn't he said *we're not all married?* Okay, room for misinterpretation there, but now she realized he was banking on that very thing.

She reached for her phone and realized she'd left her little purse on the bar with Nick. Crap! She closed her eyes and steeled herself as adrenalin-induced-sobriety allowed her to throw her shoulders back and walk through the front entrance of the bar. She scanned the room and spied Leigh, who was now wearing both her own and Jayne's bags over her shoulder.

Jayne retrieved her purse and yelled over the music, "Thanks for grabbing this for me. I'm heading back to the island."

Leigh looked straight at her, a frown creasing her brow. "What's wrong?"

"I'm just done in. I'll leave the light on for you gals. I'll text you when I get to the cottage."

"You're not walking back to the boat alone. Give me a minute to powder my nose and I'll join you."

Jayne nodded, fully intending to scoot away the minute Leigh was out of sight. It was only a three-block stroll, well-lit and completely safe. When she saw Leigh disappear around the corner, she turned to escape and slammed right into Nick's chest, his hands immediately on her shoulders. She jerked away and shot him a scathing look.

Nick caught her arm, his eyebrows raised. "Where are you going?"

She yanked her arm away. "Let *go*. Party's over, Nick. Find some other fool for your weekend." Now that the song had ended, her voice was too loud, causing people nearby to stare, but she couldn't contain the rage that vibrated with every syllable.

He stepped back with his hands up, a bewildered expression on his face. "What the hell are you talking about?"

"I told you earlier that I don't get involved with married men. You could've at least had the balls to be honest about it and admit that you have a wife."

Jayne sputtered the words, deciding it was her turn to douse *him* with a drink. If he hadn't cleared her path, she might've followed through. Instead, she whirled and pushed through the crowd and left out the front entrance.

She was half a block away when she heard Leigh shout. She stopped, dismayed to see her friend bolting toward her. As Leigh neared, Jayne said. "Well, shit. Now I've ruined your night, too. I really wish you'd stay here with Meg and Cara."

"Cara told me what happened." Leigh threw her arm around Jayne's shoulder. "Wanna talk?"

"Not really. I'm over-served and I fell for a lame line…"

"No you didn't, but we can discuss that tomorrow. Let's go back to the cottage and dive into that stash I put out of Cara's reach. Food is always a great therapist, and I'm starving. You?"

"I can always eat…" Jayne laughed, hooking her arm through Leigh's. "Thanks for being such a great wing man."

"Leigh! Jayne! Hang on—"

As one, they turned to see Brandon jogging toward them.

"Can I interest you ladies in an escort to the dock?"

"Sure, Brandon. Thanks." He slid between them and they hooked onto his arms.

Following Jayne from a safe distance, other pedestrians made him invisible. The tall woman had practically bowled him over as she galloped past, so Halverson quickened his pace to remain within earshot. Now some other guy was with them. At this rate, he'd have to be more creative if he wanted to get her alone.

Watching Jayne dress Nick down was a rush. The venom in her words radiated all the way to where he stood, hidden in the shadows, giving him a high nearly as good as using his riding crop on a naked ass. God, his cock was still like concrete.

Ten years and he hated McCord more every day. Tormenting him by taking Jayne would be fun. An ancillary move, but a bonus all the same. She'd be the cherry on top of the sundae. Once he enticed Jayne to his bed, she'd never be satisfied by the likes of McCord. He'd make sure of that.

The water taxi was idling at the dock, ready to depart as Jayne, Leigh and Brandon rounded the corner. Racing down the gangway, the women yelled for the first mate to wait while they bid Brandon a hasty goodbye. Jayne opted to stand on the fantail for the ride over and leaned against the rail, the water inky and splashed with streaming moonbeams below her.

She heard additional footsteps hurrying across the gangplank, Halverson's voice coming from behind her, and she groaned inwardly. The one she'd wanted was a liar, and the one who wanted her was simply not her type.

"Well, hello again. Didn't realize we're staying at the same resort. I should've come with you. It's not safe to walk alone this late at night."

Jayne turned to face him as they stood at the rail, admitting he was very handsome. Had she been wrong about Greg Halverson? He *was* trying awfully hard...

"Thanks, but I wasn't alone." She gestured toward Leigh and turned back to the water, exhausted and overwhelmed by the events of the last thirty minutes as the adrenalin rush ebbed. Her shoulders slumped as Greg addressed her friend.

"Greg Halverson. Jayne and I met this afternoon."
"Leigh Wallace."

Jayne remained silent, listening as Leigh made small talk with Greg during the short ride. He seemed pleasant, convivial even, as he discussed the regatta with

Leigh. Maybe they should accept his invitation to watch the race. A regatta party might be a great way to put put tonight's disaster behind her.

Then her thoughts drifted back to Nick, triggering a fresh bloom of anger—for giving him a second thought *and* for being stupid enough to let him get to her.

Dammit. This weekend is too short and I won't waste energy on a lying jerk.

They stepped off the boat, following other passengers up the gangway. Jayne listened as the soft strands of a lone guitar wafted from the resort's bar.

Halverson waved his hand toward the ocean-front patio to their right. "It appears Latitudes Bar is still serving. Join me for a night cap?"

Feeling the need to let the ocean breeze blow off the stench of the night's events, Jayne raised her eyebrows at Leigh. "I'm up for one if you are, Leigh."

"Why not?" Leigh said, nodding.

Jayne followed Leigh up the steps to the door of their cottage, anxious to find her pillow. Clicking the lock on their door, she leaned against it and exhaled, "I'm sorry...that was a mistake..."

"No need to apologize. He's charming at first, but then something else takes over. Can't quite put my finger on it, though." Leigh frowned, flipping on the kitchen light. "But I'm betting he's got a dark side, if my instincts are correct."

"You're probably right, but I'm too wiped out to give it another thought tonight." Jayne pushed herself off the door and started for the bedroom. "Two for two in the day one—talk about batting a thousand. Can't wait to see what Friday has in store..."

SEVEN

Bells, distant and drawing closer, pulled Jayne from a catatonic sleep. They persisted as she grabbed toward the sound, knocking everything off the night stand onto the travertine floor with an ear-splitting clatter. Shaking off her mental cobwebs, she squinted toward the floor and grasped the cord, dragging the phone receiver to her ear.

"'llo..." Her mouth was glued shut.

"Jayne?"

"Hmm."

"Have breakfast with me."

Groggy, Jayne grumbled, "Who's this?"

"Did I wake you?"

She finally recognized the sexy baritone and snapped awake, feeling the throb of a headache slam against her temples in a hateful cadence. The mocking, deep-throated chuckle brought the previous night's events spiraling forward.

"Wrong number." She slammed the phone down on its cradle. Rolling over, Jayne squeezed her eyes shut, cringing as images of Nick emerged.

The phone rang again. Jayne picked it up and set it right back down before it could wake Leigh, snoring soundly in the next bed.

It rang a third time and she grabbed the receiver, hissing, *"Are you impaired?"*

"Jayne?"

It was a different male voice she didn't recognize, but she didn't mask her impatience as she struggled to sit up. "Yes."

"Good morning. It's Greg Halverson. Wonder if I might interest you and Leigh in a little sailing this afternoon after the race."

"Greg, sorry, I was asleep. Sailing? Thanks, but we have a full schedule today."

"Tomorrow then?"

"Greg, I don't mean to be rude, but please understand—we're booked for the rest of our time here. I'm afraid we won't be able to join you."

"You're tough on a guy's ego, Jayne. One way or another, I'll find a way to get better acquainted with you—guess I'll have to keep trying."

He chuckled low and the hairs on her arms rose. "I'll let you go, but I've got you on my radar screen."

"That's very flattering, but I'm not a good target. You should plug in some different coordinates."

"You're cute, and I love the analogy. So I'll just leave you with a thought. I've got you filed on my flight plan. I'll talk with you later."

Jayne hung up the phone and shuddered. Halverson was nothing she was interested in, especially after having a drink with him last night. And now he was starting to creep her out. Between him, Nick and the stupid amount of vodka she'd consumed, her head was about to splinter open. She eased back onto her pillow. It would take way too much energy to locate her bottle of aspirin.

She'd just re-settled in her bed to steal another hour of sleep when the phone rang for the fourth time.

Exhaling loudly, she answered, "Concierge Desk."

"Don't hang up." Nick's voice projected both plea and command.

"Guess I need to take the phone off the hook,"

she growled.

"I'd like to talk to you about last night. Have breakfast with me."

She leaned over and squinted at the clock on the floor, then looked over at the other bed where she heard a moan coming from the stirring lump. Keeping her voice low, she spat, "Bad idea."

"I disagree," Nick argued.

"Too bad."

"Tell me why."

Fury rebounded in her gut. "Figure it out."

"I think I have."

There was a pause and her heard him exhale, rather loudly in fact. "Jayne, I know you're pissed, but there's been a misunderstanding. I'm not married. Let's talk over breakfast."

Jayne's eyes pinched shut—her stomach rolled with renewed disgust. God, this guy was arrogant. Wasn't last night enough? Were all men just assholes when they were on vacation? She covered her eyes with her hand. This was *not* the way she'd planned to spend this particular weekend.

"Nick, let's chalk last night up to too much alcohol and let it go at that. No blood, no foul."

"No. Let's straighten this out."

"Nothing to straighten out. I'm sure women fall at your feet all the time, but I've already told you where I stand."

"I know you did. And I'm not married. I don't know where you got your information, but I'm divorced."

Jayne was incredulous. Did he figure her for a gullible idiot? "How convenient."

Nick snorted, "Not really. Trust me, divorce is never convenient."

Jayne wrestled between the temptation to slam

down the phone again and allowing herself a smidgeon of inclination to believe him.

But why *should* she believe him?

Was it because she intuitively knew he was one of the good guys? Every signal she picked up on told her so. That must be why last night felt so awful. She'd always had good instincts, and she trusted them.

He finally broke the silence. "You're going to make me grovel, aren't you?"

The sound of his throaty chuckle made her stomach dip in spite of her anger. "Nick, we only met yesterday, so you don't owe me an explanation for anything you do."

"Jayne, give me an hour and hear me out. I'd like to get this cleared up."

His determination was maddening, but Jayne heard something else in his voice. Something that told her she should hear what he had to say. Everyone made mistakes, right? Who was she to be so self-righteous? And why did he care so much about what she thought of him?

Because only someone honest cared enough to vindicate himself.

"I've gotta hand it to you, Nick McCord. You're very persistent and that's a bit compelling. But there's no way I can make breakfast. I just woke up and I've got a headache that you're making worse."

He laughed. "Okay. Lunch?"

"Oh...*all right*. If you're so determined, I can make the eleven o'clock boat. You get one hour, unless you piss me off again and I shorten the deal. Agreed?"

"Agreed."

"And Nick, you're asking me to simply take your word for the fact that you're divorced. That's a lot to ask of someone who doesn't know you."

"I understand. And thanks for at least giving me the benefit of the doubt. Where should I meet you?"

"At the marina behind the Westin Hotel—where the Sunset Princess docks. You'll see the sign."

Nick clicked off his phone, not at all happy Andy had overheard.

Andy raised an eyebrow. "What's the deal?"

"No idea. I should have my head examined. What I can't figure is why she's so convinced I'm still married. Doesn't make sense. One minute she's kissing me, the next she's calling me a liar."

He'd stewed about it the rest of the night and was still fuming when he woke up. Man, she'd been pissed, but where had that come from? He shook his head. He'd had his fill of irrational, bitchy women for a lifetime. Was Jayne just another Jekyll and Hyde? He didn't think so and it bothered the hell out of him that she thought he'd deceived her. One thing for certain— he wasn't a liar or a cheat and whether he saw her again or not, he wanted to set the record straight.

Andy shook out a shirt, pulling it on. "Lots of guys lie. I'm surprised she agreed to meet you. Bet she stands you up."

"How much?"

"Hundred bucks."

"You're on. I'll be spending your cash before the day ends." Nick grinned. Something about Jayne told him she'd keep her word. He was good at reading people and even though she misunderstood what was going on, it spoke volumes about her integrity, and that's what made him want to straighten out this mess. That, and something about her had settled in the back of his mind. He'd never met anyone quite like her. Too bad the last thing he wanted or needed in his life was another woman.

Andy was mixing a Bloody Mary and leveled a look at him. "The guys will be busting your balls over this. She ripped you a new one and now you're taking her to lunch? Looking a might whipped, if you ask me."

"Wasn't asking you." Nick pulled a shirt and shorts from his duffle bag, shaking out the wrinkles.

"But I'm telling you, just the same. You're never gonna hear the end of it."

"Only if you open your big mouth—"

Andy grinned, obviously enjoying Nick's dilema. "Oh, you can count on it, buddy. Good for her, though. At least you can see what she's made of, even if she was as drunk as Cooter Brown."

"Hell, we all were. She sounded a little rough—admitted to a headache."

"She's not alone. Hoping this hair of the dog puts me right." Andy offered a silent toast and tasted his drink. "Ahh, this'll do it."

"You're a lost cause." Nick confiscated Andy's Bloody Mary and headed to the shower.

"Takes one to know one." Andy yelled through the closed door. "At least I'm not panting after a long-legged blonde."

Nick chuckled and yelled back, "You would be if you were single. Good Bloody, by the way."

"You're welcome, by the way."

Jayne groaned and hugged her pillow, "*Aargggh...*Leigh, what am I doing?"

She found if she kept her head perfectly still, the throbbing wasn't unbearable. About her queasy stomach—she couldn't decide if it was because of Nick or the amount of alcohol she'd consumed. Both were bringing on waves of nausea at the moment.

Leigh stirred and sat up. "Is this rhetorical or do

you want to talk about it? Did I overhear you make a date with Nick?"

"I guess."

"Care to dish?"

"He wants to clear up our misunderstanding. Says he's newly divorced. Oh, and Greg Halverson called to invite us to go sailing, but I declined. Hope you don't mind."

"Not in the least." Leigh yawned and stretched, "You've had a busy morning and you haven't even gotten out of bed."

"No joke." Everything she'd hoped to avoid this weekend had landed right in her lap in the form of two men she would've been just fine without meeting. Now they'd both insinuated themselves into her time away.

"Nick strikes me as a decent guy." Leigh frowned, slightly shaking her head as she plumped her pillow and settled back against it. "Oh, God, where's the aspirin. Remind me to avoid alcohol today." She shifted and asked, "Do you believe him?"

Jayne paused before she spoke, "As much as I want to, you can't make up the fact that someone's married. I just found out by chance, so lucky for me it was before I made an even bigger fool of myself."

"You didn't make a fool of yourself."

"Oh, I'm pretty sure I did." She could feel the heat rise to her face as she recalled how drawn she'd been to Nick, how good it had felt to let loose and enjoy the attention of a strong, handsome man. "He kept saying it was a misunderstanding. If nothing else, he's determined to make me hear him out." Jayne leaned forward and looked at Leigh. "What do you think?"

"I'd give him the benefit of the doubt. As I was racing out of the bar, he said the same thing to me but I didn't give him time to explain."

Leigh motioned for Jayne to join her and patted a

spot on the bed. Jayne complied, feeling Leigh's arm wrap around her shoulder, giving her a squeeze.

"You need to ease up on yourself. As far as last night goes, you're only human and he'd be hard to resist. Mmmmm, can't you just imagine grabbing those curly locks and hanging on for dear life?" Leigh sighed, "I sure wish Charlie had hair like that." Then she laughed. "Hell, I wish Charlie had *hair*. Tall, dark and dangerous sure has it going on."

Jayne leaned against Leigh, bumping the side of her head against her friend's blonde bob with a groan. "Thanks for the visual... "

"Yeah, the rest of us coined him as the Marlboro Man with a Sam Elliott voice," Leigh laid her hand across her chest and offered a stage sigh, fluttering her eyelashes.

"That's funny. Marlboro Man was the first thing that came to my mind when I met him. And you're thoroughly enjoying this, aren't you?" Jayne threw her head back against the pillow, wincing as the movement caused pain behind her eyeballs, but relieved that Leigh had the same read on Nick.

"More than you know. But there's something else going on here, isn't there? He has you *undone*." Leigh frowned. "What aren't you telling me?"

Jayne hesitated, blowing out a breath. Should she admit what had initially pulled her into Nick's orbit? Would that seem pathetic or creepy? Hell, it was a little weird to *her*. "Okay, here's the deal. I didn't see it at first, but as the night rolled on, I could see some of Mack in him—like an older brother. I'd see him from the corner of my eye and my breath would catch in my throat. The way he cocks one eyebrow, the way he laughs, the green eyes...and then he had on Aqua di Gio." Jayne rolled her eyes as she saw the odd expression on Leigh's face. "Don't look at me with that barrister's skepticism, Leigh."

"You surprise me. A guy catches your eye and the first thing you do is try to talk yourself out of him by comparing him to Mack. *Stop feeling guilty.* So what if he has the same look—a lot of men do. And it's a good look."

"I know, but it *did* make me feel guilty. Guilty about comparing Nick to Mack, guilty about comparing *anyone* to Mack… But the more time I spent with Nick, aside from appearance, he's very different from Mack." Jayne threw up her hands, words escaping her. "Hell, at least I'm consistent…"

Leigh sat up. "Explain."

Jayne gazed at the ceiling. How could she put this into words? This type of emotion was hard for her to translate, especially where Mack was concerned. She finally said, "Mack was hot. No doubt about it. Handsome and full of this walking-on-a-high-wire energy. The world was his oyster and his enthusiasm was contagious. He was invincible—like Superman. He made me feel safe—and adored. You couldn't help but want to be around him."

"And Nick?"

"He's confident. Gives you the impression he can handle anything. Like Mack, I think Nick would make you feel protected, too. The difference? Nick's an all-grown-up kind of smokin' hot. I like the creases around his eyes—the way they crinkle when he laughs. Everything about him screams success—but he wears it like a pair of old jeans. And that, Mrs. Wallace, is about as sexy as it gets in my book."

"I agree. And since I didn't know Mack, I can't get a read on this, but it must feel a little weird for you." Leigh headed to the bathroom and started brushing her teeth. "Gawd, how does so much wool grow on your teeth overnight?" She spat, and moved her hand in a circle. "Keep going."

"Okay. Am I giving Nick an advantage he hasn't earned—because of the resemblance?" Jayne sat up, cradling her temples. "Am I nuts?"

Talking over her toothbrush, Leigh shook her head. "Not at all. You're fair enough to see Nick for who he is, rather than who you'd like for him to be. Besides, he seems pretty great without any help from your imagination."

"Hope you're right. And his eyes...I caught a glimpse of him while I was singing and I could swear he was about to devour me with them—just licking his chops for good measure." Jayne laughed. "Thought my knees would give out right then and there."

"I *saw* that look on his face. I remember thinking his grin could charm the panties off a nun."

"Nearly charmed them off *me*. I was holding my own until he kissed me..." Jayne sighed as a quick recollection of his lips, warm and possessive, made her heart flutter.

"Don't let me piss you off, but from my vantage point, you didn't seem to be putting up much of a struggle. Looked like you were kissing him right back."

"Dammit, I *was*. That's the problem. Then Cara tells me he has a wife and I wanted to strangle him." Jayne got out of bed. "I need coffee. And where is that damned bottle of aspirin?" She paused in the doorway, turning to catch the bottle Leigh tossed her way. "Maybe I shouldn't go. You know I've been here before and it was a disaster."

"One married jerk in the past ten years doesn't make you the Scarlet Woman. That asshole lied to you. Don't compare this situation to that one. You're older, wiser, and you know how to put this into perspective. You agreed to hear him out, and I think it'd be a mistake to cancel. After all—it's daytime and you're sober. Those factors alone could make all the difference."

Leigh followed Jayne to the kitchen. "Just for the record, I gotta ask —does he kiss as good as he looks?"

Jayne shook her head, laughing, "You're *such* a bitch."

"And proud of it. Answer the question."

"Oh, yeah. He gets a five-star rating in that category." Jayne downed her aspirin and half a glass of water. She wiped her mouth and looked at Leigh. "Every time I get close to him, it's like a shock wave. So you're right...I'll go."

Hearing the cottage doorbell, Jayne padded to the living room and peeked through the glass panel on the door. A bellman stood on the porch, nearly hidden by an enormous bouquet and an ice bucket holding a bottle.

Jayne swung the door open, "Wow. Aren't these gorgeous? Let me help you. Who're they for?" She retrieved the flowers and set them down on a table while the bellman placed the ice bucket on the counter.

"Jayne Morgan. She's in this cottage, right?" the bellman checked his ticket.

"Sure. That's me. Hang on a minute." She raced to her room to grab some money from her wallet and returned, handing him a tip. "Thank you."

She closed the door behind him and opened the card, the smile falling from her face as she read the card.

Happy Birthday, Jayne. Flowers to celebrate your beauty and champagne to celebrate your sparkling personality. Cheers, Greg Halverson.

"Leigh, check this out."

"Oh, my. These are fabulous." Leigh walked over to examine the bouquet. "That is one big-ass bunch of flowers. And Dom Perignon? Nick making amends?"

"No. Read this," Jayne said as she offered the note.

Leigh's eyes scanned the card, then back at Jayne, her face grim. "Appears he's now your admirer...or *stalker.* Any idea how he found out it was your birthday? I don't recall mentioning it last night."

"We must've said something. Doesn't matter. He's imposing himself a little too much."

"So it seems. Trust your gut on this guy, too. We'll make it a point to keep our distance. You gonna call and thank him?"

Jayne chewed her lip, considering. "No, I'll write a note and drop it off at the desk—have a bellman deliver it." She stepped over to the desk and retrieved a card and envelope from the guest service packet.

Jotting the note, she looked up. "This sound okay? Greg, thank you for the champagne and lovely bouquet. Very thoughtful of you. Sincerely, Jayne Morgan."

"Perfect. And we need to figure out what you're gonna wear. If you're gonna make the man crawl, make him pant a little too."

Leigh reached for the coffee pot. "Cara left us a note. She and Meg suggest we get our asses out to the pool pronto—or to quote, *lazy* asses. If they get too smart, we won't share this bottle of Dom with them," Leigh chuckled, pouring a liberal amount of cream into her mug. "Now, how about a cup of this to go with your shower?"

"Sure, but go easy on the cream. Maybe I can get out of here before I have to face that particular court of inquiry. Tell them I'll explain about the Hog's Breath later, and you can fill them in on my lunch date with Nick." Jayne took a sip, heading toward the bedroom.

"Oh, you can bet on it. Your ears will be burnin' kiddo."

EIGHT

Nick leaned on the rail, his gut tight. When was the last time he'd been on a date? Was that even what this was? A smart man would leave well enough alone and spend the rest of the weekend chilling. But nooo, here he was...

And he was highly pissed at his ex. She'd called to accuse him of having an affair while they were married. Now she was threatening to challenge the financial disbursement. *Good luck on that.*

Nick stepped closer to the gangway as the boat made its way into the berth. What on earth was he doing? He had no business chasing after a woman right now. Kidding himself that he just wanted to straighten out the misunderstanding was merely postponing the inevitable truth. He may have only been divorced for a couple of days, but he'd been alone for the better part of a year. Just being with Jayne last night made him painfully aware of how lonely he was, physically *and* emotionally. Nick blew out a breath, the knot in his stomach tightening as he caught a glimpse of her.

Jayne stepped off the gangplank, and from behind his sunglasses he performed a visual checklist. Her legs, miles long beneath her short skirt, were even better than he'd imagined. Continuing upward, his eyes roved to the bit of cleavage showing at the dip of her tank top. Intriguing. Her hair, glistening in the sunlight, was clipped up and looked cute, even though he wished she'd left it down. She seemed completely unaware of how beautiful she was. Big plus on that. Nothing about her screamed for his attention, but her actions whispered—*and he could hear every word.*

He noticed long scars spanning both of her knees and a couple of long scars running down her right calf—major scars, but old ones. Sports related injuries? Something they might have in common if the conversation lulled.

When she turned to him, a tentative smile played across her face, seeming to warm as she drew closer. The ire Nick expected to meet was surprisingly absent, thank God. But did she regret coming? Although sunglasses hid her eyes, he knew she was assessing him, maybe wondering why she'd come, same as he had.

"Hi. You look great." He leaned down to buss her cheek, disappointed when she stiffened at his touch. He groaned inwardly as he caught a whiff of her perfume. Damn, she smelled good.

"Thanks. Good morning."

"What do you say we take a walk and get the story straight over lunch?"

"No, I think we should get the story straight right now."

He nodded, leading her out of the traffic flow. "I figured as much." He pulled a piece of paper from the back pocket of his walking shorts, unfolded it and handed it to her, "Take a look at this."

"What is it?" Jayne glanced at it, then leveled her gaze at him.

"Proof."

Jayne scanned it, then handed it back to him, "This doesn't even have a signature. And most of it's blacked out."

"This is just the first page of a financial

disbursement statement. It's all I have with me, but if you take a look at the top paragraph, it shows that it's the result of a divorce decree. I just blacked out the numbers. That's personal."

Jayne took it back, removed her sunglasses and squinted at the page. He watched her eyes flick back and forth. She folded the paper and handed it back to him, her face a mask. "Okay, so why are you showing this to me?"

"Because a lot of men lie." He shrugged as he put the paper back in his pocket. "I don't. I want you to know that. Figured you wouldn't be convinced unless I showed you something concrete. And I want to erase all doubt." Nick cocked an eyebrow. She'd either accept the truth or she wouldn't. At least she'd shown up—that had to count for something.

"You're right. A lot of men do, so I apologize for jumping to conclusions based on hearsay. And thank you for caring what I think."

"So how about some lunch?"

Jayne smiled and tilted her head to the side, offering what he interpreted as a conciliatory smile, and slipped her hand through the arm he offered. "Okay."

"How does the Conch Republic Seafood Company sound? We can sit near the water and watch the boats."

"Perfect."

Strolling through the bustling streets of Old Town, Nick decided Jayne was easy company. She seemed relaxed in spite of the tenuous high wire he knew he still walked in her mind. They dodged the tourists who crowded the streets, some boarding bright yellow Conch Tour Trains and others leaving cruise ships to ride around on the orange and green Old Town Trolleys.

As they crossed Front Street, a group of girls went

flying by on red scooters, beeping their horns and howling in contagious laughter, one careening toward Jayne.

"Look out!" He yanked her up on the curb as the riders sped past, pressing her against his side.

"Whew! That was close." Jayne exhaled. "A little out of control, but they're sure having fun."

"Maybe we should rent a couple and zip around the island this afternoon," Nick suggested, warming to the thought of spending the afternoon with her. "I've never considered it before, but I'd be game."

Jayne laughed as she said, "After riding that big-ass Harley, I'm surprised you'd consider down-sizing. As tall as you are, you'd probably look like a grasshopper on one of those things."

They walked along the waterfront and paused here and there to admire the dozens of handsome sailboats and yachts, several of which were in town for the regatta, sporting various sponsorship decals along their sides. Up and down the pier, the chatter of fishing boat captains hawking charters smacked against the hum of idling diesel engines.

"Ever been fishing down here?" Nick asked as they made their way past one particularly aggressive captain.

"A few times. You?"

"Yeah. We usually go for half a day. One of the guys is setting it up for tomorrow morning if the weather cooperates. I don't care whether I fish or not, I just enjoy being out on the water."

A Border Collie, sporting a flowered visor and sunglasses, bounced to greet them with a bark and a thumping tail.

"Oh, look. Isn't he adorable?" Jayne paused to kneel next to the dog, accepting his licks on her fingers.

The pup's human companion was a street musician, unkempt and filthy, strumming an old guitar.

Jayne pulled a five dollar bill from her pocket which the dog promptly carried over to drop into his basket, returning to Jayne in hopes of an encore.

She scruffed his ears. "What a good boy you are." She looked over at the musician. "How's it going?"

Nick watched the kindness and affection Jayne lavished on the dog, and her lack of judgment for his ragged owner, her stock growing in his book. You never knew what road a man had walked. The animal had a happy disposition, but he had a ratty coat and smelled to the heavens. Most women would've shunned the creature. He squatted to pet him, giving him another bill, earning more wags and a bark.

Jayne turned to him as they continued down the wharf. "I'm a sucker for a dog of any kind, and that little guy was a sweetie. Can you imagine how cute he'd be if he was groomed? At least he appeared well-fed."

"Too bad you can't say the same for his owner." Nick stopped at the open doorway of the restaurant, deciding he'd order a sandwich for the fellow as they were leaving. "Here we go." He placed his hand at the small of her back as they entered.

Jayne flinched as the sizzle slid down her spine. Every time he touched her, a shot of heat and energy zoomed through her blood.

She glanced around the restaurant. It was a warehouse of sorts with concrete flooring and large garage doors on three sides. Hemmed in by the marina on two sides, the doors stood open to allow a warm breeze to filter through.

She excused herself and went to the ladies' room to rinse her hands, then returned to find Nick looking into the gigantic salt water aquarium. Movement at the bottom of the tank caught her eye and she spied a sinister eel skulking around the coral. For some strange reason, it brought Greg Halverson to mind, along with an involuntary shudder.

Guitarists in the corner crooned a James Taylor song, softening the echo in the cavernous facility. A hostess led them to a waterfront table with an impressive view of the marina, spectacular yachts bobbing in moorings just a stone's throw away.

Nick studied Jayne as she studied her menu, curious about the various expressions he'd watched cross her face in the last half hour. What was going on in her mind? She was a contradiction, or maybe a kaleidoscope. One minute she seemed open, the next she wore a mask.

She looked up and offered him a quick smile. Now that her sunglasses were off, he had the chance to really look at her eyes. Wise, with a twinkle that invited mischief. He couldn't decide if they were blue or green. Either way, they were lovely and they had a way of filling in the gaps of what she didn't say.

"You like shrimp?" she asked.

God, she was pretty with the light reflecting across her face. "Sure. Let's order some." Nick could care less about what they ordered. He was busy falling into the dimples that braced her grin. And then his eyes shifted to her lush lips. Better not go there—that's what got him into trouble in the first place. That and alcohol. Shaking off the thought, he decided he should stick with iced tea for a while longer.

Nick signaled the waiter and placed their order, then took a breath and met Jayne's eyes. "Let's talk about last night. Get it out of the way."

"Okay."

"If I'd been clear from the start, this conversation wouldn't be necessary."

She started to say something and he held up his

hand. "Let me get through this. I told you that not all of us were married and that's true. I didn't go into detail because I didn't think it mattered. I had no intention of getting to know you or any other woman on this trip. My wife and I split a year ago, but the divorce wasn't final until this week."

Her brow creased. "Oh, that *is* recent. I don't mean to pry, but I'd like to hear what happened if you're inclined to tell me."

"All right." He thought for a minute, searching for an answer. He really hadn't talked about it much with anyone.

"Life." He shrugged his shoulders. "I mean, you build a business, raise the kids—you're so busy that everything gets your attention but each other. Then you wake up one morning to find you're living with a stranger. We'd become two very different people with separate interests and only our kids in common."

"So you just decided to call it a day?"

He was hard pressed to come up with a good answer for this one. Finally, he said, "Let's just say we've decided to move on in separate directions due to irreconcilable differences."

He took a breath and met Jayne's gaze, continuing, not at all inclined to further elaborate. "There comes a point when you need to be moving forward rather than constantly looking back. When you can't do that, you need to own your part, cut your losses and move on. Better for us, better for our kids."

"How many children do you have?"

"Two. My son, Jamie, is in his second year at university and my daughter, Katherine, is studying art and design in Paris this year."

"How are they handling the divorce?"

"As well as can be expected, I guess—my daughter's doing better than my son, so I've tried to spend more time with him in the past few months. He seems to be getting through it."

"From what I've seen, divorce is tough on everyone involved." Jayne took a sip of her tea. "Honestly, Nick, I figured you'd tell me you were separated. Most men have a habit of using the word *separated* as a euphemism for time away with the boys, and they often lie about being divorced. I almost didn't keep our lunch date, but I'm glad I did."

Nick grinned. "Me, too. You saved me from losing a hundred dollar bet to Andy. He figured you'd stand me up."

"Pretty sure of your powers of persuasion, huh?" Jayne teased, then tapped her finger on the table. "Okay, since I've got a stake in that C note, looks like you'll not only be buying lunch, you'll also be buying drinks later."

"You're on."

Nick watched her face redden as the words left her mouth. Obviously she realized she'd just tipped her hand. Drinks later, huh? So their thoughts were on the same wave length. He fought to keep from laughing while she busied herself making space for their food, focusing on the pewter platter of iced shrimp the server was placing between them, looking anywhere but at him.

"Look at these prawns. They're huge." She plucked one off the platter and began peeling it with her fingertips. She dipped it into sauce and sucked on the end, taking a bite, moaning, "Oh, you've got to have one. They're delicious."

She was delicious, and watching her take the large prawn between her lips made him shift uncomfortably, the blood pooling in his lap. He pried his mind away from that trend of thought, focusing on his seared tuna.

Shit, that just made it worse. What was going on

with him? At this rate, lunch was going to be torture.

Taking his last bite, he wiped his mouth and tossed his napkin on the table. "Okay, I need to finish. When I kissed you last night and suggested we go somewhere, I didn't mean to offend you. I was drunk and you're gorgeous—simple as that. Sorry I pissed you off. I don't know who said what, but you must've misunderstood something to get the impression that I'm still married. All the guys know about my divorce."

"Some guy from Toronto recognized you, and told Cara that he knew your wife. When Cara told me, I had a bad acid flashback of something that happened to me a few years ago and it triggered a nasty reaction." She winced. "Spilled over onto you. Guess I'm guilty of jumping to conclusions before checking the facts, so I apologize for the hateful way I behaved."

He had to laugh, remembering the scene. "No problem, but I think there's a chunk of my ass still missing. Remind me to stay on your good side." Sobering, he said, "You don't owe me an apology. And we probably wouldn't be having lunch if you hadn't gotten so upset."

"How's that?" Her eyebrows shot up.

"You showed a moral compass." He took a bite, swallowed, then said, "Long story I'll save for another time. Let's just say that's a rare thing these days. Your reaction when you thought I was married…"

"Thanks, but don't get the wrong impression about me. I'm no angel, Nick. You could say I have a past interesting enough to keep me company in my old age, and I hope to continue adding chapters to the book for several more years. I just draw a line when it comes to married men. Years ago, I made the colossal mistake of falling for a man who was *going through a divorce*." She used her fingers in mock quotation marks to make her point. "I was naïve enough to trust a liar. When he called me on Christmas Eve to tell me that he was moving back home to his wife and kids, I realized what was going on. I was the other woman. I felt so cheap—the kind of cheap that doesn't go away. And his wife didn't deserve that kind of treatment. Anyway, I was so ashamed that I swore off any man who remotely appeared to be involved in a relationship."

Nick nodded. "Now I understand—"

Jayne continued, "I know I over-reacted last night. It *was* just kissing..." She threw up her hands. "I was drunk and I thought you'd deliberately deceived me. I'm sorry."

Relief showed on his face. "Me, too. Looks like we're clear on this, eh?"

"I'd say so."

"One thing still bugs me. I can't figure out who recognized me." Nick frowned.

"I have no idea. Cara mentioned that he works in the construction industry."

"Well, it was an honest mistake. My ex and I were fairly visible in Toronto, and our divorce is so recent that the news isn't out. He probably thought I was picking up a hot babe while I was out of town. Not an impression I'm happy with."

A couple slowed at their table, and the woman said to Jayne, "You sang at the Hog's Breath last night, didn't you? You were terrific."

Nick was paying the check and glanced up in time to watch Jayne smile at the pair, thanking them as her face grew deep pink under her tan. He nodded and looked at them. "I agree."

The couple departed and he turned back to her. "That brings up another topic. I know very little about you other than you have an aversion to lying assholes and you're greedy with shrimp. Why don't we start with

93

the Hog's Breath? You owned that stage—I take it you've done that before." He stood and helped her with her chair, grabbing the to-go order for the street musician.

"That's a long ago and far away story. You'll have to take me for a motorcycle ride to get that one out of me."

"Would you like to do that?"

"I'd love to. I haven't been on the back of a bike in a long time."

"That's more than doable. You just say when. But for now, tell me about Jayne Morgan."

"Hmm, surely we can find something more interesting to talk about."

"Somehow I doubt that…" He looked up and surveyed the sky as he put on his sunglasses. "God, what a great day. And it's snowing in Toronto."

"In Kansas City, too. If we could bottle this weather, we could retire." Jayne pulled on her sunglasses as well and inhaled. "Ah, the smell of salt and sea." Then she crinkled her nose. "And dead fish…"

Nick took a whiff and laughed. "Oh, yeah…" He offered his hand. "Now let's take this food to that musician and his dog. Then I suggest we take the long way back."

☼☼☼

"Okay, Nick. Enough about me."

Nick smiled. "Not at all. You lead an interesting life."

Jayne smiled and nodded. "So far. Now tell me what you like to do when you're not working."

"I golf and I have a cottage on a lake about ninety minutes north of Toronto. That's where I go when I need to clear my head. A few of the guys I'm with this weekend have places up there as well. We do a lot of racing around on our Snow Cats in the winter and we boat and water ski in the summer. It's a great area."

Jayne nodded. "Sounds like. My folks had a place on the Lake of the Ozarks when my brother and I were growing up. Just a little cabin, but we loved it. Went every weekend. I was a wicked water skier back then."

"Still do any skiing?" Nick asked, thinking how great she'd look on a pair of water skis.

"No. A leg injury several years ago curtailed several of my sporting hobbies. I still manage to play some golf though."

"You any good?"

"I hold my own on the course..." Jayne flashed a challenging grin at him.

Nick took the bait, cocking an eyebrow in her direction. "What's your handicap?"

"Golf," she teased.

"Mine, too." Nick laughed and shot her a high five.

They walked in closer proximity to one another than they had before lunch. Jayne seemed unconcerned about the direction or the time and they had long since blown through the hour she'd allotted him. When she bumped into him to avoid another couple, he grabbed her hand to steady her and held it for a few seconds longer than necessary. He was surprised that this slight bit of contact drew protective, possessive inclinations that weren't unwelcome.

The more time they spent together, the more he saw how different Jayne was from his ex. She had a way of putting him at ease, conversing easily on any topic he'd mentioned. When she asked basic questions about his work, they were intelligent without being personal. And he answered without hesitation—something he rarely did. It seemed odd to be having so much fun—

that hadn't been high on his priority list lately. Letting loose and laughing felt great. Since meeting Jayne at the dock, his barriers were lowering more than he'd allowed them to in the past year.

Somewhere along the way, he'd reached for her hand and kept it. It was a friendly gesture, not quite romantic, but he liked the way it felt to have the physical attachment to her.

A large group of Harleys roared past them and Jayne squeezed his hand. "Nick, tell me about your motorcycle trips…"

As they strolled, Jayne lost track of time until she heard a church carillon chiming. Her eyes rounded as she glanced at her watch. "I can't believe it's three. Maybe we should get back. Are the guys looking for you?"

"No. We pretty much do what we want to do on these trips. And honestly, there's no place I'd rather be and nothing I'd rather be doing. I don't have many days when I can kick back without an agenda. How about you? Are you supposed to be somewhere?"

"Not really. And isn't this what vacation's all about? Taking a detour and seeing where the road goes? Let me send Leigh a quick text message telling her I've altered my plans a bit." She typed the note on her cell phone then looked up at Nick. "Okay, now that we've wound our way to the Southernmost Point and back, would you be interested in splitting some Key Lime pie with me?"

"Sounds good. But are you one of those women who say they'll split dessert and then eat one or two bites?" Nick asked, a mock frown on his face.

"Do I look like a woman who forgoes dessert?" Jayne laughed, patting her hips.

Nick grinned and performed an exaggerated full body assessment, his eyes sliding from her face to her toes. "I'd say you look perfect, whatever you do with dessert."

A quick pang of desire spread through him, taking him down that road he was trying to avoid. He was more than a little irritated by his body's immediate response to Jayne. Obviously his mind and his body were at odds where she was concerned and it seemed to be getting worse.

Jayne seemed oblivious and pointed out things of interest as they strolled. Stopping for a traffic light, she quizzed, "Do you specialize in commercial or residential construction?"

"Mostly commercial, though we build some specialty homes once in a while for the right customer."

"What defines the right customer?"

"One that will pay, for starters." He laughed, then continued, "And it needs to be a big enough project to warrant the allocation of resources."

"That makes perfect sense. Who's the most interesting person you've ever built something for?"

"Bryan Adams—we designed and built his recording studio. Great guy." *And a palatial estate for Celine Dion, a twenty-four-thousand-square-foot lakeside cottage for the former prime minister...* No, he'd sound like a name-dropper if he mentioned these clients or projects. One was plenty.

"Sounds like you build on a large scale."

You have no idea... "Yeah, we handle some big projects and stay busy..." He kept his answers short and basic. Better that way. He liked spending the day with someone without the accoutrements of money or status clouding the view. He hated to wonder about motives.

Stepping up to the outdoor counter of the Key Lime Factory, Jayne studied the menu on the wall then raised an eyebrow at him. "My treat. What looks good to you?"

You do... "Oh, I guess I'll just have the basic slice of pie."

Addressing the woman behind the counter, Jayne said, "Make that two please, and two bottles of water."

Nick took the plates and led Jayne to a little table on the edge of the sidewalk. Pulling out a chair for her, he sat opposite and took a bite. "Ummm, this is good."

"You're so right. This is one of my downfalls when I'm here. I could go face down in this stuff."

Why did so much of what she did and said make him think about getting her naked? *Dammit.* Before lunch, he'd categorized her as a woman he needed to see to clarify a misunderstanding. At some point in the past three hours, she'd cozied into his subconscious. Now she perched just beyond his ability to evict her. Too bad he liked her too much to consider something casual for the weekend. That left him only one viable option—distance. And the sooner the better or he'd be a lost cause. Resigned, he exhaled and pushed back his chair, coming to a conclusion. "We should probably head back."

Jayne grabbed their trash and tossed it in the can, a confused expression on her face that shot a dagger to his gut. Too bad. Better now than later.

Nick turned, slowing at the corner of Duval Street. "Let's go this way. Sidewalks aren't as crowded."

Jayne paused. "Nick, it isn't necessary for you to walk me back."

He turned to look at her. "Why wouldn't I walk you back?"

She took off her sunglasses and squinted up at him, slightly frowning. "You seem to be in a hurry all of the sudden. I'm practically jogging to keep up with you. If you need to be somewhere, please go ahead. I can get back to the dock just fine on my own."

He detected a bit of irritation in her voice. He *had* been walking fast, his strides long and inconsiderate. Seeing the hurt expression in her eyes, he kicked himself. He needed to get away from her, but he was acting like a jerk, motoring along and going silent. She didn't deserve this, but dammit, he didn't want to *want* her. He blew out a breath. "I'm sorry. We can slow down." He turned to start walking again but she remained rooted.

"Nick—did I say something that offended you?"

He paused, looked up at the sky for a couple of minutes and exhaled as he shook his head. "No. Just some things I'm dealing with."

"Wanna talk about it? I'm a pretty good listener. Neutral ear and all that."

"No, but thanks." Like he could tell her that he was the last man she should be spending time with. That she was wasting her time if she thought he was worth her trouble? He held out his hand in a simple peace offering, relieved when she finally smiled at him and accepted it, holding it as they continued down the street.

Half a block later, strains of a familiar song floated through the air. Jayne pulled him toward the open doors of a small bar. "Listen. This guy's really good."

Nick leaned forward, cocking his head to the side. "Old Santana. Man, he's knocking it out." His eyes rested on Jayne as she stood there in the doorway, the breeze teasing her hair. He brushed an errant strand from her face, the contact making his heart do a quick tap dance. As hard as he tried to ignore it, she was still pushing down his defenses.

He pulled back, again needing a distraction. "Let's head down Whitehead Street—check out who's playing at the Green Parrot tonight."

"Sure." Jayne nodded.

So easy. Jayne had a way of making his every suggestion sound like a brilliant idea, but she wasn't false about it. She was game and agreeable. Total opposite of his ex, who made *contrary* a pseudonym.

A block down the street, Jayne pointed to a large Banyan tree, its roots and limbs reaching down like fingers and knuckles to anchor the sidewalk, "Aren't these the most magnificent trees?" She climbed onto its roots, reaching up for a low-hanging branch. "My brother and I loved climbing onto them when we were kids."

Nick inspected the giant trunk, then leaned against it as Jayne grabbed branches. She yelped, careening sideways and he sprang to grab her around the waist to keep her from falling.

"You okay?"

Laughing, she said, "I'm fine. A Gecko slithered across my foot and startled me."

Now that she was in his arms, he had no choice but to forfeit his feeble effort to distance himself. She fit his hands perfectly and without a word, he lowered his head to kiss her, finding her lips soft and warm, tasting of Key Lime and peppermint. It turned into a long, slow, wet kiss that could've gone on for the rest of the afternoon if he'd had his way, other thoughts crowding his brain. If she made love like she kissed...

After a moment Jayne pulled back and locked eyes with him and he felt her fingertip graze his cheek, sending his heart stuttering as she whispered, "Let's consider that our first kiss."

He ran his hand over the back of her head, his fingers sifting through the strands of satin that fell loose from her clip, deciding his frame of mind was a little dangerous. "Okay by me."

She grasped his neck, pulling his head down,

pressing her lips against his again. Her tongue teased his lips open, her mouth inviting his to join in a playful duel, nipping his lower lip as she pulled back. When she ran her fingertips along his scalp and pressed firm curves against him, a tremor slid down his spine, the blood from his brain racing southbound again.

"You're killing me…" he laughed, wondering if she'd noticed his obvious reaction to her kisses.

She laughed. "You do the same thing to me."

God, I hope so. "Let's keep walking or I'll get us arrested."

They retraced their steps and were soon along the waterfront, pausing at a pier. Nick took a deep breath, enjoying the warm breeze blowing across the Gulf.

She leaned over the rail, pointing down into the shallow water beneath the dock, "Check out those Tarpon. Aren't they amazing?"

Nick peered over to see several long, slender fish ranging from five to seven feet in length gliding in the clear water. "Wow. I see at least twenty or thirty. They must feed here."

Jayne waved at a schooner under full sail gliding past. "Look. Someone's getting married. What a beautiful afternoon for a wedding."

Nick squinted toward the horizon, his eyes landing on the formally clad wedding party waving from the deck of a boat. "You ever been married?"

When she didn't answer, he turned to look at her, wondering if he'd just stepped on a land mine. He watched the shadow of sadness float over her features.

A slight frown creased her brow, then she looked away. "It's part of that long ago and far away story."

"Okay…" He read the sorrow in her eyes and could sense someone or something in her past had hurt her deeply. "I didn't mean to pry."

Jayne was quiet for several seconds, then finally

spoke. "You didn't. It's just—sometimes your past reaches out and pulls you back even when you think you're safely away. And that seems to be happening to me over and over this weekend." She was silent for another moment, then she smiled and looked at him, squeezing his arm as she continued. "But right now, I'm enjoying your company. It's been a fun afternoon and I don't want to spoil it. Another time?"

"Of course." He pursed his lips and nodded, wrapping an arm around her shoulders. He sensed something sad rather than bitter. Women who'd been married were one or the other. Only a few were neutral. He hated the thought of Jayne ever being hurt, but he doubted he'd hear the story. Besides, he didn't want to get too involved in the details of her personal life. If he let her get too close, he could become one of those bad details and he didn't want that to happen.

Jayne watched the boat, wishing she hadn't allowed Nick a glimpse of her past. She kept the remnants of that tragedy tightly locked down. She'd made a point of forming new friendships and told few details. The last thing she wanted or needed was him or anyone else feeling sorry for her. The less he knew about her, the better. But this particular form of grief was a volcano that had been sitting dormant for years, and if she wasn't careful, this recent collision of elements could trigger an eruption she wouldn't be able to contain.

She sighed. Nick was perceptive. His eyes, so clear and honest, invited trust, and he didn't press her. To his credit, he'd offered understanding by laying his arm across her shoulders and kissing her on the forehead. That simple act told her he had a compassionate soul— and was a man who would zealously shelter those he valued.

At once, her head swam with the realization that

she could fall in love with him.

They came to the corner of Front and Simonton Streets and stopped, waiting for a delivery truck to lumber past before they could cross. Jayne turned to her left and stopped short. Nick watched her expression grow sober and he looked to find what had drawn her attention. She was looking at a young woman who wore a scarf tied around her bald head, her skin an ashen shade between tan and gray.

He shook his head, painful memories surfacing to sock him in the gut. He grimaced as he said, "God bless her. Cancer's a wicked disease. Lost my youngest sister to breast cancer a few years ago."

"You did?" Jayne blanched. "How old was she?"

"She was thirty-four. She fought hard and we thought she was going to make it, but they found it too late." Nick shook his head. "She was my baby sister. It was hell watching her go through something I couldn't fix."

"Oh, Nick, that must've been awful for you. For your family." Jayne laid her hand on his arm.

"It was—and on her husband and two little boys. They were only five and seven when she died. She was beautiful and so positive. If they'd found it sooner, she probably could've made it." He grew silent, his face a mask. "We'll never know."

"I'm so sorry."

"Me, too. When she died, I prayed I'd never again watch someone go through that. Especially someone I care about. You feel so helpless."

"I can only imagine." Could it feel any worse than being the one who was sick? Jayne wasn't sure, but she suspected so.

NINE

"As Jimmy Buffet says, it's five o'clock somewhere. Time for a cocktail?" Nick suggested, grabbing her hand and pulling her along, needing to lighten their mood.

"Surely it's past time," Jayne laughed.

"We need to break out that C note you helped me win off Andy."

"Save it. Something tells me you're going to need it before the night ends. Besides, it's really two hundred. The hundred I saved you and the hundred Andy owes you."

"You caught that, eh. Figures I'd pick a woman who's good with math."

"When it comes to money, my math has always been good." Jayne bumped shoulders with him, laughing.

As they neared the street, honks and yells shattered the quiet afternoon. In a blinding pink blur, a pack of scooters screeched to a halt in front of them.

"Ah ha! We found you!" Andy hollered as Jimmy and a few of the other guys yelled greetings and continued to beep their horns.

Jayne's mouth fell open. Cara and Meg were smack in the middle of the Canadian wolf pack.

Nick greeted Andy, "What's all this?"

Jayne circled the group, relieved by the greetings thrown her way from Nick's cohorts—especially after her behavior last night. Nick must've done some damage control earlier.

Jimmy waved her over and gave her a tight one-armed hug from the seat of his scooter.

She grinned at him. "Hey there, trouble. Looks like you've been leading my friends astray."

"Other way around. You and Nick get things sorted out?" He peered over the top of his sunglasses at her.

"We did." Jayne grinned and turned to Cara. "What a pair of biker babes you make."

"Oh, my gawd. We've had the best time this afternoon. These guys kidnapped us when we ran into them at the Schooner Bar after lunch. We've been all over the island and just for the record—they're certifiably insane. I've never screamed or laughed so much in all my life." Her eyes were still watering as she swiped at them. "See. Meg's laughing so hard she still can't speak."

Jayne turned and could see Meg, shaking, no sound escaping her mouth as she tried to catch her breath.

Pointing at Cara, Jimmy said, "This one's dangerous, eh? She's got a death wish or something—and she's no fun at all. We're trading her in."

A bearded guy whom Jayne didn't recognize jumped in, "Yeah. She nearly got us all killed. *Several* times. And she kept coming back for more." He stuck out his hand. "We haven't met. I'm Brad."

Jayne shook his hand. "I'm Jayne. Glad to see you managed to survive."

Cara was still gulping for air. She finally choked out what she'd been trying to say for the past few seconds, "Hollywood, it was all your fault that I kept running off the road." She pointed her finger at Jimmy's chest.

He grabbed it playfully and pronounced to Nick, "These girls are keepers. They can roll with the best of 'em."

105

Jayne patted Jimmy's cheek and teased, "Well, obviously they did just that if they kept up with all of you, sugarpie."

"Awe, listen to you sucking up. Trying to get in good with us to make points with the boss….. " Andy chuckled and wrapped his arm around Jayne's shoulder.

Meg finally caught her breath and was chatting with an auburn-haired hunk Jayne hadn't met. She looked pretty, the slight pink across her cheeks and her relaxed posture were a nice change from her usual reserved countenance. Her thick dark hair was back in a messy ponytail and her long legs stretched from her cargo shorts.

Seeing Meg let loose and engage in a conversation with a man, and a handsome one at that, was encouraging. Even after three years, Meg was slow to converse with men outside the boundaries of business. Her asshole of an ex-husband had really done a number on her self-confidence. But it appeared she was making headway.

Meg caught Jayne's eye, speaking under her breath, "It's been a really good day. You should've been with us—we missed you. Everything go okay with you two?"

"Just great. Looks like *you've* been having fun." She quirked an eyebrow, delighted when Meg blushed.

Jayne turned to the fellow Meg had been chatting with and introduced herself.

"I'm Sean." He smiled and grasped her hand, nodding.

His voice was a low rumble, matching his sexy amber eyes, and he had some serious guns bulging from the sleeves of his tee shirt. Lotta brawn going on, and what a nice smile.

Andy slapped Nick on the back and pointed to the scooters as he suggested, "Don't you think we should trade in the Harleys? We look fabulous in pink."

Andy's large frame more than dwarfed the scooter. The mere sight of him in his floral Tommy Bahama shirt straddling the tiny bike made Jayne laugh and envision the clowns in the Shrine Circus. All he needed was a big red nose.

She glanced at her watch and called out, "Anyone up for a toddy on the Sunset Pier? I'm buying."

Roaring their approval, the riders zoomed to a nearby parking area, obnoxiously beeping their horns the entire way as Jayne and Nick led the way to the pier.

A gusty breeze cooled the afternoon, raising goose bumps on Jayne's arms as wave runners and lazy sloops trolled back and forth in front of the long dock. She looked across the wooden structure jetting out into the water where turquoise umbrellas poised over tables of yellow, coral and lime, deciding it looked festive—a perfect match for her mood. The tin twang of a steel drum band and the occasional shrieks of pelicans and sea gulls provided the soundtrack.

Nick draped his arm across her shoulder as they walked, the gesture casual, but it was enough to raise more goose bumps that had nothing to do with the cool breeze. Locking eyes with him for a couple of seconds, a palpable vibration resonated between them. Then she heard her name. Looking around, she spied Leigh seated at a table midway down the pier, her cousin at her side.

"Jayne. Nick. Over here!" Leigh called again, waving her arm in the air.

"Hey Leigh, what are you up to? Hi, Brandon." Jayne greeted the pair as Nick leaned in to shake his hand.

Leigh signaled the waitress. "We heard the commotion in the street. Should've known you'd be in the middle of it."

"Nope. We were innocent bystanders this time."

Jayne slipped her credit card into the server's palm. "Please open a tab."

Brandon rose to help Nick pull additional tables and chairs together as the rest of their friends paraded toward them in a noisy cluster. In the afternoon light, Jayne studied Brandon's athletic build, thinking Liz needed to meet him. Liz was partial to blondes—Brandon's hair, shorn to Navy standards, and his riveting hazel eyes—would definitely appeal to her friend. Easy to see how a gal could go head over heels for this one, and from the stories Leigh shared, many had. But Liz was more than capable of handling a lady slayer.

Plopping in a chair between Leigh and Nick, Jayne asked, "Did Liz get here yet?"

Leigh leaned back and crossed her legs. "Yes, ma'am. Just after you left this mornin'. She had a lunch date with some fella she met on the plane, then she crashed at the pool. She should be heading this way shortly."

Cara was on her phone, just joining the group. "Found Liz." She pointed to the street. "Here she comes."

Jayne followed Cara's gaze, gave the server her order and excused herself, strolling to the end of the pier.

Liz Carson raced toward her, statuesque in a white cotton shirt knotted at the waist, short denim skirt, and high heeled wedge sandals, her mass of dark auburn hair flying from beneath a straw cowboy hat. "Hey Jayne. Glad you could finally join us."

"Back at ya, Red. Good to see you." Jayne pulled Liz in a tight embrace, soaking up the residual exuberance radiating from her friend. "You look fantastic. As always. And your timing is perfect. We just got here. The guys we met last night are with us. I'll fill you in on the dirt later, but you'll get a kick out of them." Then she added under her breath, "And you need to check out Leigh's cousin."

"I got most of the scoop at the pool earlier." She linked her arm through Jayne's as they headed back to the pier. "So what's the deal with this guy you met from Toronto? Is he fabulous?"

"You tell me. I'll introduce you." Then she called out to the group, "Here's our late arrival, Liz Carson from Chicago. Liz, these are the Vespa Boys and our token Naval aviator." Jayne ticked off names as Jimmy and Andy positioned a chair between them for her.

Standing to bow in the direction of the chair, Andy gestured. "Here Liz. We invite you to be a Canadian club sandwich."

"Best offer I've had all day, handsome." Liz sat, grinning at the group. "And there appears to be a whole lot of mischief going on around here. Can't say I'm surprised, but I've obviously got some catching up to do. Hear you killed a few brain cells last night…"

Happy to watch Liz jump into the melee without missing a beat, Jayne winced as the decibel level grew proportionately to the exaggerations as the day's scooter escapade unfolded. Jayne chuckled as one by one, the rowdy men fell prey to Liz's mesmerizing vixen charm. She was flirtatious, brazen, and could make any man feel like he was a combination of Superman and James Bond with a single look. Likewise, she could level a man's ego with a single word. Depended on her mood. And she was as smart as she was sexy. Not many chemical engineers could pull off short skirts and four-inch heels with a cowboy hat. But Liz Carson could. Divorced for twelve years after what she referred to as a very expensive mistake, she had no intention of ever marrying again, but made no bones about the fact that she loved men—just didn't want one underfoot for any length of time.

Jayne was amused to watch Andy zero in on Cara. "Where do you Americans learn to drive anyway, blondie? Birds and animals were running scared."

"It wasn't our driving that scared them. They heard about your twisted sexual proclivities," Cara mocked.

"Pro—what?" Andy yelped, looking at the other guys, "How'd you find out about Jimmy and small animals?"

Jimmy countered, "Hey, hey, beats what we hear about you and large farm animals, Jameson."

Roaring, the guys shot barbs at one another as Jayne swiveled her head back and forth, trying to follow the volley. She looked sideways at Nick as she wiped her eyes. He was laughing with his head tossed back and his mouth wide open. *What a great laugh he has.* At that precise moment he looked at her and offered a conspiratorial wink, making her heart thump a little faster. She grinned, giving him a nod. At some point during their long walk while talking about everything under the sun, they'd bonded. And his crew knew it because they'd started referring to her playfully as Nicky's girl.

She caught Liz's eye and leaned close to ask under her breath, "So what's this I hear about you having a lunch date not an hour after you landed? That's pretty quick work, even for you."

Liz offered a sly grin. "Couldn't help myself. Met him on the plane, but he didn't turn out to be very interesting. Then I met someone at the pool this afternoon. Oh, hey, that reminds me—," she turned to address the Canadian contingent. "I met a guy from Toronto this afternoon—said he owns a large construction company. Any of you know a Greg Halverson?"

TEN

Jimmy's beer came out his nose and Andy was still choking as Jayne shot Leigh a look, offering a slight shake of her head.

"Isn't he the guy that—" Cara jumped in, stopping short when Jayne shook her off.

Jayne saw the men look at one another, then finally at Nick, whose eyes had narrowed as he said, "Yeah. We know Halverson."

Though Nick's response was neutral, the set of his jaw and the dark expression clouding his face implied otherwise to Jayne. She threw a frown at Leigh and received raised eyebrows in return. What was this all about?

Andy jumped in, his voice demanding as he leaned toward Liz, "Where'd you meet *that* asshole?"

"He's staying over at Sunset Key. We met at the pool and he invited me and my cottage mates to watch his boat race in the regatta tomorrow. He's supposed to call later. You obviously don't have a good opinion of him, so what's the story? I'd appreciate a little intel here, guys." Liz looked from Andy to Nick.

Nick slowly shook his head, and it appeared to Jayne that he wasn't inclined to say anything. Maybe she should follow his lead and keep her mouth shut as well, for now anyway.

Jimmy finally filled the silence. "He's slime. Let's

just say you'd be better off keeping your distance. He's the last guy any of you should ever want to know."

Liz shrugged her shoulders. "He seemed okay, but I'm not stupid. If you black ball the guy, that's good enough for me. Thanks for the heads up. Maybe later you can fill—"

"Are ya'll aware there's a noise ordinance on this pier?" Steve Mitchell's voice boomed as he walked up behind Jayne and squeezed her shoulders, cutting off the tense conversation.

"Of course we are. Come help us continue to violate it," Cara said as she scooted her chair over to allow Steve and Mike Vincent to join the circle.

"Hey, how's everybody doin'? What'd you think of our gal last night?" Mike asked the group. "She knocked 'em out, didn't she?"

Jayne felt the heat collect in her cheeks as her friends offered agreement, and finally murmured her thanks.

The server arrived with their tray of drinks. Nick handed Jayne her cocktail along with her credit card as he said to her in a stage whisper everyone could hear, "I retrieved this from the server. Drinks are on Andy for being such a pain in the ass. Don't tell him. It's going to be a surprise, eh."

"You guys play this little game of spending each other's money and no one seems to care. Guess that's how it goes with the big money boys' club, huh?" Jayne slipped her card back into her pocket. "I'll just grab a tab later this evening. You guys bought last night. It's our turn."

"It's only money, babe," Nick said, tapping his beer to her glass.

"Yeah. *Mine*," Andy whined.

Mike tapped Jayne's arm and announced, "We think Jayne should sing with us again tonight. Ya'll agree?"

"Oh, no. *No way*. I winged my way through last night because you guys are *so* good and all the patrons were *so* drunk. I'll never be able to pull that stunt off twice." Jayne shook her head.

Leigh argued, "Aw, give yourself some credit, kiddo. I vote yes."

Meg jumped in. "Me, too. Your fan club," she spread her arms to indicate the group, "will be clamoring for you, and Liz is dying to hear what we've been raving about. Let's just say you owe us for keeping us in the dark."

"For that matter, we're still in the dark..." Cara said.

"Okay, okay. Let me think about it." Jayne threw up her hands, surrendering to the onslaught of comments. Nick's warm hand closed over the top of hers, warmth spreading from his hand to her veins, and she turned to him. His eyes were twinkling as he nodded. "You should. You were great."

Unable to resist the invitation in his eyes, she tilted her head. "I'll think about it."

"Hey everyone, it's time for sunset."

Heads turned toward the western sky to confirm Cara's words. The sun, slipping behind crimson ribbons that stretched along the horizon, cast its spell as onlookers up and down the pier cheered.

How lucky I am to have just another day in paradise. Jayne bit her lower lip, looking at the final bow the day was taking and squeezed her eyes closed. *God, please let me return to this place, with my dear girlfriends. Let me have many more sunsets like this.* The cheering of the crowd pulled her back and she joined in, contributing her famous farm-hand whistle.

The temperature went down with the sun and the wind kicked up in earnest. Jayne looked at the group, wrapping her arms around her chest. "As much as I hate to be the party pooper, we should think about heading back to the island."

☼☼☼

Nick and his fellow scooter riders strolled by their hotel pool and Nick heard Colin calling his name from the vicinity of the hot tub. Before he could respond, an out-of- sync, off-key quartet was crooning, *"Going to Kansas City, Kansas City, here I come..."*

"You guys better keep your day jobs." Nick shifted direction and shook his head, grabbing a beer from the cooler sitting beside the tub. He pulled a chair to the edge and sat, leaning forward with his arms resting on his thighs.

"You were gone a long time for lunch, boss," Colin chided.

"Service was slow..." Nick chuckled and turned to look at Sean, who'd taken the chair beside him. "Looks like you locked onto a doll."

Sean gave a slow nod, accepting the beer Colin offered.

"You know the girls always go for the silent, athletic types," Andy chimed in. "I should have played professional hockey, too."

Sean shook his head. "Yeah, well those days are long over."

Nick watched Sean rub his hand across a scar on his temple, a result of an errant puck years earlier and wondered for the millionth time how he would've handled having his career ended by a fluke shoulder injury.

"Hey, can you believe that prick Halverson is here and hitting on Jayne's friend?" Jimmy shot Nick a sideways look.

Andy piped in, "Speaking of hitting...I heard Halverson's ex filed a restraining order. Guess he beat the shit out of her. Asshole strikes me as the type that could hit a woman. Probably has a little bitty dick." Andy twirled his pinky, bringing a snicker from the crew.

"That is one twisted piece of shit." Colin shook his head. "He better never let me catch him touching a woman."

"Yeah. I'd have to destroy both his kneecaps and castrate the bastard," Jimmy declared, standing.

Andy nodded. "For starters. And ten to one, we'll run into him tonight."

Nick stood, grimacing. "Something I'd rather avoid. We don't need any hassles down here in the States, but we need to make sure he doesn't cause problems for Liz."

"Surely she'll blow him off after your warning."

"If she's smart, she will. Anyway, what's the plan tonight?" Andy asked.

Gene scurried toward them, calling out, "Hey. You're back. I looked all over town this afternoon and never seemed to find anyone."

"We saw you first," Andy kidded.

Ignoring the jibe, Gene continued, "I set up three boats for eight tomorrow morning, so be sure to put your wake up calls in before we go out or you'll forget. And don't get drunk. You'll either be too hung over or you'll blow it off." Gene hesitated, then said, "On second thought, I'll set up everyone's wake up calls. Seven o'clock."

Colin laughed, "I thought I left my wife at home."

"Yeah, me too," added Jimmy, offering Gene a beer from the cooler. "Here, have a beer, dear. And would you please shave your legs before we go out tonight?"

"Fuck you guys," Gene snipped, twisting the top off the bottle. "You laugh, but you wouldn't get shit done without me."

Nick stepped in. "Right about that, Gino. Sounds like a plan. So let's meet in thirty minutes and go to the raw bar for dinner."

Walking down the corridor to their room, Andy commented, "Looks like you and Jayne sorted things out."

"You owe me a hundred bucks."

Andy reached in his pocket and peeled off a bill from his money clip. "Never figured to lose this bet. Find out what set her off?"

"Yeah. Some guy from Toronto recognized me. Told her friend I was married. Said he works in construction, too."

"Hmm. I don't remember seeing anyone familiar last night. Think it could've been Halverson?"

"Nah. One of us would've seen him." Nick shook his head, pulling out his key card and opening the door. "I'm gonna hit the shower." He hollered from the bathroom, pulling off his shirt as he flipped on the shower head, "Sounds like you guys had an adventurous day."

"Those girls are a kick. We got the third degree from that sassy blonde—she's a pistol. Quizzed me and Jimmy. Wanted the inside skinny on you. Gotta tell ya, buddy, if you fuck this up, there'll be hell to pay. I think they'd track you down and skin you alive—or worse. They're pretty thick."

Nick lathered up and showered quickly, assessing Andy's pronouncement. He stepped out of the steamy bath, wrapping a towel around his waist. As he reached for his razor and wiped steam off the mirror, he continued to mull over Jayne and her crew. He knew about loyalty. He and his mates could give each other hell, but let an outsider say or do something against the grain and they formed a united front. Like they'd done for him with Halverson. Wiping his chin, he called into the other room, "And just how much did they get out of you?"

"Told 'em you were a skirt-chasing booze hound with a gambling problem, five ex-wives and twenty kids that you knew of. Now hurry up and clear the bathroom or our wife is gonna be wringing his hands."

"All yours, big guy." Nick vacated the bathroom and winced as he heard Andy's off-key version of Garth Brooks' *Friends in Low Places* coming from the shower. He pulled on jeans and a black long-sleeved tee shirt with a Harley-Davidson insignia on the breast pocket. Then he raked his damp hair straight back with his fingers, and frowned. *Man, I need a haircut.* Slapping on some cologne, he relocated his money clip to his front pocket and slid into his flip flops.

Retrieving a Heineken from the mini refrigerator, Nick stepped onto the balcony and dropped into a patio chair. He surveyed the pool deck, letting the warm breeze and the briny scent of the ocean skim over him. Resting his head against the back of the chair, he closed his eyes as the echoes of lapping waves tumbled from the darkness, lulling him. He took a swig of his beer and reviewed the day. *Jayne Morgan.* What a complete surprise. There was so much more to her than he'd first thought. So much more that didn't play into his idea of casual.

And that wasn't good. She was a keeper and he wasn't looking for something permanent. But putting distance between them now seemed futile. He'd tried, and had failed miserably. Jayne had him hooked on a three-hundred pound test line, reeling him in whether it was her intention or not...and damned if he could figure it out, but he no longer cared to put up much of a fight.

He reflected on a conversation he'd had with Andy during the flight down when he'd finally declared himself officially single.

Andy had said, "Buddy, you've been single for the past year."

Nick hadn't argued with him. Too much trouble to try to explain that even though he was separated and living alone, he was still married. He couldn't consider himself a free agent until the divorce was official. Not that it had stopped women from throwing themselves at him. He hadn't been able to make it through a week without some gal slipping him her card or her number, suggesting dinner, or more. Women he thought were his wife's friends suddenly shifted loyalties, declaring him open season. He wasn't interested then, and he wasn't interested in dating now. *God, what a word.* He was forty-two—too old to be *dating*. But Jayne had him rethinking his position on the matter.

Andy rumbled around in their room, buttoning another of his loud Tommy Bahama shirts. Their room phone rang. He laughed. "Twenty bucks, it's Gino."

"That's a sucker bet."

ELEVEN

Liz filled their wine glasses and waved toward the bouquet on the counter. "Gorgeous flowers. To whom, from whom?"

Jayne pulled the card and handed it to her. "Liz, I didn't want to say anything on the pier, but those are from Greg Halverson."

"Soooo...you've met him, too?" Liz raised her eyebrows, then peered at the note. "Hmm. You obviously made quite an impression." Then she burst out laughing. "This is hilarious. What a bird dog. I guess I'm first runner up."

Liz was unfazed that Jayne had caught his eye first, her confidence and common sense coming to the forefront of a ridiculous coincidence. Jayne proceeded to fill in the gaps, and heads started bobbing around the circle of friends lounging on the couches in the great room of the cottage.

"We've got to figure out a clever way to let him know the two of you are friends," Leigh said. "Make him squirm."

Liz offered an evil chuckle. "Oh, that little man has no idea he's tangled with the wrong pair of women."

Jayne patted Liz on the shoulder. "While you plot, I'm heading for the shower."

Finally alone in the confines of the bathroom, Jayne allowed her façade to slip. She'd done pretty well today, all in all. Only one moment when she'd almost crumbled. That moment when Nick had said, "Cancer is a wicked disease."

She'd wanted desperately to reply, "Yes. It. Is. *And I'm so scared.*"

Leaning back against the cold, wet tile, Jayne couldn't shut out the images flashing against her eyelids…images of doctors and hospitals and hideous scars. Of the woman she'd seen on the street.

Oh, God, why? WHY? Tears stung her eyes and she fought to keep them at bay, but her efforts were futile. Sliding down the wall, Jayne curled her knees against her chest, hoping the roar of the spray disguised the sobs that racked her body as she let loose.

How long would it be until she became that woman she and Nick had seen? That woman without hair, wearing a scarf over her bald head, dark circles outlining her eyes, her skin a pasty shade of gray…

Bitterness ricocheted through her system, making her want to bellow to the heavens.

As quickly, abject sadness took over and eclipsed the anger, enveloping her in a suffocating bubble of fear. God, she'd give anything if she could turn back the clock, or simply wake up to realize this was just a very bad dream.

And what about Nick? Of all the men she could happen to meet this weekend, she ends up with one whose sister lost the battle. *How ironic.*

She'd never considered telling him, but it underscored the fact that he was the last man she should be spending time with. Too bad the day with him had been better than she'd expected. It would be so easy to let him get into her head, and into her heart for that matter. But she couldn't, if for no other reason than he'd been through this struggle before with his sister, and he shouldn't have to go through it again with someone else.

Besides, what man would want to look at her body

after a double mastectomy? As her hand slid to the small lump, bile lodged in her throat. Tentacles of fear wrapped slimy fingers around her, confining her, tormenting her with tiny voices whispering that she was sick, that she'd be disfigured...*that she might not survive...*

It's so unfair... How could she ever agree to the bilateral mastectomy her oncologist and surgeon had recommended?

How could she *not?*

Three weeks...not much time to pray for a miracle—but an eternity while cancer grew unchecked in her body. Three weeks until her life changed forever.

No. My life changed forever the day I found the lump.

Jayne dragged herself upright and stood while the spray mingled with her tears, finally washing them away along with the remaining strands of self-pity. She shut off the water and grabbed a towel.

Spirited heckling seeped through the closed door, teasing her about taking too long to primp for Nick and complaining about running the island out of hot water, etc.

Jayne quickly took a wash cloth to her face, removing the mascara smeared around her eyes. Clearing her throat, she called through the door, "Alright, alright. Settle down, girls. Takes a lot of time to work magic in here."

She'd pull it together, apply concealer under her eyes, and no one would be the wiser. But keeping this secret was so much harder than she imagined. Would it be better if she shared this with her friends? Allowed herself to take solace in their support?

She chastised herself. Maybe for her...but not for them. She couldn't do this to them. Not yet.

As she dried and curled her hair, she put her mental affairs in order. The major affair being Nick—

now relegated into a realistic compartment confined to this weekend.

But since he could easily be the last man she'd spend time with before surgery, before she could no longer experience the raw pleasure of pressing her breasts against a man's chest as he danced with her, as he pulled her close for a kiss, she would allow herself the joy of spending time with him for the next couple of days. What harm could come from that?

She mentally shook her head...Oh, *lots* of harm...Getting involved with Nick for the weekend was the proverbial double-edged sword. On one hand, it was a bad idea on every level in the universe. But on the other hand, he might be able to provide the distraction she needed right now.

And he'd be great for her mental memory book. Flashes of kissing him that afternoon kept drifting through her mind. She'd had a moment of pure bliss in his arms—a moment she'd relive again and again. That had to be worth something.

Stop! Balling her fists and shaking her head, Jayne stared into the mirror, hating the weakness staring back at her. She had to be positive, strong, and not let the bad thoughts enter her brain. Cancer may have invaded her body, but she wouldn't let it take over her mind. At midnight, she'd be celebrating another trip around the sun, and she might not have another birthday like this ever again. *Make the most of it, girlie.*

Determination pinned down the last vestiges of despair and Jayne looked into the eyes staring back at her, knowing what she had to do. She'd suck it up. She'd catch up with Nick, and he and her girlfriends would help her make this her best birthday yet.

It required extra effort to cover the puffy circles under her eyes, but Jayne emerged from the bathroom absent the traces of her meltdown. Another night, another mask.

Her complete ensemble awaited her, pressed and laid out across the bed. Flashing Leigh a smile of gratitude, she whistled. "I see my wardrobe fairies have been hard at work."

Leigh, busy at the ironing board, glanced up. "Meg got the same treatment. Now it's Cara's turn."

Checking out the selection, Jayne nodded. "I approve—right down to the lingerie. This is exactly what I had in mind for tonight. And thanks for giving everything a quick press."

Cara, dwarfed in a spa robe, peeked in from the doorway, a pretty package in her hand. "We want to be sure you're sinfully suggestive with a whisper of understated elegance, birthday girl. Here's a little something I made for you. Happy birthday."

Jayne took the box, always touched by her friend's generosity and felt her eyes sting. She was so fortunate to have these friends at her side.

And she was such a liar, pretending everything was hunky dory. "You shouldn't have, but I'm always so glad when you do. I love wearing your creations."

"Purely selfish on my part. I want you wearing my designs for the paparazzi. Bragging rights, you know. And now that you're a singing sensation as well as a famous author, I'm sure we'll need to ramp up production."

Jayne smiled, shaking her head. "You know how much I love your jewelry. Rarely wear anything else." She untied the ribbon and opened the box, gasping as she lifted the lid. "Oh, Cara, these are beautiful." She pulled out a short necklace of woven jet beads and a matching bracelet and set of earrings. "Simply fabulous. Thank you so much." She hugged her friend, holding a little tighter than usual as she fought to control her raging emotions.

Leigh examined the set. "You've outdone yourself, you little Texan. This will be perfect with the outfit we've picked out for our girl."

Meg was standing in the doorway, fingering another of Cara's creations that graced her neck. Jayne recognized it as the one Cara had worn when she'd been photographed for her cover story in *Forbes Small Business*. Meg had admired it and Cara has simply taken it off and fastened it around Meg's neck. Cara's modesty and generosity were a couple of the qualities Jayne most admired about her friend. Her jewelry designing hobby had turned corporate heads, with *Forbes* touting her savvy as she turned a kitchen table business into a small goldmine, yet Cara was as unassuming, enthusiastic and genuine as ever.

"Jayne's always easy. Anything black works right into her wardrobe."

Jayne grinned as she fastened the bracelet. "It's my signature color. And to think, I knew you when you were stringing beads and watching soap operas. Now you're on the newsstands."

Cara grimaced, "Yeah, right. If I'm so famous, why the hell am I still doing laundry and cleaning up puke when my kid gets sick?"

"Joys of motherhood." Meg threw her arm around Cara's shoulder. "And last week, I'd have gladly traded you my hormonal sixteen-year-old daughter for your puking seven-year-old son."

"Is Reagan at it again?" Cara asked.

"Started at thirteen and hasn't stopped. Nothing we can't get through, but teenagers these days. Ugh…" Meg turned as Liz joined them. "Wow! Call nine-one-one. This gal's on fire."

Liz exaggerated a model's haughty pose in the doorway, stunning in a tight black knit dress with a leopard print belt, her mass of curls tied back loosely—the veritable seductive siren.

"Thanks, doll. Thinking I might weave a web for a cute flyboy. With your permission of course, Leigh."

"Go for it. And I'm guessing Brandon will be putty in your hands when he gets a load of you in that dress. My, you do know how to make heads turn."

"Figure I'll need all the ammunition I can muster," Liz said, a cocky smile plastered on her face. "Taking my notes from Jayne Elizabeth, here."

"Doubt you ever needed lessons in seduction," Jayne laughed.

Cara nodded. "That flyboy is gonna be begging for mercy. Now I need to get myself dressed. Thanks for the ironing job, Leigh. 'Scuse me, girls."

Jayne slipped into her jeans and a sassy black and fuchsia low cut animal print sweater. Perfect with her new jewelry. As always, Cara's knack for taking the simple and making it remarkable blew her away. She slid into a pair of her Jimmy Choo high-heeled sandals and added a spritz of Burberry Brit cologne, then headed to the living room where the girls were congregating.

As she entered, Meg caught her eye and tilted her head toward the porch.

Jayne followed her out the door. "What's wrong, Meg?" She searched her friend's panicked face for a clue.

"Oh jeez, Jayne. I might as well be riding my first bike without training wheels. This is so awkward for me. I haven't been out more than a couple of times since I left Richard, and I've forgotten how to act around men. I never know what to say. Now Sean's texting me to meet him for drinks and or dinner."

"Okay, let's get you settled down and put this in the proper perspective, sweetie. I think it's great that Sean is interested. Why wouldn't he be? You're pretty and you're smart. And you seemed to be getting along well with him this afternoon."

"He was just being nice."

Jayne tilted her head to the side, squinting, then shook her head, saddened that her friend had such little self-confidence. "Bullshit. Men are never just being *nice*. It's against their owner's manual. He was interested or he wouldn't have asked for your number or texted you."

"You think? I'm so out of touch…"

"Absolutely. Did he say anything earlier about getting together?"

"Well, he did ask if I wanted to grab a bite of dinner, but I told him I had plans with all of you." Meg shrugged her shoulders.

"Have you answered his text?"

"Yeah, I told him we'd be at the Hog's Breath or at Sloppy Joe's later."

"Did he respond?"

"He said he'd find me." Meg frowned, shaking her head, "After being married for fifteen years, it's taking me a while to get my legs under me. I'm somewhere between rusty and rusted out."

"Oh no, you're not. Consider this another step in your life-after-Richard recovery plan." Jayne hugged her friend. Man, she'd like to get her hands on Meg's asshole ex and personally strangle him for everything he'd done. Thank God Meg had finally gotten away from him. But she was a long way from mastering self-confidence and trusting her own judgment.

Liz and Leigh stepped out in time to hear the last of the conversation, so Jayne explained, "I was suggesting Meg should get to know Sean. It's time for the next stage of her liberation plan. She's changed up her wardrobe, added a bit of color to her hair, and painted her toenails. Now it's time for Confidence and the Art of Flirtation One-O-One. Liz, this is where you take over."

"With pleasure." Liz turned to Meg and placed her hands on her shoulders. "For starters, you're gorgeous and you need to figure that out. You're one of the smartest, kindest women I know and men are drawn to you like moths to a flame. You simply don't see it. It's high time for you to roll with it and have some fun. You're way overdue."

Meg smiled, relief evident on her face. "This is way out of my comfort zone. But I'll give it a shot as long as I know you guys have my back."

Leigh hugged her. "You got it, kiddo. Now let's go eat. I'm starving."

"Leigh, it's a wonder you aren't as wide as you are tall. I don't know how you manage to stay so slim as much as you eat," Liz whined, following Leigh down the path.

Jayne leaned toward Liz and asked, "What's your brilliant plan for Greg Halverson?"

"He called earlier and I told him I wasn't available. I know you already blew him off. So here's what we'll do if you're game..."

TWELVE

The blonde woman snapped her phone shut and tapped her fingernail on the counter, addressing the Westin desk clerk. "I need a key to my room, please. The room's under Halverson. Greg Halverson."

The clerk tapped a few keys. "Your name, ma'am?"

The blonde gave a curt reply.

"I'm sorry. Mr. Halverson didn't indicate another party on his reservation and I won't be able to give you a key. Let's try calling his cottage." He held the phone receiver to his ear, shaking his head, "There's no answer. We can leave a message for him to contact us when he returns. Does he have a cellular phone you can call?"

"That's what I've been doing. I need to store my bags. Is there a decent place to have dinner at this time of night? I'm about three hours late getting here."

"The hotel restaurants are closed, but we have twenty-four-hour room service. If you'd like to go out, Bagatelle is close. You go two blocks up Green Street," the clerk pointed out the front drive, "to Duval Street and turn left. It's on the right side of the street."

"Thank you." Turning on her heel, the blonde pushed her bag and a couple of bucks at the bellman. "I need to store this until I know my room number."

Clicking down the street, she wrinkled her nose, the smell of coconut, fried seafood and stale beer assaulting her. She dodged foot traffic, muttering and shaking her head, "Nasty, rank place."

Her head swiveled from side to side as she searched the street, making her way down another block. Why would anyone want to come here? She peered into the dark cavern of Captain Tony's Saloon, waiting for her eyes to adjust as she took in the walls littered with business cards and the rafters dripping with every type and size of bra. Several patrons, but no Greg.

At the corner of Duval, she looked up and down the street and shook her head. Just another Bourbon Street.

A hand clamped her shoulder and she jumped with a shriek, turning to find a grizzled old guy with a ratted beard offering a toothless grin. She sped away, his cackle ringing in her ears. *God, get me out of this hell hole...*

Wishing she had on anything but high heels and white silk slacks, she careened along the choked sidewalk until she spied the restaurant. Climbing the front steps of the old mansion, she paused in front of the hostess. "Table for one."

"Certainly, follow me." The young woman led her up another flight of stairs and out onto a balcony with several small tables. "Here you are. You'll have a nice view of Duval Street while you dine."

She surveyed the street below. Maybe coming down here had been a mistake. After all, Greg had told her he'd be busy. But they hadn't spent a lot of time alone recently and she was feeling neglected. She summoned the waiter, insisting he wipe down the seat cushion before she sat.

Watching the parade of tourists and locals below, she searched for Greg's figure on the off chance he'd be strolling along the main thoroughfare. Why on earth wasn't he answering or returning her calls or text messages? She wasn't having any problems with cellular coverage.

The waiter reappeared at her side.

"I'll have a Caesar salad with shrimp, dressing on the side, no croutons, and a glass of Cakebread Chardonnay."

She settled in to wait for her food, nibbling on a piece of warm sourdough bread. Fidgety, she picked up her phone and punched in Greg's number, hitting *end* when it again rolled to voicemail.

Her salad arrived and while she picked through it, she decided she'd better call the Westin and reserve a room. She'd need somewhere to stay if she didn't locate Greg. Where the hell was he, anyway?

☼☼☼☼

Knee deep in gin, Halverson walked out of the regatta reception, stumbling on the uneven sidewalk. He'd grown weary of the shallow young women who flocked to the party. Half-naked, brainless, reeking of cheap perfume and blathering on about the most inane things, they were mind-numbing.

But he was going to have to use a different approach if he wanted to get to Jayne Morgan or Liz Carson. The sting of rejection throbbed with growing vigor as each moment passed. Only weak men failed. That had been whipped and drilled into him since he was knee high. According to his father, failure was *unacceptable*. And Greg had the scars to remind him. All over his back.

Breathing in the night air, Halverson took a moment to think about the two women. He preferred Jayne. She was less of a siren, more suited to his taste, and now that Nick had an interest in her, she was the perfect quarry. But Liz was stunning and would do if he couldn't find Jayne. Yes, indeed. Nothing wrong with that one. Either way, he might need to tip the odds in his favor a bit, but he'd become very good at that. He just needed the right setting and opportunity.

But he was restless and all this could take time. Given his mood and growing level of impatience, if he didn't do something soon, he'd have to find an...*outlet*...someone a lot more exotic and talented than those mindless coeds he'd just escaped. Maybe later, Bennett could arrange for a woman who would suit his needs...someone bought and paid for who'd do whatever he wanted without complaint. It just cost a little extra to find one who'd accommodate his special preferences. A specialist who could take the edge off...

Full of anticipation and concentrating on the sidewalk, he heard his name and looked across the street. His captain and crew of the *High Class Looker* were standing in a huddle. He hailed them and watched as they dodged traffic to come to him. Assessing the stalwart group, a dark pinch of envy for their youth and well-sculpted bodies squeezed the breath from his lungs. Their vigor, emphasized by the custom Beretta crew uniforms of black shorts and wind shirts, prominently sporting the logo for Halverson Companies Limited, ground on his ego.

"Hey Mr. Halverson. How's it going?" His captain, a Nordic hulk in his late twenties, pumped his hand. "Join us. We're celebrating today's victory."

"I'm busy later, but I'll join you boys for a quick drink." Halverson nodded, emphasizing the word boys to place the necessary distance between him and his hirelings. He wouldn't tolerate familiarity from his inferiors, but he needed their loyalty for what he wanted them to accomplish. Forcing a congenial expression, he asked, "Where to, Captain Andersen?"

"Anywhere. We're doing the Duval Crawl, just going from bar to bar to take it all in."

"Your crew performed exceptionally today. And I'm expecting another win tomorrow. I want that trophy." His gave the captain a look that left no room for misinterpretation.

"Sir, we have every intention of winning. Consider it done."

Halverson caught the wink and nodded. "Good. I see we understand each other."

Following his crew into the Hog's Breath Saloon, he glanced toward the stage and stopped short. He looked again, blanching. There stood Jayne Morgan, belting out an old Motown hit. She looked gorgeous, but how could she be doing something so public—so *common*--exposing herself to every drooling miscreant in the bar. It sickened him that she could portray herself in such a cheap manner. And as quickly, the nausea in his stomach turned to anger. *She shouldn't be doing this...*

"What's wrong?"

"Nothing, Captain Andersen." Halverson snapped.

"Okay, sir. We'll be at the bar."

Halverson studied Jayne. His blood pressure was climbing at a rapid pace. This was bad. *Very* bad.

Glaring as his phone vibrated, he recognized her number. Fifteenth call since morning. Why was she so ridiculously persistent? She should know by now he didn't want to talk to her today. He clicked the mute button and crammed the phone back in his pocket.

He focused on Jayne and fought to steady his pulse. Maybe if he imagined she was only singing for him, he could get beyond the cheap display. He tried shifting, but she never looked right at him. When the song ended, he started toward her but she started singing another song.

Blowing out a breath, he imagined punishing Jayne for being so pedestrian. That was the best way for him to channel his anger. He imagined her begging for him to forgive her, and his pulse finally slowed. Riding crop? No, too mundane. But maybe a throat clench just to the point of a faint? Shutting his eyes, he pictured clamps on her nipples and smiled. He could add just the slightest touch of current? He felt himself stiffen. *Hmmm, there we go.* Halverson watched Jayne for another few minutes, relishing the throb, then changed direction and joined his men. God, he needed a drink.

He tossed his credit card to the bartender. "Open a tab. Whatever these boys want, and I'll have a Bombay Sapphire on the rocks. Make it a double and don't be stingy."

His phone vibrated deep in his pocket. He yanked it out, aiming for the off button when his eyes landed on the screen, a satisfying tremor sizzling through him as he pictured the auburn-haired siren on the other end of the line. Maybe he could save the night after all. Might have to improvise, but in a pinch he'd take a redhead over a blonde and forego the punishment. Maybe...

Cupping his hand over one ear, he stepped away from the noise. "Well hello, gorgeous."

"Hi Greg. My plans changed at the last minute. Can I buy you a drink or are you tied up?" Liz purred.

Not yet but it's a definite possibility..."No. I've been hoping you'd change your mind. Where can I meet you?"

"Back bar at the Hog's Breath?"

"I'm already there." Halverson clicked off, excitement pulsing through his veins. Once she arrived, they'd go elsewhere. He couldn't let Jayne see him with another woman and he didn't need the crew ogling Liz, distracting her. No. He wanted her undivided attention.

A swift image played out in his mind. He'd have Liz on her hands and knees, opening to him as he pounded into her. He'd yank her head back by that tangle of red hair, making her cry out in pain. Ah, *that* image certainly succeeded in making his dick twitch and grow. A satisfied smirk slid over his face.

Checking his pocket, he palmed the small vial of powder. If Liz played coy, he'd simply change her mind.

Leaving the restaurant, the blonde peered up and down the street. Where on earth was Greg? Green-eyed daggers stabbed her. Was he with another woman? A niggling worry tingled along her spine. If she caught him with someone, she'd strangle him. No way would he get away with dumping her after all she'd gone through to be with him. Gritting her teeth, she crossed the busy thoroughfare, dodging pedi-cabs and motorcycles. Music floated from a bar across the street, inviting her to follow the sound.

Pausing just outside the entrance of the Hog's Breath, she glanced at the stage. Deciding the music was good enough to warrant a drink, she chewed her lip, her eyes moving over the patrons. No Greg. She spied an empty bar stool, grabbed napkins from the counter and wiped it off. Sitting to face the stage, she eyed the bartender and tapped her finger on the counter. "Chardonnay."

Watching Halverson click off his cell phone from her vantage point, Liz winked at Leigh. "Be sure to fill everyone in and tell Jayne what she needs to do as soon as she's done singing. I'm going to leave through the side entrance and come around to arrive through the front."

Slipping around, Liz greeted the bouncers at the main entrance, tossed a signal to Jayne, and sashayed to the back bar, pretending oblivion to the heads turning in appreciation.

Spying Halverson perched on a stool, she sauntered up, cooing, "Hello, Greg. I'm so glad I caught up with you."

He stood, pulled out her bar stool and leaned down to brush a light kiss on her cheek. "You're looking exquisite."

"Flattery will get you everywhere, handsome."

Shit, she'd need more than a loufa sponge to wipe the smarm off after spending thirty minutes with him. She steeled herself against the gin and cologne wafting toward her in a gagging fog. Gazing at Halverson with what she hoped was just the right touch of implied interest, she placed her hand over his. "Had I known I was going to see you, I would've paid more attention to my appearance tonight."

Liz knew full well she looked every bit the seductress. She leaned toward him to offer the full effect of her brand-new 36D's and from the direction Halverson's eyes strayed, they were working their magic.

"Why don't we find somewhere more intimate so we can...get better acquainted," Halverson suggested, skimming her shoulder with his fingertip.

"Oh, if you don't mind, I'd like to listen to the band for a little bit. That singer is great, don't you think?" Liz purred, silently relishing the game.

"Oh? I hadn't noticed. Alright, then, what can I order for you?"

"Grey Goose martini, *dirty*." She arched an eyebrow as she said the word. God, he was so easy...

Greg's hand strayed from grazing along her shoulder, to a fingertip brushing her collarbone. Steeling herself against the repulsion, Liz was lifting the glass to her lips when she saw a flash of blonde hair flying toward her from the corner of her eye.

Before the image could register, Halverson careened into her, knocking her backwards, the stool tumbling over. Liz grabbed hold of the bar to keep from going down, proud that she'd managed to hang on to her martini and stay balanced on her heels. Righting herself, Liz winced when the blonde woman flew at Halverson again, grabbing his shoulder and knocking him into her a second time.

Halverson's elbow slammed sharply into Liz's upper arm as she struggled to keep from losing her footing. She yelped, helpless to keep her drink from flying through the air in a wild spray, the glass shattering on the brick pavement.

The blonde woman shrieked at Halverson, "You *asshole.*" Then, jabbing an index finger toward Liz, she hissed, "Is *she* why you haven't answered my calls? Is *she* why you didn't want me here?"

Halverson lashed out, grabbing the woman's arm and twisting it, "What the hell are you doing here?"

The woman pulled away, stumbling back, tilting awkwardly in her spike heels. "Good question." Tossing her head in Liz's direction, she spat, "Talk about trading down."

Rounding the corner, Jayne stopped short when Halverson landed against Liz, sending her drink into the air. Jayne rushed to her friend, stunned to see a blonde woman smack at Halverson and hurl hateful accusations toward Liz. Halverson's eyes blazed, and he was raising his right hand, rearing back as if to slap the woman.

Jayne jumped forward, crying out, "*No!*"

Halverson's arm paused mid-air, and he turned to Jayne with crazed eyes. "Jayne—don't misunder—"

"Who's *she?*" the woman demanded. "Another one of your whores?"

Halverson whirled, his jaw set in a sneer as he sprang at the woman, grabbing her by the shoulders and shaking her violently, making her head bob back and forth. His face had flushed a dangerous red as he snarled, "Shut up! *Shut up*, you stupid bitch. You shouldn't even be here!"

Jayne and Liz jumped back, astonishment freezing them in place for a full second. Then Liz grabbed Halverson's drink off the bar and threw it in his face, making him sputter and release the blonde woman.

Spinning on Liz, fury and indignation contorting his dripping face, Halverson bellowed as he lunged for her arm, "Why the hell did you do that?"

Jayne shoved Liz behind her. "Stop! *Stop* it, Greg!"

Locking eyes with Halverson, Jayne froze, knowing the slightest flinch could trigger another outburst. His expression, menacing and cold, scared her like nothing she'd experienced before. She held his gaze and true fear engulfed her. This was a man capable of doing bad things—had more than likely already done bad things. Her knees threatened to give way but she couldn't let him call her bluff. She needed to grab Liz and get away from here. Thank God the blonde woman had finally stopped yelling.

Nick walked in the back entrance, laughing at Andy's complaints about Gino as Jimmy brought up the rear. His eyes landed on Halverson, and he blinked, not trusting what he was seeing. Halverson was shaking a blonde woman by the shoulders and Jayne's friend was throwing a drink in his face. Jayne jumped in front of Liz, defending her from what he could see.

Blades of white hot rage shot through his system, spiking when he recognized blonde woman's face.

Alynn? What the fuck? Adrenalin propelled him into their midst, an intense desire to rip Halverson's jugular consuming him as he read the fear in Jayne's eyes.

"So Greg, is this your wife?" Liz waved her hand toward Alynn.

Nick stormed at Halverson, ferocity radiating from him as he stepped in front of Jayne. "No. She was *my* wife." Nick glared at his adversary, daring him to take another step.

Andy and Jimmy were on either side of him, each grasping firmly to his arms to restrain him. More to keep him from doing something stupid than anything else. They despised the prick as much as he did.

Nick shook them off. "I've got this, guys."

Andy addressed a group of younger men collected behind them, "Show's over boys. Move on."

Nick glanced back at the group of men clad in crew uniforms. The big blonde fellow ignored Andy's command and stepped toward Halverson. "Come with us, sir."

Nick didn't budge.

Wiping dripping liquid from his face, Halverson slithered past Nick, his eyes thin slits as he spat, "You should thank me—she's a useless whore."

Nick roared, lunging against the restraints imposed by his friends. "*Fuck you, Halverson!* Come near any of these women again, it'll be the last thing you do."

"You don't scare me, McCord," Halverson heaved.

The prick was full of bravado now that he had some muscle backing him up.

"Then you're a fool." Nick's growl was low and he could see he'd hit his mark by the quick blink of fear in Halverson's eyes.

"Get him out of here. *Now.*" Andy bellowed at the large blonde fellow, drawing the attention of several patrons and a couple of bouncers.

Nick turned to the trio of women. "Anyone hurt?"

Alynn looked at him, defeat and embarrassment had replaced the fury in her eyes. "You're the last person I expected to see."

"Likewise. What are you doing here?" God, he absolutely did not need any of this.

She shook her head and looked down. "I have no idea."

Out of the corner of his eye, Nick caught Jayne and Liz nodding to one another and backing away. Shit, this had to look bad. Especially after the conversation they'd had over lunch. Signaling to Jimmy to keep an eye on Alynn, he caught Jayne's arm. She looked down at his hand, then up at him, her eyebrows raised.

Dammit. Here we go again...

He dropped his hand. "Sorry you got caught in that." He searched her eyes for a read, surprised to see concern and contrition rather than disgust and anger.

"Don't be. It's mostly our fault. We were setting Halverson up—there's more to this story—when your wife—"

"*Ex*-wife."

"Okay, when your *ex-wife* arrived on the scene and everything blew up. Greg Halverson is a maniac. He went from zero to asshole in one point five seconds."

"Yeah, I saw that."

"What's the deal, Nick? What's going on?" Jayne frowned.

Nick couldn't tell if she was asking or accusing. He shook his head and pursed his lips. "Halverson and

Alynn..." Then he held up his hand to signal he didn't want to discuss it, "Long story..."

He wouldn't elaborate. Not the time or place, but he detected comprehension in the softening of the crease across Jayne's brow. And pity. Damn. That was something he didn't want or need. He couldn't let her see him as some jilted, damaged loser. But God, he was exhausted, and the thought of trying to explain everything was overwhelming. He was so tired of the angst that had eddied around him for the past year. Would it ever end? Couldn't he just put his life on cruise control for a while?

Coasting without a woman in the mix—the idea appealed to him on several levels and now was as good a time as any to put some distance between him and Jayne. Better for both of them. She deserved more than he was willing or able to offer. And after witnessing this mess, she'd be thrilled to give him all the distance he wanted.

Jayne was talking but he hadn't heard a word.

She grabbed his arm. "Nick, listen up." When he finally met her eyes, she continued. "I know this is awkward for you, but your *ex* needs a friend right now."

Why did Jayne have to be so nice? It'd be a whole lot easier to disappear if she was a bitch. He nodded, turning to go. "She does." He stopped and turned back to her. "I'm really sorry about all of this."

"Nick, this wasn't your fault. Go take care of her." She hesitated, then locked eyes with him as she continued, "And be kind. No matter what, she's been publicly humiliated and she's got to be feeling pretty low. Will you call me later?"

Should he just tell her he was going to call it a night? Lie and say he was tired when the truth was, he was simply tired of the aggravation and drama women seemed to carry around by the truckload? Or should he

140

tell her that even though she seemed to be the exception in his book, he had to keep his distance or they'd both regret it? Clamping his mouth shut, he shook his head. "Most women—"

"I'm not most women." She gave him a lop-sided grin.

"Understatement. I have no idea how long this will take. I'll call if it's not too late."

There. His options were still open and he hadn't done or said something he could regret. He needed to get away and think. He kissed Jayne on her cheek and left her standing there with a hurt expression on her face. Nothing he could do about it now.

Returning to his friends, still posting guard over his ex, Nick ran his hands through his hair and rubbed his neck. "Alynn, what are your plans?"

"I've got a room at the Westin for tonight, and I'll try to get a flight home first thing in the morning. You don't need to worry about me. I'm a big girl. I can take care of myself."

Was that embarrassment and vulnerability in her defensive response? He exhaled and threw his hands up. "I know, but I'll still walk you to your hotel."

"I can walk her over," Andy offered.

Nick shook his head. "No. I'll catch up with you two later. Thanks for backing me."

He led Alynn out the back door and onto the street. The silence was thick between them until she finally broke it.

"Is that the woman you've been seeing? The one in the picture I received?"

Nick stopped and made Alynn face him. "About that picture—where the hell did that come from? I only met Jayne this weekend—she's a nice lady I'm getting to know—nothing more. I wasn't sleeping around on you when we were married. Never did. Never would've.

You should know me better than that," anger edged down his spine, his words clipped.

"No, I know…you didn't." She blew out a breath. "Greg sent me that photo. It's obvious he's still trying to sabotage you."

Nick nodded. *Halverson. Should've known.*

Alynn looked down. "Nick, I'm so sorry. After what just happened, I finally understand how you must've felt in Paris last year when you found me there…*with Greg*. You have every right to hate me. But here you are, stepping up to the plate one more time." She finally looked him in the eye. "You're a good man. I guess it took tonight for me to see the light. I'm very sorry I hurt you. More sorry than you'll ever know. Can you ever forgive me?"

"Already have. We were both at fault, Alynn. We grew apart and waited too long to fix it. I'm sorry, too." He hesitated, chewed his lip as he measured his next words. "I know you don't want to hear this, Alynn, but you should stay away from Halverson—he's…unstable. He could hurt you."

"I can see that now." Alynn sighed.

They walked the rest of the way to the hotel in silence. Nick opened the lobby door for her. "I'll walk you to your room."

"Not necessary. The bellman will escort me."

"You're sure?"

"Yes. I'll call your cell if anything goes awry. Fair?"

"Fair. Good night." He leaned down and kissed her on the cheek. Turning to walk out the door, he stopped and turned back. "Alynn?"

She turned around, and he saw her eyes welling. "Yes?"

"I'll check on you in the morning. If you can't get a commercial flight, I'll call the jet down from Orlando to take you home."

"Thank you, Nick."

She turned away abruptly, and he was certain she was trying to hide her tears from him. He shook his head. Some lessons were tough, and they'd both learned so much in the past year.

Striding down the hotel's front drive, a wave of liberating forgiveness washed over him—forgiveness for Alynn—and for himself. The blame he'd shouldered for the past year tumbled off his shoulders and he realized he'd been holding himself hostage for the failure of his marriage. Guilt that he hadn't done enough to save it in the beginning, and guilt that he'd fallen out of love with Alynn had festered and grown. Sure, he knew he'd only been half of the equation, but knowing and accepting were two different things. The night's events had opened his eyes.

He took a deep breath, savoring the heavy night air. Alynn would always be the mother of his children, and she'd hold a place in his heart accordingly, but now he was truly a free man. And that thought led to Jayne. Time to find her and get the night back on track.

Heading down the alley to Sloppy Joe's, his mind on what he'd say to her, he heard someone call his name from a doorway. He turned, and there was the huge fellow who'd championed Halverson in the Hog's Breath, a smirk planted on his face. Then two other guys, smaller but wiry, stepped from the shadows.

Ah, shit. Not this. Not tonight. Nick faced them head on and calculated his options.

☼☼☼

Halverson slammed through the door of his cottage, spewing, "That fucking son-of-a-bitch McCord. How the hell does he always manage to get in the middle of everything?" He threw his assistant a withering glare. "And what the hell is Alynn doing down here? Did you know anything about this?" He sloshed gin in a highball glass and tossed it back. "So where have *you* been all night, Bennett?"

"Sir, I've been right here. And no, I wasn't aware she was here until an hour ago when I got the message she left for you on the cottage voice mail. I called you several times and sent you text messages."

Halverson yanked his phone out of his pocket and scrolled through his message screen, loathe to see several missed calls and texts. He paced, then stopped in front of Bennett, pointing a finger into his chest. "Dammit. You should've tracked me down when I didn't answer. Tonight was a disaster!"

He paced, his fury growing with each step. "Nick McCord had no business insinuating himself into my affairs tonight. He'll pay for this. And I'm not done with Jayne Morgan, either. Not by a long shot. She picked the wrong player and she's just changed the rules of engagement." He spun and headed for the master bedroom.

"Sir, I'm afraid the night isn't over."

Something in Bennett's tone made him stop in his tracks. He turned and glared at his assistant. "Now what?"

"You got a call from the chairman of the regatta committee about fifteen minutes ago. The *High Class Looker* has been disqualified. Seems a member of your crew was caught tampering with the rudder of the *Bold Scotsman*."

"Son. Of. A. Bitch!" Halverson grabbed the gin bottle off the bar and splashed another shot into his glass. He took a slug, then hurled the glass against the wall, sending crystal shards and liquid flying. Was everyone who worked for him incompetent? Or were they just complete idiots? Probably a lot of both. Good thing damage control was his strong suit.

And getting even…

☼☼☼☼

Nick sized up the odds, playing out each option in slow motion. No doubt Halverson had sent them. He was too much of a snake to confront Nick directly. Three to one—not terrific, but not insurmountable. Unless more were coming. That could be bad. Either way, he'd need to take out the big one first.

Nick let his arms rest easy at his side, but his fists were knotted. "How's it going, fellas?"

"Better for us than you, McCord." The big Nordic fellow took a step forward.

"Doubt that."

"You should keep your nose out of Mr. Halverson's business."

"That so?"

He had a split second to plan his moves before the big one charged. Nick sidestepped a solid jab intended for his gut. The hulk's movements were slightly off and delayed, probably due to alcohol consumption. Nick spun and zeroed in with a hook to the fellow's jaw, snapping his head back. He got behind the guy and propelled him forward into one of the wiry men, sending them both careening to the ground. The third had slipped back, deciding he wanted no part in this little scuffle. Gotta love loyalty.

A pair of uniformed officers appeared in an instant. "What's going on here?"

Nick stepped toward them, shooting a warning look at the three crewmen. "Just a little misunderstanding, officers. Too much alcohol and not enough common sense. There's no cause for concern. We're just heading back to our hotels."

"All right, then. See that you do, or we'll find another place for you to stay. We'll get you a cab if you need one."

Nick walked toward the curb. "That'll be great. Thanks." Nick shook the officers' hands, noting blood on his knuckle, and jumped in the back of a taxi that had magically appeared. Maybe going back to his hotel was a good idea after all. It had been a long night and could've been a lot longer if those guys had caught him in a different place or under different circumstances. He'd need to do something about Halverson. And soon. The guy was psycho. If he'd been a dog, he would've been considered rabid and put down.

THIRTEEN

"How's everyone this morning?" Jayne called, dumping her canvas bag on an empty chaise lounge. "Let's see...we're reading, floating, and—" chuckling at Leigh's soft snore, "napping. Perfect morning in paradise."

"You were the only thing missing." Meg grinned.

"Correction. You and *cocktails*," Cara said. "Now that you're back from the base, your birthday can officially start and it's time for screwdrivers and mimosas. Let's find the server."

"So, birthday girl, how was it? Are those fighter jets everything you thought they'd be?" Meg asked.

"They're amazing. My brother flew the F-16 when he was in the Navy, but the F-18's are even more impressive. I owe Brandon big time for the sneak peak. So what's been going on around here?" Jayne untied her sarong and settled onto her lounge, a sigh of pleasure escaping her lips as her limbs relaxed.

Liz rolled over and stretched. "I filled everyone in on what happened last night and then Halverson had the balls to send both of us flowers, which I refused. And then he called to apologize for what he referred to as *the unfortunate incident*." She used her fingers as quotation marks to emphasize the term. "Then he called back, looking for you. I answered and clued him in that he was calling you at our same cottage. He hadn't figured out that we're friends—idiot. Anyway, gave him a piece of my mind and told him in no uncertain terms that if either of us saw or heard from him again, I'd call the authorities and press charges for assault." Liz turned to show nasty black fingerprints on her forearm. "Look at this. Everything happened so fast that I didn't even notice this until we were having breakfast. Meg snapped a photo in case he decides to cause any more problems."

Jayne leaned closer for an inspection, then grimaced. "Damn, that looks painful. We need to treat last night as a nightmare we woke up from this morning. No more Greg Halverson and good riddance."

And obviously, no more Nick McCord. It hurt that she hadn't heard from him after he'd left the Hog, but she wasn't going to let it get to her. After everything that had happened, she wasn't all that surprised. Just disappointed…and angry with herself that she was.

Liz settled back on her lounge. "Isn't it weird how some men become so much more determined when we're not interested?"

Leigh stirred from her nap and groaned as she rolled. "Age old story of the cave man. He's a hunter and wants to club us and drag us back to camp."

"Speaking of which, Leigh, I wouldn't mind getting hauled back to camp by that cousin of yours. He waltzed in and took my mind right off the Halverson mess last night," Liz said. "Diversionary tactic of the best kind."

"Must've been that sexy black dress," Jayne said.

"Brandon's a handful, but I'm betting you're just the woman who could take him to his knees, so to speak." Leigh looked over the top of her sunglasses at Liz.

"At the very least." Liz chuckled. "We're meeting for sunset cocktails this evening. So, Jayne, was he looking delicious this morning, or wearing the effects of last night? We closed the Green Parrot at three, then took the long walk back to the dock."

"He looked great, none the worse for the wear. I'm surprised you haven't heard from him yet. He asked about you—wanted to make sure you're okay. I'm telling you, if he runs across Greg Halverson, it'll be ugly. Talk about silent and lethal. Anyway, it was great of him to take me out to see the jets. They make my Baron look like a wind-up toy," Jayne said, pulling a magazine out of her bag.

Leigh added under her breath, "Albeit a very expensive wind-up toy…"

Jayne watched a sleek private jet fly low overhead, on final approach. "Speaking of expensive, check out that Gulfstream. Now *that's* an airplane. Some celebrity must be arriving."

Meg handed Liz her tube of sunscreen. "Mind hitting my back?"

"Only if you'll scoop us on what happened with you and Sean last night."

"I'll tell if she doesn't." Cara splashed Meg from the side of the pool.

"Tell what?" Meg asked, her face turning as red as the hibiscus blooming beside her.

"That you were making out with him on the dock."

Hoots of laughter erupted and Liz smacked Meg's foot as she eased by. "Busted."

"We never did get those drinks ordered. Who wants what?" Meg stammered, standing and inching toward the bar. "Need to toast Jayne's actual birthday. It *is* today, isn't it?"

"I think so, but we've had so many shots and toasts since we got here I've lost track," Jayne laughed. "At midnight last night I was certain the Canadians were trying to poison me. Funny how I manage to keep my drinking to a minimum the rest of the year, but I get down here and we start drinking earlier every day. We should just book next week at The Betty. I'm pretty sure we'd qualify for a group discount."

"Yeah, but I hear they search your luggage at check in," Leigh said as she sat on the side of the pool.

Liz stood. "Rules me out."

Cara groaned as she pulled herself out of the pool, "But nobody knows how to celebrate a birthday quite like you, Jayne. Promise that we'll always get to help turn your birthday into a birth week."

"You got it, and this birthday girl gets the privilege of buying the first round for the confessional. I'm thinking a little truth serum might be in order. Who wants what? Meg—you're off the hook for now, but later we want to hear the sordid details."

Jayne hailed the server, then whispered to Meg out of earshot, "So….fess up. We lost track of you after you left the Green Parrot. Anything happen?"

"Not really, we headed down Duval and then he walked me to the pier. We sat and talked…"

"And made out…"

"Yeah, there was that…it just took us a really long time to say good-night."

"Fun?"

"Oh, yeah."

"Good for you." Jayne winked at her friend, placed their order, and stepped over to the side of the pool to sit down and dangle her feet in the water beside Leigh.

At least someone had a good night. As much as she'd tried not to, she'd kept her eyes peeled for Nick the rest of the evening. She'd been aggravated with herself for letting her disappointment dampen her mood, doing everything she could to hide it from the crew.

Even Andy and Jimmy, who'd been her steadfast arm amenities into the wee hours, had been sneaking looks at their cell phones, trying to send discreet texts. It was obvious they were as curious as she was about Nick's whereabouts. The man had pulled a regular Houdini act. Maybe he'd ended up spending the night with Alynn. How divorced was he, anyway? She'd seen it happen before, and things had certainly gotten weird after the confrontation with Halverson. She couldn't fault Nick for coming to his ex's rescue. Hell, she'd practically insisted he do just that, but the thought of him doing more than just walk Alynn back to the hotel gnawed at her.

Leigh interrupted her thoughts. "And you were also very late coming in. Or should I say, very early?"

Jayne bumped her shoulder against Leigh's and whispered, "I could tell you the boring truth, but it's much more fun to let your imagination run wild."

"So where'd you go after I signed off?"

"Andy and Jimmy corralled me and made me their mascot. We cruised down Duval, hit Cowboy Bill's and the Green Parrot, and then we ended up closing Willie T's. They filled me in on the story between Nick and Halverson. We had a slice of pizza at Angelina's on the way back. I ran into Liz on the dock. Once we got back here, we sat on the porch and talked for a while."

"Nick didn't come back? Did he call?"

"No." Jayne shrugged, hoping her disappointment wasn't too obvious. She needed to put it behind her. Not that he owed her anything, but she thought they'd formed some kind of bond during their afternoon together.

Leigh shot her a sympathetic look. "Not to worry. I'm sure you'll hear from him. So what's the deal between him and Halverson?"

"Remember when that shopping center skywalk collapsed in Toronto a few years ago?" When Leigh nodded, Jayne continued, "Seems Halverson's company owned the project and his brother was the project engineer. Nick was appointed by the province court to chair the investigative panel after the accident, and they discovered Halverson's brother incorporated inferior materials that wouldn't tolerate the weight loads. He'd bribed inspectors to look the other way. His greed cost six people their lives and several more were seriously injured. The court imposed heavy fines and charged his brother with gross negligence and involuntary manslaughter, sentencing him to six concurrent ten-year prison sentences. Their company went under and it's taken Halverson all this time to recover and rebuild. Now he's on a mission to ruin Nick because of his testimony."

"Wow." Leigh blew out a breath. "So he's shifting blame. Typical narcissist." She shook her head. "And then he puts the moves on you and you end up with Nick. Talk about a crazy set of circumstances. You can't make this shit up."

"Wild, huh? Seems we were right about him from the beginning."

"Unfortunately. But on another note, you promised to tell the girls your story today." Leigh twisted around to face the rest of the group. "Gals. Circle up. We've finally got Jayne to ourselves, and she's gonna tell us a story."

FOURTEEN

Jayne looked at her friends, wondering what they'd think once they knew of her past. Would they understand her reasons for remaining silent for so many years? Had enough time gone by that they wouldn't treat her differently, like so many had back then? She was an onion, ready to shed a layer. But there were still so many.

The idea of telling them made her heart jump to her throat, but one look at their expectant faces told her everything would be fine. These friendships, forged with love, understanding and a heavy dose of humor, had withstood far worse.

Jayne grimaced and began, "As you've probably figured out, there are some things about my past I've, ah, *refrained* from discussing. Seems it caught up with me this weekend. When I'm done telling you, I hope you'll understand why it's taken me so long." She took a drink. "You guys know I'm a story teller at heart, and a little windy at times. Are you sure you're up for this?"

"Let's see." Liz made a big show of looking at her watch. "It's eleven. As long as you can wrap it up by six. I have a social engagement, you know."

"Well, that means I'll have to make it the condensed version..." Jayne grinned, her heart swelling with love for these spirited women. Good times and bad, their wit always surfaced, taking the sting out of the worst of situations. She'd be counting on that in future months.

She paused, closed her eyes and exhaled as she willed her heart to slow. She drew her knees to her chest, wrapping her arms around them, forming a shield of sorts as she began, "You know I was married when I was younger." She looked around the circle at the bobbing heads and continued, "There's more to that story. You've allowed me the privacy I've needed for a long time, and it's meant a lot to me that you've never pried or asked about Mack. I've put most of it behind me because it's too painful to talk about."

Jayne read curiosity in their eyes, but everyone remained silent as she continued. "I was just finishing my senior year of college when I met the man of my dreams...Macklin Harrington Payne, the Third. He was Trey to most of his friends, but he was Mack to me...he was a musician..."

☼☼☼

Wiping a smattering of tears from her cheeks, she said, "Can you understand why I don't talk about any of this?"

Cara blew her nose, got up and gave her a hug. "Of course we understand. We're your wingmen, and we love you."

"How could we even think of being upset with you? You're the one who's been through hell and back." Meg blew her nose. "Maybe it's time we take a little break. Anyone care to join me for a quick dip? I need to cool off a bit." Meg put her sunglasses back on, patted Jayne's leg and headed over to the water's edge.

"That sun is definitely hot today. I'm joining you." Jayne followed Meg, wishing she could sneak away, find a cool dark room and indulge in an all-out crying jag. But she couldn't. The days of running away were over. Now that she'd gotten through this, should she go ahead and tell them the rest while they were together with no interruptions? It would surely make things easier for her, but it would be selfish to ruin the rest of the weekend for everyone else. It would definitely change the tone and focus of the rest of their time together. So she'd wait…

Liz was right behind her as she walked around to the zero-entry end of the pool. Jayne's nerves were ragged and she jumped when Liz laid her hand on her shoulder and spoke quietly, "Sweetie. It's okay if you need some space. You've had a lot come at you in the past forty-eight hours."

You have no idea…"Thanks, Red, but I'm fine. What would I do without you guys?" Jayne smiled, throwing her arm over Liz's shoulder. She was so lucky to have these women in her life—such good, understanding friends who constantly humbled her with their huge hearts. She pulled away and plunged into the chilly water, resurfacing to splash some water at Meg and Liz, finally laughing. "This feels great." She floated on her back, staring at the fluffy clouds scattered lazily across the brilliant blue sky, feeling her sadness ebbing with every kick that took her to the end of the pool.

"How 'bout I order us a round of frozen lemonades? Spiked with vodka, of course. " Leigh called out to them from the side of the pool, then turned to pounce on Meg. "And you—we let you off the hot seat earlier. Now it's time for you to 'fess up. What's the story on Sean?"

Meg was crimson, her eyes begging Jayne for another rescue when Jayne heard the trill of her cell phone, "Cara, could you grab that for me?" She swam to the side of the pool.

"Diva Central. State your purpose." Cara paused to listen and then giggled. "Careful, this isn't Jayne. It's

Cara, and I'm not sure this call's gonna pass muster. Let me check with the Queen Diva."

Looking over at Jayne she mouthed, "*Nick,*" and in a stage whisper she relayed the message, "Some guy says his purpose is purely illicit. Maybe I'd better screen this call...."

Jayne stepped up on the ladder and took the phone. "Illicit, huh? What can't you share, Mr. McCord?" Careful to keep her voice neutral, she wanted to hear what he had to say but she wasn't letting him off the hook this easily. Nor did she want him to think she'd been eagerly awaiting his call.

"I'd prefer to tell you in person, Ms. Morgan. That is, if you want anything more to do with me after last night."

"Why would you say that?" Damned if she'd let on that his disappearing act had bothered her.

"I'm sorry about last night. I ended up heading back to my hotel after I walked Alynn to the Westin. And happy birthday."

She accepted the apology, but what she couldn't understand was why he hadn't called to tell her he was signing off for the night. Then again, he *was* a man. At least he hadn't stayed with his ex. She wasn't sure whether she was irritated or relieved. Maybe a little of both. "Thanks."

"How's your day shaping up?"

"Great. How was the fishing expedition?"

"Wild. And early. We managed to catch a lot of fish in spite of our hangovers and lack of sleep. A couple of the guys on another boat got sick and came back in after an hour, and now most of us are just relaxing by the pool."

"So, who were the puking fishermen?"

"Gene and Jimmy. But Sean was looking pretty green. They won't live this down any time soon. What are you up to?"

"I got up early and went to the Naval Base. Brandon took me to see the F-18's. Now we're poolside, in various stages of recovery from last night's antics."

"Hmm. Nice image. Better than what I'm looking at over here," Nick laughed. "Had lunch yet?"

"Just finished a salad and was deciding whether a nap or a book would be the plan for the next couple of hours. You mentioned a proposition?"

"I did. I want to make amends for last night. Care to consider a third option?"

"Maybe. Is it an illicit option?" Jayne teased, aggravated with herself that she was so happy he cared enough to try to make it up to her. She grabbed a towel and sat on the side of her chaise lounge.

"Would that increase my chances of you saying yes?"

"Maybe." God, the low rumble of his voice was sexy, and just the image of doing anything illicit with him was enough to make her want to jump in the pool to cool off again.

"Well—I was going to invite you to go out with me on my bike this afternoon, but if you'd rather do something illicit, I'm game—"

*I'm sure you are...*Jayne swallowed, her mouth going dry. "Okay, okay. Twist my arm. I'll let you off the hook this time and we can go for a ride. When?"

"When can you be ready?"

Jayne looked at the clock on the bar and answered, "I'll need about forty-five minutes by the time I change and catch the boat. Say, two o'clock?"

"Perfect. Wear jeans, and boots, if you have them."

"Sure. See you at the dock."

Clicking off, Jayne realized her friends were staring at her with raised eyebrows. "What?"

Cara was the first to speak. "You are nothing but a twitter-pated school girl. You should see your face right now. You're grinning like the Cheshire Cat."

"Nick wants me to go for a ride this afternoon."

Her friends burst out laughing and Liz sputtered, "I'll bet he does."

"Well, he actually said a ride on the bike, but I'm pretty sure the other offer is on the table. Hope you guys don't mind if I go. I should be back in time for sunset and dinner with you—or at least those of you who aren't otherwise engaged." She tapped Liz's leg as she squeezed by her lounge. "I can't imagine we'll be gone more than an hour or two."

Was she crazy to want to go with him? Probably. But after last night's fiasco she didn't want him to think she was avoiding him for something that wasn't his fault. And after baring her soul to the divas, she really needed to clear her head. This would be perfect.

She stepped out of the shower and toweled off, then tugged on a pair of jeans, boots and a long-sleeved, v-necked knit top, pushing the sleeves up to her elbows. She dried her hair and pulled it back into a pony tail, then applied a bit of mascara, lipstick, and perfume. Giving a quick turn in front of the floor-length mirror, she nodded. Not bad for twenty minutes. She grabbed her jean jacket and crammed a few essentials in the pocket, and slid on her sunglasses. She glanced at the clock on the night stand—right on time to catch the boat. Maybe she *was* crazy. But as she'd always said, crazy was good.

Feel the fear and do it anyway...

FIFTEEN

"Jayne, wait up."

She turned as Meg pulled the cottage door closed and hurried toward her, dressed in similar attire. "Hey. Where are you headed?"

"Sean called about the same time you were leaving the pool and invited me to take a spin as well." Meg was beaming. "I think we're joining you."

During the boat ride, they stood out on the covered fantail. Several sailboats were racing in the distance, their pristine sails stark against the dazzling turquoise water. Jayne's thoughts drifted back to the story she'd shared that morning. Funny how life can deal you such a mixed hand.

Meg touched her arm. "You're awfully quiet. You all right?"

"I was just thinking about the twists and turns fate casts our way in a lifetime. Some of us get so much good, some get a mixed bag and some get nothing but crap. When it comes down to it, I'm one of the lucky ones in spite of everything."

Meg put an arm around her shoulder. "We both are. It's okay to be sad about someone you loved so much. Funny, but I'm even sad about Richard at times. Not because it's over, but because there was once a part of him I loved with all my heart. We're who we are today because of our yesterdays, good or bad. I probably know that as well as anyone. Can you put the sad part of you on the shelf for the afternoon? There's a handsome guy standing at the top of the gangway, and he's looking forward to your pretty smile."

"You're right, and thanks. We've both gone through a lot, and we're stronger for it. Let's go. As my friend Chris Filer says, it's time for a joy ride." Jayne grinned, shaking off her funk, thinking about the words to one of her friend's first recordings. *Take a joy ride, leave your cares behind...* Turning back as she stepped onto the dock, she lowered her voice. "P.S. I like Sean and I'm glad you're having a good time with him. He's nothing but delicious, Meg."

The men stood at the top of the walkway, clad in jeans, Harley T-shirts and boots. Jayne watched other women casting appreciative glances at the pair, a possessive schoolgirl thrill rolling over her knowing she and Meg were claiming the prizes.

Nick offered her a broad grin and pulled her close for a hug and kiss. "You look terrific. Glad you were game."

She inhaled the scent of his cologne, her pulse quickening. "Thanks for asking."

Sean greeted Meg in a similar manner, giving Jayne a chance to look him over more thoroughly than she'd be able to the previous day. His tee shirt really emphasized some serious pecs and biceps, and a navy bandana around his neck added a roguish quality she hoped Meg could appreciate. He was quiet, but his caramel-colored eyes took in everything and right now they were devouring Meg.

Jayne patted his cheek. "Sean, I see you've managed to lose the green pallor."

"You're cruel," he chuckled.

Nick laughed. "You have no idea." He laid his hand on Jayne's shoulder as they headed for the hotel's front drive. Leaning close, he purred into her ear, "You make a really hot biker babe, but there's something missing."

"And that would be?"

"Leather."

"How do you know I'm not wearing leather lingerie?" She flashed him a wicked grin.

"You're good at this game, and you're killing me."

He turned to her with a more serious look on his face. "Need to know—you or Liz have any more problems with Halverson?"

"He called our cottage this morning while I was over at the Naval base. Liz threatened, he retreated. Enough said." Jayne frowned and shook her head. "But you should see the bruises on her arm from where he grabbed her."

"I can only imagine. I saw him at the airport this morning. He was filing a flight plan and getting his plane refueled."

"Did you have another run-in?" She stopped, frowning. "Wait. You saw him at the airport?" Halverson's plane was at the private terminal. What was Nick doing over there?

"Yeah. I helped Alynn get back to Toronto this morning."

Nick hesitated and Jayne could see his discomfort. She raised her eyebrows as a question mark, willing him to elaborate.

"She couldn't get a commercial flight so I had my company plane fly down to pick her up. It was already in Orlando—"

"What do you fly?" Under other circumstances, that would be a gauche question, but as a pilot who owned planes, it was standard aviation speak and she thought nothing of asking.

He hesitated again, then said, "Gulfstream. A G-Four."

Jayne didn't let on that she was impressed, knowing it would embarrass him. "I think I saw it come in earlier. Those are great jets. You fly?"

"No, though I'd like to learn at some point." Nick shrugged, "It's a perfect size for my team and it comes in handy when we need to get to a construction site quickly."

Jayne sensed his unease sharing the trappings of his success, so she shifted the conversation. "It's good that you could help Alynn out. How's she doing?"

"Embarrassed. And Halverson ducked out the minute he saw me. He's spineless."

Jayne nodded. "He's a lot of bad things. I'm surprised he's leaving before the end of the race."

"I overheard the guys working the desk saying a couple of his crew members got caught tying a bucket to the rudder of one of their main competitor's boats last night and his crew and his boat were disqualified."

"A bucket?"

"Yeah. One of the oldest—and dumbest—tricks in racing. You tie a five-gallon bucket to the rudder with a half inch cord and it drags, slowing a racing boat enough to make a big difference. Hard to detect unless you're under water. Can't say I'm surprised. It's Halverson's style, though he'll never admit blame. He'll accuse the team and deny he ever knew a thing about it. And they'll pay hell for getting caught," Nick said. They rounded the corner to the front drive and he led her to his bike. "Here we go."

Jayne stood back to check out the handsome machine. "This is sharp, Nick. Love the black. Looks like you spit polish it daily." She checked out the fine stereo, wondering what he listened to while he rode. The chrome upgrades shone in the sunlight and were gleaming so brightly she could see her reflection. She circled the bike, squatting down to get a closer look at the engine. She nodded her approval as she muttered, "Ultra Classic with the one-ten twin cam—Screaming Eagle package... *nice*..."

His eyebrows shot up. "You know bikes?"

"I know I'm looking at some serious upgrades and custom work. Handsome bike. How much does she weigh all rigged out like this?"

"About eleven hundred pounds."

God, where had this woman been all his life? She actually recognized what she was seeing. Even knew the lingo. And she looked smoking hot just walking around it, sliding her fingers across the leather seat, caressing the chrome trim. For a split second, he wanted to trade places with his bike. His mouth went dry. "So how is it you're so familiar with motorcycles?"

"I did research for a story a couple of years ago. Ended up spending a weekend in Sturgis at the annual run, talking to riders. Then I met with a woman who owns a very large dealership in Kansas City. She filled in the technical gaps."

"I'm impressed. Ever ride one yourself?"

"Not yet. Just shotgun so far."

And it had been a long time. Turning over control to Nick had her nerves on high alert—made her heart stutter at the thought. She'd been freakish about it since the accident, but today she was determined to fight down the panic. Squelching the dive bombers attacking her stomach, she returned her attention to his bike. "You must love this. Blasting down the road at eighty."

"Or a hundred."

She nodded without blinking, relating to his love of speed. "Or a hundred. Give me the down and dirty."

"Once I get on, you just step on this bar." He flipped down a foot rest. "And climb on behind me. When I lean, lean with, not against me. If you need me to stop and I can't hear you, just tap my leg."

"I can manage that." She glanced over at Meg, climbing on behind Sean, the rumble of his engine drowning out further conversation. Sean's bronze Heritage Soft Tail was equally impressive with similar upgrades.

Nick climbed on and hit the ignition, adding the reverberating growl of his motor to the din. At his signal, Jayne climbed on and nestled against him, his raw strength evident as he straddled the big bike. These were heavy suckers and though they were fairly easy to balance, this one would be hard to manage due to sheer weight if it started to get squirrelly and go over on him. She put her hands firmly on his waist, again fighting the panic building in her gut.

She wasn't sure how she'd manage this, another wave of panic washing over her. Had this been a mistake? She'd always been a control freak, but after the crash her neurosis blossomed. Now, anyone who knew her at all simply understood that Jayne would be behind the wheel or the stick, though only those in her inner circle understood why. And forget driving in rain, snow or ice storms. Valium wasn't strong enough to get her through that.

Closing her eyes and saying a quick prayer, Jayne forced her shoulders to relax. *Suck it up—everything's going to be fine.* This would be a fun afternoon. She had no idea where they were going, and she didn't care. Being with Nick, the wind whipping her hair and the sun beaming down on her face was a perfect way to spend her birthday.

Between Nick's broad shoulders and the windshield, the wind was manageable. Sean and Meg roared up beside them as they left the island, heading north on Highway One. She caught Meg's eye and gave her a thumbs up. So far, Sean appeared to be the antithesis of Meg's ex.

She fought to relax, but her fingers clutched tightly to Nick's waist. She rolled her shoulders, willing them to loosen. Nick's confidence and experience became more evident with each passing mile. And she *did* trust him or she wouldn't even be here with him. He handled his bike as expertly as she flew her planes. She leaned back and let the wind buffet her face, focusing on the tiny whitecaps dancing on the water. Would she ever figure out how to let someone else completely take charge for a change?

The sun blazed, playfully glistening across the water on both sides of the road as they passed through Big Pine Key. Jayne could see Nick's chiseled profile in his mirror, sheer pleasure etched across his face. He pointed out different things as they rode, leaning back into her in the way of unspoken communion from time to time. To a fair degree, she was managing to stifle her issues, white knuckles her only concession to the anxiety that remained.

Coming upon Summerland Key, Sean signaled to Nick and slowed, pulling into the lot by a weathered, water-front shanty. Climbing off first, Jayne ran her fingers through her tangled hair and re-tied her pony tail, grinning at Nick. "That was awesome. I usually fly down here—I'd forgotten how much I love the feel of the wind and the smell of salt water. Really makes you come alive, doesn't it?"

Nick's dimples deepened. "That it does."

Unbelievable. Those were his exact thoughts during the ride down. And Jayne wasn't bitching about what the wind was doing to her hair. Bonus points for that. If only she could relax. She was holding on so tight he figured she'd be ready to head back the minute he pulled over.

"It's time for a beer. Name your label," Jayne tossed over her shoulder as she headed to the rail of the outside bar.

Nick followed her into the bar. Meg was equally unconcerned about how the wind had trashed her hair. He caught Sean's eye and nodded. He could get used to spunky women who were so busy living they ignored the trappings of vanity. Tally mark for these girls.

Jayne approached the squatty, bald bartender. "Hi there. What's the coldest beer you've got?"

"Corona and Michelob."

Jayne slapped a fifty dollar bill on the bar. "I'll have a Corona with a lime, if you've got one, and whatever these pirates are having."

"Make it two." Meg joined Jayne at the bar and leaned against it, laughing. "Holy crap. This is almost better than sex. Just the rumble of the engines—what a rush. Isn't this just the best day ever?"

"Ever." Jayne nodded. And she truly was having fun, in spite of herself. "You should have bugs between your teeth the way you've had the perma-grin going for the last half hour."

"My face hurts from smiling so much. You know, we may need to buy a couple of these bikes for ourselves. Wouldn't that be a kick?" Meg lowered her voice, "I know Sean's nothing serious, but I really like him."

"You're long overdue, my friend. I didn't get the Cliff Notes on last night's *late night*....but he seems to be a good guy."

"He's definitely a book worth reading. There's a lot more to him once he opens up."

"You'll have to fill me in later." Jayne headed outside to the patio where Nick and Sean leaned on the rail overlooking the inlet. She sidled up to Nick and he turned and made room for her next to him.

"Having fun?"

"Just hating every minute of it." Taking a pull on her beer, she peered over at the small marina below her. "Don't you love bars like this?"

"Definitely," Sean said, joining the conversation.

Jayne studied Sean's profile as he watched the water, likening him to a panther. All sinewy muscles that moved in fluid, sexy stealth. He'd be the type who would observe, form his opinions, and if he found you worthy, he would be a rock solid ally or partner. His quiet demeanor made him that much more intriguing.

"Sean, have you been riding long?"

"Since I was fifteen."

"Where do you like to ride?"

"Anywhere." Sean grinned, taking a pull on his beer.

Jayne realized Sean wasn't aloof, just efficient with words.

"What's the best trip you guys have ever taken on your bikes?" Meg asked.

Nick answered, "A few years ago we toured the Colorado Rockies—took a day off riding to white water raft down the Colorado River. Fantastic trip."

"Yeah, that was a good one. So was that trip through eastern Canada last fall. The Sugar Maples were turning. Amazing," Sean added.

Sean's deep quiet voice had a rich timbre, and Jayne enjoyed listening as he elaborated on other rides and his collection of vintage motorcycles. As Meg said, there was a lot more to him once he opened up.

They finished their beers and headed out to the parking lot.

"Sean and I thought we'd take you to a little bar we found in Marathon for some Florida lobster. You two comfortable riding that far?" Nick asked.

"I'm game," Meg answered.

Jayne nodded. So far, so good. No way years of fear would be gone in a single afternoon, but her phobia was ebbing.

After another hour of blazing up the highway, they crossed the Seven Mile Bridge. A few miles later, Nick slowed and turned onto the parking lot of a turquoise cinderblock building. It had a corrugated tin roof and stood poised over the water on stilts.

Jayne climbed off, noting an interesting collection of bikes parked in the lot. "Yet another great joint. This is a new one for me."

Nick faced her and placed his hands on her shoulders, his eyebrows arched. "You okay?"

"Great. Why?" *Dammit, he must be tired of me squeezing the daylights out of him.*

"You seem a little tense. Does riding with me scare you?"

"I'm sorry, Nick. I have a little trouble giving up control. Please don't take it personally. I'm having a great time."

"If you're sure…"

"Positive. I'll explain another time, but right now I've gotta find the little girls' room." She gave him a quick peck and followed Meg to the entrance.

Sean knelt next to his bike, frowning.

Nick joined him, looking over his shoulder to examine the engine. "What's going on?"

"There's a popping sound when I accelerate. Probably nothing, but it doesn't sound right. Feels a little sluggish."

"Bad petrol?"

"Maybe, but we filled up at the same place. You notice anything with yours?"

"Not at all."

"I'll watch it on the way back and have Jimmy take a look at it in the morning. If there's a problem, he'll find it."

They were wiping their hands on a rag from Sean's saddle bag when Nick looked up to see Jayne standing at the entrance. They headed to the door, checking out the other bikes in the lot. There were some upgrades he liked and some he didn't. Nick smiled at Jayne, laying his hand on her shoulder as they walked into the bar. No harm staking his claim.

"Everything okay with Sean's bike?" she asked.

Nick stopped in the foyer and faced her. "Hope so. He noticed it running a little rough. Hungry?"

"Sure, and thirsty."

"Let me wash up. I'll join you in a minute."

Meg was waiting for her at the bar. Jayne looked around the room at the different groups of riders, knowing a certain amount of camaraderie and respect existed between them as they assessed one another—from the bike, to the rider, to the gear.

She turned to Meg, chuckling. "Did you see the way all these guys sized up Nick and Sean? It's like women meeting at a black tie event for the first time. Only we check out the jewelry, the escort and the label on the gown. Same game, different playing field."

"Hadn't thought about it quite that way, but you're right."

"Try this on for size." Jayne leaned toward Meg, speaking in a low tone, "In that far corner are the older, over-weight weekend warriors trying to look tough, but looking silly in their spanking new biker togs. Their wives humor them, but are secretly embarrassed for them." She nodded toward the back room. "Shooting pool in the back are the rough, gang-type riders. Probably own those custom choppers in the lot. Prison tats and police records are a membership requirement, so we'll give them a wide path. Their women are mean, fight dirty and like to mud wrestle."

Meg was nodding and laughing. "And they probably wear tube tops. No wonder your books do so well. Your imagination is outrageous."

Jayne laughed and continued, turning toward the outside bar, "And those fellows on the deck? They're more like Nick and Se—" Jayne grabbed Meg's arm. "Oh, *hell*."

"What?"

"I know one of those men."

"So? Who is it?"

"Come on, I'll introduce you. Nick doesn't know about my pen name and I'd like to keep it that way—for now, at least. May need your help." Jayne strode to the back of the bar and stopped at the foursome, tapping one fellow on his shoulder. "You can run, but you can't hide."

The silver-haired man looked up, surprise spreading across his face as he rose to hug her. "Jayne. What in the world brings you down here? Research?"

"Naw, just taking a little walk on the wild side. How are you, Jim? You look pretty righteous in the leathers. New hobby, or are *you* doing a bit of research?" She laughed as he rocked her in a hug.

"You'll just have to wait and see." He stood away, his eyes making a quick trip from her head to her boots, "Don't need to ask how *you're* doing—you're gorgeous as ever, kid. Let me introduce you to my friends."

As they exchanged introductions, Jayne pulled Meg forward. "This is my good friend, Meg Ewing."

"Meg, Jim Hathaway. Glad to know you." He offered a hand.

"It's a pleasure. Love your work."

"Thank you—always appreciate a beautiful fan. Will you ladies join us?"

"Oh, thanks, Jim, but we're with friends and I think they've already ordered. We don't want to intrude..." Jayne inched away, intent on catching Nick at the bar before he headed toward them.

"Not at all." Jim pulled back the table while the other fellows grabbed a couple of extra chairs. "There's plenty of room."

Jayne bit her lower lip, her stomach a jumble of nerves. This could be tricky. Keeping the conversation away from their professions would be akin to hoping for a winning lottery ticket.

Sean, leaning on the bar, nodded to Meg's signal and joined them. Jayne saw the intent look on his face and knew he'd recognized Jim. Meg made the introduction as Jayne looked around for Nick, relieved to hear the men discussing their bikes and respective destinations.

Nick, toting four beers, strode to Jayne's side. He handed out the beers and shook hands with the trio of men, turning to catch the passing server, "Let us have a couple of your sampler platters." He slid into the seat next to Jayne, resting his arm across the back of her chair. She tensed and held her breath as Jim turned to address Nick.

"Nick, what do you do in Toronto?"

"I'm in commercial construction. And you're *the* James Hathaway?"

"Guilty as charged. That's how Jayne and I met."

Jayne's heart was thumping murderously. She had to steer the conversation to a new topic before Jim spilled the beans.

Sean folded his arms on the table and looked at Jim. "Really like your work. I just finished your last Corrine Logan novel. Any more in that series?"

"Thanks, Sean. Absolutely. The next comes out in May. She's one of my favorite characters. I'll bet you like Jayne's Blair Harper, then?"

Jayne cringed, waiting for the light to go in Nick's eyes, but he merely frowned. She could tell his mental gears were turning, but he hadn't connected the dots.

But Sean exchanged a look with Meg and she read his lips as he mouthed to her, "You need to fill me in…"

Platters of seafood arrived and Jayne could've kissed the server. It shifted the conversation from books and characters to the delicious array of appetizers.

"Jim, is your next book set here in the Keys?"

Crap. Meg couldn't let it go.

"No, but I'm betting Jayne will be writing about rugged men riding Harleys."

One of Jim's friends looked at Jayne. "Did I miss something? You're a writer, too?"

Jayne took a swig of beer and answered, shooting Jim a look, praying he was perceptive enough to follow her lead. "Oh, Jim's in a whole different league. There's no comparison."

She watched the confused expression cross Jim's face, relieved when he gave her a sly wink. He turned to his friend and said, "You gotta love a gorgeous woman who's modest. So Jayne, did you come down in your Baron or did you slum it and fly commercial?"

Good grief. This conversation was a literal mine field of information she'd intended to keep under wraps. Embarrassed by the tidbit that slipped out, but relieved the topic was no longer about books, she rolled her eyes at her friend, shrugging her shoulders. "You know me, Jim. I'll find any excuse to fly the Keys. I visited my brother in Ocala for a couple of days and came down Thursday."

"We need to go flying again soon." Addressing the group, Jim said, "Jayne and I met up in Palm Beach about a year ago. We took her plane over to Naples one day to have lunch and play eighteen holes. She beat the socks off me, but we had a ball. I'll warn you fellas, if you play golf with her, don't let her talk you into making any wagers."

Nick couldn't keep his notes straight on everything Jim was saying about Jayne. They'd spent hours together and there was a lot she still hadn't told him about herself. She obviously wrote more than magazine articles and she was a pilot. What other surprises did she have up her sleeve? He couldn't wait to find out.

Jim's friend who'd quizzed Jayne looked at Sean, squinting. "Hartung. You seem familiar. What do you do?"

"Custom cabinetry."

The other friend, huge with hands the size of boxing gloves, squinted at Sean. "*I know you.* You played pro hockey—Toronto Maples Leafs, right?"

Sean nodded. "Yeah. Ten years. How'd you know that?"

"I was a forward for the Red Wings and we played against each other a few times, in Toronto and Detroit. I thought your name sounded familiar."

"You have a better memory than I do. But now that you mention it, I *do* remember your name. Didn't you retire due to an injury?"

"Yeah. In my eighth season, I had to have my knee replaced. Sure miss it, though. Now I coach a group of high school kids in my spare time. You blew out your shoulder, right? You still play?"

"Right. I play with some guys in a small league. We don't play for blood."

"*Bullshit.*" Nick nearly choked on his beer. "I play on the same team with this guy. He's merciless."

"Old habits die hard." Sean chuckled and tapped his beer to Nick's.

Laughing, Jim glanced at his watch. "Hate to end the fun, but we're expected for dinner at the Ocean Reef Club in a couple of hours."

Nick looked at Jayne as they stood. "We better get going, too." But he wouldn't mind if the afternoon went on a lot longer.

Once in the parking lot, Jayne pulled Jim to the side, hugging him as she whispered, "Thanks for not outing me in there."

"Honey, I damn near did."

"I know, but it'll be okay. I just haven't told these guys very much about myself yet. Nothing to hide, but it's just...you know."

"I sure do. You take care of yourself and tell Leigh hello for me. Let's try to catch up for another game of golf the next time you're in my neck of the woods."

"I'd love it."

"And Jayne, I like your big fella. He seems quite taken with you, and that makes him A-plus in my book."

"Thanks, Jim. You guys be safe and *try* to behave," Jayne gave him a final hug and waved as the men roared off, a cacophony of beeping horns as they hit the northbound lane of Highway One.

Nick waited astride his bike, the engine rumbling. Jayne turned and walked toward him, surprising him when she leaned down and took his face in both hands and kissed him hard on the lips. Something about her was slipping under his skin. Whether her casual manner or her sexy confidence, he couldn't be sure. Both were playing havoc with his determination to keep from getting too close. So much for keeping this a strictly fun, making-amends type of afternoon. He was already panting after her like some school boy with a raging crush.

She pulled back and flashed him a dazzling smile, her dimples deep, her voice a sweet purr. "I know I'll tell you this later, but thank you. I'm having a great time with you."

"Pleasure's all mine." *Damn*. His reaction to her was immediate. He shifted uncomfortably on the seat, tasting her lip gloss that lingered on his mouth. *Easy boy...* She climbed on, making matters worse as she pressed against his back. With a groan, he revved the engine and signaled to Sean, rolling southbound toward Key West. *Time to get back to Key West and put a little distance between us...between my back and her breasts for starters....*

Ten miles down the road, Nick glanced in his rearview mirror. Sean's headlamp flickered in intermittent intervals and he and Meg were lagging behind them. He slowed, waving for Sean to come up beside him, signaling to pull off at the large service station just ahead.

Nick waited as Jayne climbed off. "We need to see what's going on with Sean's bike."

"I saw his headlight dimming in your mirror. Could it be his alternator?"

"Could be." Nick stepped over to Sean's bike, offering Meg his hand as she swung her leg around. Sean remained on his bike, revving the engine while they listened. Nick heard the weakening in the rumble, then knelt to check the fuel line, shaking his head. "You're not leaking petrol, but you're losing power. Bet it's your stator."

Jayne watched and listened, picking up on the weak whine underneath the rumble of the engine. Years of flying mandated a keen ear for the slightest deviation in an engine's hum, and a working knowledge of carbureted and fuel injected engines. "What's a stator?"

"They're what replaced alternators in the newer bikes," Sean answered. "Not easy to find at this hour of the day."

"I'm going to check in with the gals while you figure out what we need to do," Meg said as she walked toward the convenience store, punching in numbers on her cell phone.

Jayne followed, overhearing Meg tell Leigh about their eventful afternoon.

Meg spoke for a few minutes, then waved Jayne over, passing off her phone. "Leigh wants to talk to you for a second. I'll grab waters for us."

"Hey, Leigh. All quiet on the western front?"

"Very. Meg said you ran into Jim Hathaway."

"Oh, that was entertaining."

"I'll bet. So—how are Meg and Sean getting along?"

"Good. He's a sweetheart. His voice is deep and quiet—he should use it more often. It makes my toes curl and I'm not even interested. I'll let Meg fill you in, but he's sharp, educated, and they seem in sync."

"Great. We've been wondering. How's *your* date? Still on probation?"

"Naw—he's a good guy and I'm pretty sure he's legit."

"To say the least. Hope you don't mind, but I spent some time on the web this afternoon. Did a bit of checking on him and Andy."

"You beat me to it. Find anything?"

"A lot. Ready for this? Nick is founder and CEO of one of the largest construction companies not only in Toronto, but in Ontario and beyond. McCord Consolidated is huge and it has subsidiaries in other portions of the construction industry. He sits on a couple of boards, both professional and altruistic. To his credit, he's a lot more than he appears to be—seems as if the two of you are playing the same game. I've been chuckling to myself all afternoon. Here you've been hiding your success, and he's been doing the same with you. I'd love to be the fly on the wall when you two finally open up to each other."

"I had a hunch there was more to him than meets the eye. That Gulfstream that flew in this morning? It was his. I'll fill you in on that later. Have you mentioned any of this to the others?"

"No. This is just between us—a little something to put in your back pocket."

"What about Andy?"

"Similar story, not quite as much info out there, but he's the head of a big electrical contracting company."

"Nice to know they're telling us the truth. Albeit an edited version."

"Sounds familiar…"

"On that note, I need to go see what's happening."

"Let me know if we can help you out."

"Thanks. Stay tuned."

Jayne pushed through the large glass door to find Nick pacing, talking on his cell phone, and Sean kneeling beside his bike with two men in leathers leaning down to confer. Meg was looking on from a vantage point slightly behind them.

"….yeah….Right…If you can't, let's get one here as quick as you can………That'll work…..right. Let me know."

Nick clicked off his phone and turned to Jayne. "It's like we thought—the stator's gone out. That was Andy and he's trying to locate one in the area, but I doubt we'll be able to get it this afternoon. According to these guys," he pointed to the two strangers, "there aren't any dealerships in this area and it's already after four." He raked his hand through his hair. "If we can't get one today, we'll have one couriered down first thing in the morning. Only option on a Sunday."

Meg had been standing beside Jayne, listening. She said, "Well, why don't we wait at that place across the road until Andy calls you back."

SIXTEEN

"My kind of place," Sean said as he headed toward four empty stools at the corner of the bar, pulling one out for Meg.

Jayne agreed, taking in the strands of vintage Christmas lights bound in the rafters, hulls of old fishing boats converted to tables, buoys tethered to the support columns and rusty corrugated tin walls with weathered marine rope. She slid onto the stool next to Meg as Nick settled beside her. There was a decent gathering of customers, and the happy hour music echoed just a notch below loud as Stevie Ray Vaughn vibrated an old jukebox perched in the corner.

Sean beckoned the bartender and turned to the group. "Same poison or are you guys ready for something different?"

"Corona for me," Meg said.

Jayne nodded. "Same, please."

"So if you can't get the part today, what *is* the plan?" Meg took a sip, looking at the men with raised eyebrows.

Ticking off options on his fingers, Nick answered, "We can rent a car at the Marathon airport but I'm not crazy about leaving the bikes here. Or you girls can drive back in a rental car while we stay here with the bikes tonight. Or, we—"

"*Or* we can stay here *with* you and the bikes tonight. This could be a fun place to hang out. I'm sure we could find a little motel in the area," Jayne offered, hoping to alleviate some of Nick and Sean's stress over the situation.

"Well, *that's* definitely an option...." Nick looked surprised, his eyes meeting hers.

Jayne held his gaze for a fraction of a second longer that she should've, and knew Nick was reading her mind. Had that been her subconscious intention? She squirmed, that private little tingle announcing that her body was sure as hell on board with the notion whether she was consciously willing to admit it or not.

He chuckled, and the deep, mellow rumble vibrated along her skin just before he leaned down to kiss the side of her head, whispering in her ear, "That's an excellent option."

The tickle of his warm breath on her ear and the caress of his fingers on her neck shot her into hot, wet, overdrive. Feeling awkward and exposed, she looked at Meg and the uncertain expression on her friend's face brought Jayne back to a sober reality.

"Meg, would you be okay staying here tonight?" Sean asked.

Meg studied the rafters, her face turning pink, then said, "I'll let you all decide...."

Catching the bartender's eye, Jayne asked, "Is there a motel or resort nearby that you recommend? We've had a break down and might need to stay in this area tonight."

"Sure. If you're looking for cheap, there's the Gulf Breeze Inn about a quarter mile south. Nothing fancy but it's clean. If you want something real nice, the Southern Cross is about four miles north of here in Duck Key. One of the managers is sitting right over there. He'd probably cut you a deal. I'll get him."

The diminutive brunette spoke earnestly to a man seated in a small group. He rose and joined them.

He stuck out his hand to Nick. "Don Holder. I'm the Director of Sales at the Southern Cross." He shook hands with the rest of them and then reached into his inside blazer pocket, pulling out business cards to pass around. "Sorry to hear you're in a bind, but I'll be happy to help you out. Two king rooms?"

Jayne opened her mouth to protest, then clamped it shut, feeling her face heat up. Meg's eyes bored into her and Nick was the one who rescued the awkward moment.

"Don, we're not sure we'll need rooms. We need a plan in case we can't get a part for one of the bikes until morning. We should know shortly. The rest of our crew is in Key West working on that for us."

"I'll set up the rooms so you have the option. We can help you out with necessities like toothbrushes and razors, and there's a shop just off the lobby that stays open until ten o'clock. You'll find just about anything you need to survive." He was already dialing his cell phone. "Be right back."

Nick, again chuckling at the expression on Jayne's face as Don suggested the rooming set up, decided this turn of events could be fun. She was a deer caught in headlamps, but she hadn't corrected the man.

Even if they stayed, sharing accommodations with Jayne wasn't a given. If anything happened between them, it would happen on her terms. He'd never take advantage of this situation. She was great, no question. And the ongoing flirtation was a kick. If they took things up a notch, it wouldn't be casual. Guess he'd sit back and let the night play out, but he couldn't help hoping they'd end up in bed. If not, he'd be taking a cold shower. Maybe two.

Don returned a moment later and said, "Use my card. I set up rooms under my name at the special rate we extend to family members. Advise the desk staff that you're my guests. When you're ready to head over there, call the resort and our driver will be happy to pick you up."

He passed another card to Nick, pointing to a number. "When you figure things out, just call the desk to let them know if you'll need the rooms. And I know the owner here. He'll have a secure place for your bikes. If those are your Harleys with the Canadian plates, you've got some seriously nice rides that you'll want to lock down."

Nick shook his hand, offering his business card. "Don, thanks. If you're ever in Toronto, let me buy you dinner. Call any time."

Sean shook Don's hand, passing over his card. "Likewise. Thanks again."

Jayne scribbled notes on a receipt, planning an article for her next submission to *Travel and Leisure,* then said, "Don, thank you. You've been extraordinarily kind. I almost hope we have to take this unexpected detour." She meant it—the best times in her life had been those when she'd been forced to take an alternate route, and this side trip was turning into a doozy.

"My pleasure. You guys have a great evening wherever you end up. If you head to the resort for dinner, I recommend The Grille. It's on the water— great food, nice view and it's very casual. You'd be comfortable in your jeans. Good luck with the bike."

Nick's phone rang. He glanced at it and started for the door, signaling to Sean. "Thanks again, Don." He turned to Jayne and said, "It's Andy. We're going outside where we can hear."

Jayne caught the bartender's eye. "Send a round to Don's table from us, please, and a platter of appetizers. Tell him it's sent with our sincere thanks."

Jayne winced as Meg's fingers clenched her arm.

"Do you really think we should stay? What if Sean doesn't want to be stuck here with me? I'll feel like I'm being pushed on him," Meg whispered, her eyes clouded with doubt.

"We won't stay if you don't want to. But, Meg, can't you see Sean's crazy about you? He's probably more afraid that you don't want to be here with *him*. Besides, all this may be moot—salvation may be on the way this very minute." Jayne took a sip and turned to face Meg straight on. "I'm sorry if I screwed up. Staying seemed to be the easiest solution, and the guys seemed to be stressing. How 'bout you and I share and we'll let the guys bunk together. Or if you want, we can rent a car and go back. Let the guys stay with the bikes."

"You'd do that?"

"Of course. We'll do whatever you want." Jayne paused, then laid her hand on Meg's arm. "For the record, we're big girls and we don't need our training wheels any more. No one's judging you, Meg. Talk to Sean, then decide what you want to do." She winked and tapped her glass against Meg's. "Fair?"

Blowing out a breath, Meg finally smiled. "Fair. You always make things seem easy."

"When you've been single as long as I have, you learn that once in a while you need to trust your gut, close your eyes and jump. What's your gut telling you?"

"That Sean's a good guy and he'll respect my feelings."

"That's my impression, too, so seize the moment. Sleep with him, don't sleep with him. It's your choice to make. But make it for the right reasons. If you're inclined, what's the harm? You're both single, consenting adults, and it's not like you're drunk in a bar and you're picking up some guy at closing time. You've already made it clear that you care about him on some level. Given the right circumstances and the right man, we should get over that *good girls don't* mentality that brainwashed us as we grew up. Good girls do, and we enjoy it."

Hmmm, maybe she should listen to her own advice.

"We don't have long, but I need to say something else." Jayne looked over her shoulder and then continued, "After what I shared with you earlier, you should realize that everything can change in an instant." She snapped her fingers for emphasis. "And you need to seize as many moments as you can in this life. So I think we should play tonight by ear and see how it goes. Hell, they may be the ones putting on the brakes when it gets right down to it."

Jayne stopped, looked at Meg and they both burst out laughing. "Yeah, right."

Striding into the parking area, Nick shouted into his phone, and covered his other ear with his hand, "Okay Andy, now I can hear you. What'd you find out?"

"I'm putting you on speaker phone so Jimmy can hear. Hang on." Andy continued, "The dealership in Orlando has the stator. We couldn't get actual courier service until Monday, so I bought one of their employees an airline ticket to fly it down first thing in the morning. Should be here about seven." Andy chuckled. "Tell Sean I spent some of his money. Should be in Key West at seven. Now that we've got that figured out, let's talk about tonight. We can be there in a couple of hours to get you guys. I called Hertz and they have a Ford F350 Club Cab available. The four of us should be able to get the bikes in the back without ramps, don't you think? And the six of us should fit in the cab."

"We might stay here tonight and have you come up in the morning. It'll be dark soon and we've been drinking."

"What about the girls? They good with this plan?" Jimmy asked.

"Think so. We've got a line on rooms at a nearby resort," Nick answered, his tone as neutral and nonchalant as he could make it, knowing the guys would jump all over this.

"Okay, Nick. Picture me rolling my eyes," Andy chortled.

"I know. I know. Get it out of your systems right now and keep a lid on this. Comprende'?"

"Listen young man. Mind your manners and be sure to say please and thank you."

Nick choked out a laugh. "Yes, Mrs. Jameson."

Jimmy jumped in, "Nick, you owe Sean *big time*. This is kind of like running out of gas on a country road…."

"Alright, alright, you two. We'll let you know if anything changes. Otherwise, call when you head out. We'll be at the Southern Cross Resort in Duck Key. Few miles north of Marathon."

Nick ended the call and looked at Sean. "So?"

"So." Sean stared out at the horizon and said, "I'm good either way. Not sure Meg is. Maybe I'll rent a car and take her back, then I can drive up with the guys in the morning. You and Jayne can stay with the bikes."

"Or you could take my bike." Nick pulled the door open, allowing Sean to head in before him. "Let's see what they've decided. Maybe we'll all stay."

"Okay, but you and I may end up as bunk mates." Sean tossed a skeptical look over his shoulder.

"Could happen. I'm winging this myself. Either way, it's time to switch to scotch. Let's find that bartender. Hell, if things start going south, we'll just sit here and drink all night."

"Wouldn't be the first time." Sean slapped Nick on the back.

Jayne met Nick's eyes. "What's the verdict?"

Nick filled them in, outlining Andy and Jimmy's offer. He shrugged his shoulders. "So we'll let the two of you decide."

Sean stood beside Meg and leaned down with a serious expression on his face as he spoke, though Jayne couldn't hear his words. She was curious to see how Meg responded to him and was praying Sean could prove to Meg that good men still existed.

Meg had come a long way, but she had miles to go to overcome years of enduring a controlling, insecure chameleon of a man who treated her like she was insignificant and worthless one minute, then like a valued treasure the next. She'd been kept off balance, and for nearly fifteen years she'd believed she wasn't worthy of more. But Richard slapped her once too often and she finally snapped. While he was at work, she packed up and fled, taking her daughter to hide at Jayne's family's place on Hilton Head while she put her affairs in order. He'd begged and cried, but *that* time she held strong and filed for divorce.

Jayne marveled that Meg was doing so well after enduring so many years of criticism and abuse. Four years and thousands of dollars in therapy stood between Meg and her ex, and Jayne was proud of the progress her friend was making. Seeing her enjoying Sean's attention was proof that she was finally mending. *God, please let this man be worthy of her.*

Nick touched her arm. "You okay?"

She smiled up into his eyes. "Sure. I was just watching Meg and Sean. I'm a bit over-protective of her, for obvious reasons. Please tell me he's a gentleman."

Nick bristled. "Of course he is. We both are, for that matter." Nick frowned at her. "If there's a question in your mind, we should head back now."

She winced at his tone. *Great.* Now she'd insulted him. "No Nick, I wasn't implying that you're not." She laid her hand on his arm. "I don't know Sean as well, and after what Meg's been though I'm cautious. Don't be offended by that."

She'd told Nick about Meg's situation yesterday while they'd walked. Surely he could understand. And the last thing she wanted to do was get cross-wise with him when the afternoon had been so perfect. But apparently, a perceived challenge to his honor brewed a storm.

He laid his hand on top of hers, his expression softening. "Can't blame you. Truth is, he's offering to take her back."

"Good. That'll make all the difference in the world. She'll be fine as long as he lets her decide. I agreed to room with her if she was uncomfortable sharing with him."

"Same with us. What are *you* thinking?" He leaned against the bar, searching her eyes.

What am I thinking? I'm thinking you're addictive and I'm way more attracted to you than I should be. She read curious intensity in the green depths and the electricity leapt from them to spark through her like a brush fire.

"What am I thinking about staying?" She took a sip, hoping he wouldn't notice that her hands were shaking.

"Yeah. I realize you were trying to be a good sport when we were listing our options."

Jayne swirled her beverage, staring at the crystals of ice going round and round, then set her glass on the counter. Meeting his eyes, she said, "I was, but I wouldn't mind spending more time alone with you." There. She'd said it. No going back now.

Nick's heart sped, but he hid his surprise and nodded. "Let's stay, then." He cocked an eyebrow at her. "We sharing a room?" Everything about her and this situation made for a night he couldn't conjure up in his wildest dreams. Stuck overnight at a resort with a gorgeous woman and no interruptions? Nothing wrong with that picture.

Except. If she was looking for something beyond this weekend, she'd end up hating him, and that was the last thing he wanted. He met her eyes, trying to read her thoughts, but they weren't giving much away.

She hesitated, looked at the ceiling, then back at him, pressing her hand against his chest. "Nick, I don't want this to ...you know, imply expectations? We can stay together, but I'm not in a good place to get involved with anyone right now. I'm really attracted to you, but I'm not casual about sex and I'm not a tease. So where does that leave us?"

"Doesn't change a thing. I won't tell you it hasn't crossed my mind more than once, but either way, I'd like to have a night with you away from the crowd." *And maybe you'll change your mind...*

Here he'd been worrying that she'd want more from him than he could give, and now she was taking words from his script. He should be relieved, but he wasn't.

He put his hand on her shoulder and leaned to her ear to murmur, "I'll let you set the pace. But given the chance, I'll make you beg for mercy......"

"Threat?" She turned and cocked an eyebrow at him, her eyes twinkling.

He winked. "Promise."

SEVENTEEN

Jayne climbed out of the resort's SUV at the front entrance and did a quick three-sixty, admiring the vibrant blooms and lush landscaping surrounding the resort's pristine buildings. The sun was low, gleaming across the calm waters of the marina where impressive yachts swayed in their moorings.

"Welcome." A silver haired woman in a tailored suite greeted the foursome at the door to the lobby. "I'm Grace, please come in and we'll get you registered. Mr. Holder explained that you're accidental tourists."

"Thank you, Grace." Jayne accepted the woman's outstretched hand.

"I hope you'll be pleased with your accommodations—Mr. Holder arranged for you to have a couple of our very nice villas, and I've taken the liberty of sending over a few sundry items in light of your circumstances."

"How thoughtful. We figured we'd pick up what we needed in your gift shop," Meg said, shaking Grace's hand, following Jayne into the reception area.

"It's our pleasure. If there are things you still need after you get settled, you can certainly let me know or stop in the shop just across the way. May I assist you with dinner suggestions or reservations? We have some terrific options here at the resort, or I can help you with something in the Marathon area. Our driver will be happy to take you."

They followed Grace to the desk where she had paperwork waiting. Sean flipped out his card, waving Nick off. "I've got this. My bike's the reason we're here."

Nick acquiesced and turned to Grace. "Don suggested The Grille. Can we get a table at eight?"

Jayne studied the spacious lobby, admiring the travertine floors and mahogany furnishings, deciding they'd entered a Rudyard Kipling novel. She was relieved they'd decided to forego the bar scene. Loathe to admit it even to herself, she was feeling the strain of the long day. Fatigue pulled on her, making her want nothing more than a hot bath and a nap. Where on earth did Nick get so much energy? He was still at Grace's desk, talking and nodding.

Nick returned to her with a broad grin stretched across his face. "We're all set." He shook the concierge's hand. "Thanks for your help, Grace."

Following the bellman down a path lined with fragrant shrubs and flowers, they walked to a row of stucco structures along the marina and stopped at the first building. The bellman opened the door, stepping aside to allow Jayne and Nick to enter.

Jayne wandered in to find a spacious two-room villa. French doors divided a charming sitting area and kitchenette from the bedroom.

Walking on in, Jayne discovered a sleigh bed in gleaming mahogany topped with bedding that resembled a cloud. She ran her fingers over the cream silk shantung duvet, goose bumps rising on her arms. Matching shams and pillows were stacked atop the bed, inviting the nap she craved. This comfortable elegance suited her.

Nick was reading a note that accompanied a bottle of wine and a cheese platter perched on the bar. "Don doesn't miss a beat. Card says, *Enjoy your detour.*" He examined the bottle, adding, "Nice choice of wine."

"He's very good with details." She laughed, and turned to flip on the light to the bathroom, stopping short. "Wow."

Understatement. This bathroom fell into her Nirvana category, and easily among the best she'd yet to encounter.

Nick followed her through the bedroom. He glanced at the bed and instantly fell prey to some steamy images. None of them involving clothing. Then he entered the spacious bath. On his left was an all-glass shower that could hold a football team, and further down in the corner was a huge whirlpool tub. A vanity with twin artisan glass bowl sinks were on his right. High-end travertine and granite covered the floor, walls and countertops. He recognized quality materials and good workmanship, nodding his approval.

"We could just stay here. Who needs anything else?" *Get you naked and I'll die a happy man.*

Jayne laughed as she stepped into the enormous shower, "The things you could *do* in here. And that tub—they should post a lifeguard. Did I mention I have a weakness for fabulous hotel rooms? Mix that marshmallow of a bed with this bathroom and I'm a goner. It's just way too sexy."

Nick joined her and sized up the space. "I know *exactly* what we could do in here…."

"Okay, you tell me and I'll tell you." She hooked her finger in his belt loop to pull him close for a quick kiss, releasing him to step out of the shower as she headed back to the bedroom.

Damn, she did have a way of getting his attention. "I'd rather *show* you..." He followed her, eyeing the soft curve of her backside, deciding *she* was way too sexy.

"No doubt..."

He caught the crooked grin she threw at him and tossed back a challenging wink. So far, he was enjoying this little game of cat and mouse...

Absorbing the seismic charge in the air, the last thing he expected was to see Jayne turn, jump, and pounce on the bed like a little kid, completely altering the tone of the moment. She landed and threw her arms out and lazed back, giggling, "Ahh, this is unbelievable. Mind pulling off my boots?"

"Certainly, your highness." Nick accommodated and then kicked off his own, falling on his back beside her, lacing his fingers behind his head. "If you'd told me when I was heading out to go fishing at the crack of dawn that I'd be here with you tonight, in this place I'd never heard of, I would've called you crazy."

"Isn't life more interesting on days filled with good surprises?" She turned on her side, putting her hand on his chest as she said, "And just for the record, crazy is *good.*" She leaned in to kiss him lightly on his nose. He shifted, so she kissed his lips, playfully at first but when he pulled her closer and let his mouth linger, the playfulness of the moment fled. Everything about her was a warning that if she got any further under his skin, he'd never be able to let her go.

Nick let her lead, feeling her deepen the kiss, her tongue sliding over his lips and slipping into his mouth, her body melting as he pulled her closer. As he wrapped her in his arms, he could feel her body's soft shudder. He reached up and pulled her hair loose from the band. Holding the back of her head, he wove his fingers through the silken strands while tracing the outline of her lips with his tongue. He rolled onto his side, wanting the full contact of her body, needing this connection. She tasted and smelled so good he couldn't get close enough. As their chests pressed together, he groaned. Even the way she kissed aroused him—first teasing, then aggressive as her tongue parried and her teeth lightly nipped. He grazed her neck with his lips while he followed the outline of her face with his fingertips, slowly etching a path down her neck and chest, stopping to cup her breast. He felt her breath catch and heard a small moan, heat coursing through him as she tossed one leg over his hip.

He blew out a laugh. "*Again*, you have no idea what you're doing to me."

"Oh, I think I do. And *again*, you're doing it right back to me," she purred, nibbling on his ear. "At least we're not standing under a Banyan tree on a street in Key West this time."

He felt her grasp the hair at the nape of his neck as she kissed him. Her other hand splayed across his chest, and his nipples tightened as the warmth of her fingertips crept through the knit of his shirt. He willed her hand to go lower, needed her to take hold, whispering as much. Her leg locked around him and he literally ached with the sensation of her pressed against his groin. He could imagine how warm and wet…how sweet she'd taste…

Flipping her onto her back in a playful maneuver, he slid her shirt up, exposing her stomach. It was tan and smooth under his tongue and fingers as he leaned down to kiss her navel, working his way up and pushing her shirt further to reveal her bra, and his breath caught. He needed to slow down, but he wanted to rip the thing off. He cupped her breasts in his hands, the silky lace at the edge of the satiny fabric taunting him to uncover what swelled beneath.

He let his eyes feast and then he unfastened the front hook of the garment, letting her taut, full breasts spill into his hands, the pale sight of them glorious, accentuated by the tan of her swimsuit line. *Gorgeous.* Nothing short of perfection...even more beautiful than he'd imagined.

He leaned down to taste one nipple while he kneaded the other breast with his hand. Her heart raced beneath his fingers and when he looked at her face, she was leaning back, watching him with her eyes half closed and her lips partially open in a smile. God, she was something. Desire roared in the pit of his stomach. It had been such a long time since anyone had made him feel this good.

"I need to feel you against me." He leaned up, pulling his shirt over his head and her hands were immediately swirling through the hair on his chest, her fingertips caressing his pecs, brushing over his nipples. He uttered a quick oath, then crushed her against him, taking possession of her mouth as need racked his body.

Pressed against her breasts, he caught his breath and kissed her temple in an effort to gain control again. Was she running her tongue along his ear just to be sure she had his complete attention? He imagined her doing that to his dick and nearly came.

Then he sensed her hesitation. Her movements had slowed, and her hands were on his cheeks. He knew the signs. She was having second thoughts. He pulled back and their eyes met. Then she looked away, her face flushed.

"What's wrong?" Was he moving too fast? Was he pushing?

"Nothing, but..." She exhaled and whispered, "I'm sorry, Nick, but I'm not ready to step off the high dive..."

Taking a breath, he groaned, pulling her with him. "Like I said earlier, it's your call." He took her hand and pressed it against his erection. "But just to be clear, I'm ready to jump off that high board when you are."

"I understand, and I'm not being fair...you probably think I'm just leading you on."

"You're not leading me anywhere I'm not willing to go." He kissed her lightly and took her face in his hands. "We're fine, whether or not anything happens. Let's take our time and see where this goes."

Her smile was wistful, making him wonder what was really going on in her pretty head. She murmured a soft apology and a thank you into his neck. He returned the kiss and forced his body to relax, as much as he could with a pair of naked breasts pressed against his chest.

"Can we at least get this out of the way?" He tugged on her shirt, now wrapped around her neck.

She complied and pulled it over her head. He slipped her bra off her shoulders and pulled her against him, hugging her to him as their bodies melded. She seemed to relax, making him that much more determined to be a gentleman. He fought the urge to slip his hand inside her jeans, wondering if she was as hot and wet as he imagined. And damn, he wanted to taste her. Gentleman or not, if he didn't call a halt to this torture, he'd explode. He rolled over on his back and blew out air.

Her voice, a low coo in his ear, offered salvation, "Maybe we can just test the water..."

Shock and needles of intense pleasure rocked Nick as he felt Jayne's hand slide down his stomach and begin stroking him.

He tried to concentrate on the ceiling fan blades to stave off the painful need for release, but he was keenly aware of every move of her hand as she unfastened his belt, unbuttoned and unzipped his fly, and wrapped strong fingers around his cock as it sprang free of the restraints.

Clinching his teeth, he uttered a tight moan under his breath, "Sweet Jesus..." He buried his face in her hair and stilled as she moved her thumb in a small circle over the tip. Her hand was smooth and firm, and hell, she knew what she was doing as she slid it up and down his shaft. *Keep this up and it won't take long.*

"Oh, my...this is *nice*..." she purred, nibbling on his lobe.

"*Nice, hell.* I want you naked beneath me. Now *that'd* be nice," he muttered into her ear, choking on a laugh. He held his breath as her hand continued stroking, but after a moment of enduring excruciating bliss, he closed his eyes and whispered, "Babe, I'm gonna be a goner if you don't stop."

"Would that be so bad?"

Nick opened his eyes to find Jayne staring at him, her eyebrows raised. She still had a firm grip on him and damn, the way she applied just the right amount of pressure...ah, he liked the way her mind worked. Offering her a grin, he groaned and closed his eyes again as her hands and lips began working their magic. He slid his hands through her hair, clasping the silky strands as her lips ran a scorching path from his mouth, across his chest, teasing his nipples into tight nubs. She kissed a trail down his abs and paused, shifting lower on the bed. Nick was more than a little stunned, but in no way disappointed as her intentions became apparent. He couldn't remember the last time...

He let out a low, appreciative chuckle, "You're wicked."

"You have no idea..."

Jayne was curled inside Nick's arms, half asleep, when her cell phone rang.

"You not really going to answer that, are you?" Nick muttered, also half asleep.

"Choose a cell phone over *you*? Not in a million."

The cell phone went silent, replaced by the ringing of the phone on the night stand. Jayne squirmed out of his grasp and flipped over to crawl to it, giggling as he grabbed for her, catching the waistband of her jeans and hauling her back as she grabbed the receiver, yelping. "But maybe a room phone. Hello."

"Sounds like I'm interrupting," Meg teased.

"Hi Meg. Actually…"

"Sorry. I'll be quick—do you need anything from the gift shop? Sean and I thought we'd hit the hot tub after dinner so I'm looking for swimsuits. Want me to pick some up for you?"

"Hang on." Jayne cupped the phone and peered at him, "I think I'll run to the store with Meg. You need anything?"

He shook his head. "Probably, but I'm not sure what."

Returning the phone to her ear, Jayne said, "Meet you in ten."

She hung up the phone and relayed the conversation."

"I won't need a swim suit to go to the hot tub. You don't either as far as I'm concerned…"

"You may not think so, but the other guests might appreciate it. You're a thirty-two?"

"Thanks, but probably a thirty-four. I'll just stay here and relax. Here." He grabbed his money clip off the night stand, peeling off bills.

"No worries, I'll get it."

Jayne pulled herself together and scrutinized her reflection in the mirror, deciding she looked none the worse for the brief romp. Surveying the basket on the bathroom counter, she called, "I think the hotel covered the critical items—toothbrushes and toothpaste, razors, deodorant. If you think of anything else, call my cell." She gave him a quick kiss and headed out the door.

She found Meg waiting on the sidewalk. "Where's Sean?"

"Snoozing."

"So is Nick, and I'd like to be doing the same. Now fill me in. What did Sean say to change your mind about staying?"

"He said it was my choice, and if we stayed together, there were no strings attached. He was worried that I was just being a good sport." Meg laughed, music in Jayne's ears. "It's like we've become conspirators in this little side show."

"Terrific, Meg." She gave her friend a little hug across the shoulders. "So what do you think of the rooms? Nice, huh?"

"Oh yeah. Sean took one look at the bed and bathroom and said they just invited trouble."

"That's funny, we said the same thing. I'm having a hard time keeping my head on straight where Nick's concerned."

Jayne headed for the rack of men's swim shorts. She selected a couple and held them up for Meg's approval. "How about these?"

"Great. And I found this for me." Meg held up a cute blue two-piece. "And this for you."

Jayne burst out laughing as Meg twirled a tiny bit of strings and macramé. "Perfect. Who needs the pill with that for birth control? Not since I was sixteen, thank you." She pointed to another suit. "Just grab that black bikini in an eight, will you?"

"Sure. Think we should we pick out clean tops to wear tonight? Maybe sweat shirts for all of us? It'll start cooling down soon."

"Good idea. And I'll grab four pairs of flip flops. I'm over these boots for the day."

While Meg checked out the liquor selection, Jayne slid a box of condoms under her stack of items as the clerk totaled her bill. Dividing her purchases into two bags, she slid half of the condoms out of the box and into Meg's bag.

Meg walked to the counter, arms laden with bottles. "I'm not letting you pay for everything. How much do I owe you?"

"Not a dime. You get the booze and we're good." Jayne hefted the bags and headed out the door, struggling to keep a straight face.

"Let me take that bag with my swim suit and you take this one with your vodka and tonic." Meg glanced at her watch. "I've got time to take a quick shower and check in with my daughter. Why don't you guys swing by and we'll have a cocktail before we go to dinner."

"That sounds great. See you about seven-forty-five."

Jayne tip-toed through the villa, Nick's snores drifting from the bedroom when she peeked in on him. Warmth spread through her as she gazed at his peaceful expression. God, he was handsome. She couldn't get over it and she couldn't put her finger on exactly why, but she liked the familiarity of sharing space with him. Maybe liked it too much—the cozy way the two of them blended. One started where the other finished.

She retrieved a Diet Coke from the small refrigerator and slid open the door onto their patio. Settling onto a chaise lounge to gaze at the boats bobbing in the marina, she took a moment to will some sense into herself, knowing full well falling for Nick was sheer stupidity. She rolled her shoulders and punched in the number for Leigh's cell phone.

Leigh answered on the first ring. "Talk to me, you scarlet woman."

"It's *Whore of Babylon* to you, counselor. What's going on?"

"We're having cocktails and discussing where we're having supper. Looks like Antonio's wins the vote. Any chance you'll be joining us?"

"Oh, man. You're going there without me?"

"I take it that's a *no*."

"We decided to stay near Marathon at the Southern Cross. Nice little resort."

"Will you be co-habiting with a handsome man tonight?"

"I will."

"Will you be fornicating with a handsome man tonight?"

"I hope."

"So that means Meg and Sean…?"

"It does…"

"Hot damn. I'm gonna see if Liz or Cara will buy my dinner in return for the scoop."

"You're a mercenary old bitch, you know."

"Damn straight," Leigh laughed.

"Oh, and I bought condoms for Meg and stuck them in a bag with her purchases. She's gonna stroke out when she finds them. With any luck, Sean will be looking on."

"She's gonna kill you."

"Probably."

"Thanks for checking in. Be safe and give me a call when you figure out what you're doing in the morning. We'll be waiting with baited breath for the low down. Oh, wait. Cara wants to talk to you. Hang on."

"Hey, you. Are you having a blast?" Cara asked.

"Absolutely. What have you been up to this afternoon?"

"Worked on my tan, then Liz and I ended up hanging with the boys from Toronto. With you and Meg gone, and Leigh on a conference call half the afternoon, we were left to our own devices. We ran into Andy and Jimmy while we were having lunch and they convinced us to join them for an afternoon pub crawl. I got the scoop on Nick for you." Cara went on to tell her Nick's background and Jayne didn't have the heart to tell Cara that she already knew most of what she was relaying.

"All in all, I think you're in good hands, my friend. But you must've already figured that out. Leigh told us about your break-down. Is this one of your famous detours?"

Jayne laughed, "You know it, girlfriend."

"Good. We're rooting for Nick. He could end up being your John Wayne. *Carpe Diem*, Miss Jayne. And just so you know, you *will* be in the confessional tomorrow. Count on it."

"Understood. Are you meeting up with the Toronto terrorists again tonight?"

"More than likely."

"You guys have fun tonight and keep it down to a dull roar. When you run into them, play dumb. Only Andy and Jimmy know about our stay up here."

"Okay, but it's gonna cost ya. See you in the morning."

Jayne clicked off her phone and closed her eyes, allowing herself a ten minute respite. A gentle breeze soothed her senses and in her dreamlike state, Mack sat at the foot of her chaise, then stood and kissed her on the forehead as a noisy seagull squawked, startling her awake. She remained perfectly still for another minute, warmed by the image.

Dragging herself to the shower, Jayne found a plush sueded silk spa robe in the closet. Nick was still sleeping soundly so she slipped into the bathroom, careful not to wake him. She flipped on the twin shower heads and stripped, rinsing her panties in the sink and hanging them across the towel rack before she stepped into the enormous shower.

Mango filled the room as soon as she coated her body in the silky bath gel, and her muscles yielded to the needles of hot water. Her body ached with fatigue, and the night hadn't begun. Her energy level had been declining in the past few weeks—probably part of the deal.

She finished showering and shut off the water, then wrapped a bath sheet around her. Applying lotion to her body, her hand slid to the small lump on her breast. *The alien.* Touching it had a way of energizing her into action. *Dammit, something this small will not win.*

She took a sip of her Diet Coke, and faced the mirror. *Every day is a gift...put all this away for now. Tonight you're here. It's your birthday, and you're with a dreamboat. Revel in it. Squeeze every ounce of happiness out of every minute...*

She found the hairdryer under the counter and dried her panties. After applying mascara and lip gloss, Jayne looked in the mirror again. She was as good as she could get, given the circumstances. Now if she could only do something with her hair...

Nick awakened to the roar of a hair dryer, momentarily disoriented. Then thoughts of Jayne and their situation slid across his mind. He stretched and stood, then tapped on the door and peeked in to find her drying her hair in front of the mirror. Standing there in her lacy lingerie, she looked sexy as hell and he tried to be casual when all he really wanted to do was explore every inch of her. Instead, he asked, "Can I fix you a drink?"

She turned off the dryer and flashed him a dazzling smile. "Sure, but would you put some lotion on my back first?"

And then can I toss you on the bed and ravage you? "Sure. Looks like you got some sun today." He stepped over and picked up the little bottle, warming the lotion in his hands before he smoothed it over her warm back, slipping his fingers under her bra straps, and then easing up and over her shoulders. Such a small act, but it was intensely intimate. His restraint was running thin, so he finished and leaned down and gave her a little kiss on the neck. "For the record, you're beautiful....and to quote you, *just way too sexy...*"

Their eyes met in the mirror and a sharp twinge swirled deep within her. Standing there without a shirt, the top button of his jeans undone, Nick looked entirely edible. She wanted nothing more than to run her hands over the contours of his chest, twirling her fingertips in the veil of dark, wiry hair covering it. She was teetering on the edge of throwing caution to the wind and making them late for dinner, but she steeled herself. She hooked her finger in the top edge of his jeans and pulled him close for a slow, wet kiss. "So are you."

"I'll get drinks."

Nick's words were a bit strained, so she figured he was making a sacrificial retreat. In fairness, she hurried to get her top and jeans on before he returned.

He returned with her drink. "Shame you had to go and cover up that nice scenery. I was enjoying the view."

Maybe too much for our own good. She took the glass and sipped. "Umm, thanks. How was your nap?"

"Great. That bed is awesome. Can't believe I slept so long. How was the shopping?"

"Good. Let me show you what I found." She retrieved her bags from the parlor and began holding up her purchases. "I bought you a sweatshirt, a T-shirt, swim shorts and a pair of flip flops. I'll return anything you don't want. It's cooling down so we thought sweatshirts might come in handy if we end up down at the beach later."

"These are perfect. Think I'll follow your lead and take a shower. You know, I would've been more than happy to join you—"

"If you had, we would've *never* made it to dinner and I'm hungry." She laughed and tidied the sink area where she'd been getting ready. "Here. Let me get out of your way."

"You're fine. Go ahead with what you're doing."

As Nick undressed and got in and out of the shower, she caught herself stealing glances in the mirror, feeling like a voyeur, yet enjoying the view of his well-toned body. She finished her hair and stepped into the bedroom, grabbing a magazine off the night stand and plopping in the chair, resting her feet on the ottoman.

Nick emerged from the steam, wrapping a towel around his waist. He sorted through the basket on the counter and came up with a toothbrush. Talking around it as he brushed, he stepped into the doorway and said, "Great shower. I'm glad we opted to come on over here rather than staying at that bar for dinner. I can only take so many nights of howling at the moon." He spat and rinsed out his mouth. As he grabbed a razor, he chided, "I started to shave in the shower but you used that razor on your legs. That's hell on a face, by the way."

"Duly noted. Guess that's why they gave us two of them, huh," Jayne teased, tossing her reading aside. She joined him in the bathroom, hopping up to sit on the granite counter while he shaved. That same cozy feeling she'd experienced earlier hit her sideways. Weird, but she'd loved the small everyday things that were so intimate, but not sexual, when she'd been married to Mack. Like brushing their teeth together at bedtime, him shaving while she fixed her hair, or the way he would perch on the side of the tub to visit with her while she put on her make up. Little bits of connection during an otherwise disconnected day. And here she was, sharing the same type of intimacy with a relative stranger as if she'd known him forever.

Nick grabbed a hand towel and wiped the remaining shaving cream from his neck, realizing he liked that she'd come in to keep him company... and he especially liked her casual attitude. He ran his fingers through his damp hair, and she reached over to push back a couple of errant strands. Her touch seared his skin, sending a bolt of desire straight through his system. What was it about her that had this effect on him?

He stepped over, positioning himself between her legs as he took her face in his hands for a kiss. "This is nice. You're easy to be with." He leaned down and covered her lips with his, feeling her soft, sweet response. He meant it. He couldn't remember the last time he'd so been so relaxed, or had so enjoyed sharing his private space with a woman.

Jayne scrunched her nose and nodded at him. "I know. You're so familiar to me in the oddest way. Just like this." She patted his chest and the feel of her fingertips put his libido into overdrive.

"Exactly." He breathed against her ear, his lips grazing her neck.

"As much as I'd like to stay right here, we're expected for cocktails in ten minutes. I'll let you get dressed." She started to hop down.

"Not just yet." He wasn't ready for her to be away from him. He was savoring this moment. Putting his hand on the back of her neck, he pulled her close for another kiss and deepened it as she twined her fingers into his hair. Damn, she might has well have been sliding her hand up his inner thigh. He grazed her neck with his lips, thinking they should cancel their dinner plans, and his body was in complete agreement.

She pulled back. "There you go, getting me all stirred up again."

"You? Check this out," and he pointed down to the protrusion in the front of his towel.

"Hold that thought," she laughed and winked.

"Why don't *you* hold that thought?"

"Already did." She shot him the same wicked grin that had been his undoing earlier. "Are you being greedy again?"

"Absolutely. I'm now your humble servant."

"Okay, my slave...but later." She laughed and gave the bulge a lingering pat. "Now please get dressed or we'll be late." She hopped off the counter and headed for the parlor.

He chuckled to himself as he pulled on his jeans, willing his erection to subside. This was a fun little game—Jayne was quick and clever, a bit naughty without being crude, and she made his blood race. This was so much better than if they'd hurried into the sack. Delayed gratification could kill a guy, but what a way to go.

EIGHTEEN

"Very funny…" Meg pointed a finger into Jayne's chest in mock disgust.

"What're you talking about?" Jayne raised her eyebrows.

"You know *exactly* what I'm talking about."

Jayne couldn't keep a straight face any longer. "Just watching out for you, my friend."

Sean leaned back against the bar and crossed his arms. Grinning, he shook his head at Jayne and said, "Knew I liked you."

"Gotcha covered, big guy."

"Literally."

"You guys gonna fill me in or what?" Nick looked from Sean, to Jayne, to Meg, a bewildered expression on his face.

"I just added a little something to Meg's shopping bag this afternoon." Jayne spied one of the Trojan packets that had fallen under the bar stool and swept it up, tossing it to him.

Nick caught it, inspected it, then leaned his head back, laughing. "That's funny."

Meg's face was scarlet but she was smiling. "Glad *you* think so. I dumped my bag on the bar and they went everywhere."

Sean passed out drinks, chuckling. "You should've seen her. She was grabbing them so fast it was a blur,

208

and her face was the same color it is right now." Sean slid her arm around Meg, hugging her to him. "Jayne, I figured you must've had something to do with it. It was great. So many of them I wasn't sure whether to be flattered or scared."

"At least I bought you the good ones. Ultra-thin, ribbed and everything," Jayne teased. She liked kidding around with Sean. His dry, quick wit belied his quiet countenance and her confidence in how he'd treat Meg grew.

"That's what I said…among other things." Sean nodded, winking over at Meg.

That last comment made Meg blush even redder which brought another peal of laughter from the trio and Sean wrapped his arm around her again. "You're fun to tease, sugar."

Sugar? Jayne could feel the change. A more relaxed side of Sean was emerging, and she was happy to see that he and Meg had formed an alliance. She might be blushing, but she wasn't running away.

"Okay. Okay." Meg threw up her hands, laughing. "Joke's on me. Tally mark for you, Jayne. Now…isn't it time for dinner?" Meg sashayed to the door and Jayne mentally cheered the spring in her friend's step.

☼☼☼

"Look at the moon. Isn't it gorgeous?" Jayne pointed as they strolled across the pool deck. The huge slab of butter was peaking over the eastern horizon, offering an invitation to chase its beam across the inky water.

Nick and Sean were brandishing wine bottles, a corkscrew and plastic cups. Jayne and Meg were on their heels with towels. Steam rose from the hot tub, situated in a secluded area off the pool deck. Jayne flipped the control to turn on the jets, glad no other guests were present.

"Great dinner. My lobster was one of the best I've ever had," Sean declared, uncorking a bottle.

"Same with my sea bass." Jayne agreed. She grabbed Nick's hand and squeezed. "That was one of the best birthday dinners I've ever had. Thank you again. The cake was perfect."

Nick kissed her forehead. "You're welcome. Everyone needs a birthday cake."

"With candles to make wishes on," Meg added.

Hope my wish comes true… Stars twinkled above, even more brilliant for the lack of lights in the area. One skipped across the sky before falling to earth and Jayne closed her eyes. *I wish for more nights like this…* Two wishes for the same thing…maybe there's magic in that.

A chilly breeze assaulted Jayne's skin as she shed her robe and eased her way down the steps into the bubbling water. Her knees had a way of telling her when the weather was about to change, and tonight they were screaming. She settled next to a set of jets, hoping they'd provide some relief.

Meg gave her a worried look. Jayne nodded and smiled, trying to waylay her friend's concern. Until today, Meg only knew she'd demo'd her knee in an accident. Now that she knew the whole story, Jayne feared the sympathetic looks would come more frequently.

Nick settled between the women and proposed a toast, "To faulty stators and detours."

"I'll drink to that," Jayne laughed, touching her glass to the other three. "Okay, Sean, tell us about your time on the ice. Such a coincidence that Jim's friend played against you…"

Sean gave a full account of his time as a professional hockey player, including his career-ending injury, evidenced by a diagonal scar that extended across his shoulder from his collarbone.

"More wine?" Nick got out of the tub and opened the second bottle.

"Sure. We're not driving and we're not far from our hangars," Jayne agreed.

Sean turned to her. "Speaking of hangars, it's your turn, Jayne. You haven't said a word about yourself all evening. How long have you been flying planes?"

"Since high school. Strictly recreational, mind you."

"That's so cool. I've wanted to get my pilot's license since I was a little kid. I'd love to see your plane," Sean said.

"So would I." Nick nodded. "As soon as my schedule slows down, I'm going to learn to fly. We saw this nice looking private plane circling low above us as we crossed the Seven Mile Bridge on our way down here. Don't know why, but I had to wave, and the pilot dipped his wing. Made me decide I'd like to be able to do that."

Jayne started laughing and said, "*Her* wing, Nick. Pretty sure that was me."

"No way." Nick cocked an eyebrow and looked at her. "Seriously?"

"Yeah. About three o'clock Thursday?" Nick nodded, so she continued. "You looked like you were having such a great day." She shook her head. "That's wild." A little zing snapped through her. *No such thing as a coincidence...*

Sean looked at her, flashing an ornery grin and she knew it was her turn in the hot seat. "You're not done, girlie. What was going on this afternoon? You gave Jim Hathaway the evil eye every time he mentioned your writing. Meg stone-walled me—said I had to ask you. Then I thought about something Jim said about a character of yours. I've read a series of suspense novels with a main character named Blair Harper by M.H. Jaynes." Sean's eyes twinkled as he gave her a wink. "Wouldn't be a connection, would there?"

Surprised by the flow of words from the quiet man, Jayne figured he must be feeling the effects of the wine. She looked up at the moon, then at Meg, and finally at Sean.

Sean blinked a couple of times, then shook his head. "*Wow*. I've read all your books."

Nick frowned. "I need to start reading something other than reports and blueprints."

Jayne gave Nick's thigh a pat. "Don't worry. A lot of people don't have time to read fiction."

"How'd you get started? Whole story," Sean demanded.

"I've been writing all my life, but took it up seriously about ten years ago. I started by writing articles for magazines, and then a friend encouraged me to submit my first manuscript to her friend, Leigh Wallace—that's how Leigh and I met. Anyway, a couple of months later Leigh called me and offered to represent me, saying she thought the manuscript would sell. This was a very rare occurrence. Most writers receive *stacks* of rejections before getting a nibble. I just happened to get lucky. And it didn't hurt that we had a good friend in common. Greased the wheel, so to speak."

"Then what happened?" Nick asked.

"We met and two months later we contracted with our publisher. It took me about six months to get it edited and revised, and a year after that it was released." There was a whole lot more to it, but she wasn't going to bore these guys with the harsh realities of getting a book on the shelves of a store.

"That was *High Speed*, right?" Sean asked. "And your second was *Low Drag*, right?"

Nick refilled their glasses. "Why the pen name?"

"Privacy. And to keep neighbors from reading themselves into my stories." Jayne laughed. "I couldn't have the little ladies at church painting a scarlet letter on my chest because of the steamier aspect of my books." She didn't add that she'd wanted to have a masculine name for her genre or that she'd used Mack's initials to somehow keep him alive in her work.

Sean grinned, "I can see that, but I'm blown away. I read a lot and your books are great."

Jayne, uncomfortable being the center of the conversation, said, "Thanks, Sean. I'm flattered—it's so nice to know when someone enjoys my stories."

"So, how do you come up with them?" Sean asked.

"I meet interesting people when I travel, then I listen to the news or read the paper. And the stories create themselves. You take a headline, add a dose of imagination, asking *what if* and off you go. I know a couple of retired military guys and have friends in law enforcement. They help with the technical details once I've got the basic story laid out."

"Amazing." Sean was still shaking his head. "My son's going to be so impressed that I know you. He turned me on to your books."

"Then let me send him a signed copy of my latest novel when it comes out in early May."

"That'd be awesome. By the way, he's convinced you're a man. Do you mind if I tell him the truth? He'll never believe I was in a hot tub with his favorite author. Authoress?"

"Either way. Sure you can tell him—but tell him it's a big secret." Jayne laughed. "Maybe we should wait and let me meet him. That'd be a bigger surprise."

"Speaking of which, Meg's going to join me in Mont Tremblant the second week of March to do a little skiing. My son and a couple of his friends from university will be there, too. I have a cottage at the base of the slopes and there's more than enough room for all of us. Do you ski, Jayne?"

"Not anymore. Knee injuries put a kibosh on the downhill runs for me. But I'd love to see Mont Tremblant sometime—I just can't swing it in March. Rain check? March is insane. I've got a couple of deadlines and a launch looming in the next two months." How easily the half-truth slid off her tongue...

Sean turned to Nick, "What about you?"

"I could probably figure something out." He turned to Jayne. "You sure you can't swing a long weekend? Work a little double time between now and then? We could go out on Snow Cats or do some cross country skiing if you're up for it."

Jayne gave Nick a smile and shrugged. "Let me see what I can work out."

"Jayne, it looks like you've had your knees either rebuilt or replaced. What type of sports did you play?" Sean asked.

Meg winced at Sean's tone and question. Jayne appreciated her friend's protective nature, but she was accustomed to the questions and the natural assumptions.

"Just rebuilt, Sean. I was in a car wreck several years ago."

"Oh, sorry. Didn't mean to be rude."

"Not at all. People ask me all the time."

Nick pulled his knee out of the water to show his long suture scar. "My souvenir of university rugby."

"Oh good grief, we sound like poster children for a sports rehab facility." Meg chided, earning a laugh and a splash from Sean.

Jayne stifled a yawn but Nick caught her. The jets stopped and he stood. "Don't know about you guys, but I need to crash."

"I think we all do. Been a long day." Sean stood and pulled Meg up by the hand.

Nick climbed out and grabbed a towel, wrapping it around his waist. He offered his hand to Jayne as she stepped from the tub, then held a robe for her as she slid into it. Wrapping his arms around her from behind, he gave her a hug as his lips brushed her temple.

Jayne hooked her arm through his and leaned against him, strolling toward their villa. Feeling the effects of the wine and the whirlpool, her feet were moving through quicksand.

When they entered their villa, the red light on Nick's cell phone was flashing. Checking the screen, he picked it up and punched in a few numbers, listened, then said, "It's a message from my son. I need to call him back. Mind?"

"Not at all. I'm going to shower this chlorine off." She grabbed a bottle of water from the fridge. "Want one?" He nodded and she tossed a bottle to him. "I'll leave this packet of aspirin in case you need a couple." She popped two into her mouth and took a swig as she headed into the bathroom.

The room attendant had turned back the bed covers and tidied the bath with fresh towels. Shedding her swimsuit, she showered and got ready for bed in record time, then slid into one of the spa robes hanging in the closet. Nick was still on the veranda talking to his son, so she curled up on the sofa and flipped on the news. Settling into the soft cushions, she fought the temptation to close her eyes as the weatherman droned on about the storm front heading their way. *Could've told you...*

Nick's voice carried into the room. "...as long as you're safe, Jamie. That's all I care about. That's why we have insurance. No...I'm glad you called...Love you, son."

Nick clicked off his phone. God, where had the years gone? In the blink of an eye his kids had gone from crawling to carousing. How could his son be nineteen already? Only yesterday he was taking his first steps.

Nick was sitting on the side of the patio lounge chair, leaning forward, elbows on knees. He could see Jayne curled up on the couch. The notion that she deserved more than he could offer kept rolling through his head. But now they were alone. And she was gorgeous.

God grant him strength.

So he just sat there, looking at her, weighing the options. She was Alynn's antithesis—on every level. And she was perfect—all soft and curvy. And he wanted—no, he *needed* to feel her body against his again.

So why was he rooted to this chair?

Because of that damned ache in his gut, telling him this went beyond something physical.

He'd been numb since the day he'd caught Alynn with Halverson in Paris and this nagging sensation that she was more than a passing attraction was all but foreign. Now he had to figure out what to do with it.

Nick stepped back inside and started to tell her about his son's mishap when he heard a soft, feminine snore. The little purr was rather endearing. She looked so peaceful that he wasn't inclined to disturb her, especially when he noticed the dark smudges shadowing her eyelids. What a trooper. Jayne was exhausted, but she hadn't uttered a solitary complaint.

Moving through the villa, he extinguished all but the light in the bathroom and then showered, brushed his teeth and peeled the covers back on the bed. He went to Jayne and slid one arm under her knees and one around her shoulders, picking her up.

She roused and he kissed her temple, "Shhh, I've got you."

When he placed Jayne on the bed, she immediately rolled to her side and grasped her pillow, settling in. He tucked the covers around her and got in on the other side. The cotton sheets were a caress, crisp and cool on his bare skin as he crawled between them, a thoroughly erotic sensation, heightened when he slid over to spoon up against Jayne's backside, the feel of her sueded robe putting his nerve endings on high alert in spite of the fatigue. He wrapped his arm around her waist and nestled, breathing in the fresh scent of her.

Damn, he needed a physical release. He was so hard it hurt, and imagining the warm, slick sweetness beneath her robe made him groan. It had been a long time since he'd been inclined to share a woman's bed. Now, here he was with someone he cared about, and he craved the pleasures of her body. Their little prelude before dinner burned in his mind, making him harder still.

But her slow, even breathing drew an unexpected grasp on his heart and made it swell, inciting pangs of something altogether contradictory. Consideration for her comfort shouted down his physical need. The way she slept, so quiet and relaxed, nudged his protective side, making him want to take care of her.

Nick couldn't quite absorb these new feelings. He'd never been inconsiderate, but thinking of Jayne in this manner was throwing him off balance. This was a long way from what he'd had in mind when he'd decided to spend time with her this weekend.

He liked her. *A lot*. Wanted to know her beyond this weekend. On what level, he couldn't say. The only thing he knew for sure was that he needed to learn to be alone—needed time to adjust. Too bad his heart missed that memo.

Holding her would be enough for tonight. The fact that he was rock hard was a bit of a nuisance, but hell, every time she touched him, he got hard. His response to her was becoming automatic...like a damn teenager.

Jayne stirred, trying to shift in his arms. He kissed the back of her neck and whispered, "Shhh, just go to sleep."

She started to turn toward him, but he remained resolute and held her tight, groaning inwardly. Her slightest movement challenged his control, and he fought the desire that rolled over him in waves—a desire to possess her, to take pleasure in her body.

He managed to conquer the selfish urges. "Just sleep, babe. I'm not going anywhere," he whispered, softly kissing her ear before he relaxed against the pillows. He stopped in wonder. Would those words prove prophetic? Jayne was immediately peaceful and he could feel her heart beating against his hand, realizing that even their heartbeats were in sync.

Jayne woke with a start, disoriented. Lying perfectly still, she concentrated until her surroundings became clear and her heart slowed. Nick was next to her, snoring. She was on her side, wrapped around him, positioned in the crook of his arm with one of her legs thrown over his and her hand splayed across his chest.

His naked chest... *his naked body*. And she was in a robe that was half off her. She pulled the robe around her, the chilled air giving her goose bumps. *I've made myself right at home, haven't I?*

She settled but couldn't fall back to sleep. Nick had carried her to bed? She vaguely recalled that he'd nestled against her, but she drew blanks after that.

He hadn't tried to awaken her. A twinge of disappointment washed over her—this wasn't exactly how she'd seen the night playing out. But maybe this was for the best. Any way she viewed it, she and Nick couldn't come to anything. He was either a perfect gentleman or he'd come to his senses and decided to cool this off a bit. Probably a little of both.

Closing her eyes, she eased away, careful not to awaken him. She settled on her side of the bed, willing herself to go back to sleep, but thoughts of their time together plagued her. And now that their bodies weren't touching, the distance between them felt like the Grand Canyon, but she stayed put.

If she wasn't careful, she could fall in love with him. Maybe she already had.

But dammit, she knew better. Romance in this setting was all smoke and mirrors. It was a fantasy you could indulge in for a few days, everything put into an intensified, fast-forward mode. But reality would bite you in the ass the minute your plane touched down in the land of alarm clocks and obligations.

Even if she could convince herself to accept this brief interlude as a consolation prize for what was ahead of her, she knew she couldn't be capricious about Nick. Her heart wouldn't allow it. No, she'd keep things light, then she'd say goodbye. He'd head back to his demanding empire and she'd head into the frightening world of cancer treatment.

She didn't need a crystal ball to figure out that having both breasts removed would change her...both inside *and* out. Her soul wept, counting the days until she'd be...*mutilated.* That word ripped through her mind over and over, even though she knew it was wrong. She just hadn't found a better word to describe how she felt about losing her breasts. Maybe in time...

Jayne knew she was being ridiculous since it was a matter of life and death, but she would mourn the loss of her breasts, mourn the loss of the physical pleasure a man's touch could give her. She had a chest men admired, but she'd never been vain. Nick's comments had hit hard, but he had no idea what he was doing to her. No man could fully understand how his admiration for a part of a woman's body could end up driving an emotional wedge between them if that part of her went away. She'd always think she was less in his eyes if that part of her was gone. He could tell her a million times he didn't care, that she was beautiful, that it didn't matter. But she'd always wonder.

Why was she thinking this way? She had to be wrong. Men didn't care if breasts were real, did they? If a man really loved you, he wouldn't care if you even had breasts. Right? Wasn't love supposed to transcend physical form? She'd have loved Mack no matter what. And he'd tell her the same if he was here.

Ah, the shit that crosses your mind at three in the morning.

Dammit, she had enough to think about without over-thinking Nick McCord. Even though she hadn't had sex in eons and every fiber of her being wanted him, she'd be crazy to let this go any further. The price tag would be way too high. So she'd put him in her memory book as her all-time best detour.

But this particular detour will take a chunk of my heart with him when goes.

NINETEEN

No matter how Jayne tried to wrestle down the demons, sleep was elusive. When slivers of light eventually snuck through the plantation shutters at the windows, Jayne gave up and slipped from the bed, careful not to disturb Nick. Her knee was killing her and her thoughts about him were nearly as agonizing. She had to put some space between them before she threw her resolve out the window.

She padded into the sitting area, closing the French doors behind her before starting the coffee maker. There was time to enjoy the little courtyard before Nick woke. Before too long, they'd be hearing from Andy and the day would be off like a rocket. While the coffee brewed, she snapped on the Weather Channel. Last night's forecast was becoming a reality. A line of yellow and red, flashing on the Doppler radar, signified a front out in the Gulf heading in their direction. If Andy and Jimmy didn't arrive shortly, getting back would be dicey.

She clicked off the television, downed a couple of aspirin for her knee and took her coffee to the chase lounge on the porch. Lulled by the twittering of the birds welcoming the day, Jayne sipped her coffee and as the cobwebs cleared, guilt, thick and heavy, replaced them, along with a large dose of shame. Why had she even come here with Nick? What on earth possessed her to think staying last night was a good idea? She'd only teased and led him on, and he was too good to call her bluff. Nick deserved so much more than she could give, even on this temporary basis. Knowing the score, she should've steered clear of him that first night. It was pure narcissism—all take and no give on her part. Is this what finding out you had cancer did to you? Did you become selfish and inconsiderate? God, she hoped not. She needed to set things right, and soon.

She was in the bathroom, dressed and brushing her teeth as she heard Nick's cell phone ring on the other side of the door. It went silent and started ringing again as the room phone rang. Before she could pick up the receiver at the other end of the tub, she heard Nick's voice, full of gravel and sleep.

"McCord."

There was silence and then he said, "Well, it *wasn't convenient* to get up and get it. What's the story?" Another silence, then, "....You're *here*? Right. We'll be there in a bit."

She opened the bathroom door to see Nick climbing out of bed, and she was momentarily riveted by the vision of his broad, tan shoulders and chest. He caught her eye and she smiled.

"Morning, handsome. How'd you sleep?"

"Like a rock. You're up and at 'em early."

He moved across the space and was in front of her, naked and glorious, and the proximity was rattling.

"You're looking rested and very pretty this morning." He pressed a kiss to her lips. "Andy and Jimmy just arrived. Shame they got here so early. I was hoping for a different start to the day."

His fingers tangled in her hair, sending a tremor through her system. Fighting the desire that contradicted her decision, she laughed and rolled her eyes as she pulled back, tapping her fingertip against his chest. "Honey, it's not that early. It's after nine."

"Seriously? I never sleep this late." He pulled on his jeans, then grabbed a toothbrush and positioned himself at the sink beside her.

"Me either unless I'm on vacation. Obviously we both needed it. I was so tired, but I woke up early. Thought I'd let you sleep as long as you could." She pressed a hand on his shoulder, pulling him to her so her lips could brush his jaw. "I'm sorry I wimped out on you last night. I'm some date, huh?"

"You're a great date. No apology necessary."

He leaned over and gave her a kiss that underscored his words, his mouth soft and warm on her lips. "Rain check?"

Jayne forced a smile, deciding the little white lie couldn't hurt. "Absolutely."

"Speaking of rain check, Andy said there's a front heading this way, so we should get going."

☼☼☼

Comingling, the aromas of freshly brewed coffee, bacon and pancakes wafted through the air when Jayne and Nick entered the cafe.

Andy hugged her, then signaled the waitress to bring more coffee as he started talking. "Here's the deal. We can change the stator here, but I think we should load up the bike and take it back to the hotel. We can work on it this afternoon in a covered area and our mechanical gurus will be on hand if we need some help. Both bikes aren't going to fit in the truck, so Nick, your bike needs to be driven back after all."

Jimmy nodded. "Yeah, and the weather is turning to shit fast, so we need to get loaded up and out of here. If you guys want to go back in the truck, Andy or I can ride your bike back, Nick."

"Nah, I'll ride it back, but thanks. Jayne, it's up to you if you want to ride with me or in the truck. Think about it—we can decide once we're loaded—take another look at the weather."

Turning to Jayne and Meg, Jimmy laughed. "And I'll have you know we managed to keep your friends entertained last night. They should be suffering the effects of over-indulgence and very late hours just like the rest of our crew. None of our guys ever figured out you were missing."

"Yeah, when you've got a bunch of drunks who can't find their own asses with both hands, it's easy to keep them in the dark," Andy chuckled.

"Eh, it became quite the game and your friends played right along. Oh, and that pilot chap, too," Jimmy chuckled.

☼☼☼

"We picked up some straps, so let's try to center it and we'll attach it to both sides," Andy said, lowering the tailgate.

Jayne and Meg stood off to the side while the four men hefted and secured the bike. Jayne leaned toward Meg and said in a low voice, "Everything seems good with you and Sean."

"Very good," Meg whispered, her face turning pink.

"Great." And it *was* great to see Meg's radiance.

"I'll have to fill you in later, but I'm glad you convinced me to indulge in some new lingerie. Not sure, but I think the earth moved..."

"...so *that* was the tremor that shook the building..." She laughed as Nick looked over and she winked at him.

"That should do it," Jimmy said, giving the straps one last tug. He looked at the weather on his phone. "We should be able to make it back if we leave now."

Nick crossed to Jayne. "Are you riding with me, or in the truck?"

"If I'm going to slow you down, I'll ride in the truck. Otherwise, I'm game." She had nearly mastered her fears yesterday and she was anxious to get back on the horse to see if her confidence held.

"Good enough."

Andy pulled a yellow bundle from the truck's back seat and handed it to Jayne. "I threw in a slicker set for you. Just in case. If it starts raining, you can climb in with us."

"Thanks, Andy. You always seem to have my six."

"Yeah, 'cause it's such a nice view...." He gave her a quick hug.

Nick took the bundle and packed it into his saddlebag, shaking his head as he pulled on his jacket. Andy was such a hound. He shook hands with his mates and climbed onto his bike, starting the engine as the others got into the truck. Jayne pulled on her jean jacket and climbed on behind him, waving as they pulled onto the highway.

Although the sun blazed, the wind had a chill not evident the previous day. Nick kept his eye on the dark thin line along the far western horizon. Doppler and his knee were right on the money. He leaned back and patted Jayne's leg. She leaned up, giving him a squeeze around his waist, so he sped up. It would've been nice to take their time riding back, but riding in a storm was miserable...and dangerous.

As he accelerated, she tucked in tight behind him and he knew she was trying to escape the biting wind. They made it as far as Big Pine Key when the front arrived, delivering icy whips of air and ominous, rolling thunderheads.

Racing the storm, Nick thought they would just make it, but fat cold drops contradicted him a couple of miles north of Key West. Before he could even think about pulling over and letting Jayne hop into the truck, the sky opened up and dumped harassing, stinging shards. He grabbed her leg when Jimmy flashed his lights, but she hunkered against his back and indicated for him to keep going, her hold so tight he was convinced she'd draw blood. The water pelting against his face and running into his eyes minimized his view, but he managed to follow tail lights to the hotel's covered garage.

Nick parked at the end of the line of bikes and shut off the engine. Jayne was still clinging to him, her grip as tight as before and when she made no move to get off, he steadied himself and clasped her clinched fingers. They were icy and shaking. He shot a look at Jimmy and Andy, now climbing out of the truck. Coming to either side of the bike, Nick felt Jayne's grip loosen as Andy helped steady her.

"Hey gorgeous, let's get you off this thing and warmed up."

Andy was using the voice he used on his little girl when she was afraid, immediately putting Nick on alert.

Jimmy steadied her as she climbed off, then put an arm around her. Nick swung his leg around, startled by the vacant look in her eyes. She was soaked and shivering, her face ashen. He was freezing, but her expression made him forget his misery. Her eyes weren't seeing him and then she started shaking uncontrollably, scaring him into action.

He grabbed a sweatshirt from Meg and wrapped it around her shoulders. "Jayne, here, let me warm you up." He forced a smile and flexed his frozen fingers before wiping some of the water off her face. He ran his hands up and down her arms, then hugged her to him in spite of the wet clothing, trying to bring her back into the real world. When her shaking subsided, Nick leaned back and looked into a pair of terrified hazel eyes. What in the world?

He decided to try talking through it. "Shit I'm glad we're finally here. That last bit was no fun at all, eh?" He wrapped his arms around her again and rubbed her back, his eyebrows up as he looked over the top of her head at the rest of their friends. "Jayne? Babe, are you all right?" This was the last reaction he'd expected. She simply stood there in utter silence and he was at a complete loss as to what had brought this on. He continued rubbing her back and arms. "You'll be fine once we get you warmed up."

Jimmy looked at Jayne, a frown creasing his forehead. "We should've made you get in with us when it started raining. You're soaked and you need some dry clothes, girl."

"We were s-s-s-o c-c-lose…"

Nick leaned back and assessed her eyes. Strain had replaced the unseeing glaze, but he was worried. This was more than sodden misery. This was something altogether different. "Here, let's get you out of this jacket." He peeled it off her and took the dry sweatshirt Meg handed him to wrap around her shoulders. "Here you go. This will help. I'll take you upstairs as soon as we get this bike unloaded."

Sean stepped over to them. "No. You go on. We've got this."

Andy and Jimmy were removing the straps from Sean's bike as Nick jumped into the bed of the truck, leaving Jayne in Meg's care for the moment. "This will only take a minute. Besides, the two of you can't handle it. This sucker weighs a ton, and it's wet and slick."

Jayne fought to silence her still-chattering teeth. Being out on wet pavement in that deluge had thrown her into a bone-deep panic that had her needing Meg's arm and one of the support pillars to remain upright. Her heart was finally slowing, but she could still feel its irregular rhythm pulsing in her ears.

Meg's voice was full of worry. "I'll get Nick's key—we need to get you dry and warm. *Now.* I just talked with Leigh and boat service is suspended until the storm lets up. Brandon's over there watching football with her. Cara and Liz are upstairs in a poker game with the rest of this crew. They got stranded over here after breakfast. Looks like we'll be staying here for the time being."

Jayne was mortified by the worry still filling Nick's eyes as he handed Meg his key.

"Jayne, I'll get Andy's key and be up as soon as we're done here. Grab one of the bathrobes in the closet and crawl to my bed to get warmed up." Then he kissed her forehead and returned to his task.

Meg started for the elevator. "I'll come with you, kiddo."

"Thanks, but I'm fine...or I will be soon." Jayne offered Meg as much of a smile as she could muster. "Call you later."

She punched in the floor number and waited as the car slowly ascended to the top floor. The corridor was open and the wind and rain provided a second drenching as she hurried to Nick's room.

Jayne's teeth chattered anew when she opened the door and encountered the icy blast from the air conditioner. She located the thermostat and clicked it off. As the roar shut down, she could hear mellow rock flowing from the overhead speakers.

She entered the bathroom and zeroed in on a large soaking tub with whirlpool jets. *There we go...* She plugged the drain while flipping the faucet on full blast and adjusted the temperature to a notch beyond warm. Taking a whiff of a bottle sitting on the side of the tub, Jayne added a splash of the key lime bath salts. She'd been on autopilot for the past fifteen minutes, afraid to let go of the tenuous hold on her emotions. The knots in her shoulders were finally ebbing.

Setting a towel to the side, she began peeling and prying off layers of soaked garments, and with each layer, a bit of her stability returned. Jayne took the dryer to her hair and fluffed it for a few minutes, then grabbed a pencil from the counter and twisted her hair with it and anchored it up on her head.

She balanced on the side of the tub, swung her throbbing knee around to the water, then eased into the steamy bubbles. Resting back, she let her eyes drift shut as suds tickled her shoulders. Don Henley was crooning from the speakers as she caught the tune and hummed along. Words from the song found her lips, *"...love you, like nobody's loved you, come rain or come shine..."*

The outer door clicked and she opened one eye as footsteps sounded in the entry.

"Hey you," Nick said as he leaned around the corner. "Don't stop. You sound great."

He came in, looking quite soggy, and put his hands on his hips. He shook his head, grinning. "Lovely picture, eh? Only a couple of things missing—"

She raised an eyebrow.

"Toddies and me. Care if I join you?"

TWENTY

She sipped the vodka on ice Nick handed over, liquid fire flowing down her throat, warming her insides as the hot soapy water warmed her exterior. "Ahh, that hits the spot." Between the vodka and Nick's gaze, she was warming up at the speed of light.

Nick shot her a look. "Good. You were frozen when we got here. Now your color's back. I was worried about you." He was peeling off his soaking clothes and hanging them over a towel rack next to hers, then gave her a cautious glance. "You okay?"

"I'm sorry about all that, Nick. I'm fine now. This tub is just what the doctor ordered." She sipped and tried to look anywhere but at him as he stripped, but his erection caught her eye and her mouth went dry. Impressive. Astonishing, really, especially in light of what they'd just been through. Sure, she'd had a preview yesterday, but she was still in awe. If she hadn't been sitting down, her knees would've buckled. Thank God he didn't realize she'd noticed.

He stepped over the edge, easing into the water opposite her. "Big tub. And this feels *good*. Damn, I was cold. A day or two in here and I might unthaw. Cheers." He touched his glass to hers and sipped, "Ahhh." He sank further into the soapy water until she could only see his head above the bubbles. "Is this what you'd call another detour?"

"Or a side trip on a detour that's been underway for the last twenty-four hours…"

He took her feet in his hands and pulled her legs up over his, then settled in with his Glenfiddich. She had the cutest toes, tipped in red. He leaned back and closed his eyes. Maybe he could interest her in some water sports? Hell, he was hard as a rock and she was all nice and slippery. Not a stretch to imagine her wrapped around him as he sank into her.

"Penny for your thoughts?"

He opened his eyes and winked at her, took another sip, then said, "Ah, but they're worth at least a quarter." He studied her face. She was such a curiosity to him…relaxing there in the bubbles with her vodka. "You're awfully quiet yourself."

"Just enjoying the view."

"Back at ya, babe."

Was there a side she hid? Most women were on good behavior in the beginning, but once they had you hooked, the other side emerged. Often an ugly one. He'd watched it happen time and again with other men. Hell, it had happened to him to a degree. But Jayne seemed genuine. She wasn't clinging, trying to turn the weekend into something more. In fact, she seemed to be holding back. Why wouldn't she let her guard down?

He finally said, "Tell me about you. There's a lot I don't know. You keep surprising me. We're a lot more alike than I would've guessed."

"How so? We meet in a place we both enjoy, so from the start we have things in common."

"There's that, but I'm talking about the important things. Your personal code, how you treat people, the friends you have. Big differentiators. And I've learned that when you meet someone's closest friends, you can tell a lot about that person."

She nodded. "I agree. Judging by your friends, you get my vote." Nick shrugged off the compliment, so she continued, "...in spite of your tendency toward roguish behavior a time or two in the past couple of days..." Jayne splashed a little bit of water at him.

Nick chuckled and nodded. "You bring out my evil twin..."

"And I'd be lying if I didn't admit that I like him, too."

They both laughed as he refilled her glass. "We keep drinking and you'll meet him here in this tub..." He touched his glass to hers and winked. Damn, when she moved and he caught a glimpse of her breasts, he wanted to touch and taste them again.

"About the time I've got you figured out, you do something that adds another dimension. Like your writing. And singing with the band. Tell me about that."

Jayne bit her lip, squinting, "Okay, but you go first. Tell me how you got started and then I want to know what you want to do with the next fifty years of your life."

"This could take a while. Do we have enough booze and hot water?" He laughed, and started from the beginning. How when he'd nearly flunked out of university, a summer job his dad had orchestrated convinced him he didn't want to spend his life on the wrong side of a shovel. Then he'd gone into architectural engineering thanks to his wise old man.

Nick proceeded to give her the down and dirty of the early days of McCord Construction and the transition to McCord Consolidated.

Jayne was certain he was playing down the years of hard work, and she didn't *ooh and ah*. Not her style.

What he'd amassed was impressive, but she was more interested in the how and why of what he'd done. So she asked and wasn't surprised to hear of his visionary tendencies.

"Nick, you should be proud of your accomplishments. Sounds like you're just hitting your stride, and there's so much ahead of you."

He tipped his hand back and forth, "You never know, but thanks. Anyway, I'd rather focus on the here and now. And on you."

He pulled her to him for a lingering kiss, then exhaled and leaned back. "By the way, I'm applying for sainthood after this weekend."

She raised her eyebrows, confused.

"Just saying...I want you, and if there's a doubt in your mind, I can show you right now. But I'm not casual about sex, never have been and I know you aren't either. I care about you, and I'm not about to do something that'll cheapen what's going on with us." He offered a wink and a wicked grin. "Sitting here in this tub with you is killing me, but knowing our friends are two doors down, doing anything about it would seem sleazy."

"Thank you. I know I've sent mixed signals, Nick. I'm not a tease, and I care about you, too. And you're right, I'm not casual either."

The fact that he was being so decent wasn't making it any easier. If he'd acted like a jerk, tried to persuade or push her, she'd have hung on to her resolve with ferocity. But his attitude made her want him more because he respected her feelings. Now, sharing this tub with him...

Shaking off the image of what she'd really like to be doing with him, she realized the vodka was talking a little too loudly. She rambled on, needing to explain herself further, "As I said yesterday, I'm in a lousy position to get involved right now. And I have no illusions about this being anything more than time away for either of us, no matter what we say. Next week we'll swallow a big dose of reality. Keeping in touch will be tough."

"You honestly believe that?"

"I'm a realist Nick." *And I have cancer and I can't let you too close...*

"So am I, and I'd like to stay in touch. I'd like to see you again. Why don't we try for Mont Tremblant in late February? No strings."

"I wish I could, but I've got a deadline that'll pose a problem until April. I know I won't be able to come up for air until after that." It was time to change the subject, so she took another sip and said, "We'll see. Now it's your turn. Ask away."

He was silent for a few seconds, probably processing her response. Then he looked at her with a grin as if he'd just come up with the perfect punishment.

"Okay...for starters, how'd you end up singing at the Hog's Breath."

Jayne blew out a breath. "Really? Isn't there something else about me you'd like to know?"

"Nope. Your turn. Tell me."

"It's a long story—you sure?"

Nick was grinning and nodding, but he wouldn't be for long. He thought this was a lark, but once he knew...God, was she up for this again so soon?

"You asked me if I had ever been married. I was, back in my early twenties. I met Mack in college. He blew me away in the first five minutes. Truth is, you remind me of him."

Nick's gaze didn't waver, and he gave her a slight nod and squeezed her foot.

"After we got married, we lived in Kansas City, near my parents because I'd landed a great job with an ad agency. Mack's family was old Chicago money and they wanted him to join the family's financial business there, but Mack was a talented musician and he wanted to pursue a music career. His dad pretty much disowned Mack. But money was something he could relate to, so we figured once Mack made a name for himself, he'd come around."

"So that's how you came to sing with the band the other night?"

"Yes. Steve Mitchell was a guitarist with Mack's band. I hadn't been in touch with Steve in nearly twelve years." She paused and took another drink. "I'll speed this up."

"Don't." Nick shook his head. "I want to hear the whole story."

"Then we need more hot water and alcohol. I'll handle the water. You fill the glasses." She continued while the water cascaded into the tub, "Mack and I co-wrote some songs that ended up doing very well. But again, I wanted to remain anonymous, so we published them under a shell name and I received credit in the contracts. We were in the process of signing a big recording deal when I found out I was pregnant."

"I didn't realize you had children."

She shook her head, the pain in her heart palpable. "I don't, but I'm getting ahead of myself." She turned off the water and leaned back.

"My parents never judged Mack's folks—did their best to help smooth things over, and they convinced us to go see them to tell them about the baby. I was four months along by then and felt great, so we decided to head up." Jayne paused, recalling the first flutter of the baby moving inside her.

"We were going to fly our plane but the weather was sketchy—thunderstorms all over the Midwest—so we decided to drive. I'd set things up with Mack's mom—she was thrilled. The mess between Mack and his dad had been really hard on her."

Jayne took a big drink and paused, a vivid memory slicing through her calm, almost stoic narration. They'd departed early and driven into a blazing red sunrise, and Mack had joked about the old adage, red sky in morning, sailor take warning. If only they *had* taken warning.

She stared into her glass and chewed her lip. Even now, recalling that horrible time in her life ripped her to shreds. Pretending it was one of the books she'd written was the only way she could manage to keep going.

Jayne shifted to stretch her leg a bit and continued, "As predicted, the weather tanked that afternoon. It rained from St. Louis on, and at times it came down so hard you couldn't see twenty feet in front of you. We got through most of it, but the weather slowed us down. It was dark and we were going through a construction area when we hit another torrential downpour. Mack was driving and I remember suggesting we'd be better off stopping for the night as soon as we could find a motel. And that's all I can clearly remember." She exhaled and took a sip before she continued.

"Next thing I knew, I was in a hospital in Chicago. Mom was holding my hand. I'd been unconscious for two days and I woke to excruciating, all-consuming pain. My head throbbed like a spike was being pounded into it and my legs screamed like they were being ripped from my body. When I tried to sit up, it only intensified."

"The scars on your legs?" He lifted her right leg to take a look, then returned it to a comfortable spot with his hand on it.

She nodded. "I was in and out of consciousness for the next couple of days. I guess I kept tossing around and crying out for Mack to the point they had to keep me sedated to prevent further injury. Mom and Dad never left the hospital, and my brother flew back on emergency leave from Germany. That's when I sensed things were bad, but I couldn't find my way through the fog."

Jayne could still see the look on her dad's face, his haunted expression that told her nothing would ever be okay again.

"I finally realized Mack was gone. My dad's face said it all. He just held my hand and shook his head. I totally lost it and the nurse had to sedate me again."

"When I came to, I made my mom tell me what happened. By that time I was in traction and couldn't move. I couldn't react, and Mack was gone. A day later I found out I'd lost the baby, too." Jayne felt a couple of tears start rolling down her cheeks. "I really thought I'd die at that point. I know I wanted to…"

Nick's eyes were so full of understanding that she stopped fighting and let her tears stream unchecked. "I'm sorry, I thought I could tell you this without falling apart."

He leaned forward and cradled her face in his hands, gently wiping the tears from her cheeks with his thumbs. "Shhh, go ahead. You have every right."

Jayne hiccupped and sniffed. "You must think I'm a mess."

He tipped her chin up, forcing her to look into his eyes. "No. I think you're amazing."

Jayne shook her head, embarrassed. She'd done nothing more than survive. "No, I'm not, but maybe now you understand why riding through the rainstorm caused me to freak." She rolled her eyes and fought to regain her composure. "I don't talk about the accident because I hate being pitied, and it's always seemed easier when people didn't know."

"Jayne, we're all entitled to our secrets." He caught one last tear with his fingertip. "I'm glad you told me."

Nick's compassion was slowly unraveling the armor she'd built around her heart. Sharing the story with him seemed to have a dismantling effect. For the first time since the crash, she was talking about this to a man she cared about, stunned to find it liberating. Nick clearly had the wisdom and compassion to understand how hard it had been for her to tell him. But more importantly, he understood who she was because of what she'd been through.

"How long were you in the hospital?"

"About six weeks the first time. I had to stay in Chicago because they didn't want to move me. They transferred me by helicopter from the first hospital to a trauma center. I had several surgeries on my right leg. Infection set in and I nearly lost it, but my parents wouldn't let the doctors give up. Dad found a specialist at Johns Hopkins and moved heaven and earth to get him to Chicago on a consult. Dr. Landers took my hand and said after all I'd been through, I'd have enough emotional scars that I didn't need the loss of my leg as another reminder of the accident. He said he'd give it his all if I'd give it mine. That was a pivotal moment for me. That's when I started to fight."

"So how'd the accident happen? Did you ever find out?"

"I get bits and pieces in flash backs, but the highway patrol report said a teen-aged boy in a pickup was driving too fast for the road conditions and hydroplaned, throwing him head-on into a semi. We ended up wedged between the semi and the concrete barriers. Mack must've tried to veer to the right—witnesses said it looked as if he tried to protect me by taking the brunt of the impact. My side of our Jeep hit the concrete barricade, crushing the engine back into the front seat, which is how I was pinned. They said it was a chain effect, total chaos in the storm. Fourteen cars in all. Four people died. I understand it took quite a while to extract us from the Jeep once the emergency crews arrived. Mack died before they could get him to the hospital and they weren't sure about me because I'd lost so much blood—I'd started hemorrhaging."

She paused, swallowed and said quietly, "I lost the baby en route to the hospital."

Nick closed his eyes and shook his head. "...I can't imagine."

"It was a nightmare. I look back and it's surreal. Our lives unraveled in so many ways. My parents put up a good front, but they couldn't get beyond the fact they'd encouraged us to take the trip. And Mack's dad was never the same—but how could he be? Can you imagine having harsh words with your son and never seeing him again? Never having the chance to set things right..."

"No, I can't."

Jayne took Nick's hand and squeezed it, feeling a burden lift from her shoulders. For such a long time, she'd been half crazy with grief and anger, questioning why God had taken Mack *and* her baby. Her heart and soul went into the ground with them. She'd recovered, albeit slowly, and built a shell around this part of her past, isolating her from the pain. Now, it was truly lifting away.

She leaned back, offering him a wistful smile. "So *that's* how I came to be singing at the bar. Am I off the hook for a while?"

"One last question—you said some of your songs had been published. Anything I'd know?"

"Hmm—here's one for starters." She swallowed, cleared her throat and started singing a song she'd sung for Steve the first night, "*All I needed was some time away, time to clear my head, time to clear my heart...*" She finished the first couple of stanzas. "Know that one?"

Shock was all over his face. "*You* wrote that?"

"I wrote the lyrics. Mack wrote the music."

"That's a *great* song. Now I'm in a tub with a famous songwriter?"

"Two-timer." She leaned forward and motioned for him to lean toward her for a kiss. A quick peck turned into a kiss with more serious intent as he responded in kind. "Whether I'm a songwriter or an author, I'm definitely a prune. Let's get out of this confessional."

"And just when things were getting interesting...." Nick laughed and pulled himself out of the tub, wrapping a towel around his waist. He offered Jayne a bath sheet and then his hand. As she stepped out, he wrapped the sheet snugly around her and hugged her from behind. Nuzzling her neck, he purred, "Thanks for sharing the tub and the stories."

"What happens in the bathtub, stays in the bathtub..." She turned and gave him a quick peck and grinned. "Now, do you think you have something I could wear?"

"Nothing you'll look as good in as you did that tub...."

TWENTY-ONE

"Look who's here." Jimmy grinned while chewing on an unlit stogie, cards in hand. "You sure look better in those jeans than Nick ever could."

"Well, they're certainly tighter across the ass," Jayne joked, slapping her backside. "So how's everyone doing? We decided it was high time we crashed this very loud poker game."

She took in the enormity of the suite and the span of ocean beyond the wall of glass. "Nice digs, Gene. This is bigger than a lot of the houses here in Key West."

Jimmy chuckled. "Actually, it's bigger than some third world countries."

Nick had told her Gene usually reserved and stocked a palatial suite as a place for the crew to congregate. He wasn't kidding.

"Anything smaller, this wrecking crew could cause damage." Gene looked over the top of his cards to wink at her.

Jayne stepped behind Cara. "Are you cleaning them out?"

Cara sipped her beer, studied her cards, and nodded. "Was there a doubt in your mind?" She looked at Jayne with creased eyebrows and mouthed, "You okay?"

Jayne nodded at her friend, wondering what had been said, then turned as Colin tugged on her shirt tail.

"We're convinced your friends are card sharks." He threw in his hand. "I fold."

"Sounds more like piracy to me." Jayne ruffled his mane of white hair.

"Speaking of piracy, you seem to be one yourself. Always making off with the boss."

"No, I'm the pirate." Nick chuckled and handed Jayne a bottled water. He shot a look at Andy. "Sean's bike good to go?"

Andy nodded. "Yep. Piece of cake."

Cara opened the sliding door. "Looks like the weather has cleared. Maybe we can get back to the island." Then she added in a stage whisper to Jayne, "And we've got to high tail it out of here before they calculate their losses."

"When are we gonna see this island?" Jimmy asked.

"Why don't you go over with us now? It's what, three-thirty? We'll get happy hour started early," Cara suggested.

Andy looked at Nick. "What'dya think? I'm game if you are."

Nick met Jayne's eyes, questioning her approval.

A nap would've been her first preference, but she wouldn't be the one to put a damper on the fun. "Why not? We have a full bar and God knows we've got enough food to feed an army. Be a nice chance to clear out our kitchen before we check out tomorrow."

"Then we'll go to Blue Heaven for dinner." Jimmy stood, throwing down his cards. "I fold."

"I'm out." Gene pitched his cards to the center, his head bobbing. "Yeah. We decided at breakfast this morning. Nick, you and Jayne are coming, too."

Cara and Liz picked up their pile of winnings and Liz knocked her knuckles on the table. "This booty from our afternoon of piracy goes toward drinks tonight. Fair?"

"Atta girl." Andy threw his arm around Liz's shoulder, giving her a hug. "You're good sports. You can play in our sandbox any time, even though I think we've been hustled."

"Stick with me, pal, and I'll teach you all the tricks," Liz teased as she pinched his cheek.

"Lobby in ten minutes," Andy called out, leading the group out the door. "I need to grab some cash. That little poker game put a dent in my walking-around money." He pulled out the lining of an empty pants pocket for emphasis as he bumped shoulders with Jayne. "But we had a ball. Your friends are okay, Jayne."

Nick leaned in to her other side. "Like I said, you can tell a lot about a person by the company they keep."

Jayne rolled her eyes. "Then we're both in big trouble."

She cornered Nick while Andy was in the bathroom. "This plan all right with you? Or do you want your last night on the island to be a guy thing?"

"You're kidding, right? Even if I did, I'd be the odd man out. The guys are having fun hanging with your crew. What about you?"

"Fine by me. We get the best of both worlds as far as I'm concerned."

Nick leaned down and kissed her lightly. He had on Armani cologne again and just the way he smelled

243

made her head swim. As she leaned toward him for another kiss, the bathroom door opened.

Andy looked from one to the other, then chuckled. "I gave you half the afternoon alone in here. Wasn't that enough?"

"Not nearly." Nick shook his head as they headed out the door, muttering, "If you only knew…"

Jayne called Leigh to advise her of the plan, then looked around and counted heads. "Eight. Who's missing?"

Jimmy looked around. "Guess this is it. Some of the guys are opting out of our little adventure. It's just the A team tonight."

"Talk about nice digs." Nick wandered around, looking over the cottage.

Leigh, brandishing a jigger, winked at Jayne and caught Brandon's eye. "Put yourself to good use, cousin. Hand these drinks to Cara and Meg."

"You put together quite a spread, Paula Dean," Brandon said as he popped an olive in his mouth, taking the beverages from Leigh's hands. Then he turned to Liz, an eyebrow cocked. "What'll it be, gorgeous?"

"Vodka tonic." She flashed a smile at Brandon, then raised her voice to catch everyone's attention, "Meg and I are going to give a quick tour of the resort for anyone who's interested. Grab your drinks and join us." In a lower voice, she said to Brandon, "Private tour for you later if you're inclined."

Jayne, a little surprised by the exchange, whispered to Leigh, "What have I missed? I'm sensing some sizzle between those two."

"Well, last night they disappeared. She's as wily as he is, and they seem to be the quintessential challenge for each other. If anyone can put a harness on that mustang, it's Liz, but I'm almost afraid to watch. Whether it's fireworks or grenades, it'll definitely be explosive, so stand back." Leigh handed Jayne two drinks. "For Gene and Jimmy."

Jayne walked to the deck and handed the drinks to the men as they set off on their tour. Catching Nick's eye, she asked, "What's your poison?"

"Scotch, if you've got it."

Jayne headed to the bar as the majority of the crew filed out. She grabbed a glass and poured Glenfiddich over ice and handed it to Nick.

"How about showing me around?"

"Follow me." Jayne wiggled her finger and she felt him grab her belt loop as she turned. "Let's do the upstairs first." At the top of the steps she paused, "Liz drew the long straw and won the rights to the master suite for the weekend." She tilted up her face, inviting him to kiss her. She managed to push aside the warm rush and pulled him forward. "Want to see the rest?"

"I want to see your room while everyone's gone. And I want to lock the door."

His knuckle caressed her jaw and down her neck, pausing just above her breast, searing her skin and making her want to drag him to her room to do a whole lot more than lock the door.

"Like the way you think." She tapped her finger into his chest and he caught it in his hand, holding her captive, a wicked grin spreading across his face.

Jayne led him back down the steps to the room she shared with Leigh, opening the door to let him walk in ahead of her.

Folding his arms over his chest, his eyes skimmed the room, then settled on her bed. "That's seriously inviting...but a little small."

"Oh, I imagine we could make it work…" The image of crawling all over him played through her mind.

"That's what I was just thinking. How do we get rid of your roommate?" He laughed and pulled her close for another kiss.

"I'm sure she could be bought."

"What?" Leigh walked in at that moment. "I think I heard that."

"How much will it cost me to trade roommates with you?" Nick asked. "Sky's the limit."

Andy peeked in and Leigh locked her arm through his. "You're just in time. There's a serious negotiation underway and you could capitalize on this if you play your cards right, Mr. Jameson. Nick, here, is trying to sell me the rights to a night alone with you. How much are you worth? And what's your cut?"

"Honey, I'm free, but we'll never be able to afford my wife's or your husband's attorneys."

"Ah, so true, but it was nice to imagine for a brief moment." Leigh grinned, turning to Nick. "Mr. McCord, I'm afraid you're going to have to come up with Plan B while I show your roommate around." She winked at Jayne and pulled Andy along. "Follow me, big boy. We aren't welcome here."

They trooped out of the room and Jayne turned to Nick. "I need to change before we go out tonight. You're welcome to keep me company or join Leigh for the tour. Either way, would you mind shutting the door?"

"I'll relax on the deck." He took her chin in his hand. "Your eyes look tired even though your smile pretends otherwise, sugar. Take all the time you want. If we need to let the others go ahead, that's fine. We can catch up with them later."

"Thanks. I'll be fine. Maybe I just need a little caffeine. Maybe a Diet Coke."

"I'll get one for you."

Nick pulled the door closed and Jayne exhaled. She needed a few minutes to catch her breath and get her act together. But it would probably take more than caffeine and time to get the job done. Somehow, she'd will some energy into her tired body and enjoy the now. She flipped through her closet and pulled out a pair of jeans and a black top. Clean, dry jeans—something she'd never considered a luxury before today.

She looked up as Nick tapped on the door and opened it.

Clearing a spot on the night stand, he set down the icy beverage and a plate with some cheese, crackers and strawberries. "Here you go. Thought you might need a little snack. Whistle if I can get you anything else. And like I said, take your time. I'm not going anywhere."

His words, familiar for some reason, brought a smile to her heart. It would be so nice if it was true. Or if just for tonight, she could pretend it was true. Hmmm, where had she heard those words before? *Oh, well. Nice thought...*

Jayne popped a strawberry in her mouth and shifted her focus to getting dressed, selecting a delicious set of lacy black lingerie. Such a nice change after wearing and washing the same set three times. She applied a bit of makeup, curled her hair and slid into her clothes. One glance in the mirror said she needed a belt and her Manolo Blahnik sandals.

Leigh tapped on the door and stepped in. "Well, well. Sensational results in a flash."

"Thanks. I'm feeling less than sensational." Jayne shot her friend a wan smile. If anyone could be trusted to understand, it was Leigh.

"Are you kidding? You look terrific and a charming, spectacularly handsome man is falling hard for you if my read is correct. And on that note, I've been dying to hear about your last twenty-four hours. You and Nick seem very *simpatico,* shall we say."

"We are."

"Have you two opened up to each other yet?"

"Yeah, this afternoon—for about an hour and a half while we soaked in a giant bathtub. It's pretty funny. Andy's got the impression we've been screwing our brains out, but all we did was have this great heart-to-heart talk."

"Oh, my. And…?"

"Seems I'm hanging out with a bona-fide tycoon."

"And he's hanging out with a celebrated author."

"And songwriting pilot."

"Oh. So you told him *everything?* And nothing's happened between the sheets with you two? How'd you keep yourself from jumping his bones during all that time alone with him?"

"I had to use every ounce of restraint I could muster, believe me. We've been *this close* a couple of times," Jayne pinched her thumb and index finger almost together for emphasis, "but only managed to test the water. This afternoon would've seemed so *frat party* with everyone playing poker two doors down, so we used the time to get to know each other." She sighed. "Believe me, it was one of the most erotic and romantic afternoons I've ever spent with a man. Could've easily led to more, but we agreed time and place seemed off, and I think he knows as well as I do that this can't go anywhere."

Leigh shot her a look and Jayne held up a hand to ward off a comment. "He's a busy man with an empire to manage. I'm sure there are hordes of gorgeous women swarming around him, right in his own backyard. I'm geographically undesirable, as they say."

"Or so you're trying very hard to convince yourself. Appears to me the guy is smitten. Like I've said from the start, I think Nick's different. You should keep your options open."

Jayne smiled and shrugged her shoulders. "Perhaps."

"Jayne, I know you, so don't you give me lip service. I really like him and I like his friends, especially Andy and Jimmy. Nick's a keeper. Play this out and see where it goes. You don't have to buy the car. Just drive it for a while."

"Leigh, I *know* this is a seriously good guy and a chunk of my heart will be heading north on a Harley tomorrow. But there's no way in the world anything's going to come of this."

"So say you."

"So say me." With a pert nod, Jayne pulled the bedroom door open. She couldn't make Leigh understand without telling her everything, and it was too soon for that.

☼☼☼

Nick spied the sign on the weathered gate at the restaurant's entrance. "Ah, here we are. After you," he stepped back to let the women enter the enclosed courtyard and patio area first.

His eyes shifted from the mismatched tables and chairs filling the patio to the striped sail lashed high above them between tree trunks. He nodded his approval. "This place has *character*."

"It sure does, and the food is fantastic. Be sure to save room for dessert—but this time we can share."

Nick followed Jayne to the bar while they waited for their table. She was studying the singer, perched on a stool, strumming a guitar. The makeshift stage was nothing more than an elevated platform the size of a postage stamp. Nick couldn't decide whether the woman was nervous or simply lacked talent, but her music wore on his ears. She butchered an old Joni Mitchell song and was struggling through Van Morrison as Jayne stepped closer to listen. He followed and stood behind her, as Meg and Leigh joined them.

When Jayne heard a few off-key notes, her heart went out to the woman. The rest of the crowd pretended to ignore the music. Guessing the singer was about her same age, Jayne spied evidence of a tough life in the woman's eyes and by her unkempt fingernails as they strummed her guitar. Ill-fitting clothes magnified her ample size and didn't improve the impression. But Jayne knew stage fright, and this woman was terrified.

She caught the singer's eyes and nodded with a smile. The woman's face brightened and the smile that crept onto her face made her pretty. That ounce of understanding seemed to bolster her confidence, and Jayne watched her blossom as her voice strengthened.

Jayne signaled Leigh and Meg to join in with her as she hummed along. Then the three of them started singing along with the lady, though Jayne was careful to keep her volume low.

Nick watched the interaction between the women with interest. He stepped beside Jayne and laid his arm around her shoulder, whispering, "You're a kind person."

Jayne looked up at him and shrugged. "We girls gotta stick together."

The hostess called their name and he watched Jayne drop a twenty in the tip jar on her way to their table. How easy it would've been for her to ignore the struggling singer, or to show scorn, yet she offered encouragement. He marveled at her behavior. She was kind even when no one was looking.

Once the waiter took their orders, Cara addressed the table, "Let's play a supper club game."

Jayne winced and started shaking her head. "No Cara, let's not."

"Oh, come on. This will be fun. Don't be a buzz kill, Jayne," Cara chided. "Each person gets to ask a question and then we go around the table and everyone has to answer. The only question you don't have to answer is your own. I'll go first. Where's the most interesting place you've ever had sex."

Nick shot Jayne a grin. "This could be fun. Let's play. Come on, be a sport."

So they played, and when it was Jayne's turn, she asked, "Who was your best first kiss and where did you kiss her?"

Jimmy was the first to respond. "That's easy. My high school girlfriend, Robin Meyers and I kissed her on her hoo hoo."

Jayne smacked Jimmy's arm and could barely be heard over the roar of laughter. "You know that's not the *where* I meant."

"Yeah, but that's why it was the best first kiss."

Nick didn't have to think. Easy question. "Jayne Morgan at Sloppy Joe's Bar and she nearly kicked my ass for doing it."

Jayne's mouth dropped open. She whipped her head around and looked at him. He returned her stare, a smile torturing the corners of his mouth. Heckling from everyone else at the table kept the moment light, but he'd bet money she was shocked.

She leaned over to him and said under her breath, laughing, "Suck up."

"Maybe, but I speak the truth, sugar."

☼☼☼

"Let's go dance this dinner off. There's supposed to be a great salsa band at the Green Parrot. Anyone game?" Cara called out, receiving unanimous approval.

Nick led the amoeba of rowdies as they made the two-block jaunt, weaving and laughing their way to the bar, a glorified concrete slab and cinder block pool hall. He looked around and surmised the crowd was mostly local residents with a few adventurous tourists mixed in. And the band was fantastic. The small dance floor was packed.

Nick grabbed Jayne's hand. "Come on."

Jayne followed him in a spirited Samba. Nick's lead was smooth and easy—he'd done this before. They danced in silence for a few minutes and it was easy for her to slip into sync with Nick, her skin humming as he held her, intoxicatingly content in his arms.

The song ended and they started to exit the dance floor when Jayne recognized the start of *Hold On*, an old song Carlos Santana had recorded. She decided it was ironic that a Canadian had written it. "Do you mind dancing one more? I love this song."

"Sure." He pulled her back onto the floor. "Oh, I know this one. Actually know the guy who wrote it."

"You know Ian Thomas?"

Nick nodded and slid his hand to the small of her back.

Jayne closed her eyes and listened, the words settling over her like a prophetic shroud. Ian Thomas could've been writing this very song for her and Nick.

She hated the pace of her relationship with him. She wanted to slow everything down, and savor each moment for what it was…commit every single second to memory.

She looked up and was surprised to find him studying her face. He gave her a questioning look and then hugged her close as they continued dancing. Was he hearing the same meaning woven through these words?

Would she be able to remember every nuance of his face and memorize how he made her feel, or would time prove to be a hateful thief?

Jayne glanced at the bar while they danced and her heart stopped. Staring back at her, leaning on the bar, was someone who looked uncannily like Mack, offering her a nod. Her pulse raced and she blinked, focused on that spot at the bar again, but there was no one there. She shook her head, feeling goose bumps raise on her arms. *I'm truly losing it…*

When the song ended Nick leaned down and gave Jayne a lingering kiss, her lips soft under his. He couldn't read her expression. Her eyes were distant and gave nothing away. He hugged her and led her back over to their group. *Where does she go when she disappears that way?* Maybe someday he'd know.

It was much later when they trooped to the Hog's Breath Saloon. Jayne led the group through the entry and blew a kiss to Mike and Steve.

Mike nodded a greeting in their direction. "We're the Mike Vincent Band from Atlanta and this is our last night here in Key West. We've had a great time and I see a friend of ours just walking in." Mike pointed at Jayne and waved her toward the stage. "Some of you have already heard the sexy and fabulous Jayne Morgan.

For those of you who haven't, fasten your seat belts. Jayne, come on up and join us."

He squeezed her hand and murmured into her ear, "Knock 'em dead, babe. Sing one for me."

She shot him a quick smile and turned to accept Steve's hand, stepping onto the stage.

Jayne hugged Steve and Mike, feeling that familiar rush of adrenalin as she took the mic. She laughed as she heard Andy whistling, and Jimmy and Colin yelling, "Yeah, Baby. You go, Girl."

Mike leaned toward her to suggest, "How about *Joy Ride?*"

Jayne nodded. "Perfect." Then she said into the mic, "This one's for the Vespa Boys. It's a hit written by some drinking buddies of mine back in Missouri. I'm sure you've heard this Chris Filer hit a time or two."

She tapped her hand against her leg as she sang the words, "It's been a while since these miles have been a friend. Some days this road just goes around and back again...So can't we quit trying to make sense of this. Let our hearts just run, and drive off into the sun. Take a joy ride, leave our cares behind..."

Man, this was such a kick. She couldn't ask for a better way to polish off the trip.

Nick pulled Leigh to the dance floor, keeping one eye on Jayne. Tough to believe the weekend was over. He wasn't ready to say goodbye, and as much as he'd learned about her in the past twenty-four hours, there was so much more he wanted to know. But she'd be insane to want anything to do with him right now. And he'd be crazy to jump from the frying pan into the fire. It was way too soon. All the same, he couldn't imagine not seeing her again after tonight. He'd figure something out.

The song ended and he heard her chuckle into the mic, "This one's for my crew. Remember, Divas, what happens in Key West, *stays* in Key West."

He laughed out loud when he recognized a song Carrie Underwood had made famous as Jayne started singing *Don't Even Know My Last Name* in an exaggerated manner.

She winked at Nick and mouthed, "This one's for you," and broke into Bonnie Raitt's *Something to Talk About*. She watched a sloppy grin stretch across his face and managed to get him to step close to the stage by wiggling her finger. The crowd played along as she made it obvious she was singing it to him. Then Nick surprised her by pulling her off the stage to lead her in a quick dance spin with an elaborate dip at the end. She was breathless and laughing when he gave her a quick kiss and a bow. Thunderous applause greeted them as she blew a kiss to the band.

How on earth could she say goodbye to Nick? They'd barely said hello and he'd crawled into her heart and set up residence. Jayne hopped back on the stage to hug Mike, and then kiss Steve's cheek.

She whispered, "Lunch tomorrow?" At his nod, she said, "Call me and we'll set it up."

Nick took her hand and helped her down, giving her a hug. "You were great. Ready for a drink?"

"No, *you* were great. Nice moves, biker boy. Order me a vodka tonic and I'll follow you anywhere."

"Not until I get an autograph."

"So it's *still* all about the negotiation?" She shot him a suggestive look, one eyebrow cocked.

"You betcha, babe…"

TWENTY-TWO

Jayne listened to the rhythmic slosh of waves lapping the shoreline as the mellow shades of morning glowed across the water. Clad in her pajamas and a cozy robe, she lounged on the porch in a big Adirondack chair, one knee pulled up to her chest, her head resting on it. *Nicholas James McCord.* She was definitely in like, and a bit in love with him. And it had only been four days. *But I fell in love with Mack in four hours.* Saying goodbye had been torture, but she couldn't change the circumstances. *It is what it is...* She sipped her coffee and glanced at her watch, finding it hard to breath. He'd be leaving the island in a short while if they stuck to their intended schedule.

The vibration of her phone on the armrest of the chair made her jump and she looked at the screen, her heart skipping a beat.

"Morning, Biker Boy," she sighed, realizing that she was using her voice for the first time that morning, finding it raspy and hard to speak with any volume.

"God you sound sexy. I wanted to call before we head out. How're you doing this morning? "

"I'm fine, I guess. I always hate saying goodbye to everyone. How are *you*? Are you okay to head out on an all-day ride? You didn't get much sleep last night. It

seemed to take us a very long time to say goodnight."
Or, goodbye…

"That it did, and I got less sleep than you know. I kept rolling over, looking for you."

"Blame Andy and Leigh." She laughed, then said, "Regardless, Nick, I had a really good time with you this weekend. You've been one of the best detours I've ever taken."

Her low chuckle, warm and mellow hit all the right buttons, giving him an image of how she'd look all soft and sleepy at this hour and he had to fight his body's immediate response. Spending another day with her was far more appealing than the eight-hour ride ahead of him. He didn't have the words, so he borrowed one of hers, "Ditto."

Why wouldn't she agree to make plans see him again? Did his recent divorce scare her? Or was she like him—skeptical of a connection forged so easily and so quickly. But what could be the harm in getting together now and then?

If he read her right, Jayne was running scared.

Jayne felt the uncomfortable silence stretch, yet she was unable to figure out what she could say that would appease him. Not agreeing to make future plans left a gaping void between them. It was truly goodbye rather than a preceptor to future conversations. Finally, she settled for the benign. "Are you all packed up?"

"Yeah. We're ready to pull out. Gene's nagging at us to be on our way or we won't make Islamorada by lunchtime. God forbid we get off schedule. Like the plane won't wait for us."

"Yeah. I hear the guy who owns that bird is a real hard ass," she teased. "Best you be going, then. Wouldn't want to upset Mother." She laughed and he joined her. She heard the rumble of the throaty engines in the background and pictured the group, clad in leathers, rugged and restless as they checked tires, wiped down chrome and stowed gear.

Despondency, painful and potent, closed over her as she imagined him roaring out of sight, disappearing from her life.

"Jayne, I've gotta roll. I just wanted to hear your voice. Enjoy the next few days down here. Think of me freezing in the tundra while you're still basking in the tropics."

Her mouth was dry. "Nick, be safe and have a great ride. Call when you make it to Orlando. Let me know you're safe."

"Will do. Bye, babe."

"Bye." She disconnected the call and he was gone…like smoke through a key hole.

Looking out at the waves, the quaking in the pit of her stomach took on an aggravated cadence. Time and place were everything. Why would Fate pick now for Nick to cross her path—now when neither of them was emotionally available? She sighed and closed her eyes, leaning back to rest her head against the cushion. *Lousy circumstances.* Bile welled up, depositing a bitter taste on her tongue. *This is all so unfair. First Mack. Now Nick.*

Her eyes burned and she brushed at a couple of tears that escaped to roll down her cheeks. Spending the next few days down here working had seemed so perfect. Now that wasn't possible. Without her friends to distract her, she'd end up dwelling on two things. *Cancer and Nick.* Maybe she should head home early.

"I like him, Jayne."

Jayne started, her breath lodging in her chest. She looked around, sheepish, certain she'd dozed off. *I really am losing it…*

Then the deep, gentle timbre of Mack's voice fell on her ears again. "You're not crazy, even though *crazy is good.*" A chuckle, low and melodious floated on the air, the tone of his voice unmistakable.

"Mack?" Jayne whispered, afraid to believe, her heart thundering in her chest. "Are you here?"

"I've always been here. Watching you when you sleep, holding you when you cry, laughing at your jokes…"

Still whispering, Jayne knew she was in a trance and the slightest movement would wake her from this dream, but what a sweet dream, "Why haven't you talked to me before?"

"Oh, I have. Lots of times. Maybe you need me more right now, so you're listening. "

Jayne's common sense wrestled with her desire to believe. Was exhaustion and despair manifesting itself, or could she trust the loving calm that embraced her? This moment vibrated and hummed with something truly spiritual, and in that moment she knew beyond anything she could explain that Mack's spirit was with her, on some level.

"This isn't the first time I've needed you…God, Mack, I've missed you more than you can understand…so much has happened and it's been so long…"

"I know, honey. But time here goes so fast. I can't stay so let's get to the important stuff. I know you're sick, but you're strong and you're tough. You're gonna be fine."

"I am?"

"Not that I know these things, but that's what I'd tell you if I could still be there to help you through this. And about the cancer—I always loved the twins, Jaynie, but they're not worth your life. Go for it. Get rid of 'em. You're so much more than that gorgeous pair of ta ta's, and any man worth his salt isn't going to be thinking differently about you if they're replacements. Trust me on this."

"So you know about these decisions I'm facing?" Jayne looked out at the water, speaking softly, tears flowing unchecked.

"Sure. I've been with you through it all. I'm so sorry you're facing this without me, and I wish I could be there to help you, take care of you, be with you as you meet with the doctors, and kiss away your fears. Just know that until you're out of the woods and you have someone else to love and care for you, I'll be right beside you."

"I've dreamed that you were sitting on the side of the bed talking to me. It was really you? Did I see you the other night?"

"Yeah. I couldn't stay away. And I really can't move on until I know you're well and in good hands. Speaking of which, as I said before, I like Nick. He's the only man you've met since me that's worthy of your heart. Timing may not be right, but the man is."

"How do you know?" Jayne frowned, wiping off her cheeks.

"I just do. You two need to figure it out. It may take a while, but he's a good man and he'd never hurt you. And you've said it yourself—he's a whole lot like me. By the way, you sounded great at the Hog. That was a kick, getting to watch you on stage with Steve. How cool is it that you ran into him down here? You should sing like that more often. You're still the hottest ticket in town." Mack chuckled, his voice a sexy breath on Jayne's ears that had her heart skipping, mere pebbles across the water.

Jayne heard the creak of the door as Liz stuck her head out. "Hey girlfriend, how about some coffee?"

She sniffed and called back, "Sure, I'll be right in." The door closed, and she prayed she wouldn't be met with silence. "Mack, are you still here?"

His voice melted in her ear, velvet and silk as the softest of kisses, the mere flutter of a butterfly wing touched her cheek. "I'll always be right here. Any time you want to talk, I'll listen. You go on in with the gals, now. Enjoy the rest of your time here and then go home and concentrate on getting well. Consider what I've said about Nick. I want you to be happy because I love you. Always have, always will."

With the breeze, he was gone. Jayne sat there, loathe to break the spell as voices carried from inside. Closing her eyes, she allowed the rest of the tears to slip down her cheeks while his words and voice swam over her, strengthening her. It was comforting to recall the nights she'd assumed she was dreaming, certain now that Mack had always been watching over her...that she hadn't been alone after all.

Shaking her head, a slow smile creeping to her face. *Men.* No matter what form they came in, they always had a way of making things seem uncomplicated. Like her situation with Nick. And the decision about the surgery. But Mack was right about one thing. Nick and he were a whole lot alike. Mack may be right about him, but so much more was involved. She simply couldn't explore that possibility right now. It would be too unfair to Nick, and maybe to her.

Pulling onto Highway One, Nick could almost feel Jayne tucked in behind him. He wasn't happy about the way he'd let her settle under his skin, so he focused on the road. It was time to get his head straight and put things into perspective. She was phenomenal. No

261

question. He'd like nothing better than to spend more time with her. But he had to get back to work. Get used to being *divorced.* God, he hated that word. He might as well use the word *failure.* Same difference.

It was obvious Jayne hated the word, too. Hadn't she told him that she'd never met a man who didn't need at least two years to get his act together after a split up? She'd used different wording but the meaning was the same. He had to agree with her on that score. As insane as he'd be to let her get away, she'd be even more insane to bet on the chance that he'd be worth a damn for quite a while. She kept telling him he needed time. Maybe she was right. A twenty-two-year marriage would take time to get over.

He shook his head, an ache settling in his gut. Five days with Jayne would take time to get over, too. He replayed their first encounter at the Hog's Breath. Nothing more than a mutual flirtation—he was playing the wolf to her vixen, enjoying the game as they matched wits, never intending this dance to be more than a mutual ego boost. But when she'd taken off that first night, he had to track her down and straighten things out. He'd been kidding himself that it was only about clearing his honor.

Sometime over the last couple of days, the dynamics shifted. He couldn't pinpoint when, but the dance had changed tempo, upping the stakes. He'd been thinking about Jayne when she wasn't around, wanting to hear what she had to say, and he realized he was as attracted to her mind as he was to her body. He'd become protective, and even a little possessive of this woman. Thinking of her in that way changed everything. He blew out a breath and groaned. *Shit!* Whether he liked it or not, she was on a loop that would keep playing through his brain.

☼☼☼

Jayne panted and pulled herself out of the pool. She toweled off and grabbed a bottle of water, settled on a lounge chair and grabbed a pen and a folder of manuscript pages from her bag.

Moments later, Leigh and Meg arrived and tossed towels into the chairs beside her. She put on her baseball cap and took a swig of water. "I can't believe you made me exercise alone."

"I'm still on vacation and that's not on my agenda until I return to reality," Leigh groaned, plopping down. "Tomorrow will be more than soon enough. Besides, Andy kept ordering drinks for me last night. I feel like nine kinds of hammered shit."

"Need some hair of the dog?" Meg asked.

"Probably. As long as I don't have to drink alone."

"You won't be. Thinking a Mojito sounds good," Meg said.

"Ooh. I think that's what poisoned me, though I lost track," Leigh grimaced. "What the hell. Get one for me, too"

"Jayne?"

"No, I may be flying this evening and I have a twelve-hour bottle-to-throttle rule. Mind getting me a frozen lemonade?"

"You're flying today? I thought you were staying until Friday?" Leigh raised her eyebrows, looking over the top of her sunglasses.

Jayne fought to keep her voice light and neutral. "I've pretty much decided to head back—fly as far as Ocala tonight, stay at my brother's, then on home tomorrow. It's just not as much fun down here without you guys." *Or without Nick...*

Meg handed tall, frosty beverages to Leigh and Jayne and held up her glass. "To another great diva weekend. Cheers."

"Cheers. So, Meg…did you give the man a proper send off? You two seemed to vanish after we left the Hog's Breath," Jayne asked.

"Yeah, well…we didn't think we'd be missed…" She stammered and laughed, "In my wildest dreams, I didn't imagine meeting someone during this trip. Not sure where this will go, but I'm going to take your advice and take this little joy ride. He's going to meet me in New York during my business trip in a couple of weeks, and then we're planning to ski in March. You and Nick really should join us. Leigh, you and Charlie could come, too."

Leigh shook her head. "Thanks all the same, but I prefer warm weather vacations. Let me know when you plan something involving a beach and I'm your gal. But I definitely like Sean."

"And all of this happened because of a spilled drink." Meg shook her head.

"Maybe, but somehow I think we would've ended up meeting them regardless of the drink incident. Two big groups are bound to collide in a place as small as Key West," Jayne mused. "Just think about the other fun groups of people we've met over the years. And we tend to run into them from year to year."

"Yeah, I've thought of that. But these guys were far more memorable than any of the others. I'm still having a hard time figuring out why we haven't met them before. We always come down at the same time and so do they, within a week or two. Doesn't it make you wonder that we might have seen them before? Oh well, this was our lucky year."

Was it a twist of fate—this innocent encounter that led to so much fun? Meg had met Sean. Liz had met

Brandon. And she had met Nick, and learned that she could feel that *buzz* again. In spite of her own heartache, she was happy they'd bumped into the Canadians.

Leigh stood to stretch. "Boy this place seems quiet now that Cara and Liz are gone. I miss Cara's energy already. I always get a little depressed on this last day, too. Just hate to see all the fun coming to an end. I guess that's why I always take the last flight out." Leigh tapped Jayne's foot. "You're sure quiet this morning. That tall drink of water holding you hostage? I checked the clock when I heard you sneak in last night and it was way past your curfew."

"Yeah, people were getting on the boat to leave for the airport as I was coming in. Gotta admit, that was a first." She sobered and added, "It was hard to say goodbye."

"How did you two leave things?" Leigh asked.

"He wants to stay in touch but I didn't commit to anything. He's a busy man and he's far from ready to get involved with someone. Hell, the ink isn't even dry on his divorce and you guys know my rule—two years recovery, *minimum*."

"I agree with Leigh that Nick may very well be the exception," Meg said.

"Maybe, but I'm not willing to take that chance. Timing's just bad. If we'd met a couple of years from now, who knows? But for now, I'm not planning to keep in touch with him. I just can't." She fought to keep the emotion from her voice, but she couldn't fake it with these two. Her control ebbed as an errant tear slid down her cheek, quickly followed by another. She saw Leigh and Meg exchange a glance as she tried to brush them off her cheeks but they were falling in earnest and she couldn't stem the tide. Everything she'd been feeling was hitting the surface and she couldn't push her disappointment and her fear back into their hiding place.

"You don't need to rush into anything. Nick may need time to adjust to the idea of being single, but I think he's crazy about you, whether he's figured it out or not." Meg paused, then laid her hand on Jayne's arm. "Don't do anything right now. Okay? Think about it for a few days."

Leigh frowned. "Why don't we talk through this? It might be time to lower your guard and let your heart take the lead. I don't think he's going to disappear, so you don't need to beat him to the punch by pushing him away first." She paused, then exhaled, concern apparent in her eyes. "Or is it something more?"

Jayne could lie and fabricate every reason under the sun for pushing Nick away, but they'd never believe her. Her strength was evaporating under the weight of what loomed ahead. It was time to tell them—she couldn't hold it in another minute. As much as she hated it, she'd just have to risk putting herself back in her old shoes where everyone worried about her.

Right now, Leigh and Meg needed to know. Then maybe they'd understand why she was separating herself from Nick. Her heart was hollow and empty and she wanted their support. Of all the women in her life, Jayne knew her four dear friends would honor her confidence and be supportive without making her feel isolated. She needed them, not for their sympathy, but for their strength. She could read the concern etched across their faces. Swallowing, she braced herself, struggling to form the right words.

Leigh patted her arm and asked, "Jayne, talk to us, kiddo."

Jayne gulped, tears forming anew. "I need to tell you guys something. I planned to wait until after this weekend—tell all four of you at the same time—," She took a breath, closed her eyes for a second, then looked from one to the other. "I've been diagnosed with stage three breast cancer."

Time stopped as the full weight of her words hit like a wrecking ball, smashing and crushing their perfect world. She watched the shards of fear, anger and worry play across their faces as the news fully registered.

"Oh, my God...I can't believe it..." Meg was shaking her head back and forth, her words disjointed. "Jayne, I'm so sorry."

Leigh, stunned to silence, finally looked at the sky and closed her eyes, whispering, "No...no, no, no.... this can't be." Leigh moved over to sit at Jayne's feet, her eyes filled with pain and concern. "Why didn't you tell us sooner?"

Jayne shook her head, fighting back a sob. "I just couldn't. After everything we went through when Maddy got sick, I didn't want to ruin our time together this weekend. We're finally to the point where we can talk about her without crying, and I didn't think I could handle having this become the topic of our time away. I don't want to be the girl everyone's tiptoeing around, like I was after the accident." Jayne looked from one friend to the other. "I simply *cannot* do it again."

Meg's voice was low as she said, "You've hidden it so well the whole weekend. I wish we'd known." She hugged Jayne to her. "You're going to get through this just fine. *We're* going to get you through this just fine. Women win this fight all the time and you will, too. But for this minute, I need to cry and hug you because I need to get the shock out of my system. Then we're going to join forces and get you well." The tears were now running down Meg's face and she held Jayne tightly.

"Amen, Sister." Leigh nodded, swiping at the tears in her eyes. "How long have you known?"

"Just three weeks today."

"Do you want to fill us in, or do you want to table this until later?"

"Now's fine. Reader's Digest condensed version, okay?" When her friends nodded, Jayne continued, "About a month ago my underwire broke on my bra and wore a spot under my left breast. When I rubbed it, I found a lump. Thought it was from the underwire poking me all afternoon. Well, it was still there the next morning so I went in for a mammogram that afternoon. Preliminary results were inconclusive, but I had a bad feeling. Since Mom died of cancer, my doctor scheduled me for an ultrasound the next day just to be on the safe side."

"You were so smart to follow your gut. So many women don't." Meg nodded.

"It was a good thing, because during the ultrasound, the radiologist saw something suspicious and performed what they called a *needle guided biopsy* of what they originally saw on the mammogram, which turned out to be a three centimeter tumor. He placed a marker in the site and sent the tissue to a pathologist.

Jayne blew her nose and paused. That two-week period had been a nightmare. Telling it now was nearly as surreal. "When I didn't hear back regarding the lab results by the end of that week, I called my doctor's office. She was gone for the afternoon, so I spoke with one of the nurses who is a friend of mine. Because it was late on a Friday and the results said there was no malignancy, she broke the rules and told me so I wouldn't worry over the weekend."

Leigh tilted her head to the side, eyebrows arched. "If the results were negative, what's the deal?"

"Lab error. After I spent a weekend thanking God and spending a small fortune on a celebratory shopping spree, I got a call that Monday from my doctor asking

me to come to her office. Three weeks ago today."
Jayne shook her head, recalling the day in horror. "I
didn't want to rat out my friend so I played along,
convincing myself that my doctor just wanted to deliver
the good news in person."

Her hands were shaking, making it hard to hold
her glass. "I was in denial. Big time. You guys know as
well as I do that doctors don't invite us to their offices
to give us good news. When she delivered the verdict, it
was like I'd been on a week-long roller coaster ride that
screeched to a halt in mid-air—me hanging upside
down. Seems there was a coding error at the lab, and
my test results had been mishandled or something."

Jayne wiped her nose and continued, "No one can
prepare you for the words, *you have cancer.* I managed to
hold it together until I pulled into my garage. Then I
completely lost it. It was one of the worst days you can
imagine." Her stomach quaked with nausea as she
remembered sobbing in her car, wondering if
asphyxiation might be an easier solution.

"You should've called me. I would've been on the
next plane."

"I know, Leigh, and I almost did, but I needed to
come to grips with this before I could tell anyone.
Somehow telling it makes it real and I wasn't ready for
that. I didn't even tell my brother and sister-in-law until
last Wednesday."

"Did you find a good surgeon?"

"Yes. And trust me, I've done my homework."

"I'm sure you have, but I hate that you've been
dealing with this alone. You *did* get a second opinion?"
Leigh asked.

"And a third." She pursed her lips and gave a nod.
"I'm having surgery in three weeks." She went on to
explain the decision looming before her. Consenting to
the bilateral mastectomies the oncologist had

269

recommended would take every ounce of courage she could muster. But this was an invasive, fast-growing cancer. A lumpectomy would be quicker to recover from, but the chances of the cancer coming back with a vengeance were too strong to ignore.

Meg's mouth fell open. "Wow. That's soon."

"Not soon enough when you know you've got a deadly tumor in your body. You just want it *gone*. But getting everything scheduled seems to take *forever*..."

"I'll fly in to be with you," Leigh said.

"And I'll tag team with you, Leigh. We can coordinate our schedules." Meg nodded. "That way, you'll have someone with you during your recovery and then we'll figure out what works best for you. I have lots of vacation time. How long before you'd go for the reconstruction?""

"It'll depend on the chemo. Initially, they'll insert tissue expanders. Then I get to decide what my new ta-tas will look like." Jayne rolled her eyes. "And no, I'm not planning to go bigger."

"You wouldn't need to. But I'm thinking we should pick up a couple of Penthouse and Playboy magazines so you'll have plenty of inspiration," Leigh teased. "If we'd known sooner, we could've stopped by one of the strip clubs and taken a vote."

"Thank you. I knew I could count on you for support. In its many forms." Jayne rolled her eyes. "Now I'm *glad* I didn't tell you sooner. Seriously, I will need you. I just didn't want to tell you down here. This is our happy place. I don't ever want anything bad to be part of our time in Key West. And I have one huge favor to ask."

"Name it," Meg said.

"I want to keep this as quiet as possible, for as long as possible. Okay? As I said, I don't want to be on the receiving end of everyone's concern and sympathy again." She hated seeing the worry and fear in anyone's eyes. It suffocated her. She knew it sounded horrible and ungracious, but after the accident, just the thought of going through it again was unbearable.

As both friends nodded their vow, she continued. "Now do you see why I can't keep in touch with Nick?" Jayne asked and blew her nose.

Meg frowned. "I think he'd be hurt to know you weren't willing to share something so important after all the time you've spent together."

Jayne chewed on her lower lip. "But we've only known each other for a few days. We haven't even had a chance to be alone for any length of time. Nick and I may only be the proverbial vacation fling."

"I think you're lying to yourself." Leigh pursed her lips. "But I think you already know that."

"No. This is way too heavy to lay on someone who's not already part of my life. It's simply not fair." If she told him now, he'd either disappear or feel obligated to stick around and be supportive. She couldn't bear the thought of either reaction.

Meg shook her head. "You may be selling him short. He may want to be there for you because he cares."

"Or because he feels sorry for me. I'd never know the truth, and I couldn't stand that." She exhaled. "Besides, I've got some very big decisions to make and I *cannot* let the possibility of a relationship influence me. And it could, on several fronts. Believe me, it's better this way." Jayne shrugged her shoulders, determined to maintain her resolve. "Think about it. He's on the heels of a divorce and hasn't had time to come to grips with that emotionally. Then here I am, dealing with cancer and going through treatment. Bad combination. Better to make a clean break now." She grimaced, then lowered her voice, "Besides, he lost a sister to breast cancer five years ago and pretty much said he never wanted to go through that again. It must've been horrible to watch someone you love suffer and lose the battle, so I completely understand where he's coming from, and I'd hate to put that on him again."

"Surely you misunderstood what he meant, so don't be hasty. Give yourself a few days to think it over," Leigh said. "Either way, you're not alone. We're here for you no matter what."

Meg nodded. "We're stuck to you like Gorilla Glue, girlfriend. But you really should reconsider telling Nick. At least at some point if he stays in touch."

"Believe me, I've thought of nothing else since the moment I met him. He and I crossed paths during an impossible time for both of us." Jayne stood and hugged her friends. "So, let's put all this on hold for now. You have no idea how much I appreciate knowing I can count on you guys. I'll need you, and I love you for your willingness to help and support me." She picked up her towel and bag. "Now that I've made a colossal mess of the rest of our day in paradise, we need to get ready for our lunch date with Steve. He's meeting us in an hour. Where should we go?"

"I think I hear a burger and some greasy fries calling my name," Leigh announced, grabbing her bag.

"Ditto." Meg nodded and slid into her flip flops.

"Then it's unanimous. That's one thing I've enjoyed about this weekend. For the first time in my life I haven't worried about eating too much or gaining a little weight. I figure once I start chemo, my appetite won't be all that great and I'll be fighting to keep weight on. So I've been eating like a horse and enjoying every calorie. I'm sure Nick thinks I'm a gluttonous pig." She laughed, relieved that she'd finally come clean with these two. "Dessert without guilt. Small consolation prize, but I'll take it."

"In that case, I think we should go to the Hot Tin Roof and have a piece of their cashew crusted key lime pie after lunch," Leigh suggested.

Jayne hugged her two friends. "No. I think we should have it first."

☼☼☼

Between the Stones, U2 and INXS, Nick tried to blast thoughts of Jayne from his mind in the first fifty miles. But the farther he rode, the more he dwelled on the unfinished conversation between them. There were just too many words left unsaid...or too many words they'd avoided. He was blown away by the fact she could dismiss him without so much as a backward glance. They shared too strong of a connection for either of them to just walk away without having a discussion about seeing each other again. Images of her had idled in his head off and on for the past three days and they were still motoring around. It wasn't just physical with her. That was clear since they hadn't even had sex yet.

In that precise moment, he knew he couldn't just walk away. But damned if he could decide what he should do.

Distracted and cranky, he hit the brakes, catching Jimmy's signal too late. He squinted at the sign, surprised they were already nearing Islamorada. He made a U-turn in the next crossing and rode back to the parking lot, stopping his bike next to Andy's in front of the Lorelei Bar and Grill.

"What's up with you?" Andy sidled up to him as they strode toward an outdoor table overlooking the inlet.

"Huh?" Nick turned, frowning. "Oh, I didn't see Jimmy's signal."

"You're zoning, man. Have been since we pulled out. Not like you to miss a signal. "

"Just tired." Nick pinched his forehead, frowning.

"*Bullshit.*" Andy was shaking his head as he signaled to the waitress. "That birddog won't hunt. This is *me* you're talking to."

Andy was right. He *was* full of shit and he was pissed at himself. For the confusion that played havoc with his brain. For wanting more time with Jayne. For not making a plan to get together with her again to see if there was something real between them.

But she'd shut him down. He'd looked at it from every angle for the past two hours and he still couldn't figure it out. Maybe Jayne figured he wasn't worth it—that he'd spend his next two years carousing and chasing skirts. If she knew him better, she'd understand that wasn't his style.

Give it a rest, McCord. He shifted his attention to the sandwich in the basket before him, his appetite non-existent. He tried listening in on the conversations around him, but Jayne had already settled down in the back of his mind. And if he was a betting man, he'd bet the house she'd be rattling around there for a while. *A long while.*

He left most of his sandwich in the trash and followed Andy to the parking lot. Gino was yapping about making up lost time and Nick tuned him out as he revved his engine.

Nick followed the pack onto the highway, determined to shake off the funk that rolled over him. He wasn't a scorned teenager. He squared his shoulders and blew out air. He'd get back to work and be too busy to give any of this a second thought.

From any angle, Jayne *was* the kind of woman he'd be looking for if and when he decided to allow someone back into his life. She was someone he

274

genuinely liked. He wasn't worried about the physical thing. He knew they'd have been good together, given the chance. Her intellect was what drew him in—he wanted someone he could talk to and share ideas with, someone he

could laugh with, someone who didn't take herself or him too seriously. As he ticked off his mental list, Jayne scored on every bullet point.

Timing sucked. But a thought had taken root in the back of his head and a voice in his gut nagged and hammered away. *Stop. Turn Around.* What was it Jayne had said? *Feel the fear and do it anyway?* He should listen to that voice, to his gut telling him he needed more time with her. Would another couple of days make a difference? Would that be enough time to figure things out? Maybe. Maybe not.

Only one way to find out.

In the long run, it'd be a small price to pay for peace of mind. Just how many second chances did a man get? Would he ever find anyone else that made him feel as alive, as excited about living his next thirty years as Jayne did?

Feel the fear and do it anyway. If you let her out of your sight, you may never see her again. He scowled, fighting the obvious conclusion. He'd built an empire by trusting his gut, so why shouldn't he listen this time?

Because this was foreign territory and he didn't have a map...

Two miles south of Florida City, Nick absently clicked the change button on his bike's stereo and the first notes of Santana's version of *Hold On* triggered a vision...dancing with Jayne at the Green Parrot. As the song implied, why should he let her get away just because of lousy timing? Why shouldn't he be the one to say when he'd had enough...

And dammit, he hadn't had nearly enough of her...

He signaled to Andy, pulling over on the shoulder of the highway just south of the Florida turnpike entrance. Andy pulled up beside him while the others roared past, looking over at Nick with raised eyebrows.

Nick nodded once and said, "I'm going back. I'll call my pilots and tell them you'll be taking the plane without me."

TWENTY-THREE

Jayne beckoned to the bellman, pointing to the luggage. "These bags, please and I'll meet you at the boat."

Her phone buzzed, Nick's name flashing on the screen. He couldn't be in Orlando yet. "Hi. How's your ride going?"

"Great. What're you up to?"

"Just checking out of the cottage. I'm flying out this evening."

"Really? What changed your plans?"

"Oh, I've got a pile of work sitting on my desk and I'm antsy." Just the sound of his voice on the other end magnified her loneliness.

"When are you taking off?"

"Couple of hours. I need to check out, then I'm meeting my friend Brian and his partner at the Schooner Bar for a quick visit."

"Sounds like I caught you at a bad time. Let me call you later."

"Not too late. I'll be in bed early tonight."

You read my mind... Nick glanced at his watch. Much longer and he would've missed her. He made the turn down Duval Street and drove to the end, pulling along the front of the Ocean Key Resort. He entered the lobby, the lime green and blue walls startling, but not nearly as unusual as the light fixtures over the front desk—hanging globes with metal octopi draped on them. *Huh...*

Nick secured an oceanfront suite for two nights, with the understanding his stay could be extended, and made parking arrangements for his bike. He followed the bellman through a confusing labyrinth of walkways and lifts to his door and palmed him a bill. He should've left a trail of bread crumbs...

He entered to find a startling riot of bold tropical colors, similar to the lobby. Furniture painted in wild Caribbean designs sat on tile flooring. An enormous bed draped in mosquito netting anchored one side of the room while a sitting area faced a set of glass-paned French doors on the other. He opened the doors and stepped onto the balcony, taking in the span of blue water. Then he glanced at the eclectic collection of vendors setting up for the nightly sunset celebration below him on Mallory Square, the pinging tin of steel drum reggae music filtering through the afternoon. The view alone made this room worth the hefty price tag.

Checking his watch again, Nick grabbed his duffle bag and stepped into the large marble bathroom. He turned on all three of the shower heads, deciding it was more of a glass-encased adult playpen than a shower. A couple of steamy images floated through his mind before he focused on getting cleaned up.

He stripped and stepped under the jets, allowing the hot water to pound his aching shoulders. God, he was tired. Long ride on top of very little sleep. But he was mentally wound up and the spraying needles had an energizing effect as he washed off the day and shaved.

He ran his fingers through his damp hair, pulled on his last clean pair of jeans and the shirt Jayne had bought him at the Southern Cross, slid into his flip flops, pocketed some cash and headed out the door.

He slowed as he neared the Schooner Bar. Voices of late-afternoon musicians harmonizing on an old Eagles song escaped the bar's confines and drifted down the pier.

Paris flashed before his eyes and a cold fear socked him in the gut. What if this turned out to be another colossal miscalculation? He sucked in a breath and shook off the memory. Arriving at the Ritz to find Alynn with Halverson was a whole different story and had *nothing* to do with coming back to see Jayne.

She was perched on a bar stool with her back to him, chatting with Brian and another guy. Nick caught Brian's eye, putting his finger to his lips and stepped closer.

Her hair, tied up, bounced loose as she spoke. Jayne gestured wildly, and was laughing and regaling them with something that had the two guys doubled over. When he got close enough to hear, he realized she was sharing the story of their detour. He listened as she chattered away, figuring that she'd noticed him when she paused at one point, stilling mid-sentence. Then she shook her head and kept talking.

"...and the bathroom was huge—a football team would've fit in the shower. Very sexy. It was all I could do not to jump his bones right then—"

Had she really just said that? His pulse sped up as he laid his fingertips on her shoulders, giving them a light squeeze, then leaned down to press his lips against her neck. "Wish I'd known that at the time."

Jayne, jumping under his touch, gave a little gasp and whirled, her eyes widening as she grabbed him. "Nick! What are you doing back here? Is everything okay?"

"Everything's fine." He pulled her close, giving her a kiss that lasted just a little longer than polite company mandated, not caring a whit as he breathed in the wonderful smell of her, fresh with just a whiff of that soft perfume he'd come to appreciate.

He turned. "Hey, Brian." He reached across the table to shake hands, then offered his hand to the other man. "Nick McCord."

"Nick, this is Andrew Spalding, Brian's partner," Jayne offered as she turned, placing her arm on Andrew's shoulder.

"Nick, it's a pleasure. Join us? Jayne's been sharing tales of your little excursion up the Keys. Sounds like quite a road trip," Andrew said, his British accent identifying him as most likely South African.

"Oh, it was." He looked over at Jayne and winked. Then he addressed the waitress who'd appeared at his side, "I'll have a Heineken." He waved to the trio. "You guys ready for another?"

Jayne's heart was doing cartwheels and she fought to still the dive bombers in her stomach. Why was Nick back? She looked around. "Where are the other guys?"

"Orlando. I'll fill you in later."

"You're sure you're all right? Where were you when you called?" She couldn't keep the worry out of her tone. What was going on? She'd just spoken with him what, an hour ago?

"I'm fine. I was just getting back. Needed to figure out where I'd find you."

Why hadn't he told her he was on his way back? She stopped quizzing him when her efforts proved futile.

Nick left for the men's room and Andrew pounced on her. "He's simply scrumptious, love. Even though

280

he hasn't said anything, I'm betting *you're* the reason he's back."

"No way." A thrill passed through Jayne, though she couldn't conceal a skeptical frown.

"Oh, *definitely*," Brian echoed. "And you need to call the airport and have them put your plane back in the hanger for at least another night. Or two…"

"I'm not so sure—"

"Are you *insane*?" Andrew hissed. "You've got Mr. *I'm So Fucking Hot For You* ready to put you on the moon and you're *not so sure*? Have we taught you *nothing*? He's been undressing you with his eyes for the past hour. You need to go *do* that man, and *do* him right. Several times, in fact…."

Jayne was laughing and she patted Andrew's hand. "You're incorrigible. But you might be right. I might be lucky enough to have him all to myself for a night."

Andrew leaned forward, lowering his voice conspiratorially, "Sweetheart, luck has absolutely nothing to do with it. And because I'm so bad, I've got to ask. Is he as good as he looks?"

"Funny, but I think I might just find out…"

"So. You two haven't…"

"No. I hadn't gotten to that part of the story yet."

"Well that needs to be remedied *immediately*. Hell, he makes *me* hard. I'll bet your knickers get wet just looking at him."

Jayne choked on her Diet Coke, laughing as her eyes watered. "Is nothing off limits, Andrew?" She pinched his cheek. "I'll give you a hint. He definitely gives me the *buzz*."

"Oh, *my*…." Andrew groaned. "Hear that, girlfriend."

"Enough, you two. Here he comes," Brian warned and sipped his drink.

"What have I missed?" Nick reclaimed his seat and reached for his beer.

"I was just telling Jayne that we need to head out. I've got an early morning at the office. Now that you're here, we won't worry about leaving Jayne to her own devices. We'll leave her to *your* devices, so to speak." Andrew chuckled, shaking Nick's hand. "Good to meet you, Nick. Take good care of our girl." Andrew hugged Jayne after she released Brian and stage-whispered in her ear, "Now girlfriend, don't do anything we wouldn't do...."

Nick grinned, pulling bills from his clip to pay the tab, shaking off Brian and Andrew as they drew their wallets. "Any objections to being relegated to my company, Ms. Morgan?"

"None whatsoever." Jayne gave Nick a playful grin. For *whatever* reason, he was back. Her resolve to push him out of her life faded into oblivion. For now, anyway.

As Brian and Andrew took off on their scooters, Jayne grabbed his arm. "Tell me why you're back.."

"Let's go somewhere private to talk. How about the Sunset Pier?" He took her hand and headed out to the docks they'd walked that first day. Was it only four days since that first lunch? Four days and she'd spun a web around his heart.

Jayne didn't press him, thank God. He hadn't figured out exactly what he was going to say and he needed these few minutes to script it out in his mind. She managed to keep it light as they strolled, but he could sense her impatience. He was half-listening as she described her day.

Turning on Duval, he led her down to the pier. He pulled out a stool for her and leaned against the rail, taking in every feature of her face. God, she was stunning. The waning sunlight danced in her eyes, turning them blue against the water's reflection. Her face had a healthy glow from her time in the sun and the look in her eyes, curious, expectant but trusting, gripped his heart, constricting his lungs. He'd been right to come back. Being here with her squelched his last ounce of doubt.

His heart, still beating a little too wildly, forced him to admit he was still nervous as hell about how she'd respond to his proposition. He ran his hand over his face, rubbed his jaw, and looked out at the ocean for a few seconds while he selected his words.

Turning to face her, he said, "I thought about you while I rode today. By the time I got to Florida City, I turned around." He tried to gauge her reaction but all he could see was the question she wanted to ask. *Why?*

He continued, "Crazy, huh?"

She smiled at his use of her term, but said nothing, so he continued, "I had no idea you'd decided to leave today. Would you consider staying a couple more days? I'd like hang out with you—get to know you without all the commotion." He swiped his fingers through his hair and raised his eyebrows at her. "Will you stay? Take another *detour*?"

Jayne couldn't speak. Her heart was pounding so loudly in her ears she wasn't sure she'd heard him correctly. The more time she spent with him, the more attached she'd become...and the more it would hurt when they parted company for good. No matter how well they got along, that fact couldn't change. Sooner than later, she'd have to walk away.

She could see his uncertainty of her answer etched on his brow, though he made a valiant effort to appear at ease. And that glimpse of raw vulnerability knocked her defenses down. No matter the outcome, she'd grab whatever amount of time she could share with him and deal with the consequences later.

"Of course, I'll stay. I still can't believe you came back." She reached up and put her hand on his cheek, cupping his jaw in her palm and looked him right in the eye. "But I'm glad you did." She pulled his head down to she kiss him in what she hoped was a convincing manner, taking possession of his mouth as her tongue teased, alluding to future pleasures as she nipped his lower lip.

Catching her breath, she pulled back. "So...we'll hang out and see if we can stand each other after a day or two? Don't know about you, but I'm a habit forming drug. I come with a warning label."

He laughed and raised one eyebrow, challenging her. "Duly noted. Gotta tell you, though, so am I."

Don't I know it. I'm already jonesing for you. "Forewarned is forearmed." She laid her hand on his chest. "Where should we stay? I've checked out of the cottage. Want me to see if they have something else available?"

"I've already got a room here." He had a sheepish grin spreading across his face as he gestured to the hotel behind them.

"Really? I love this place. I usually stay here when I'm by myself. The rooms are wonderful. Did you get a good one?"

"Of course. Knowing your hotel room fetish? Wanna see? Maybe we can come up with some way to keep ourselves entertained tonight..."

She threw him a sideways glance and raised her eyebrows, then burst out laughing. "I know what they look like and I've already got a couple of ideas...but first I need to call the airport about my plane and then I need to have my bags sent over from the Westin."

"While you're doing that, I'll get drinks." He placed an order with the bartender while she made her calls.

He returned and handed her a beverage. "And I have another idea."

"Yes?" She cocked an eyebrow, sure it would be some outrageous hanging-from-a-chandelier comment.

"Let's turn off our cell phones for the night."

"*Great* idea." Jayne made a big show of turning off her phone and slipping it into her pocket. Touching her glass to his beer bottle, she watched the evening sky claim the last moments of the day, a thin red stripe all that remained along the horizon. She sighed, "I never get tired of this view."

Nick shook his head. "Me neither." But he was looking at Jayne. He laid his hand on her arm. "Need to ask—now that you've had a couple minutes to think it over. You really okay with staying?" He searched her eyes, but they were a mask.

She went silent and his heart stuttered. Had he been wrong?

Finally, she blew out a breath and said, "I am, Nick, but I'll be honest. This scares me. *Big time.* The more I'm with you, the more attached I get. We can kid around all we want, but I can't get past the truth. You're too new to the game and I'm simply not in a position to get involved with anyone right now."

He appreciated her honesty, but it stung. How should he respond? Did her past still have such a hold on her? Was she so afraid of losing someone again that she wouldn't allow herself to consider there might be another man who was worthy of her trust?

"Jayne, I do need time to adjust, but we need to see what's going on here…with us. I can't make any promises about our future, but I promise I'll never intentionally hurt you and I'll never lie to you."

"I know that, but I've been single for a long time, Nick. I've dated men who've gone through divorces, and I've dated men long-distance. Neither successfully. You need to learn how to be alone whether you realize it or not. And there's the distance issue. Relationships, whatever the parameters, are tough. We'd compound that with distance and insane schedules. Before long, we'd fizzle out because it would be too hard. I don't want to be a casualty of timing or geography. And I don't want you to get hurt because of my issues, either."

He gripped her hand. "I'd never try to replace Mack, but you should give yourself permission to live. You never know—the right man could be standing in front of you." He blew out a breath. "That said, how about if we stop living down the road and put all this shit on the shelf for a couple of days. Just hang and see how it goes. We might surprise ourselves."

God, he hated all this over-thinking. Jayne's points were logical, but why did women always have to analyze everything to death where men and relationships were concerned? All this talk was making him crazy.

He stole a sideways glance. She was working up a slow nod, and he figured she was coming to some kind of mental compromise. Eating was always a good diversionary tactic, and his stomach was rumbling. "You hungry?"

Jayne brightened and finished her drink. "Ready to go postal. You?"

"Starving. Let's go to Michael's."

"Perfect. Let's stop by the desk on our way and have them send my luggage to your room."

Nick pulled her off the bar stool and took her hand. At least they'd cleared the air and he knew where she stood. Fair enough. She might be holding back, but what did he expect? He'd shown up unexpectedly and plopped this little plan smack dab in her lap.

He'd give her however long she needed to get comfortable with the idea. He caught a whiff of her perfume and his olfactory senses kicked in. Images of time with her at the Southern Cross played through his mind. Damn, he hoped she'd get comfortable soon.

He was determined to spend quality time and learn everything he could about her, but the anticipation of getting her naked was killing him. He wanted nothing more than to be behind closed doors, skin on skin, feeling her move beneath him as he sank into her. He fought off the thought. If he didn't focus on something else, *she'd* be dinner.

TWENTY-FOUR

Shadows cast from the single candle on their small table played across Nick's features, giving him an almost predatory look as desire radiated in the glow of his eyes.

Dinner had been a drawn-out affair featuring shared delicacies from the sea while they discussed a plethora of topics. Jayne savored the Italian merlot Nick had selected, marveling how happy she was to be sitting here with him. They never ran out of words. She'd finally come to the conclusion she'd pay whatever emotional toll came due. Staying with him was the gift she'd give herself before everything changed in her world.

The waiter topped off her wine and emptied the bottle into Nick's glass, then disappeared. Nick offered a silent toast and as their eyes met, Jayne's desire for him ignited a fire deep within her that yearned to be stoked. What they'd be doing later was a foregone conclusion, an unspoken testimony to how in-sync they'd become. But in that moment, the underlying current that sizzled between them fanned the flame and was intoxicating. Now that they were alone with the night drifting ahead of them, anticipation hummed beneath her skin. She took another sip of her wine, looking at him with a renewed awareness. Here was a man she craved and he'd traveled back just to be with her. Why on earth were they still in the restaurant? *Because he was allowing her to set the pace.*

Jayne set her glass down and laid her hand on his, offering a silent communiqué.

He took a sip of his wine and settled back, cocking his head to the side, meeting her gaze. "Dessert?"

"To go?"

Nick signaled the waiter, "Check, and two chocolate tortes to go." He looked back at Jayne, "I like the way you think."

"If you like the way I *think*, everything else will blow your mind…"

They were on the same page. No crossed signals, no interruptions, only the two of them with the night ahead. Nick signed the tab and stood, grabbed the small sack and reached for her hand. They'd walked about twenty steps when she stopped and pulled him to her, laying her lips on his, backing him into a small alcove along the façade of the building.

"Umm, feeling a little feisty, huh?" he murmured.

"I'm ready for dessert *now*."

He made a little strangling noise deep in his throat, exhaled, and grabbed her hand, heading in the direction of the hotel. "Come on…"

She wasn't sure how but they made it through the maze, up the elevator, and down the walkway to the door with their clothes on. Nick opened it and let her enter first. Then she heard the door close and the dead bolt turn. The room was spacious, but the big king bed cloaked in white linens dominated the space. Nick slid his arms around her waist from behind, nuzzling her neck and she was certain the heat radiating off him was melting her skin, and would surely set off the smoke alarm. Turning, she wrapped her arms around his shoulders and let him back her toward the bed. When it hit the back of her knees, she tumbled and pulled him with her.

Her hands were everywhere, pressing against his chest, tangling in his hair, wrapping around his back. He pressed hard and heavy on top of her, kissing her, making her skin hum as his hands slid up and down her body.

She pulled back and took his face in her hands, memorizing the way his strong, chiseled jaw met her fingers. Then she tasted his lips as they melded against hers, torturing her as he slid them down her throat to kiss her neck. His hands cupped her breasts and she arched into his palms, feeling her nipples tighten, heat spreading down her stomach, the *buzz* vibrating through her as she grew wet and slick, impatient for him. She pressed closer, telling him with her body that she craved the feel of his skin against hers, needed to let his warmth spread into her.

Nick rolled back and tugged her top up and over her head. Her breath stilled as his eyes slid from her face, down to rest on her breasts, then back up to her face.

"You're beautiful." He caressed the lace on the edge of her bra with his fingertips and in a swift movement, unclasped and threw it aside, filling his hands. He looked down, appraising. "*These* are beautiful."

It was a whisper that fell hard on her ears. *Not for long…and you're the last man I'll ever be able to share them with…*

He was gentle at first, exploring her body with his fingertips ever so lightly, then his touch grew bolder as he leaned down to lick and nip. She craved the feeling of his skin and began tugging up on the hem of his shirt. He complied and yanked it over his head, pulling her to lie on her side, face to face, hugging her to him as he whispered endearments. Soft little nothings that melted into kisses.

The tickle of his wiry chest hairs against her nipples made her ache, the pulse throbbing between her legs. She hadn't known desire this raw for so long she could barely contain it. She wanted him in her, filling her. She was an animal, out of her cage and prowling, seeking her mate.

Jayne leaned over to torment his small nipples with her tongue, instantly turning them to tight buds. When Nick gave up a groan of pleasure, she took her time and slid her hands down the planes of his stomach, finally unbuckling his belt. His hands tightened on her hair and the muscles of his stomach clenched as she opened his fly, freeing him. Clasping him firmly in her hand, feeling him stiffen even more within her grasp, she was again awed by the thick length of him. Leaning down to flick her tongue across the tip, she heard him suck in a breath as he went still.

Nick rasped, "Hang on." He rolled to the side of the bed. He stood and yanked off his jeans and boxers, then leaned over to unfasten her shorts. Pulling them and her lacy panties down her legs, his gaze nearly made her blush as he ran his hand up her leg. He paused at the juncture of her thighs, "I hope you're not in a hurry…"

Jayne locked eyes with him, whispering, "We've got all night."

They might have all night, but she wanted him *now*. She ached for that release, now barely a touch away. His glorious body, illuminated by the soft glow of the light that slipped in from the balcony, held her in a trance as she soaked up the sight. Everything about him was right for her. Solid and lived-in, Nick's body radiated a mature strength that beckoned to her. Every scar, every remnant of a life fully-lived made him so much more perfect. Her eyes fell to his erection, a smug smile tugging on her lips. *Yes, perfect.*

Nick leaned over and kissed her stomach, then pulled her legs to the edge of the bed and knelt, splaying his hands on her thighs. She quivered at his touch when he started kissing the scars on her knees, his mouth moving over her slowly, feeling her pulse quicken as she offered a soft moan. Her skin was pure satin that tasted of oranges and honey, and he took his time, licking and teasing his way up her thighs, spreading them, her skin warming under his touch as he gently picked up her leg and wrapped it over his shoulder, sliding his mouth to her center. Her hands grasped his hair and the feel of her fingernails against his scalp brought his every nerve ending to life.

He tasted and savored, intent on giving as his tongue flicked over and into her until she was fiery silk. God she tasted good and he told her so. He loved doing this and he was unhurried, intent on giving her as much pleasure as she could stand. Her moans and whimpers filled him with a deep satisfaction, and when she cried out his name, clenching and shuddering, her fingers gripping his shoulders, it drove him crazy. Satisfaction filled him, and he realized he was enjoying this more than anything he could remember.

She gasped, trying to pull from his grasp, from what he was sure were deliciously painful sensations, but he couldn't stop. She was his. He owned her body as it bucked again, her cry of pleasure urging him on as he continued to taste, torturing her as she writhed, coming a second time.

Christ, *he* nearly came when she squirmed and pressed against his face, her legs tightening around his shoulders. Her response was so pure, so uninhibited, that it undid him.

But he'd just gotten started. He knew all the right ways to give her pleasure, ways he'd been imagining all afternoon during his ride. Like she'd said, they had all night.

He crawled onto the bed beside her, feeling her heart pounding against his lips as he nestled in to kiss her throat, the sweat on her skin sweet on his tongue as she caught her breath. He let his hand rest lightly between her legs and dipped his finger, the warm wetness an invitation.

"That was…incredible." Jayne panted against his ear, her heart still hammering under his lips.

"That was…a *prelude*."

Blowing out a breath, she nuzzled his neck. "If that's a prelude, you're gonna give me a heart attack."

He chuckled. "I know CPR."

Nick rolled onto his back and pulled her to him as she kissed his face, throwing her leg over his. While she made to straddle him, he grabbed her firmly by her backside, loving the feel of her as she slid across him. He groaned at the intense pleasure of the contact, growing even more rigid. He looked onto her eyes, completely entranced by the smoldering glow of them. Her breasts taunted him as they swayed above his chest.

All Jayne knew was this moment, the powerful hold of this man who scorched her soul with his touch. She poised over him and gasped as he slid deep inside her in one swift movement, smooth and so tight. She shifted and it took her a moment to settle fully on him. She braced her hands against his chest and started rocking back and forth, finally taking him to the hilt as he took her breasts in his warm palms, kneading them, bringing her nipples to tight peaks.

He guided her strokes, grasping her backside to hold her tightly to him. She watched the play of sensations slide over his face—intense pleasure… desire…need. He groaned as she slid up and down over him. He leaned his head up and took a nipple into his mouth, making her suck in her breath. She began to rock faster, tightening around him as the initial quiver of yet another orgasm pulsed. This was crazy, she'd never had more than two *ever*. His thumb vibrated against her nub, pulling her along until shudders overtook her.

Nick flipped her over onto her back as he remained deep, and wound one of her legs over his shoulder to gain purchase as he rocked, taking longer, deeper strokes, smiling down into her eyes as his thrusts grew more insistent, groaning as she clenched around him . He murmured words, lost in the sensations rolling over and over him. He only knew how good she felt and how long it had been since he'd let himself go.

He sank deeper, thrusting harder, sensing she was on the very edge again when she cried out his name, gasping endearments as she rose to meet him. He closed his eyes. He was so close but he didn't want the feeling to end. Her intensity met his and they were lightning bolts sizzling, crashing in one unified jolt of heat and electricity. Then her spasms pulsed and tightened around him and he allowed himself one final thrust before he exploded, riding that bliss into a mindless void. Jayne cried out, clinching him tightly over and over. He remained hard within her as long as he could, felt her heart pounding against his chest as his own heart answered with an echoing quake. He finally collapsed beside her, thoroughly sated, gasping.

They lay there, the ceiling fan whirring above them, cooling their damp skin. Jayne reached up and pulled a pillow to nestle under her head as she lay on her side, her fingers absently lazing over Nick's chest, the cadence of his heart keeping time with her own.

"I'm glad you came back," she breathed into his shoulder, near tears, her heart full of contentment and wonder that these feelings had eluded her for so long.

He kissed her hair. "Should've never left…"

Nick woke, Jayne's body huddled tightly against him. Her skin was cool to his touch so he pulled the covers over them and shifted to spoon around her. Glancing at the clock on the night stand, he was surprised to see it was nearly four in the morning. They'd made love, fed each other dessert, made love again, taken a shower and fallen asleep, dead to the world. He was hard, the insatiable need for her surprising him as he nuzzled her neck, winding his arm around her waist. Nick closed his eyes, inhaling. He was drunk on this woman and his world was spinning. It would be so easy to fall out of control.

Would that be so bad for a couple of days? Or for the rest of his life?

Jayne woke to the sound of Nick breathing evenly beside her. Sunlight filtered through the blinds and she glanced at the clock. Just after nine. Wow. She'd been out cold. Somehow she'd gotten a pillow and stolen Nick's covers. Then she'd allowed fatigue and the sheer contentment of being in his arms to lull her into a few hours of dreamless sleep.

But upon waking, like all other recent mornings, her few seconds of blissful ignorance were shattered by reality. *I have cancer.* Then she added today's footnote. *And now I'm in love.*

She watched him, fascinated by the lines etched across his face, the stories of his life imprinted there. How she wished she'd known more of him—more of how those lines had come to be. Then her eyes followed the line of his neck to settle on the masculine contours of his shoulders, so powerful, yet so peaceful in rest. *The lion sleeps...*She was overcome with a sense of completeness and fought to stifle the stirrings in her heart. Nick's words came to mind. *Live where you are...don't live down the road.* She'd need to enjoy this time with him and stop worrying about next week or next month. For now, they were here together and that had to be enough.

He stirred beside her, stretching. Leaning up on his elbow, he kissed her shoulder. "How'd you sleep?"

"Like a baby. You?"

"Great. You wore me out. And you snore." He grinned, kissing her shoulder again.

"Back at ya, fella. If it bothered you so much, you should've done something to make me stop."

"I did. Twice."

Jayne laughed and smacked him with her pillow. "Must not have been too terrible. You're still here."

"And I plan to stay. Worked up an appetite, too. Room service?"

"How 'bout I take you to Blue Heaven for some lobster benedict and homemade banana bread," Jayne suggested, then kissed the tip of Nick's nose.

"You're on."

"Race you to the shower."

"Not just yet..."

"What a gorgeous day." Nick turned his face to the sky. "Not a cloud. While we're out, I need to pick up a couple of shirts and some shorts. I'm out of clothes. Anything in particular you want to do?"

"Nothing and everything. What would you think about making a list of things we haven't done down here and only doing new things for the next couple of days?"

"I like it. But as many times as you've been here, we may need to get a little creative..."

"That's the fun part." Jayne bumped her shoulder to his as they strolled down the sidewalk holding hands. "And you've never had breakfast at Blue Heaven, so we're off to a good start."

"Did this morning's shower count?" Nick shot her a wicked grin.

Jayne's stomach fluttered, that delicious little twinge flashing between her legs that Nick could elicit with the slightest lift of an eyebrow. Remembering, her face grew warm but she winked at him. "Don't know about you, but it definitely counted for *me*."

TWENTY-FIVE

Jayne laid her head on Nick's shoulder and closed her eyes, resting her hand against his heart. Two days had turned into five and she dreaded the thought of leaving.

She had never known such complete contentment, and she was far from ready to go back to reality. But Nick had obligations and as much as he played down the calls she'd overheard, she knew he needed to get back to Toronto. And she had pressing matters of her own. A publishing deadline loomed, and of course she had those damned medical appointments.

She'd been tempted more than once to tell him what she faced, but she simply couldn't when it came right down to it. It would be too selfish to drag him into her drama. Knowing him as she did now, she was certain he'd drop everything to be with her—whether for support, a sense of obligation, or because he cared. Regardless of his reason, she couldn't have that. They weren't ready for something so earth quaking. Too much, too soon. He'd end up resenting her and she'd end up hating herself.

Nick stirred and shifted against her, his breath warm on her neck as he kissed her, his stubble tickling her skin.

"Good morning." She kissed his ear.

"Yes, it is," he breathed into her ear, nibbling on her lobe. His hands tangled in her hair, pulling her close, his breathing slow and deep.

Desire slammed through her. Every nerve ending tingled as his hand moved languorously down her stomach and lower to explore and tease, the sensation eliciting a shiver of pleasure. He traced hot kisses down her neck, stopping to gently bite her nipple while his hand performed magic tricks. Arching toward him, she moaned endearments, certain she'd die of the exquisite pleasure, seeking the release he so easily drew from her. She gasped and clenched against his hand, riding the waves, a tsunami of sensations washing over her.

"I want you in me, now," Jayne demanded against his neck. She pulled Nick to her, slipping her leg around his waist as he slid in, her body welcoming him as his groan vibrated against her shoulder. Knowing instinctively what he wanted, what he *needed*, she shifted to accommodate all of him, then allowed the spiking sensations to transfer from her body to his.

He stilled, then set a slow and tender pace, locking eyes with her as he took his time, stroking slow and deep, whispering tender words. He fit perfectly, and together they moved with the grace of practiced dancers, the familiarity of two who had been lovers all their lives, intimately knowing the nuances and preferences of the other's body.

Nick's long, lazy strokes, soothing and gentle, drove Jayne to another orgasm, this one so unexpected and intense that when she cried out his name and clinched, she took him right along with her. Ah, she

299

was going to miss him, and this. More than she was able to admit.

Putting the last of her clothing into her suitcase, Jayne let Nick interrupt and pull her out to the balcony of their room. "Let's enjoy this view for a few minutes."

Jayne leaned on the rail, looking toward the water as Nick stood behind her and wrapped his arms around her waist, nuzzling her neck.

"I'm glad I came back. It was a good call. We've proved something to ourselves."

Don't say it, Nick. Please don't say it. She'd been so close to saying those words herself last night and again in bed this morning, but self-preservation had prevailed. She had to put some distance between them. It would be insane to let him know that she'd fallen helplessly in love with him. She turned in his arms and gave him a conspiratorial grin. "One thing we've figured out is how to work off dessert. I've eaten my way through this island in the past five days and my jeans aren't even tight. I'd keep you around for that reason alone, biker boy."

He laughed, nodding. "Yes, we've definitely figured that out. We've had fun, eh?" He kissed the top of her head. "I'm going to miss being with you."

"Ditto. But it sounds like you've got a lot going on that needs your attention."

"I do, but that's on hold until tomorrow. We need to figure out when we can get together again. I'll look at my calendar when I get back, but I should be able to swing some time next month. We could go somewhere warm for a long weekend, you could come up to Toronto, or I can fly down to Kansas City. What sounds good to you?"

Her throat closed as she looked into his jade eyes. This was the moment she'd been dreading for five days. She'd managed to dodge his suggestions and comments until this second, but now she had to face the music.

She took a breath, going for a light brush off. "All of it sounds great. But let's wait to look at our calendars. I can only imagine how crazy your schedule must be, and I've got a serious deadline coming up on the final edits of my book that I simply can't ignore any longer. Can we talk about this next week? We'll both know more once we get back to reality."

The puzzled look on Nick's face broke Jayne's heart. Could he see right through her ruse? *No.* If he could, he'd see that her heart was crumbling. She fought the urge to come clean with him. But she couldn't. If anything, the five days alone with him had only strengthened her resolve that she couldn't and wouldn't drag him into the ordeal she faced. That would be a cheap shot on her part. He didn't deserve to face that demon again. He'd told her at length about his sister's illness and she had seen the bitterness and pain etched on his face as he spoke.

To salvage the moment, she took his face in her hands. "Nick, I'm so glad we had this little detour. It's been good for my soul."

"Mine, too. You've renewed my faith in a whole lot of things." He leaned in, kissing her.

As they pulled back, Jayne said, "We'd better get going."

"Yeah. Now that my bike's on its way to Orlando, I don't want to make my pilot wait. I might find myself on foot."

"Right. I hear she's pretty bitchy about keeping a tight schedule. And since you're paying extra for that first class flight to Orlando..."

"Gotta get my money's worth..." He grabbed her and gave her another kiss, longer, hotter. "Screw the flight. Let's just stay another day or two."

Jayne laughed and danced away, a dramatic accent to her voice. "Aw, you're way too easy. Come. Let us be away, you naughty, naughty boy. Your chariot awaits."

☼☼☼

Nick circled Jayne's plane while she conducted her pre-flight check. He looked it over as thoroughly as she had his Harley. He liked the lines of the snazzy eight-seater and recognized the quality.

He let out a low whistle, nodding his approval as they both completed their inspections, "She's a beauty. And it's obvious you're as particular about her as I am about my bike."

Jayne beamed. "Thanks. You ready?"

She crawled in and he followed. Cockpits were notoriously tight, making him feel that much broader as his shoulder pressed against hers. She leaned over and showed him how to adjust his seat to accommodate his legs.

"Here's your head set. This way you'll be able to hear the chatter between the various aircraft and the control tower, and then we'll be able to talk over the roar of the engines."

She made short work of securing her clearances and in minutes they were racing down the runway.

Her efficiency was impressive. Her command and comfort spoke to her skill. He shook his head, smiling to himself, deciding for at least the hundredth time that she was hot shit.

They flew to the east and then she banked north to allow him the preferred view from his side of the plane as she followed the coast line. The sky was particularly blue and the sun danced in shimmering streams across the water. He was taken by the sheer joy Jayne exuded as the aviator in charge.

"To quote you, I know I'll tell you later, but I'm having a great time. Thanks for this first class seat to Orlando."

She smiled broadly. "If you're having half as much fun flying with me as I had riding with you, then we're even. I'd rather be doing this than doing just about anything else."

"Really? *I'm hurt.*" He grabbed his heart and he looked at her with one raised eyebrow.

"I said *just* about. And no, this could never be as good as *that* was. *Close,* but you get the prize...."

She tossed him a wicked grin, making him groan inwardly as he paged through moments they'd shared in the past few days. He couldn't remember a time when he'd had so much fun or had so thoroughly enjoyed being with someone.

"As do you. You *are* the prize, babe.... and I can see why you love to fly. This is right up there with some of the best rides I've taken on the Harley."

Jayne hated how quickly the time passed as they covered the miles to Orlando. They were never at a loss for words, never ran out of things to discuss, and when they paused, silence was comfortable. As they drew closer to their destination, her heart ached with a pain she hadn't experienced in years.

Knowing she'd close this chapter when she watched him fly off in his Gulfstream, it was all she could do to hold it together. Oh, how she wanted to be selfish and tell him everything, make him swear to be there to hold her hand and diminish her fears.

Jayne owed him the final conversation. She'd been a coward while they were in Key West. She'd tried to explain that first night, but he'd suggested she was living down the road. After that, she'd dodged the topic for fear of driving a wedge between them during their time together. Now it was time to pay the fiddler.

Cleared for landing, Jayne put her expertise to the test as a nasty cross wind challenged her skills in setting the Baron down smoothly. Breathing a sigh and grinning over at Nick, whose face was a little chalky, Jayne said, "My first flight instructor called training in this kind of wind *character building*. You okay?"

"I'm fine. And impressed." He exhaled loudly and laughed as he rolled his shoulders. "Couldn't have done it better myself."

She taxied to the refueling area.

"Let's leave the plane here with the ground crew and grab something to eat at the diner while you check on your jet," Jayne suggested as she shut down the engines.

"Sounds great." He leaned over to kiss her. She traced his jaw with her fingertip, brushing her finger across the stubble on his chin, memorizing his face, then looked into his smoldering green eyes.

He held her gaze and started to say something, but instead leaned down and kissed her again, really kissed her as if her life depended on it. She was trembling inside and needed to get out of the plane before she lost her resolve and became a blithering idiot. Truth and tears were way too close to the surface right then.

The 1950's style diner was packed. Jayne smiled at a waitress as she slid into a booth. "Hi. I'd like a cheeseburger with the works, a Diet Coke, and a chocolate shake. Nick?"

He glanced at the menu and said, "I'll have the same, but a regular Coke." Nick looked out the window and squinted, "I think my plane just arrived."

Jayne watched the sleek Gulfstream touch down and nodded. "Talk about perfect timing. She's gorgeous. Will we have time for me to get a look at her?"

"Sure. I'll send a text to my pilots to go ahead and grab some lunch and get her refueled. We'll check her out after we finish our burgers."

"So tell me, what's on your agenda this week? Building a skyscraper, a convention center, or just some gazillionaire's mansion?"

Nick feigned a studious expression. "Couple of castles, one small city." Then he laughed. "Actually, I'm heading for Quebec City tomorrow afternoon. We've been asked to look at a site for a new hotel."

"Big hotel?"

"Yeah. It's a Four Seasons. We've built for them before, and this will be a great project. We're working up a preliminary cost analysis. The design is good, but it needs a few modifications according to my top engineer, so I want to look it over personally. What about you? What's on your docket for the next couple of weeks?"

Oh, just a bit of cancer survival prep…doctor appointments, major surgery, streamlining my life to accommodate this hideous illness…

Somehow, she managed to smile as she mentally edited her calendar. "Manuscript revisions. Lots of them. That portion of my book I gave you to read? That's my demon. I can't seem to get my arms around the resolution of that character's conflict. I know once I get back to my office and concentrate, I'll get it worked out. Those suggestions you made were spot on and I'm going to incorporate them. Fresh perspective is great when you hit a wall."

"Let me know any time you want me to relax by a pool and read your work. I'm your man. And I'm going to read everything you've written. I've got a lot of catching up to do. Can't let Sean be your biggest fan in our crew of rowdies."

The server arrived with their plates and Jayne caught a whiff of the sizzling burger. She smiled at the woman. "Thank you. These look and smell delicious."

Contemplating her shake, she said, "This is too pretty to drink."

"Watch me." Nick took a big pull on his straw.

Plucking the cherry off the top, she raised an eyebrow at him. "Bet you can't do this..." She pulled the stem off the cherry and placed it in her mouth. A couple of seconds later, she retrieved it and showed him a tiny knot.

"How'd you do that?" Nick's eyebrows shot up.

"Talent."

He lowered his voice and winked at her. "Only one of many..."

Nick's nerves were frayed and raw from the inside out as they walked toward his jet. The conversation looming before them was the proverbial elephant in the corner. He wasn't ready for their time together to end, but he had to get back to work. He'd realized yesterday that he needed to slow things down. As much as he hated to admit it, Jayne was right about his need for time. In the past twenty-four hours, the demands of his work and messages about settlement issues from Alynn had started to weigh on him. He didn't have things figured out at all.

He didn't want to be alone, but he wasn't ready to have someone in his life twenty-four-seven. Not that he was interested in playing the field. He just needed his life to slow down.

He had to come clean, or she'd see him for what he was—a liar and a coward. Either way, he'd demolish the little bit of faith and trust she'd been so hard-pressed to place in him. God, he suddenly felt ancient, and more than a little shitty.

Entering the lobby of the terminal, he spied his senior pilot standing at the counter. He extended his hand to the older man. "John, how's it going? You guys made good time."

"Afternoon, sir. Had a good tail wind. We'll pay for it on the way back, trust me."

"John, this is Jayne Morgan. She's a fellow pilot. Told her she could visit the office."

After a tour of the elegant jet, Jayne headed down the steps from the cabin, tossing him a grin. "Thanks for showing me how the other half live, Nick. She's a beauty." She glanced at her watch, dismayed to note the late hour. "I know you need to get going and so do I. Why don't you walk me back to my plane and I'll be on my way."

Nick laid his hand across her shoulder as they walked across the tarmac in relative silence. She was relieved to see the ground crew just pulling away. At least they'd have a couple minutes of privacy. Her heart hurt and there was no way around what she needed to do. He leaned on the wing and faced her as she placed her hands on his chest.

She studied the ground, then took a breath and met his gaze. "This has been the best week I can remember. I've had a great time." She leaned up and kissed him, wrapping her fingers in his hair at the back of his head, memorizing the feel of the silky locks.

He put his hands around the back of her shoulders, holding her close. "You caught me by surprise, Jayne. Meeting someone like you was the last thing I ever expected."

He was still holding her close as he leaned into her ear and said, "I'll be in touch as soon as I get back, and let's see if we can't manage to join Sean and Meg in March. I need to get used to being single, but I'd like to see you when we can figure out our schedules."

The declaration shocked her. She was so relieved that he could finally admit the truth.

"It'll be good for both of us to get back to work. Give ourselves some time away from each other to gain perspective."

"Perspective isn't going to change the fact that I care about you."

She pulled back and placed her hands on his chest as his hands rested on her waist. Looking him straight in the eye, she continued, "I understand, but we'll both get busy with our respective obligations. Let's not make promises that might be hard to keep."

"Are you saying that you don't want to at least give this a shot?" Nick was looking at her oddly.

"...Nooo." *Here goes.* She sucked in a breath, then rushed on, "Nick, I just don't want either of us to have unrealistic expectations."

It took a moment for her words to register in his eyes and the hurt she detected made her hate herself. She took his hand. "Please don't misunderstand. I *do* care about you. But you need to be fair to yourself, and to me." *And I've got to do the same...*

He chewed on his lower lip and nodded, a frown creasing his brow. "Alright."

His tone rang cold, almost dismissive, but she couldn't take her words back now. It had been hard enough to say them. And if she didn't get away from him in the next few minutes, she'd make an even bigger mess of this hideous farewell by turning into a blithering puddle and telling him everything.

She forced her brightest smile, determined to ignore the stiff set of his shoulders. "Now it's time for you to kiss me goodbye. Do it right, mister—make sure I'll miss you terribly. And I'll do likewise."

At first he resisted, the edge of his hurt feelings slicing her resolve, but she held fast as he tried to pull back. Finally, her insistence paid off and he leaned forward, meeting her lips.

His shoulders loosened as she gripped them, and after a few seconds, she was able to tease his mouth open with her tongue, and lingered to savor the warmth of his lips on hers as he finally responded with a kiss that went on and on. He seemed as reluctant as she was to end it.

"Whew." She blew out a breath and raised her eyebrows, giving him a tight hug. "That'll hold me for a while." *Or forever…*

"Not *too* long, if I have anything to say about it. If you've gotten the impression I'm just going to fly off and disappear, you're wrong. We'll just *see* how busy our calendars really are. I can be pretty creative with my schedule when I've got a good reason." He gave her a quick kiss and another hug. "Remember, you're a habit-forming drug…"

As are you, my handsome biker boy… She leaned up to kiss him one last time, and when he finally let go of her, she stepped toward the cockpit and pulled the door open, climbing in. "Give me a call later to let me know you've made it home safely."

"Likewise, babe. Safe flight. As they say in Russia, *Dosvidaniya.*"

"Yes. Until we meet again." Jayne settled in the cockpit, pulled on her sunglasses and headset in time to hide the tears threatening to spill. Nick stepped back from her plane and she started the engines and busied herself with radioing the tower for clearances. He was standing off to the side of the parking area waiting for her to depart, so she gave him a quick wave, touched her heart and blew him a kiss before she taxied away. As she sailed down the runway and her plane caught air, she glanced over and saw him standing in the same spot, waving his arm in a broad goodbye. This time she didn't try to stem the tears as they flowed freely down her cheeks. She'd just forfeited the man who had taken possession of her heart.

TWENTY-SIX

March, Kansas City

Damp, thick fog veiled her grounds, the yard lights casting eerie beams against the silhouettes of the trees and shrubs in the hour before dawn. Jayne stood at the window after finally giving up the pretense of sleep a good thirty minutes before the alarm.

Her bag was packed and her clothes were laid out—all she had to do was shower and get to the hospital. How could she have imagined five weeks was such a long time?

Jayne stepped into the shower, fighting a wave of fear and anger...*again*. No matter how scared or pissed off she was, she couldn't change what she faced or what she'd go through in a few short hours, or the next months for that matter. Allowing negative thoughts to creep in and take control was the worst thing she could do. She'd gone down this road a million times in her mind, and she'd get through it—come hell or high water.

Drying off and standing naked before her mirror, she studied her body. This was the last time she'd see it like this...whole...unaltered...*intact*.

Focusing on her breasts, she cupped them in her hands, closing her eyes as she ran her fingertips across her nipples. By this afternoon, these would be gone, along with the sensations and pleasures she derived through them. Sure, she'd have replacements one day, but they wouldn't be the same.

A flash of the nights spent in Nick's arms gripped her and lingered for a moment too long, leaving a keening pain and she reached down and gripped the edge of the vanity, her knuckles going white. God, she missed hearing his voice.

They'd talked a couple of times during their first week apart, but she'd managed to avoid his calls for the past week, dying inside every time his voice sounded on the recorder. She'd sent him a couple of perfunctory text messages, three short emails and had left him a quick voice mail when she knew he couldn't answer, but that was growing thin. She kept all his messages, listening to them over and over, missing him with every breath. His tone, amicable and warm at first, was becoming more frustrated, his impatience with her silence more apparent with each message.

Nick wouldn't keep calling. He wasn't that kind of man. His pride would force him to say the hell with her and move on. In truth, a small part of her wished he'd hurry up and get it over with. Yet her heart dreaded the day his silence was final. Jayne hated herself for what she was doing, but it had to be this way. Her predictions of the steep toll she'd pay for dropping her defenses were ringing true. Now the ferryman wanted his due.

Long moments later, she took another look in the mirror. Sure, *the girls*, as Mack had called them, looked perfect and beautiful.

But they were trying to kill her. And thinking of them this way was the only way she could get through this day. In a few hours, she'd be exchanging her breasts for another chance at life. Those were her nurse's words. And she agreed that it was a pretty fair trade.

Jayne's mouth watered as she followed the tantalizing aroma of brewing coffee to her kitchen. Unfortunately, doctor's order for clear liquids eliminated that option.

"Morning, Leigh. Ummm, that sure smells good."

Looking up from buttering her toast, Leigh frowned. "Oh, crap. Didn't even think about how selfish I was to make this pot."

"No sweat."

Leigh cocked an eyebrow. "How're you doin' this morning, hon?"

Jayne shrugged. "Okay, I guess. This is a lot harder than anyone tells you it's going to be."

"I'm sure it is." Leigh came to Jayne's side and wrapped her arm around her shoulder. "I can't begin to imagine what's going through your head, but I'm here for whatever you need, whenever you need it. For that matter, we all are."

"I know, and thank you. You have no idea how much it means to have you here today. I love my brother, but I needed a girlfriend for this."

Leigh pulled her close for another hug in lieu of more words.

Countless hours of conversation in the past two weeks had allowed Jayne to give voice to her deepest worries and hopes, forging an even stronger bond between the two of them. Leigh seemed to have a

313

knack for saying and doing exactly the right thing at exactly the right moment, which was why she had asked Leigh to accompany her to the hospital for the surgery. Her brother and sister-in-law would arrive that afternoon, but Jayne needed one of her divas for the first leg of this journey.

She blew out a breath and squared her shoulders, a forced smile on her lips. "Guess we should be going."

A low murmur of voices drew Jayne from a distant tunnel, her eyelids struggling to stay open so she could see the faces surrounding her.

"Well, Jayne Elizabeth. Looks like you're finally going to join the party." *Okay, no mistaking Leigh's drawl.*

"Hey, Sis. Good to see you." *A kiss on her forehead. That had to be her brother, Michael.*

"Hi, honey. Welcome back." *Meg? When did she get here?*

Her sister-in-law, Joanne, leaned down and kissed her cheek, squeezing her hand.

A nurse stood at her side, holding her wrist. As the room came into focus and she recalled the day's events, a stab of panic coursed through her. Glancing down, all she could see were sheets, and the tubes attached to her hand and arms forced her to remain still. Bright bouquets filled the window sills, counters and tables, taking the glare off the stark, plain walls of her hospital suite, drawing her attention from the beeping machine next to her bed.

Michael and Joanne stood beside the nurse and Leigh and Meg were on her left, offering encouraging smiles, but remaining silent while the nurse performed her tasks.

"Jayne, I'm Sue. You're back from recovery and the doctor will be in shortly to talk with you. Still a little groggy?"

She nodded, and croaked, "Yes." Her words rasped as she tried to swallow. Her throat hurt like hell.

"Here. Take a little sip."

A straw pressed to her lips and she decided Sprite was her new favorite beverage—it tasted delicious and so cool on her raw throat.

"Your throat's going to be a little sore from the vent, but by tomorrow it should be back to normal. Any nausea?"

Jayne considered the question, whispering, "A little. Not too bad."

"If you need to throw up, press this button and I'll come running. But here's a little basin just in case. Pretty normal after general anesthesia. We need to get something for you to eat. Maybe some soda crackers and more Sprite for starters, then we'll see how you're doing. Can't load you up with your pain meds until we get some food down the hatch. I'll be back in a few minutes."

The woman made a couple of notes on her clipboard, patted Jayne's leg and sailed out of the room, efficiency personified.

"How long was I in surgery?"

Leigh answered, "About four hours. Your doctor came out after surgery and told us he was pleased. Everything went well. Liz and Cara have been calling and texting all afternoon. I've let them know you're doing great and will talk to them tomorrow."

"Thanks. You guys should go get some supper. I'll be fine. And thank you for coming."

"Wow, you must still be on drugs, little sister. So formal with us," her brother laughed, "though I am pretty hungry. Dinner's not a bad idea. You probably need to rest for a while." Michael nodded at the girls. "Can I take you ladies out for a bite? And Jaynie, what sounds good to you?"

"Maybe a chocolate milkshake and fries from Winstead's?" Jayne forced a smile. Nothing sounded great, but it would make Michael feel better to be doing something for his little sister.

Jayne's doctor arrived, providing the perfect opportunity for the foursome to exit. He flipped through the chart, scribbling a couple of notes, then stepped to her bedside, offering her a warm smile as he looked her in the eye. "How're you feeling, Jayne?"

She really liked this guy. He was old enough to have great experience in his back pocket, but young enough to be progressive and up-to-date on the latest advances. And she trusted him. She met his steady gray-eyed gaze. "Pretty good, Doc. Now tell me. How did it go?" She had to hear it from him. Had to know exactly what she'd discover when the bandages came off, fear holding her hostage.

"Surgery went perfectly. The tumor is gone and we have clean margins. We performed the bilateral mastectomies, and we were able to preserve your excess skin, which makes the reconstruction easier—we won't need to graph skin from your stomach or back to make your new breasts. I inserted tissue expanders to hold everything in place until the next step. They'll be a little uncomfortable in the beginning, but worth it in the long run. You have drainage tubes on both sides, and they'll need stay in for a week or two, depending on how you're mending."

Now for the big question. She hesitated, took a breath, then asked, "Okay, so will I have to go through chemo?"

The doctor frowned and patted her arm. "I'm afraid so. We don't want to take any chances.

Everything is very positive, but you're not out of the woods just yet."

"I understand….it is what it is. So, Doc…and I know you can't say for sure, but do you feel that—"

He must've read the fear in her eyes. He took her hand and rested his hip on the bed. "Jayne, you're going to beat this. In fact, I'll venture to say you're going to knock this out of the ball park. You've still got to give it the old one-two, but you're young and strong, and we did all the right things in the operating room. The chemo will be our insurance plan."

"How soon can I go home?"

"Oh, a day or two. Let's see how you're doing. There won't be much pain, but I want to be sure we avoid infection and I want you to be comfortable with your drains and how to care for them."

A little later Jayne woke to find Harrison standing at her bedside, holding her hand. He was in scrubs with a stethoscope around his neck, a frown marring his classically handsome face.

"That bad, Dr. Carter?" Jayne smiled into his blue eyes.

"Hello beautiful. How're you feeling?"

"Not too bad. The roses are gorgeous. Thank you."

He leaned down and gave her a kiss on the cheek. "You're welcome."

"You still on shift?"

"Just finishing up. I stopped by earlier, but you were sound asleep."

She knew he'd come, knew he'd keep a vigilant watch over her, and was humbled by his support and loyalty. In spite of what had come and gone between them, she loved him, and she hoped in time he'd come to accept her as just a friend.

She'd called Harrison as soon as she'd returned from the Keys to tell him her news. He'd have been hurt if he'd found out through the hospital grapevine. He'd been clinical in his approach, and that was exactly what she'd needed. He approved of her choices in doctors and had helped her navigate the maze of procedures and paperwork. She knew he'd be there for her, no matter what, yet she couldn't take advantage of him. He was still in love with her. She could see it in his eyes every time they were together.

"I need to step into the bathroom. Would you mind unhooking my IV so I don't have to call the nurse?"

"Sure."

Jayne waited while he clamped off the tubes, then allowed him to help her ease out of bed and into the bathroom, joking with him about her stylish hospital gown, slit up the front instead of the back.

He pulled the door closed as he stepped out. "Whistle if you need me."

Jayne's phone vibrated across the bedside table. Harrison reached for it without thinking. "Harrison Carter."

There was a long pause at the other end. Finally a deep male voice said, "I'm looking for Jayne Morgan. Did I dial the wrong number?"

"No. But Jayne's not available right now."

"Okay...Tell her Nick called and I'll call back. Thanks."

The line went dead, so Harrison looked at the caller ID. Nick McCord. Not a name he recognized. Probably something to do with publishing. She didn't need to worry about business right now. If it was important, he'd call back.

Jayne's girlfriends arrived, so he set the phone down, immediately dismissing the call.

He stuck out his hand. "Leigh. Nice to see you again."

"You, too, Harrison. And let me introduce you to another of our friends. This is Meg Ewing. Meg, meet Dr. Harrison Carter, a dear friend of Jayne's."

Hmmm, so that was how Jayne described him to her friends. Disappointment washed over him, along with a grudging acceptance. He'd never understand why some women couldn't appreciate the value of having a good man in their lives. Jayne needed him—especially now. But there was no convincing her of that.

Jayne shuffled to her bed. "Hi. How was dinner? Bring me something good?"

"Of course. All your favorites so you can pick and choose." Leigh grinned and opened the bag. "And I'll take one for the team and eat whatever you don't want."

Harrison helped Jayne get settled in bed and reconnected her IV's, giving her a brief kiss. He shook his head and chuckled as Leigh set a chocolate shake, cheeseburger, key lime pie, tater tots and French fries on Jayne's tray.

"Good night, ladies." He'd never begin to comprehend the bond between these women or their weird dietary preferences.

☼☼☼

Nick paced his study. He'd been unable to reach Jayne all week, and now some guy answers her phone? Says she's not *available*? What the hell was that about? They'd both been busy since they left the Keys, but he'd had a tough time connecting with her at all. Maybe there was a reasonable explanation? Maybe this Carter fellow was a work associate who'd just happened to answer her phone...

Or maybe he was the reason Jayne was so distant...

He shook his head. No, Jayne wasn't like that. She had too much class to blow him off for another man without a conversation. But why wasn't she taking or returning his calls? He'd try one more time and if he didn't get a response, he was *done.*

He wasn't going to keep calling. She knew his number. He'd left several messages, but for some reason she didn't want to talk to him. Time to take the hint and move on. Tough to admit, but he was hurt. The couple of weeks without her had made him miss her more, rather than less. What could be going on with her?

Welcome back to the wonderful world of dating, big guy...

☼☼☼

Jayne hated riding in the wheelchair, but no amount of complaining changed the hospital's policy. So she had no choice but to allow Michael to push her to the front drive. Her nurse, Leigh, Meg, and Joanne were loaded down with vases and baskets of flowers, and she had Harrison's dozen roses in her lap. As quiet as she'd tried to keep her trip to the hospital, the few friends who knew had gone overboard.

Her cell phone rang, but it was in her travel bag and too difficult get to, so she let it go to voice mail. Once she got in the car, she found it and saw Nick's name on the missed calls alert. Then she heard the beep advising her of a new voice mail delivery. She punched the code, closing her eyes at the sound of his voice as the message began, her heart grieving as his message became clear.

"Hi Jayne. I've been trying to reach you all week with no success. I hope you're all right. I'm sure there's some reason you haven't returned my calls, but I can't figure it out. Either way, you know my number. I won't keep calling, but I'd like to hear from you. Call me."

A silent tear leaked from her eye. She hated the hurt in his voice, hated that she was the reason for that hurt. *Ah, Nick. I'm so sorry it has to be this way. You have no idea how much I want to talk to you, see you again. But this is for the best...*

TWENTY-SEVEN

Late April, Chicago

Nick settled on the tall, leather stool, sipped his scotch, and glanced into the mirror covering the back of the bar. In the reflection, he could see a few patrons gathered in groups of two's and three's in clusters of club chairs, the hum of their conversations as refined and understated as their business suits.

A startling image appeared in the mirror at the moment he heard the unmistakable twang of her accent. He stood as she strode toward the bar, grinning as Leigh's eyes widened.

"As I live and breathe! *Nick McCord.* I hardly recognized you in your Sunday-go-to-meetin' clothes." Leigh approached him and fingered his lapel. "Far cry from the leathers, Vespa boy. And my, don't you do justice to Armani. How are you, Nick?"

"I'm well, Leigh." Chuckling, Nick pulled her into a bear hug. He was happy to see this woman and hear the tones of her southern banter again. He stood back, giving her a head to toe nod. "You look fantastic." If possible, she was even more impressive in her black suit and heels than she'd been in her tailored Key West mode. He liked her style—the pearls and diamonds were an elegant touch as they graced her earlobes and draped over the front of her blue silk blouse.

"Well thank you, Nick."

"How are you?"

"Doin' fine, and better now that we've run into *you*. Let me introduce you to my husband." She turned to the man who had followed her in. "Nick McCord, meet Charlie Wallace. Charlie, Nick's one of the fellows from Toronto we met in Key West that I told you about."

"Charlie, good to meet you." Nick sized Leigh's husband up quickly as they shook hands. Slightly shorter and a couple of years older than Leigh, he was solid with a strong chin and his rugged face was dominated by piercing, intelligent eyes. His bald pate and firm grip alluded to a menacing countenance that disappeared when he grinned. The custom tailored suit screamed of Savile Row. Understated, yet of impeccable detail and quality, and Nick figured Charlie was a lot like his suit. His gut echoed the impression.

"What brings you to Chicago, Nick?" Charlie asked.

"I'm got a project meeting in the morning. You?"

Leigh answered, "One of my clients is coming in for a big book signing and launch tomorrow and I'm here for moral support."

Nick's heart quickened and his gut clenched. "Jayne?" Nick caught Leigh and Charlie exchanging the briefest of glances and he could've kicked himself for sounding so eager.

"No. It's Amanda Stewart. Jayne avoids promotions and signings. You know how private she is." Leigh offered what he interpreted as an apologetic smile. "Hey, if you don't have plans, join us for dinner. We're got a reservation at Shaw's Crab House."

"That sounds great. I was going to order room service and work for a couple of hours. This is a far better option." Catching the bartender's eye, he motioned to Leigh and Charlie. "How about joining me for a drink first?"

As they relocated to a table near the roaring fireplace, Leigh tallied her options. Running into Nick like this was such a fluke. Should she call Jayne to tell her about seeing him, or should she wait until she had concrete intel. One thing about it, Jayne was way off base where Nick was concerned. She'd been insane to push him away. Leigh understood her reasons, but certainly didn't agree with them. Nick should've been given the chance to stay in the game or bow out once he knew the score. Instead, he'd been shut out before he stepped up to the plate.

She finished her drink and caught Charlie's eye. "Think we should head on over? Our reservation's in fifteen minutes."

Nick signed the tab and stood. "Let me drop my briefcase in my room. I'll meet you in the lobby."

Standing next to her husband in the elevator, Leigh chuckled. "I can't believe this. What are the chances?"

"I like the guy. Jayne should've thought twice about this one. Too bad she had to cancel her plans to join us."

"Wouldn't that have been perfect? And sweetheart, she *did* think twice. If she hadn't been sick, I think she'd have held on to Nick for dear life. Oh, that reminds me—we need to check on her tonight. Meg was flying back to D.C. this morning, so she's alone again. This last chemo treatment knocked her down."

She followed Charlie into the marble foyer and continued, "Anyway, did you see the look on Nick's face when he thought she might be here?"

"Yeah, I caught that. But he won't bring her up again. Nick's astute enough to know it would be awkward for you. He also figures she's dumped him because she doesn't care, and no man wants to look like a fool. We've got to throw the guy a bone. I feel for him."

"I promised her that I wouldn't tell, but I can't help feeling he should know. Everything happens for a reason, and here we are with him. We've run into him because Jayne needs him whether she's willing to admit it or not."

"Honey, you *can't*. It's her business who she tells, and you've given your word—plain and simple."

"You know I'd never break my word. But I might navigate the perimeter a bit..."

Shaw's Crab House, with its campy 1940's atmosphere, drew Nick in when he caught a heady whiff of fresh bread mingling with garlic. His stomach rumbled. It had been hours since breakfast, and he was famished.

He followed Charlie and Leigh to a roomy leather and brocade banquette, mentally shaking his head at their chance encounter as he settled across from the couple. What were the odds?

"What do you recommend?" Nick looked from his menu to Leigh.

"I'm having the pan-fried sea bass. They do a terrific job with their seafood. Charlie, you having your usual?"

"Yes. I'll get the stuffed shrimp to share and then I'm having the filet and lobster."

Nick looked back at his menu, "I think I'll try the blackened grouper, and some calamari for the three of us." Nick was enjoying himself for the first time in many weeks. He appreciated Charlie's sharp intellect and Leigh's wit. The only tough part was being with people so intimately connected to Jayne. Since she'd pushed him away, he'd struggled to relegate her to the recesses of his mind. But being here with Leigh, he realized he hadn't pushed Jayne out of his thoughts at all. Instead, Jayne was the invisible fourth at their table. He could hear her laugh, think how she might respond to something he said, or some private joke they might've shared. He frowned, irritated by how she preyed on his mind. He didn't want to bring her up again, but she hovered over the table. *Not* talking about her was worse than talking about her.

Giving in to his curiosity, his heart pounding, he finally asked, "So, how's Jayne?"

Leigh's eyes brightened at the question. "She's had a lot going on recently. We're getting ready to launch her latest novel, and she's just polishing the next one that's sitting in the wings. In fact, she was supposed to meet us here for a couple of days but had to cancel at the last minute."

Nick swallowed. How would he have handled running into her? He still couldn't get a read on why she'd cut off communication with him after a few brief conversations. He figured she had her reasons, but it would've been nice to know what was really going on. They'd gotten along so well and then she'd just said goodbye.

He tabled his thoughts and said, "She let me read some chapters of *Out of Time* when we were in Florida. Since then, I've managed to read all of her books and I'll admit, she's changed my mind about fiction. They were good." Every time he walked past a book store or by an airport kiosk, thoughts of her sucker punched him in the solar plexus.

Charlie nodded. "I know. Before Leigh and I met, I only read legal briefs and the *Wall Street Journal*, but now I get a first read of some great books. It's addictive."

Leigh reached over and patted her husband's hand. "Charlie's become my acid test. If he gives the manuscript a thumbs up, it usually does very well. Anyway, I'll probably see Jayne in the next couple of weeks. I can't wait to tell her we ran into you. Can I give her a message?" Leigh looked him in the eye, unspoken questions floating between them.

"Give her my best." Then he grinned. "And tell her I'm still waiting for an autograph."

Leigh laid her hand on his arm. "I'll be happy to do that. I know she'll be thrilled to hear how well you're looking. And on another note, I've gotta know if Greg Halverson is still up to his old antics."

Nick nodded. "Of course. Even on this bid for Four Seasons, he did his damnedest to undercut my company. We've put some safeguards in place to ensure he can't do as much damage as he did previously and the word's getting out that he's crooked, but there will always be jobs he snags. And problems he causes. I'm his private campaign. His brother gets out of prison in about three years and I'm sure things will get interesting when the two team up. Until then, we're just keeping our noses to the grindstone."

"I can't believe that jerk had the audacity to try to get in touch with Jayne again," Charlie said.

"What?" Nick dropped his fork, white hot anger flashing through him.

"Not much to tell, really. Halverson managed to track Jayne down and sent flowers and cards to her home. Then he called her, and *that* freaked her out. We have no idea how he got his hands on her unlisted number. She refused the flowers and mail, and she's had her number changed. I don't think he's tried to contact her recently, so hopefully Halverson's given up."

"Unbelievable." Nick shook his head. "I had no idea."

"I'm sure Jayne didn't want to worry you, or cause more problems between you and Halverson."

"If he bothers her again, I need to know." Nick was beyond vexed. Was Halverson deliberately harassing Jayne to egg him into some type of confrontation? Not that he blamed any man for wanting Jayne, but first Alynn and now Jayne? Could there be a correlation? Was Jayne avoiding him because of the trouble she was having with Halverson? Thinking that staying away from Nick would get Halverson to leave her alone?

Charlie stepped in, looking him in the eye, conveying concern beyond his words. "I hope you know we're all worried about this lunatic. I've done a little background check on him and if he continues to harass her, we'll take legal action. And I honestly understand how you feel. We'll let you know if anything else occurs. I'm hoping he's given up and moved on." He wiped his napkin across his mouth and settled back, "But enough about Halverson for tonight. I want to hear about your bike trips. Leigh told me you fellows ride all over the continent."

☼☼☼

Leigh crossed her arms over her chest and looked at the lights flickering along Michigan Avenue, fifteen stories below their suite. She glanced back at her husband, propped up on pillows in their huge bed. This situation with Nick and Jayne frustrated the hell out of her. There had to be something she could do.

328

"You know—" Her mouth clamped shut as she frowned, rethinking her comment.

Charlie looked at Leigh over the top of his reading glasses, laying aside the contract he'd been reviewing, "What?"

"Oh, I can't help thinking Jayne is making a tactical error. I've got to do something, even if it's wrong."

"Leigh, it's not like you to meddle."

"I'm inclined to make an exception this time. Gotta ponder it, though."

"Why don't you sleep on it. Maybe the answer will come to you in the morning."

"I'm too unsettled to sleep. This is making me crazy." She flipped off the overhead lights and padded across the room, following the glow of the bedside lamp.

"Hmmm, I've got a couple of ideas if you're wide awake."

Charlie winked and gave her the devilish grin that always made her heart flip. God love this man and the way he could make her toes curl with a simple glance.

Looking at him, a throaty chuckle underlying her words, she offered, "I was just thinking the very same thing. Your place or mine?"

"Road trip."

Leigh laughed out loud. "You're so bad...but you read my mind." She stepped next to him and slowly pulled off his reading glasses, then removed the paperwork from his hand and set it on the nightstand. Her eyes lingered on his tightly muscled chest and shoulders as the butterflies raced around in her stomach. She traced a perfectly manicured nail across his cheek, then murmured, "You *do* know that I simply adore you?"

She felt him slide his thumb down the opening of her silk wrapper, then heard his deep sigh of satisfaction. She watched his face slide into a surprised smile as he discovered the sheer black lace teddy.

"Hmm, *very nice*. I see you've been shopping."

"Little present from Jayne Elizabeth. From her to you…" Leigh chuckled.

"Remind me to put her on my Christmas list."

She leaned down and kissed him fully on the lips. Even after all the years of being together, he still made her heart hammer and her breath catch in her throat. She pulled the covers back and knelt beside him, grasping his erection. Then in a slow, fluid move she took him lovingly and fully into her mouth. Knowing just what to do to push him to the brink without letting him careen over the edge, she led him on the first leg of their road trip as her tongue and hands worked in concert.

Miles later, Charlie was snoring softly beside her and Leigh's thoughts returned to Jayne and Nick. *I ran into him for a reason.* Knowing she had to figure out something, she tossed, finally slipping into a fitful slumber.

Six floors above them, Nick rambled around in a room that was suddenly too large and too empty. Jayne was right about men not wanting to be alone. Difference was, this wasn't about being alone. It was about being without *her*. He was restless, had been that way more often than not in the past couple of months. He'd tried blaming work and the divorce, but that was bullshit. Hard to admit, but there was only one real reason he was so unsettled. He missed Jayne.

There it was, and it was futile to argue the fact any longer. He'd crashed into that realization during dinner. Leigh's sass and intelligence were so similar to Jayne's, and once Charlie asked about the bikes, the stories of the weekend escapades unfolded. He'd enjoyed reliving the hilarity, but talking about it kept Jayne right beside him at the table, and that thoroughly unnerved him. His legs were as wobbly as a young colt's where thoughts of her were concerned.

Nick still couldn't understand why she'd disappeared, but time away from her had forced him to re-focus on his work and the projects at hand. He'd channeled his restless energy into his company projects. McCord Consolidated was busy and he had to stay on top of the game if he wanted to continue thriving during the economic downturn.

The term *divorced* still bothered him. It was a label he took very personally. Stupid, but there it was. He'd failed after twenty-two years, and self-recrimination wouldn't change things. Sure, he'd do things differently if he could do it over again, but all he could do now was move forward and learn from his past.

He had no interest in dating. But try telling that to the local women. Their brazen approaches blew him away. They were coming out of the woodwork, feigning concern, offering to cook for him, suggesting he needed a shoulder to lean on...he'd avoided them like the plague, finding even the most beautiful coming up short when he compared them to Jayne—which he always did.

He'd been kidding himself. His feelings for her ran far deeper than he'd been willing to admit—nothing casual or temporary there. He wanted her as much today as he did that last day they were together.

Finding out that Halverson had been stalking Jayne brought the slow, seething beast of disgust and anger to his soul. It was one thing when it was business, but this was personal and he'd be damned if that prick was going to do anything to cause Jayne pain or anguish.

And there was the possibility she was seeing someone else—maybe that asshole who'd answered her phone, telling him that she wasn't available? Was she simply trying to distance herself from anything remotely involved with the Halverson mess? Not that he could blame her, but that really had nothing to do with him. *Or did it?*

Dammit! Just when he'd managed to push her out of his daily thought process, here comes Leigh. Now here he was, spread out in what Jayne would call a *marshmallow* of a bed, wanting her. Wanting and *needing* her with an ache that made it tough to breathe. He punched his pillow and rolled over. It was going to be a long night.

"McCord."

Leigh gulped. *Here goes.* "Nick. Good morning. Hope I'm not calling too early but I wanted to catch you before you started your day. Would you have time to join me for breakfast? I'd like to talk with you about a couple of things."

"Morning, Leigh. Breakfast sounds good, but I just got back from working out. I need about thirty minutes to clean up and take care of some emails. That work for you?"

"Perfect. Let's meet at the hotel restaurant at seven-thirty."

"I'll be there."

"Thanks, Hon." She hung up the receiver before he could ask her to elaborate.

Leigh looked up to see Charlie, towel around his waist, water droplets glistening over his body, looking at her with raised eyebrows. "What are you up to?"

"As you suggested, I slept on our situation with Jayne and I think I've found a way around the trust factor. I'll let you know how it goes. And you're looking awfully cute in that towel this morning."

"I'd look even cuter out of it if you're inclined—"

"Need a rain check. Nick is meeting me for breakfast in thirty minutes and I'd hate to keep him waiting."

"You've got the rain check any time, sugar. But I'm guessing McCord's a man who would forgive the delay, given the reason." He chuckled and shook his head, lathering his face with shaving cream.

Leigh found Nick waiting at the hostess desk. She gave him a quick hug and breathed in the smell of his cologne. *Jayne's right. He smells delicious.* And he looked even better this morning in charcoal Hugo Boss, if that was possible. The gold and jade combination in his necktie reflected in his eyes, casting them an even more brilliant shade of green.

"Morning. You look lovely." Nick leaned over and bussed her cheek.

Leigh preened. "Nothing like a compliment from a handsome man—no matter your marital status or age." She tweaked his cheek. "And *you* are even more handsome in daylight, my Canadian friend."

They followed the hostess to a table by the window. Leigh looked out, assessing the day. "Great view. Such a bustling city." Listening, she mused, "Ah, Pachelbel's Canon in D Major. What a civilized way to start the day."

"Charlie already head out this morning?"

"No, but he has an early meeting and opted for room service while he reviews a couple of briefs. Besides, I wanted to talk with you alone."

"Thinking of trading him in?" Nick grinned.

"I think he's still got a few miles left. But just in case, it's nice to know if I've got options." She tapped his hand across the table with a chuckle, winking at him.

Their server arrived with coffee and took their order. Leigh stirred in cream and sweetener, making a study of it while she contemplated her next words. Looking at him, she began, "Nick, I want to talk to you about Jayne."

"I figured."

"You know I'm fiercely loyal to her, but I tossed and turned all night trying to figure out what to say to you because I know she's not thinking straight."

Nick started to say something, then closed his mouth, pursing his lips.

"Jayne is my dearest friend, and just about the best gal you'll ever hope to know, but sometimes she gets a notion and can be as stubborn as all get out. Now, I know you two haven't been keeping in touch. What I don't know for sure is how you feel about that. And I need to know before I continue."

Nick hesitated. This wasn't at all what he was expecting, not that he knew *what* to expect. "Trick question?"

"Not at all. What I'm asking is, do you care that you haven't been in touch, or was Jayne someone you enjoyed spending time with but you've moved on now that some time has passed?"

Not sure what she was getting at, he decided to play his cards close to his chest. "She's the one who's moved on. She stopped taking my calls. She said she'd be busy, but I figured we'd work out our schedules and get together when we could. She knew I wasn't ready for a full on relationship. Apparently she found someone who was."

Taking a bite of her omelet, Leigh frowned. "Jayne isn't seeing anyone else."

"You sure about that?"

"Absolutely. Where'd you get the idea she was?"

"One time when I called her, some guy answered—Harry or Harris. Something like that. He said she wasn't available. I didn't give it much thought until she never called back. Then I got the picture, loud and clear."

"No, no. That was Harrison, and it's not at all what you think. He's a friend of Jayne's. Nothing more, I assure you. She probably doesn't even know he answered her phone."

Nick shook his head. "If he's just a friend, why wouldn't he explain that and tell her I called?"

"I'm not sure, but I have a pretty good idea he was trying to be protective. Could've mistaken you for Halverson."

"That's all good and fine, but it still doesn't explain why Jayne stopped taking and returning my calls."

Leigh chewed, considering her angle. This wasn't going to be as simple as she'd hoped. Nick's feelings were hurt and he was angry. Who could blame him, under the circumstances?

She set down her coffee cup and began, "Let me try to explain. Sometimes Jayne is so afraid of letting her guard down that she closes herself off, and I think that's exactly what she's done with you. It's not that she doesn't care, she's worried that she cares too much. And there are other factors I can't get into right now."

He frowned. "Just what is she afraid that I might or might not do?"

"Be there for her. She understands what you're going through. She also understands you have a large company to run in another city...no, another *country*, and in time the challenge of keeping up with someone in another part of the continent could become taxing

335

and you'll run out of steam. Jayne's guarding her heart from becoming a casualty of logistics. She thinks you need more time to be single, and she's afraid if she lets you in, you'll end up hurting her." Leigh looked him in the eye. "Because you made it clear to her you're not emotionally available. Now...does any of this make sense to you?"

"It does, but I also think she's making me pay for the transgressions of other men."

"Probably. And losing Mack left a profound mark on her soul. But you can't hold that against her. Isn't everyone guilty of reacting to each situation based on our previous experiences? In all parts of our lives?"

"I guess you're right. I hadn't thought about it from that angle." Nick took a sip of his coffee and leaned back. "Leigh, why do I get the feeling there's something else you want to tell me?" He raised his eyebrows, his face a mask as he ran his hand across his jaw.

"You're right, Nick, but I want to be sure you'll be inclined to consider what I'm going to suggest. I watched you and Jayne during our little trip and from my perspective, you two were very *companionable*, for lack of a better word. Then she told me how well you two got along when you went back. I've known Jayne a long time and I've never seen her respond to anyone the way she did to you. And it appeared mutual. Am I right?"

Her eyes pierced his, daring him to deny the truth.

He took his time answering, nodding slowly. "You are."

"Are you in love with her, Nick?"

He gazed at the ceiling for a few seconds and then took a long breath. "Timing is lousy."

"That's not what I asked you. Besides, life isn't always about good timing. The older I get, the more I realize life's more about seizing opportunities and holding on to what's important ...what feels right in our hearts...than what we think we *ought* to be doing and feeling. *So*, are you in love with her?"

Nick sat, then leaned back and tossed his napkin on the table, offering Leigh a slight nod. "Pretty much." He couldn't believe what he'd just admitted. Until last night, he'd convinced himself to let his feelings for Jayne go, certain she'd found someone else. He'd concentrated on putting her out of his mind. Now having Leigh put him on the spot forced him to admit what he'd realized in the wee hours. She made it sound logical—though it made no sense at all.

But his gut told him this was right. And Leigh was stepping up as an ally. She'd gone way out on a limb to take the conversation this far. Now what?

Leigh smiled. "I thought so. And I'm certain Jayne feels the same way about you, in spite of her lack of contact. You should see your expression, Nick. It's something between a deer caught in headlights and a seventeen-year-old holding the keys to a brand new hot rod." She dabbed at the corners of her mouth with her napkin. "Now that we have that out of the way, I need to set some ground rules." She looked over the top of her coffee cup and locked eyes with him, "There are some things you'll learn very soon that I'm not able to discuss with you now. You have to promise me that you'll be there for her. No matter what."

He frowned. What in the world was she talking about? No way would he give his unconditional word until he knew what he was committing to.

Leigh continued, patting his hand. "I know that's a tall request, but you've got to trust me on this one. It's pivotal."

Her eyes implored him and he sensed she was making a desperate effort to keep a confidence. Was Jayne in some type of trouble? Had something happened to her that she didn't want him to know? He couldn't stand the thought of trouble befalling her. Whatever it was, whatever she needed—money, lawyers, a retreat—he'd do anything and everything within his power to help her.

He finally nodded. "Okay. You have my word."

"Thank you. Are you willing to close your eyes and jump off the high board on this one?"

He chuckled. "Probably. I've done that with her a couple of times already."

"Yeah, and it worked out pretty well. I'm not going to tell her Charlie and I saw you. She'll ask too many questions. Here's what I suggest you do, and don't dally…"

When Nick hugged Leigh goodbye at the elevator, he laid his hand on her shoulder. "I'm glad we ran into each other."

"Me, too, Nick. But as Jayne would say, there are no coincidences."

TWENTY-EIGHT

Early May, Kansas City

Jayne woke to the rumble of Ranger snoring at the foot of her bed. The big Lab was on his back, spread eagle, with one paw anchoring him to the footboard. She chuckled and crawled out of bed, stopping to rub his belly. He rolled and stretched, gave her hand a lick, and bounced down to wait at the French doors leading to the patio.

She needed to adopt his energetic disposition. At least she was better today than yesterday. The chemo tired her and though she'd gotten over the nausea, she'd been weak and had wasted the better part of the day on the couch. The constant fatigue was exasperating. She was used to accomplishing more in one day than she now got done in a week. She glanced at her errand list sitting on the bathroom counter. Bank. Post office. Nothing too taxing, but it would wear her out. Maybe she'd stop by the greenhouse to pick up something pretty for her patio if she still had enough energy.

Drying off from her shower, she stole a glance in the mirror. Looking at her chest the first time after the bandages and drains were removed was probably the toughest thing she'd yet to do in this life, and looking at her chest was still very tough. The suture lines initially appeared swollen and angry—as angry as she was about them. Now they were less inflamed, but it would be months before her chest resembled anything normal.

Her plastic surgeon had suggested she consider what she wanted her breasts to look like when it was time for the reconstruction—and to pick out a tattoo color for the areolas. Now *that* was something she'd never considered. Leigh made good on her suggestion that they review the porn magazines and brought her several as a joke, having marked pages with little captions on the sizes and shapes of the enormous breasts. Even Charlie had left her a couple of notes. They'd had a good laugh and the humor had been great for her morale, but in the end she had no desire for something different. She wanted to be as close to her former self as possible. She'd known that all along, so she'd had her doctor take reference photos before surgery.

Running her hand gingerly across her chest, she allowed herself a moment of reflection, confident she'd made the smart decision regardless of the physical and emotional pain. Shaking off her doldrums, she stepped into her closet and flipped through her jeans, finally locating a pair that didn't swallow her, a soft camisole and a roomy sweatshirt. She looked in the mirror. Aside from her chest, it was hard to look at herself without hair. Running her hand over her bald head, she frowned. How long before it stopped being so sensitive? Had she made it worse by having her head shaved? Didn't matter. She refused to watch her hair fall out. She couldn't control the way her body healed or responded to treatment, but she could control *that*.

A bark at the door alerted her to Ranger's return. She opened the door and ruffled his ears as he bounced in. Giddy, he ran to the kitchen, wiggling in front of the pantry door.

Following him, she heard the phone ring and grabbed it, seeing Meg's name on the ID. Positioning the receiver between her shoulder and ear as she scooped a measure of dog food, she said, "Good morning."

"Hi. Feeling any better today?"

"Tons. Sorry I was such a slug yesterday. That fourth day always hits me like a hammer. And thanks again for coming in. It was great having you and Leigh here—I really appreciate the company and all the help. Stella had a ball with you guys yesterday and I think she was relieved to be able to get a few additional things knocked off the list. She worries and frets over me like a mother hen."

"She's a gem. You should be paying her triple whatever you pay her."

"You're right about that. I feel like the queen of the manor. My house sparkles, the laundry and ironing are done, the fridge is stocked. And I'm betting Leigh's getting a manicure this very minute. Working in my flowerbeds did a number on her fingernails."

"No. Knowing Leigh, she probably got one at the express salon in the airport on her way home. So how's the nausea?"

"The meds are keeping it at bay. So far, so good. Have you talked to Sean since you got back?"

"He called when I got home last night. He was having beers and watching hockey with the guys."

She knew Meg avoided mentioning Nick's name. Sean had probably been with him, Jimmy and Andy. Her heart tripped at the image of him relaxed in front of a screen, trading smack with the boys. God, she missed the sound of his voice and the feel of his arms wrapped around her.

Shaking it off, she asked, "Are you two still getting together this weekend?"

"He's flying in Friday. We're doing the museum thing, then I thought we'd hike around Rock Creek Park and tour the war memorials."

"That sounds like a great time. Give him my best."

"Will do. And I'm so glad you're feeling better today. I'll check on you tomorrow."

Jayne's call-waiting tone beeped on the line and she saw Liz's name on the screen. "Perfect. Thanks, Meg."

Jayne clicked over. "Hey, Red. How're things in the Windy City?"

"Terrific. More importantly, how're *you* doing, hon?"

"Feeling good today. And I'm looking forward to seeing you Memorial Day weekend. Cara sent me an email that she's coming in on Friday. Leigh and Meg arrive on Thursday evening. You figure out your flight yet?"

"After work on Thursday. I'm arriving at the same time as Leigh. We're renting a car so you won't need to worry about shuttling us. I can't wait to see everyone. This will be fun."

"Not quite the same as our usual trip, but you guys can play my club and on a couple of the reciprocal courses. Maybe I'll drive a cart."

"Not a bad idea. You sure you're up for company?"

"You guys aren't company. You're family, and having you here will be great. Not quite the same as Hilton Head, but we'll make due."

Liz chuckled as she said, "I'd hardly call staying at your place making due. Pool and an open bar, call me happy. And it's not about where, it's about us being together."

Jayne gave Liz a progress report, got an update on some trouble she'd been having at work with an associate, and finished the call.

Pulling on her sunglasses and her signature red ball cap, Jayne headed to her garage. Ranger followed and bounced beside her SUV, his tail wagging furiously.

"Let's go." She opened the hatch and he leapt in.

Jayne opted for the drive through at the bank and the post office to save her strength. The green house was calling.

She strolled a couple of the aisles, knowing the entire place was too much to tackle today. The rows of bedding plants delighted her with their explosion of colors. Flowers made her happy, this warm weather made her happy and spring made her happy. The new greens of the landscape were such an improvement over the dreary grays of winter.

She selected two gorgeous geraniums in a color noted as tango, some lime green sweet potato vine, asparagus fern and purple petunias to pot with them. She'd do a little at a time. But at this rate, she'd be planting flowers into August. Maybe she wouldn't plant as many as usual...or, as much as she hated the thought, maybe she'd hire some help.

With flowers in the cargo area, Ranger rode shotgun. She looked over at him as he bit the wind through the partially opened window and ran her hand down his silky back. "What a good boy. Ranger, you are the best road tripper I know. Always happy for the smallest adventure." He turned and gave her hand a lick.

Jayne pulled into her garage and wheeled her red Radio Flyer wagon to the back of her SUV. Ranger barreled out to investigate his boundaries while Jayne unloaded her plants, careful of her chest as she lifted the containers. She'd pretty much recovered from her surgery, but the tissue expanders were still

343

uncomfortable and she wasn't supposed to lift more than five pounds.

She pulled her wagon around to the patio and took a moment to marvel at the transformation Leigh had wrought the last couple of days. Pots stood waiting and beds were tilled, eager for their annual adornments.

She squinted. The reflection off her swimming pool was blinding on this cloudless day. The temperature had risen nearly thirty degrees since she'd left three hours earlier, so she headed in to shed a layer of clothing.

Finding a worn long-sleeved T-shirt, she traded out of her sweatshirt. Her reflection in the mirror resembled a teenaged boy. Jayne turned on the outdoor stereo and grabbed a bottle of water and her gardening gloves.

R.E.M.'s song about shiny, happy people filled the air as she finished the second pot. Humming along, she stood back to admire her work and adjusted the position of the asparagus fern. She turned on the garden hose, giving the plants and Ranger a liberal drink of water, the tug of fatigue slowing her actions.

The warmth of the sun soaked into her bones, spreading a slow laziness that invited a break. She took a swig from her bottle of water and stretched out on a chaise lounge, closing her eyes and breathing in the heady scent of the awakening earth. Ranger nudged her hand and she stroked his ears until she fell asleep.

Nick watched the Missouri River rise up to meet him as the mechanism lowering the landing gear and wheels of his Gulfstream whined. Minutes later, they touched down at Wheeler Municipal Airport in downtown Kansas City. He checked his watch—just after one.

He instructed the pilots to hang until they heard from him regarding their ground time. A lot would depend on how well things went. His rental car was waiting at the terminal and he hooked up his GPS and punched in the address.

Forty minutes, three highway connections, and several winding black-top roads later, he spied the street sign and turned. Pulling down the long drive, he could finally see the house, mostly hidden by a line of trees. It was an impressive English Tudor, the stone and stucco façade giving it a stately, yet welcoming appearance. Stopping in the circle drive in front of the house, he looked around. Big yard. Nice landscaping. Substantial without pretense. Just like Jayne.

Christ, his hands were sweaty. What if showing up like this pissed her off? What if he did nothing more than drive her farther away? Leigh had better be right about this.

Nick sat there, fingers tapping the steering wheel. He'd survived Paris. He'd survived Key West. Whatever happened, he'd survive this as well. Taking a deep breath, he pulled the keys from the ignition and climbed out. *Feel the fear and do it anyway...*

He heard the low, threatening growl before he saw the Lab. He stood perfectly still and waited. The dog came toward him, inching his way, the hair raised on his back, the growl continuing.

"Hello, Ranger. Good boy." He slowly extended his hand toward the shiny black creature, palm up. "Good boy. I'm not going to hurt you."

Ranger stopped growling and sniffed at the hand, offering a series of low *woofs*. Slowly, his tail wagged and he took another step toward Nick. He tentatively licked the hand, standing very still, his hackles still at attention.

"Atta boy. You're okay, eh?" Nick ran a slow hand across Ranger's ear. "See. I'm a friend." Nick took a couple of steps, moving slow as Ranger remained wary. He reached the front door, took a breath and pressed the doorbell. *Here goes nothing...*

Waiting for her to answer the door, his head swam. How would she react when she saw him? What would she say? Hell, he had no idea of what *he'd* say. He'd figure that out once he gauged her reaction to seeing him on her doorstep. Leigh had convinced him to make this trip, but she wouldn't say why it was so important. He was leaving a lot up to trust this time. He only hoped whatever trouble Jayne was in was something he could fix. And that she'd let him try.

Only one thing was certain. He wanted Jayne in his life. They'd figure out the logistics later. Now, he just needed to make her understand he wasn't going away.

He rang the doorbell again. Maybe she hadn't heard it. Leigh assured him Jayne was at home this week. Maybe she was running errands or out for lunch with friends. He'd wait.

Ranger was still watching him. "Where's your girl, Ranger? Where's Jayne?"

The dog's ears perked and he tilted his head. Nick was certain the dog understood. He gave a soft *woof* and turned to go. Then he turned back as if to make sure Nick was following him. *Woof.* He turned to leave again.

"Okay, boy. I'll play. Where are you taking me?"

Nick followed the dog around the side of the house to the back where a large brick and stone patio fell into a kidney-shaped pool. He surveyed the area, hearing Adele crooning over the outdoor speakers.

Stepping onto the patio, he looked around, noting the lush landscaping and the big, empty flowerbeds. Then he spied the empty containers and the newly potted geraniums. *Dirt is my muse...*Hadn't Jayne said something to that effect? His eyes followed Ranger to a chaise lounge where a prone form slept. Hmmm, did Jayne know the kid she'd hired napped on the job?

Nick approached the form, figuring he'd find out where Jayne was and startle the boy in the process. At least make the kid feel guilty for being a slacker.

As he neared the sleeping figure, his breath caught and his heart stopped, then it crumbled as his throat constricted. *Oh, Jayne, my God...*

In the stark sunlight, he could see how pale she was. And... her hair...*what the hell?* The red ball cap she wore didn't hide the fact that her hair was gone. With lightning speed, the realization knocked the wind out of him.

Now it all made sense. *Oh, no, dear God, No. Not cancer.*

So this was why she'd pushed him away...why Leigh had been so cagey. But why on earth had Jayne kept this from him?

Remembering how jacked he'd been when she hadn't returned his calls, Nick was suddenly filled with shame. What an insensitive moron—he wanted the ground to swallow him. He should've figured something was vitally wrong...should've been here with her from the beginning.

He shook his head. She must've known she was sick while they were together in Florida. That's why she'd been reluctant to make plans. A wave of fear gripped his heart. How bad was she? He'd lost his sister. He couldn't lose Jayne, too. No wonder she'd asked so many questions about what his sister had gone through. She'd been comparing her own situation. *Dammit.* And he'd been so callous, told her he never wanted to go through this again. No wonder she'd pushed him away. She'd taken him for his word.

Nick stood still for an excruciating moment. He had to get his emotions under control before she

347

realized he was there. She needed his strength, not his fear.

Jayne wandered through the loveliest of dreams. The kind of dream where you know you're dreaming but choose to keep dreaming anyway. She was in her Baron, Nick beside her. They were floating in the middle of her swimming pool. Just floating and talking. Then he helped her out of the plane and they danced across the water, splashing and laughing, her white shirt soaked and revealing her perfect breasts. Nick reached out to touch them, but she couldn't let him. She could hear him calling her name, chasing after her, but she couldn't let him know. She couldn't let him touch her chest...

She could feel the tickle of his lips on her cheek, but she couldn't let him know. He just kept saying her name and her soul vibrated with the *buzz* as his warm lips fell on her mouth. It was so real...she could feel his hand on hers. Feel his warm breath on her skin, smell his Armani cologne.

"Jayne?" His voice was the softest of whispers. "Jayne?"

Now he was touching her shoulder. The deep timbre of his voice grew louder and more insistent. She blinked, crawling her way through the cobwebs of sleep, her vision finally clearing. She stared at the image, not comprehending. Finally, she gasped, "Nick?"

"Hi, babe."

She struggled to sit up as he wrapped his arms around her. He kissed her again, ever so gently on the mouth and lingered there. She leaned back and took his face in her hands, "Oh, Nick...why are you here?"

"I needed to see you."

He was being so gentle with her, as if she'd break. She took off his sunglasses so she could see his eyes, those gorgeous jade eyes, and the pain she read in the depths nearly killed her. Her heart was hammering so hard, she found it difficult to breathe.

His words were strained, "Why didn't you tell me?"

Her eyes welled. Would he ever understand? Could she begin to explain her reasons? How could she make him believe she'd cared too much to let him know...to drag him into all this? She finally shook her head, miserable with herself for hurting him and whispered, "I just couldn't."

"Why not? I don't understand." He was shaking his head, concentrating on her eyes. "You should've told me."

Jayne pulled herself into a more upright position and swiped at a tear that ran down her cheek. She took his hands, clenching them tightly to underline her words. "I didn't want to put such a huge burden on you. It was too soon." She paused and looked away, embarrassed to admit her vanity as she continued in a whisper, "And I was so afraid of how you'd feel about me if you saw me *like this*." She released his hand to reach up and take her hat off. "And like this." She pulled her shirt tight against her missing breasts. "I didn't want you to feel obligated, and I couldn't bear it if you walked away."

He was silent for the longest time and a fierce expression filled his face. God, what was he thinking? Had her admission made him angry?

He covered her hands with his and shook his head back and forth, very slowly.

"You underestimate me. I would've been here because I *love* you." He reached up to let his fingers gently graze her scalp. "You're beautiful." Then he lightly pressed his palm against her heart, "This is why I love you. What's in *here*. No matter what, you're beautiful to me. *Know that.*" Nick paused, then tipped her chin so that she couldn't avoid his eyes. "Never worry that I'll look at you differently, never wonder that I'll walk away, and never doubt how I feel about you again."

Tears flowed down her cheeks as she watched his face, the emotions that played across it and the intense look in his eyes leaving no question that he meant every word.

She etched his lips with her fingertips, recalling the day when she thought they were saying goodbye for good. Now words wouldn't come. She studied his face, traced his strong jaw line with her fingers. Could she believe in a future with someone she could love with her whole heart? Could she truly be so blessed to have found this man, and to have earned his love…

She was emotionally exhausted, so tired of being alone and being strong all by herself for so many years. Now Nick was here, offering her his strength. He wanted to be her shoulder to lean on, the one who'd love her through the light *and* the darkness.

An awesome calming peace settled over her, and in that instant she knew she could finally exhale and let someone else be strong for a change.

Nick lifted her hand to his lips and kissed it. Then he leaned down and kissed her mouth. He was trembling and when she pulled back, tears were rolling down his cheeks. Her heart swelled with the knowledge that he wasn't ashamed to let her see him cry. She kissed him again, taking strength from him and giving hers back in return. Oh, how she'd needed this man. But she'd been so scared of getting hurt that she hadn't been willing to give him a chance. Now he was here and she knew with certainty that he was here because he cared, because he loved her.

It was well into the night when they lounged together on her sofa, her head on Nick's chest. They'd talked though the afternoon and evening and she'd told him everything—from her diagnosis, to her current regime of chemo, to her pending reconstructive surgery. She painted as honest a picture as possible, wanting him to fully understand what she still faced.

And Nick finally admitted Leigh's role in getting him to Kansas City, but assured Jayne that her friend hadn't broken her word. It was easy to see Leigh and Meg's handwriting all over the advance work now that she knew the score. Their visit, the cleaning, the gardening, the over-the-top grocery shopping...they'd put everything in place right before Nick arrived.

Jayne's mind had been racing with Nick's vow to stand beside her. The magnitude of his words made her heart sing. Not only would she recover, she now had a brighter future. One with this wonderful man who brought love and joy back into her life.

"I still can't believe you're here, but I'm so glad you are. You have no idea..."

"I'm exactly where I want to be. No way are you going through any more of this without me."

She turned and looked up at him, her eyes growing watery again. He ran his thumb under her chin, meeting her gaze.

"It's going to be a long road."

He pulled her close and kissed her. "Not so long if we take this detour together."

Epilogue

January, Florida, the following year

Nick stood on the fantail and braced his arms on the rail, watching Key West grow smaller. A crowd was gathering on Mallory Square for sunset.

Andy leaned next to him. "Oh, man, I can't believe we're staying over here." His head shook back and forth. "We're gonna lose guys on the late-night boat. I guarantee it. They're gonna get hammered, go overboard and *drown*."

"We'll put Gino on watch. Besides, you know this wasn't my idea. Just going with the flow." Nick slapped Andy's back. "Don't *you* go overboard. We'd never be able to haul your ass back in the boat."

Andy snorted and shook his head again.

Pulling into the dock at Sunset Key, the boat slowed and the big engines reversed, then stilled. Nick waited for the first mate to secure the ropes and position the gang plank, then he crossed to the dock.

Andy followed and shook the captain's hand. "You should probably add a few life rings to your after-hours ferry, Captain…just sayin'…"

Sean and Jimmy stayed behind to help a pair of older ladies off the boat and then the four men headed up the ramp, their boots loud on the wooden planks.

Gene Caruso met them with his arms crossed over his chest. "I knew you guys didn't have time to stop at the Hog's Breath. Why do you *always* have to go there first? Now you're going to be late. I've got everyone checked in, but you need to get a move on."

Jimmy threw his arm around Gene's shoulder. "Gino, I brought my wife this time, and I sure as hell don't need *two* women telling me what to do. We gotta find you a new job, man."

Andy shot a look at Nick and muttered under his breath, "Yeah…*lifeguard.*"

Gene handed the men small packets. "Here are your keys. Now, dammit, I promised Leigh I'd get you there by six o'clock. I should've charged her overtime."

Nick slapped Gene's back. "Come on. Point us to our cottages. We gotta keep you on Leigh's good side." Laughter drifted from the bar and Nick changed direction as he recognized the southern drawl. "But we need to make one more stop on the way."

Gene spun toward Nick. "Fellas, you've only got thirty minutes to shower and change."

Sean rolled his eyes, following on Nick's heels to the bar. "*Damn*, I won't have time to curl my hair."

They ignored Gene's diatribe and pulled him along to Latitudes Bar. Charlie Wallace and Brandon Strickland stood to greet them, shaking hands all around, then introduced them to a couple of older men and a pair of Brandon's fellow Naval officers.

"Good to see you boys. How were things at the Hog?" Charlie gestured to empty chairs. "What'll it be?" Charlie waved the server over.

To Nick's great amusement, Gene was tapping his foot and checking his watch every thirty seconds. "*Gino,*

353

we're not going to be late. Just relax and have a drink."
Then he turned to Charlie. "So how are the girls doing?
Had to bail them out of jail yet?"

"At least three or four times." Charlie sipped his
scotch, then drawled, "When they're together, it's best
to just stand back. Add your Canadian gals to the mix
and we're nothing more than window dressin'."

Andy chuckled. "Yeah, and it's never good when
this many women get their heads together. Gentlemen,
we're *so screwed*."

"Big time." Jimmy chinked his bottle against
Andy's. "Shit, right now we are *so busted*."

Leigh slid in behind Charlie, pressing her fingers
on his shoulders. "Ah, figured I'd find you here." She
waved the men down as they started to stand and
pressed a kiss to Nick's cheek. "Good to see you fellas.
Charlie, honey, I'm sure y'all are solving the world's
problems, but we have a rehearsal and dinner to attend
in twenty minutes, and I want these fellas to look
pretty. Could you resume this summit meeting later?
I'm sure the last thing you want is to get on the bad side
of any of the divas—American *or* Canadian. So, in the
interest of maintaining good relations—"

Nick chuckled and took a last slug of his drink as
he stood. "Okay, mates. We don't want to create an
international incident..." And he couldn't wait to see
Jayne. The hotel in Quebec City had demanded his
attention for the past couple of weeks, so she'd come
on down ahead of him. Two weeks was a long time
without her.

Meg topped off Cara's and Jayne's glasses of
champagne, then added a splash to her own. Hoisting
her glass to the group of women gathered in Leigh's
cottage, she said, "Cheers to old friends and new,

something borrowed, something blue, and falling in love with a man whose heart is true."

Echoes of "cheers" and the chime of glasses pinging filled the room. Jayne couldn't have asked for a better way to celebrate her birthday. Sure, her original crew was here, but now their new Canadian gal pals were joining the fold for the festivities. Witty, interesting and charmingly irreverent, they fit right in, as Liz put it, like vodka and tonic.

Jayne stole back to Leigh's bathroom to check her hair and lipstick one last time.

Leigh popped in beside her. "Found the boys in the bar. Sent them off to get cleaned up. Nick should be at your cottage as we speak. He looks great, by the way."

She grabbed her lipstick tube and applied another coat. "Better than great, actually. Had to laugh...it's a wonder Gene doesn't have ulcers. Keeping up with that crew is like herding cats." She chuckled, turning to Jayne. "And Charlie's just as bad. Not sure if he's the *influencer* or the *influencee*—either way, they're going to be a handful this weekend."

"Wouldn't want them any other way." Jayne blotted her lip gloss and winked. "Next thing you know, Charlie's gonna buy a Harley and you'll be shopping for leathers."

"Only because I want to keep up with you, now that you're a bona fide biker babe. I can't wait to see it."

"Oh, it's gorgeous—totally rigged out. Nick really outdid himself."

"Just when did you decide you wanted one?"

"Meg and I kidded around about it last year, but Nick and I thought it would be fun to take a victory *detour* when I finished chemo. I never dreamed he'd surprise me like that."

"You deserve it. Can't think of a better way for you to commemorate the end of your treatment."

"I would've been fine with a party hat and a balloon. Nick spoils me."

"Get used to it. Speaking of which, let's see this bracelet." Leigh took Jayne's wrist and pulled it close for inspection. "Oh, my. That's absolutely stunning. Nick can put me on his Christmas list any time."

The diamond and ruby encrusted cuff sparkled as Jayne twisted her wrist in the light. "He's so good to me. And we just get better and better together. I wake up every morning and pinch myself. I have Nick, chemo's over and my scans are clear. Never thought it was possible to be this happy again."

"Enjoy yourself. You were long overdue."

Jayne fussed with her hair. She couldn't get used to the change in the texture since it had grown back. Now it was thick and wiry and a little darker. She'd managed to find a decent shorter style and altered the color with highlights, but she still didn't recognize herself in the mirror.

Leigh studied her and nodded. "I love the new style. I know you miss your long hair, but this is just darling. Really emphasizes those gorgeous eyes." Then she stood back and added, "And your new boobs look great. Especially in that dress. Nick's gonna stroke out when he sees you."

"I hope so. Haven't seen him for two whole weeks—we've got some serious catching up to do." Jayne gave Leigh a conspiratorial grin, then sobered. "Before we get caught up in the festivities, I need to tell you—I couldn't have made it through this past year— you have no idea—"

"Shhh. Don't you make me cry. You know I love ya, gal. We're just so glad you've won this battle."

"Couldn't have done it without you." Jayne gave Leigh a tight hug, then laughed. "Isn't there a rehearsal we should be heading to...?"

-The End-

You are cordially invited to attend a
Key West Wedding!

Watch for
Danger: Curves Ahead
Book II in the Roads to Romance Trilogy
Coming your way late Summer 2013

For more information about
Janice Richards:
Facebook: Janice Richards
www.threewritersofromance.com
or email:
Janice.Richards.Author@gmail.com

Acknowledgements

No story is ever told without experts, and so it goes with *Detour*. I was overwhelmed by the generous amount of time and information the team at St. Joseph Breast Center shared in regard to Jayne's diagnosis and treatment. These are amazing women who have lived this story and help others win this battle year after year. Thank you so very much Mary, Janie and Candy. You provided the backbone of Jayne's illness, her reactions and fears, and allowed me to give her an authenticity I could never have provided without your keen insights.

Another big thank you goes to Gail Worth of Gail's Harley Davidson Kansas City. You so graciously led me through your marvelous showroom, helping me select bikes for Nick and his crew based upon their personalities. And your mechanical experts helped me find a way to strand my crew in the Upper Keys by suggesting a bad stator. Brilliant!

Cheers with a clink of glasses to my Key West friends, among these the colorful bartenders and hoteliers: George, Ali, Brian, Paula, Dave, April, Nate…and so many others—thanks for the memories that helped me weave this story.

That goes doubly for the dear friends who have shared my trips and my enthusiasm for the Keys through the years. *You know who you are, divas and rogues…As the saying goes…names and places have been changed to protect the guilty…*

My most heartfelt appreciation goes to my critique partners, Darlene Deluca and Michelle Gray, both truly talented and creative authors. And to my beta readers, Thank you for every error you caught, and for every editorial comment I hated (but needed) to hear.

To the Beverage Brigade, you have no idea how much I appreciate you. Thanks for all the wild times we'll recall one day from our rocking chairs and for your constant vote of confidence. You're the best. "In your eye, ya'll."

And finally, to the Colonel, my very own *high speed, low drag, black pajama Ninja boy*, I couldn't have done this without you. Your unyielding support and encouragement kept me going. And your willingness to read, re-read, and re-read again, always providing honest and insightful feedback, whether near or *way* too far away, kept me on track, and was always spot on. You are my true north.